I0663120

Reckless

Elle Casey

All names, places, and events depicted in this book are fictional and products of the author's imagination.

No part of this publication my be reproduced, stored in a retrieval system, converted to another format, or transmitted in any form without explicit, written permission from the publisher of this work.   For information regarding redistribution or to contact the author, write to the publisher at the following address:

Elle Casey
PO Box 14367
N Palm Beach, FL 33408

Website: www.ElleCasey.com
Email: info@ellecasey.com

ISBN/EAN-13: 978-1-939455-04-8

Copyright © 2012 Elle Casey
All rights reserved

First Edition

Dedication

To indie author, Amanda McKeon.
I see greatness in you, girl.

Other Books by Elle Casey

War of the Fae: Book One, The Changelings
War of the Fae: Book Two, Call to Arms
War of the Fae: Book Three, Darkness & Light
War of the Fae: Book Four, New World Order

Clash of the Otherworlds: Book 1, After the Fall
Clash of the Otherworlds: Book 2, Between the Realms
Clash of the Otherworlds: Book 3, Portal Guardians

Apocalypse: Book 1, Kahayatle
Apocalypse: Book 2, Warpaint
Apocalypse: Book 3, Exodus
Apocalypse: Book 4, Haven

My Vampire Summer
My Vampire Fall

Wrecked
Reckless

Reckless

Elle Casey

A Night to Remember

CANDI STARED AT HER REFLECTION in the mirror, turning her head slowly left and then right. "Holy you-know-what, you've done it again, Sarah. It's like *magic* or something." She reached her hand up to the side of her head.

Sarah slapped it away before it could make contact with the artfully arranged and decorated dreadlocks that surrounded Candi's pretty pink cheeks and expertly made-up face. "Don't touch! How many times do I have to tell you? It needs to stay looking good for at least another six hours, and I don't want you smudging anything either."

Candi stood up instead of trying to sneak in a touch; Sarah would probably karate-chop her if she tried anyway. "Should we put our dresses on now?" She looked around the space, taking in the disaster that was her bedroom. Normally it was pretty neat, but with Sarah there doing prom preparations it had quickly turned into what looked like a war zone. Shoe boxes and shoes, tissue paper, various underthings, and snack plates littered the tabletops, floor, and bed.

"Yes. I need you to help me with the zipper on mine. Come to my room with me." Sarah left, not looking back to see if she was being followed.

Candi sighed. Pregnancy had changed some things about Sarah, but not her bossiness, that was for sure. She smiled secretly as she thought about it, knowing she wouldn't change that about her friend even if she could. It was part of her charm and usually bearable.

The former guest room of the Buckley house had become Sarah Peterson's new digs. Frank Peterson was being a total jerk about his daughter's teen pregnancy, and her mother was too cowed to stand up to him and tell him to cut it out. Candi had hope that maybe Frank would eventually come around, but in the two weeks since the news had been made public, he'd done nothing but insist she wasn't welcome in his house or his life. Sarah was handling it well, all things considered. The only outward expression of her disappointment had been to start using his first name instead of *dad* or *father*. And sometimes it came out more like *Fruck* than *Frank*. Candi never corrected her because she would probably have done the same thing if it were her. Thank goodness she had Glen Buckley as her dad. He was the most chilled-out adult in the world, and had accepted Sarah into their home and family no questions asked, just like Candi's mom had.

Sarah was standing in front of the dress that was hanging on her closet door, unzipping the bag it had come in.

Candi watched as the beautiful long black gown with spaghetti straps and sparkling black beading was revealed from within. She inhaled a quick breath, just like she did every time she saw it. "Wow, Sarah. It's *so* pretty."

"I know, right?" She looked over her shoulder and smiled before going back to getting it off the hanger. "Totally schmexy.

Jonathan's going to bust something when he sees me in it."

"I think every guy in school is going to bust something when they see you in it." Candi sat down on the bed, fighting the urge to fling herself onto her back. Sarah would kill her if she messed up the 'do.

"Have you talked to Jason today?" asked Sarah, holding the dress up to the front of her body, looking down at it while sticking out a leg.

"No. He's going to be busy getting things ready, all the way up to the end. But I'll see him soon enough, I'm sure," she said, standing again, frustrated by not being able to relax. Pretty hair and makeup was fun for the most part, but when all she felt like doing was going to bed it was a serious pain in the butt.

"You don't sound very excited about it," said Sarah, sliding her arms up into the dress from the bottom.

"I am. I just ... I don't know. I'm nervous or something."

"Prom queen jitters. I know exactly what you're going through right now." She put the dress over her head carefully to avoid upsetting her hair, and wiggled around, trying to get the material to fall down around her body.

Candi stepped over and took the bottom seam of the dress, gently pulling it down to the floor. After walking behind her friend, she zipped it up, noting immediately that it fit Sarah like a glove. *She's right. Jonathan is going to bust something.* "You don't know for sure I'm going to win."

"Everyone is voting for you, so yes, I am sure. And Kevin's going to be king. So just wrap your little fuzzy head around that and deal."

"You should be the prom queen."

"And dance with my brother? *Ew.* Too incestuous for me."

Candi laughed. "Just because you're crowned with someone doesn't mean you're romantic together."

Sarah walked over to the full length mirror on the back of the door. "I know. But it doesn't matter anyway. No one's going to vote for the pregnant chick for prom queen. Everyone's celebrating my downfall right now, not my beauty and charisma." She smoothed the dress down over her still flat stomach, turning sideways to look at her profile.

"That's not true ... don't say that. No one's happy that you're pregnant in a bad way."

Sarah snorted. "Are you kidding? Elise Winters was totally mocking me hard in the bathroom the other day. I was in a stall ralphing as usual, so she didn't know I overheard."

Candi shook her head in disbelief. "Are you serious? What a jerk. She is so incredibly stuck up, I'm surprised she doesn't get bird turds up her nose."

Sarah laughed, breaking away from the study of her reflection. "What did you just say?"

Candi shrugged, grinning back. "You know ... nose in the air ... birds flying by ..."

"Nice effort. Total fail, but nice anyway."

"Yeah, I know. I was never very good at insults."

Sarah walked over and gave her a quick hug. "Yes, and that's a compliment to your character, so don't start getting good at it. That's my department."

Candi squeezed her back. "I hope you're not suggesting that there's anything wrong with your character, because then you'd just be making me mad."

Sarah pulled back, pointing a nail-polished finger in Candi's face. "No violence. I'm a pregnant lady and responsible for bringing new life into the world, which is a privilege and a responsibility."

Candi raised an eyebrow at that. "Seriously?"

Sarah shrugged. "Jonathan's words. I thought they sounded nice." She went back over to look at her profile again. "Do you think I'm showing yet?"

"No. How can you possibly be showing when all you've done is throw up every morning and afternoon and only eat crackers? You've lost weight not gained any."

"The doctor said it's normal. And showing is baby weight, not mommy weight." She smoothed her dress over her abdomen one more time.

"Well, you're not showing. It's too early anyway. Now get your shoes and help me with my dress."

Sarah studied her reflection for a few more long seconds before sighing and turning away from the mirror. "I see a bump." She got her shoes and stood, dangling them from a finger. "Well, come on then ... let's go. I have my shoes and I'm dressed."

"Shawl?"

"Oh, yeah. Get it for me," she said, leaving the room.

Candi sighed. *The queen has spoken.* Maybe it would have bothered her a few months ago, or even on the island when they were marooned together, to be bossed around like that. But today, with Sarah carrying her brother's baby - Candi's own niece or nephew - and the fact that she knew Sarah just did this as a joke now and not because she was careless with others' feelings, Candi could just play along. It was almost like a private joke between them at this point.

Candi opened the Nordstrom box on the dresser, lifting the cashmere shawl from inside, putting it up to her cheek for a feel.

Sarah's so lucky her mom buys her presents like this.

"Don't get any of your makeup on it!" yelled Sarah from the hallway.

Candi's hand froze just inches from her face. *Dang it. How did she know?* "I wasn't!" she yelled.

Sarah's face suddenly appeared, leaning into the doorway. "Lies. You can't help but snuggle that thing every time you touch it. It even smells like you now."

Candi frowned, knowing she was busted. "But it's so soft! It was made to be cuddled!"

Sarah smiled. "I know, right? And tonight is the night for cuddling, so I'm all set. Come on," she jerked her head back, her voice coming from down the hallway already, "let's get you dressed, Cinderella."

*****

Sarah helped Candi into her prom dress. It was dark green, shorter than her own, and totally suited to Candi's new style. Her tanned legs and lean figure were perfectly displayed, the cinched waist showing off her post-island-rescue tiny size.

Returning from their temporary treehouse home hadn't caused Candi to fall back into her old ways of snacking and lying in bed all weekend. Sarah was proud that her friend had taken the tragedy and used it to turn her life around, jogging every day but Sunday and eating right.

All of them agreed that after eating castaway-style, some of the usual snacks had lost their luster. Yes, they were tired of fish; but they were definitely not tired of all the fresh foods they hadn't been able to get while they were there. Sarah and Candi were now practically vegetarians - Candi because she was making a conscious choice to eat healthier, and Sarah because almost everything meat- and milk-based made her feel nauseous.

"Gorgeous. Just like it was in the mall dressing room," said Sarah, stepping back and admiring the way the short strapless dress showed off Candi's trim figure. "Spin around."

Candi spun, the edges of the dress flying out around her to reveal the new, lacy black panties underneath, the ones they'd bought at Victoria's Secret just yesterday.

"And now the shoes," said Sarah, handing Candi the lower-heeled sandals she'd chosen for her friend.

"I'm so glad we didn't get those really high ones," said Candi, sitting on the bed to put them on. "I would have twisted my ankle for sure."

"You don't need heels to show off what you have. Your muscle tone is friggin amazing. Besides, you-know-who prefers you in the lower ones."

Candi looked up for a second to stick her tongue out before going back to buckling her shoes. "Whatever. Anyway, I told Jason to just stay out of Kevin's way as much as possible tonight."

"That's going to be pretty difficult, don't you think?"

"Maybe. But Kevin just needs to get a grip on himself and stop acting so jealous. There's nothing he can do about Jason. I want him in my life, and that's that."

Sarah held up her hands in a gesture of peace. "I know, I know. I'm not arguing. I'm just saying ..."

"Put your shoes on," said Candi, effectively stopping that subject line from going any further. "The car is going to be here any minute and so is your mom."

Just then the door opened, and Candi's mother stuck her head in. "Are you ready, girls? Sarah, your mom is on her way, and Jonathan just called ... they're about five minutes out."

"How many times has he called you with his time checks?" Sarah asked, a knowing smile on her face.

"Five times," said his mother, sighing. "That boy is so excited right now, I'm afraid he's going to give himself a headache before he even sees you." She winked. "You two look gorgeous, by the way. See you downstairs." She blew them a kiss and then closed the door behind her retreating head.

Sarah sat down on the edge of the bed. "Put my shoes on for me, will you?" she whined.

Candi sighed. "Are you serious? Don't you think you're taking this a little too far?"

"Taking what too far? I'm pregnant. I feel morning-sick again. I need help." She sighed dramatically. "But don't worry about it. I can manage." She waited the two seconds it took for Candi to become overwhelmed with guilt.

"Never mind. Give me the stupid shoes," Candi grumbled, holding out her hand.

Sarah smiled slyly. It was almost too easy. "Thanks. I'll just rest here and focus on not barfing on your head."

"Try focusing on not working this pregnancy too hard in the early stages, so you still have some bank when you're a giant roly-poly and *really* need the help. Like, to get in and out of a chair."

Sarah's mouth dropped open. She was dumbstruck for a moment before she recovered enough to smack her friend on the shoulder. "Hey! That's not nice, talking to a delicate pregnant girl like that! Where are your manners, young lady?"

Candi giggled, but wisely said nothing.

The doorbell rang, signaling the arrival of Sarah's mother.

"Time for pictures and sniffling parents," said Sarah, watching as Candi finished buckling the second sandal onto her foot. She lifted her other leg out, admiring the heels that would make her almost as tall as her date. She planned to be wearing shoes like this all the way up until the end of her pregnancy. She vowed then to be wearing them on the way to her baby's delivery.

"Yeah. I hope it's not too awful," said Candi, standing and holding her hand out for her friend's. "At least my dad won't be here. I'm glad work is keeping him busy and not here taking a million pictures."

Sarah took it and stood. "We'll cut them off after fifteen minutes. Then we're outties."

"Deal," said Candi, holding up her hand for a high-five that Sarah gladly gave her.

"Time to go blow some minds. Come on," said Sarah, taking Candi by the hand. Together they left the room and descended the stairs to the front hall.

*****

The girls joined their mothers in the kitchen where the two ladies were having a glass of white wine together.

"Oh, my goodness ... Sarah ... you look absolutely stunning," said her mother Angie, coming over for a kiss.

Candi watched at the way it stopped in the air right next to Sarah's cheek without even really touching her. She walked over to her mom and got a full hug, not caring at all that she might mess up her dress or her hair. Her nervousness over the whole event was more overwhelming right now then her need to look perfect.

"Hey! Wrinkles, ladies, wrinkles!" reminded Sarah. "Step away from the prom dress, Mrs. B."

Candace Buckley smiled, moving back from her daughter. "Yes, yes, I know. But she looks so beautiful." She was holding

Candi's hands and staring into her eyes, pride making them shiny.

"Thanks, Mom."

"I'm so proud of you, sweetie. Look at you! You're so beautiful. Absolutely stunning."

Candi smiled, but she could feel her lip tremble as she thought about her date.

"Nervous?"

"Just a little. Or a ton."

"You have nothing to worry about," said Mrs. Peterson. "I assure you ... my son will behave himself. He's had a stern talking-to from his father."

Candi turned to her. "Thanks, Mrs. Peterson. But I'm not worried about Kevin. I'm more worried about the prom queen silliness."

Mrs. Peterson frowned, shaking off Candi's concern with a casual gesture of her hand. "I hear you're a shoo-in. Just remember, shoulders back, chin up, and never let them see you sweat."

"Good advice," said Sarah, coming over to take her friend by the hand and pull her out of the kitchen. She leaned in next to Candi's ear and whispered, "I'd also add *tits out* to that list of instructions." Then over her shoulder she said in a louder voice, "Anyone who wants pictures of these two hotties needs to come to the front porch. We're only staying ten minutes after our dates arrive."

They walked to the front door, just as a limousine was pulling up to the curb. Candi saw them out the window that was just next to the front door and squeezed Sarah's hand. "Don't!" Candi yelled, when she saw that Sarah was about to go outside.

"What? What's wrong?"

"They're here!" Candi squeaked, her palms instantly going sweaty and her face heating up. She dropped her grip on Sarah and rubbed her hands together, barely resisting the strong urge to rub them on her dress.

"Oooo, let me see," said Sarah, pushing Candi out of the way so she could look out the window. "Oh. Em. Gee. Look at my date. How adorable is he?"

Candi got one eyeball into position - the rest of her view blocked by Sarah hogging the whole area - and saw her brother coming up the walk. "Oh my. He does look nice, doesn't he?" He'd been at Jason's house getting ready with a whole group of guys - the ones who'd gone in together to pay for the big limo and arranged to all eat dinner together before the dance.

"Nice? Try hot. Try smokin' hot."

"Ew. That's Jonathan, Sarah."

"I know." She looked at Candi with a cheshire cat grin.

Candi laughed. "You're a sad woman, you know that?"

"Sad? No. Just hormonal. Rawwrr," Sarah said, imitating a cat scratching and winking before going back to staring at her date as he came up the front walk.

The mothers came in as the doorbell rang. Mrs. Peterson said, "Step back, girls. Try not to look so eager."

Mrs. Buckley waved them back, gesturing for them to stand at the foot of the stairs so the boys had room to enter. She walked over and opened the door, exposing the two tall boys wearing rented tuxes, both of them carrying small plastic boxes in their hands.

*****

"Hi, mom," said Jonathan, stepping inside the foyer and bending down a little awkwardly to give her a kiss on the cheek. He set a clear plastic box down on the front hall table.

Candi watched him, amazed at how good he looked. For some reason, even though they'd been back for over a month and he'd only gone from island-fit to even more-fit - now that he was training with the rugby team - she still sometimes expected to see the skinny, pale braniac walking through the door. He was still a brainiac, but everything else about him had changed. And as soon as his eyes lit on his date, Candi remembered why.

Jonathan's face turned a pale pink below his tan. "Hello, Sarah. You look ... like the most beautiful girl in the entire world."

Sarah stepped up to him and patted him lightly on the cheek. "You say that every day." She stood on tiptoes to kiss him lightly on the mouth. He reached an arm around her waist and pulled her in close. "Okay ... how about, you are the most beautiful homo sapiens-sapiens on this terrestrial body?"

She nodded. "I like it. I can work with that." She closed her eyes to accept the kiss from her goofy boyfriend, the father of her unborn child.

Candi rolled her eyes. "You guys are dorks."

A movement at the door caught Candi's eye, making her heart stop beating for a moment. *Oh my god. He's here!* Her throat went dry and she thought she was going to choke. She coughed once, but it didn't help.

"Are you okay?" asked Jonathan, staring at her with concern in his eyes.

Candi waved him away, unable to answer verbally. The most amazing-looking guy Candi had ever known was walking through her door right now, and it literally took her breath away. Tall and broad-shouldered, blonde hair and bright blue eyes, he was every inch her dream date.

His eyes scanned the room, his gaze stopping when it reached her. She knew the instant he laid eyes on her because his relaxed stance went instantly still and tense. And then he reached up and tugged a little at his collar, the box he held in his hand tipping its contents sideways.

"Hey, Candi," he said in his deep voice.

"Hey."

He smiled, his shoulders relaxing a bit. "Ready to go dancing?"

She smiled back, only a little tremble in her lips. "As ready as I'll ever be, I guess."

"Pictures first!" said Mrs. Peterson. "Everyone out on the front lawn. I have a full battery, and I'm not afraid to use it!"

"We need help with the corsages," said Candi's date, still standing in the doorway, looking down at a plastic box on the front table where Candi had put it earlier. "The guy ones."

"They're called boutonnieres," said Jonathan, walking over and picking the two boxes up. "My mom can pin them on. Come on; we're going to be late for our dinner reservations." He looked down at his watch as he balanced three boxes in one arm, a small frown on his face. "We have exactly eight minutes and thirty-five seconds to do pictures before we have to be rolling away from the curb."

Sarah pushed him towards the door. "Tell me you didn't calculate to the second how long it's going to take to get from here to the steakhouse."

"No, just to the minute."

Sarah sighed, talking to herself. "Baby steps. Baby steps to normal, Sarah. Rome wasn't built in a day."

Before they made it all the way outside, Candi caught

Jonathan's little smile. "Who wants to be normal? Normal's boring."

Sarah pinched his butt lightly, making him jump out the door. "I'll give you boring ..."

The mothers followed them out, leaving Candi and her date in the front hall. He advanced towards her, never taking his eyes from her face. When he reached her, he looked down, towering over her at over six feet tall.

"You look petrified," he said, smiling to reveal his perfectly straight, bright white teeth.

"I am," she whispered.

"Is it me? Or just the prom in general?"

Candi nodded, unable to totally focus on what he was saying enough to formulate an intelligent answer.

He smiled, leaning down to kiss her gently. His lips were warm, and his familiar scent washed over her, overwhelming her with his maleness and the way he always made her feel so vulnerable and strong at the same time. She sighed with pleasure.

"Happy?" he asked.

"Yes, Kevin. You always make me happy."

"Wellll ... not always."

Candi smiled. "Okay, that's true. You've made me happy every day since you finally took your head out of your butt two weeks ago, and every day on the island before that."

"And the month in between those two times I made you crazy." He tipped his forehead down to hers until they were touching. "I'll never not be sorry for that, Gumdrop. I was an asshole, and you deserved much better than that. If another guy had done it, I'd have kicked his ass for you."

Candi pulled her head away so she could give him a deep kiss, filled with the passion she felt for him and the love that had never gone away, even when he'd been so heartless. When she was done, she stepped back. "Enough of the past. Now it's time to just enjoy the now and the possible tomorrows."

Kevin took her by the hand and led her to the door. "Photo session time."

Candi grimaced. "Don't remind me."

Just as she was passing through the door, the phone rang. She let Kevin go out ahead of her so she could go back quickly and answer. Their dad called home a couple times a day and had promised not to forget to call before she left. She smiled warmly as she lifted the phone to her ear, not even bothering to check the caller ID.

"Hey, Dad. Perfect timing."

A voice on the other end hesitated. A man cleared his throat. "Excuse me. Mrs. Buckley? Mrs. Candace Buckley?"

"Uhhh, no. This is her daughter."

"May I speak with Mrs. Buckley, please?"

"Sure," said Candi, resting the back of the phone on her shoulder, grabbing the nearby pen and paper so she could take a message. "May I ask who's calling?"

"Yes, absolutely. This is Agent Charles Caffey with the Federal Bureau of Investigation."

Candi's pen hand froze over the paper.

"Excuse me? Can you ... repeat that?"

"I'm with the FBI. Charles Caffey."

The pen fell out of Candi's numb hand.

"Di ... did something happen to my father?" she whispered, her heart spasming painfully in her chest.

"What? No. No, no, no, this call isn't about your father at all."

Candi put her hand to her chest, breathing out heavily. "Oh my god, oh thank goodness. I almost had a heart attack there."

"My apologies. I didn't mean to alarm you. Is Mrs. Buckley there? May I speak with her?"

"Yeah, sure. Just hold on a second, okay?"

"Not a problem."

Candi walked out the front door, stopping on the top step. All of her new friends were standing out on the front lawn. There were four couples, everyone dressed to the nines and posing for pictures being taken not just by her mom and Kevin's mom, but the other parents who'd followed the limo over. It was like a bunch of paparazzi had descended, reminding Candi uncomfortably of the days after her rescue, all those cameras pushed in her face when all she wanted to do was see Kevin - the one guy who wanted nothing to do with her. There was even a big black SUV across the street with dark tinted windows, causing her to remember how they'd lie in wait and jump out to take pictures with little warning.

Kevin saw her for a moment, looking confused. He jogged up the stairs, frowning the whole way. "What's wrong?" He pulled the tophat he'd been wearing off his head.

"It's the FBI on the phone for my mom."

Kevin turned. "Yo! Mrs. B! Phone call for ya!"

"Tell whoever it is I'll call them back! Take a message!" Mrs. Buckley shouted, staring through the lens at her son and Sarah who were posing with their arms around each other, smiling hugely.

"Mom, you have to take it now," Candi said, trying not to

sound as freaked out as she was.

Candace looked up from her camera, her head tilting to the side as she took in the image of Candi standing on the stairs with the phone held out. She lowered her arms and walked over at a rapid pace.

"What's wrong, sweetie, who is it?" she asked as she came up the stairs.

"It's the FBI," Candi whispered, making sure no one else would hear.

Candace took the phone gingerly. "Hello?" She disappeared into the house, leaving Candi and Kevin alone on the porch again.

"What's that all about?" asked Kevin, his tophat dangling at his side.

"I don't know. Just that it's not about my dad. I almost died when I thought they were calling to tell us that ..." She couldn't finish.

Kevin took her in an embrace. "Shhhh, it's fine. Come on, let's get some pictures done. If I let you cry, Sarah will kill me."

Candi choked and laughed at the same time. "You're right. She's already smacked me twice."

"You've gotten off easy. Come on," he said, bringing her down the stairs, setting the tall hat back on his head.

Candi looked up at it. "Nice touch. The hat, I mean."

"You like it?" He grinned. "I thought it was pretty cool. At least I know I'll be original."

Candi said nothing in response, joining the others and posing in several different spots with various groupings, until Jonathan announced it was time to go.

"We have exactly three minutes to get into the limo and on the way!" he said, coming over to stand near Candi. "Where's

Mom? She's missing everything."

"She had to take a call."

"From Dad?"

Candi nodded absently, knowing her brother would insist on knowing every fact about the call otherwise. There'd be plenty of time to get the details after prom was over. Her mom would text if it was something that they needed to come home for. She pushed her brother over towards Sarah. "Help your baby momma get in the car. That dress is pretty tight."

"I know," said Jonathan. "It's not very practical, but I appreciate the way it causes my heart to palpitate when I look at her."

Candi giggled. "God, you're such a dork."

Jonathan looked over his shoulder, confused. "Why? It's not like I calculated my heart rate or anything."

"Yeah, right."

Jonathan had his guilty look on now. "Okay, I might have done that when I first saw her, but I haven't since. And I won't anymore tonight. I'm just going to go with the flow, like Sarah suggested."

"Excellent advice," Candi responded, looking one more time at her house, relieved to see her mom standing on the porch and waving goodbye. The phone was still in her hand, but at least she was smiling now.

"Bye, Mom!" yelled Candi from the window, waving furiously. The sounds of all the kids in the limo made it impossible to hear anything. The vehicle pulled away from the curb, headed towards the steakhouse where Kevin said he was going to put their all-you-can-eat salad bar out of business.

Candi sat back in her seat, snuggling up to her handsome

hunk of a boyfriend - Kevin Peterson ... the boy she'd dreamed of going to the prom with for years. She watched the animated expressions on her friends' faces as they ribbed Jonathan about the itinerary he'd put together for their evening, smiling with contentment. *Life is good.*

*****

The slow song was exactly what the doctor ordered. Kevin was holding his girl in his arms, wearing a kick-ass tux with a seriously cool tophat - the only guy in the place with one - , and his sister wasn't giving him crap about anything. It was some kind of miracle the way his life had turned out. He squeezed Candi just a little tighter, overwhelmed by the protective feelings he had for her.

Out of the corner of his eye, he caught Jason Hicks staring at them again from across the dance floor. The guy was in charge of the music and had been helping the DJ all night. Kevin had already brushed him off a few times when he started walking over, looking like he was going to ask Candi to dance. The guy was persistent, and if he didn't cut that shit out, he was going to earn himself a shiner.

Candi squeezed him back. "Stop staring holes into Jason's head."

"What are you talking about? I'm not even looking at that guy."

"Don't lie, I can see you." She was staring up at him, giving him her stern look.

"The dude needs to lay off. You're my girl and not available. He's having a hard time realizing that I'm serious."

"He's just a friend, Kevin. You don't need to go all neanderthal over it. He's been very nice to me, unlike some other people around here." Candi's gaze landed on Kevin's ex-girlfriend, and he knew what was coming next.

He spun her around to avoid hearing it again. "We're not going to go there, remember? We agreed."

"Yes," said Candi lifting her chin defiantly, "and you agreed to lay off Jason if I agreed to lay off that girl, so just stop. Or I'm going to have a throw-down with her in the bathroom later."

Kevin tipped his head back and laughed. "She'll be in serious trouble if that happens. And then so will you, when you mess up your fancy hair. Sarah will kill all three of us."

Candi pressed her lips together and nodded. "You're right. I'll have to spare Gretchen the butt-kicking she seriously needs, then." She smiled, letting him know she was joking.

Kevin knew Candi would never fight another girl, even though she *was* capable of beating every girl's butt at this school. "Yes. Spare her from certain doom, oh Queen of Peanut Island."

Candi play-hit him in the chest. "Shush. I'm falling in love ...," she said breathlessly, before finishing with, " ... in love with this song, that is." She giggled.

He dipped his head and nestled his face into the side of her neck, accidentally knocking his hat off. "You're mean," he said, kissing the delicate skin below her ear and lightly sucking on it.

She pulled back, bumping into someone behind her. "No hickies!" she warned, pointing at his face.

"What?" he said, laughing. "I'm innocent." Then he frowned when he saw who Candi had bumped into. "Dude, give me back my hat."

Candi turned around to look at the hat thief.

"What's the big deal, man? I'm just trying it on," said Barry, Sarah's ex-boyfriend, the one who'd cheated on her with Kevin's ex-girlfriend Gretchen. The dude was asking to be pounded. Begging, actually.

"You've got three seconds to get my hat off your slimy head and give it back."

"Or else what?" asked Barry, puffing out his chest a little.

"You don't want to know."

"Screw you, Kevin," he spat out. "I'm not afraid of you."

Kevin lunged for Barry's shoulder, but he slipped out of Kevin's grip, taking off through the crowd.

Kevin was leaving to go after him and deliver the punishment Barry so obviously wanted, but the soft, warm fingers sliding into his hand stopped him in his tracks. He looked down to see his little sand fairy Candi in a shiny green dress looking up at him, shaking her head slowly.

"What?" he asked. "No pounding the asshole into the dirt?"

"No. No pounding anyone into the dirt or anyplace else. Tonight's *our* night, and I don't want to spend it in the emergency room."

Kevin snorted. "The only one who's going to end up hospitalized is him."

"I know. And he used to be your friend, so you'd probably end up following the ambulance so you could apologize. He's totally not worth it, Kev."

Kevin cast his eyes down, not sure he agreed with her or not.

"He rescued you from making a big mistake with the wrong girl; and he did the same for your sister, right? So you really should shake his hand, not kick his butt."

Kevin smiled. "You are positively devious, you know that?"

She sidled up to him, smiling and revealing a very small dimple in her chin. "Are you complaining?"

"Most definitely not."

"And Kevin ... I have another reason why you should be grateful to Barry for taking your hat."

Kevin wrapped his arms around her, pulling her in close. "Oh, yeah? What's that?" He lowered his head, intent on kissing her silly.

"I really hated that thing. It was soooo dorky."

Kevin frowned. "What? You hated my cool tophat?"

She laughed. "It wasn't cool. And yes, I hated it. You're much handsomer without it, trust me." She stood on tiptoe to kiss him, making him quickly forget the insult to his awesome man-attire. The song continued, but he heard none of it as he lost himself in the warmth that she brought with every touch, every kiss.

She was right. He did owe Barry for what he'd done. There was probably no way he'd ever be able to repay him for taking that airhead Gretchen off his hands and for freeing his sister to fall in love with the coolest guy he'd ever known.

*****

Jonathan was dancing like he and Sarah had practiced, swaying to the rhythm of the song, desperately trying to hide his secret.

"You're counting in your head again," said Sarah, a small smile playing on her lips.

"No, I'm not," he said innocently. *One and two and three and four and one and two and three and four...*

"Jonathan, stop counting."

"I'm not."

"Okay then, recite the periodic table to me *with* atomic weights."

He opened his mouth as he thought of the first element,

Hydrogen 1.008 ... oh crap! I lost count! He accidentally stepped on Sarah's toe.

She smacked him on the chest. "Ouch, Jonathan! Watch those giant clown shoes of yours!" Her words were angry but her tone wasn't.

He stopped moving altogether, resting his hands lightly on her waist. "I'm sorry. I ... uhhh ... lost my rhythm."

"You lost your *count*, babe. I told you. Just relax. Feel the rhythm ... sway. Don't walk. Don't step. We can just stay in one place." Her hands were playing in the back of his hair, sending chills down his spine. She was the most beautiful woman in the room ... on the planet, actually; he hadn't been lying to her earlier. And the feel of her gorgeous body up against his and her fingers on his neck were making him crazy.

He pulled away from her for a second, looking down at her now confused expression. "You'd better stop what you're doing or we're going to have a little problem." He gave her a look, trying to express his meaning.

She got that dangerous expression on her face that told him he was in trouble. "Oh, yeah?" She pulled him back up against her, moving her hips just the tiniest bit. "What kind of problem?"

Jonathan rolled his eyes as he felt the warmth come over him. "Too late. You are totally tricky, Sarah, you know that. Now you have to stay right where you are until I can control myself again."

She rested her head on his chest. "Never learn to control yourself around me, Jon. Never."

Jonathan lowered his chin gently to her head. "Never? You always want me to be a mess, unable to stop myself from getting excited just looking at you and smelling you and stuff?"

"Never. Ever, ever, ever. Never. Don't do it. Or I'll hunt you down and kill you like the dog you are."

"Oh. Boy. Okay, then. Consider me committed to being an uncontrolled male in your presence."

The sound of distant screams coming from the doorway broke into their conversation. At first Jonathan thought it was part of the song, but it didn't really match the overall beat or melody. Then the music stopped altogether and someone took the microphone.

"Everyone, please remain calm. No one is permitted to leave the building until further notice. Someone please turn on the lights." The vice principal who'd made the announcement was having a heated discussion with the DJ. After he was finished, he raced off the stage and ran around the outside of the room, back to the doors that lead to the lobby and parking lot of the hotel where the prom was being held. The lights went on as the sound of the door closing behind him echoed in the room.

"What the heck is that all about?" asked Jonathan, trying to figure out what was going on but finding no clues in the area nearby. Everyone was standing around or moving into small groups, speculating about what could have ended their prom so abruptly.

"What can you see?" asked Sarah, jumping up and down to try and see over the heads around her.

"Nothing. Just some teachers at the doors not letting anyone out."

Sarah reached into her hand bag that was hanging from her wrist and sent off a text. A few seconds later, she grabbed Jonathan's arm and dragged him through the crowd. They ended up off on the side of the ballroom, near the refreshment table where Candi and Kevin were waiting.

Kevin held his hand up for a shake and Jonathan complied absently, still trying to make sense of the situation, his eyes darting around the room. It had to be something serious for the vice principal to have gone to these lengths, stopping the music and turning on the lights. And the teachers looked like bouncers at the doors, only not letting people out instead of in.

"What's happening?" asked Candi, her tone high and nervous.

"I have no idea. Jonathan said teachers are at the doors not letting anyone out," said Sarah.

"Wait! The doors are opening," said Jonathan, noticing a hot pink dress and a bright blue one coming in by the P.E. teacher's door. "Some girls are coming in ... and ... they're crying, I think."

"Let's go see what's going on," said Sarah, grabbing Jonathan again and dragging him forward.

"Maybe we should just wait here," he said, resisting and pulling her back.

Sarah spun around. "Jonathan, I have to pee. So either you get me to those doors and through them into the lobby, or I'm going to have an accident right here on this floor and humiliate myself and never be able to show my face in school again! I'll miss graduation and everything!"

Jonathan's eyes almost fell out of his head, picturing the scene he'd have to deal with if his high-strung girlfriend wet her dress at the prom. "Coming through!" he yelled, holding his hand out like a battering ram in front of him, bumping into people left and right but not stopping for anything. "Sorry! Pardon us! Coming through! Lady has to urinate! Sorry! Excuse me! Watch out!" They made it to the doors in under forty-five seconds. He checked his watch just to be sure.

"Thank you, sweet cheeks," said Sarah, patting him on the butt. She faced the teacher who was standing in front of the door with his arms crossed. "Excuse me, but I need to get out."

He shook his head. "Nope. No one goes out until security tells us you can."

"You can't hold me in here. It's against my right to freedom, and also I have to pee. And I'm pregnant, so if you stop me from using the toilet, you're violating my right to pee as an American, and I'll sue the school."

The teacher frowned, shaking his head and looking totally unconvinced. "I teach Civics Class with Intro to the Law, young lady. You have no right to use the toilet."

"The hell she doesn't," said Kevin from behind them.

Jonathan turned, relieved to have Kevin as his wingman.

"You can't restrain her freedom of movement or it's false imprisonment. And if she suffers a humiliating event that affects her health or that of her unborn child, you and the school will be liable. The hotel too, probably."

The teacher smiled begrudgingly. "So you *were* paying attention in class, Kevin. I had my doubts."

Kevin shrugged. "I'm in stealth mode most of the time."

The teacher nodded slowly. "Listen, I'd love to let you guys out of here, but someone's been shot out in the parking lot ... a student. They don't want anyone else hurt, so that's why we're keeping you in here. We're pretty sure the threat is over, but just to be sure, I need you to stay put."

Jonathan could feel his ears burning. He put an arm around Sarah's shoulders, drawing her close to him. He wanted to take her far, far away from this place, where anything might hurt her.

"Are the police here?" he asked.

"Yes. And an ambulance."

The door behind him opened, and a police officer entered. They all watched in silence as he made his way through the groups of students who were all talking in lowered voices, heading towards the DJ table. As soon as he was there, he took the microphone and spoke. "Hello, everyone. I'm officer Sam Sheedy of the local police department. We've had an incident out in the parking lot that we are in the process of managing. I need all of you to contact your parents on your cells and let them know you're okay and to please *not* come down to the hotel. We've got the area blocked off, and they won't be able to get in anyway. All of you will be released to go in about an hour. We just want to get everyone's contact information in case we have questions for you later. When we open the doors, there will be officers standing outside to take your names and contact information. Thanks in advance for your cooperation." He signaled to the teachers at the doors. "You can go ahead and open up, but the students need to go out in an orderly fashion, one at a time. Anyone not following this directive will be detained by the police. Thank you."

The teacher looked at Sarah. "You heard the man. Go out, give your info, and I'm sure they'll let you use the toilet."

"Thanks," she said, dragging Jonathan with her through the door the teacher was holding open. Jonathan pulled back on her and stepped in front of her. "Me first. Stay behind me."

Sarah rolled her eyes but complied, putting her palms on his back. "Okay, fearless leader. Go forward. Momma's gotta pee."

Jonathan looked back and saw that his sister and Kevin were right behind him, the two guys keeping the girls between them. He smiled grimly, thinking how this reminded him of their trip through the jungle when they were running from the drug dealers with guns. It was a different time and place, but the fear was the same. And now he had one more person he had to protect - his baby.

*****

Sarah finally got into the bathroom and took care of business while Candi waited for her. Sarah was washing her hands and checking her hair in the mirror as they chatted. "So, who do you think got shot?" she asked.

"I couldn't even imagine. I'm just glad it wasn't one of us. Is that terrible to say?" Candi asked quietly. The bathroom was mostly empty, everyone else milling around in the lobby trying to figure out what was going on, but Candi looked around guiltily anyway.

Sarah didn't have time to answer before the door burst open and three girls came in all together, huddled around the one in the middle. Sarah turned to face her, the reflection of the girl's bronze-colored dress immediately grabbing her attention. *Gretchen, that cheating ho-bag.* Sarah was about to let her have it with a comment about her date, Barry, but her words froze on her tongue when she saw Gretchen's face.

Her mascara had leaked all down her cheeks, leaving streaks through the foundation and powder. Her eyes were swollen and bloodshot. Her friends were basically holding her up, keeping her from falling. They rushed her to a toilet where she vomited loudly.

"Oh, that is just ... disgusting," said Sarah, her own stomach churning.

"Shut up, Sarah!" yelled one of the friends, whipping around to face her. "Her boyfriend got shot tonight! Try to be nice for once in your life!"

Sarah flinched back at the viciousness spewing out of the girl's mouth. If looks could kill she'd be dead. She felt something on her arm and saw that Candi had come to stand by her - and she looked ready to rumble.

Sarah put her hand in her friend's and gave her a quick squeeze, letting her know she was okay before responding. "Sorry, I had no idea. Are you serious? Barry's the one who got shot?"

The other girl nodded, crying herself now too. "Yes. It was terrible. We were standing *right* there."

"Oh, my god," said Candi, "did you talk to the police?"

"Yes. But then Gretchen got sick so we took a break."

The other girl walked out of the stall to get some paper towels. She wet them in the sink before returning to the prostrate Gretchen who was still heaving over the toilet.

"Wow. That's just ... so friggin scary," said Sarah. "Did you see who did it?"

The girl shook her head. "No. We heard this loud muffler kind of sound and then this low rider car came by, the back window rolled down, and they just ... shot him." She began to cry in a soft whimpering kind of way.

Candi handed her a paper towel, looking at a loss for words.

"You should get back to the police," said Sarah. "The sooner you can give them all the details, the faster they can catch whoever did this."

The girl nodded, looking over at Gretchen.

"We'll take care of her," said Sarah, sighing. "Go on. Go back out there." She was waving the two girls away as they stared at each other, looking as if they were trying to decide whether to take Sarah up on her offer.

They both shrugged before quickly going over to the mirror. They did their best to fix their faces before going out before leaving Candi and Sarah there with a very forlorn-looking Gretchen. She was sitting on the floor now, her back up against the side of the bathroom stall, the door hanging open.

Candi went inside and flushed the toilet, putting out her hands to help Gretchen up.

Gretchen just looked at her.

"Get up," said Sarah. "Come on. You look like hell. You don't want one of those losers on the yearbook committee getting a picture of you like this."

The fear leapt into Gretchen's eyes, and she grabbed Candi's hands, getting unsteadily to her feet. One of her shoes was missing its heel. She limped over to the sink and started crying all over again when she saw her face.

"Shhhh," said Candi, rubbing her back. She looked over at Sarah, urging, "*Do* something."

Sarah sighed. "My work is never done." She dropped her little evening bag down on the counter, pulling open the drawstrings that held it shut. "Get some paper towels, Sugar Lump ... stat. We don't have a lot of time."

Candy rushed over to pull several towels out of the dispenser.

"Use this," she said, handing Candi a small bottle of hand cream. "Get all that shit off her face."

Candi dabbed some of the lotion on a towel and used it like makeup remover to take off all the mascara.

"Eyes too. All of it."

"You're trying to make me look worse," said Gretchen, suspicion in her eyes as she hiccuped.

Sarah pointed a long nail at her face. "That's what you deserve, boyfriend-stealer, but that's *not* what I'm doing. Because the fact is, you did me and my brother a favor. I owed you one, and this is me paying you back. After this, we're even, and I don't ever want to see your face again as long as I live."

Gretchen smiled without humor. "That might be pretty tough seeing as how we still go to school together and we still have one more year left."

"Yeah, well ... just stay the hell out of my way." Her mind wandered over to the situation of her pregnancy, wondering if she was even going to be able to finish her senior year with the baby being born in the middle of it. But now was not the time to be worrying about that. She had a mission to accomplish. Operation Fix Gretchen's Butt-Ugly Face was now in full swing.

"I don't have any foundation, but you don't need it so we'll just skip to the eyes. I have liner, shadow in two shades, and mascara. Your eyes will look a lot like mine when we're done, but it's the best I can do right now." She smiled wickedly as she approached Gretchen. "Besides. You like having the same boyfriend as I do ... maybe you'll like copying my makeup, too."

"Sarah!" scolded Candi. "Stop. That's not nice. She's been traumatized. Leave her alone and just make her beautiful again."

Gretchen smiled tremulously. "Sarah's right. I was a bitch. I stole her boyfriend, and I know it wasn't nice."

"Ha. Told you." Sarah stuck her tongue out at Candi before reaching over to begin adding shadow to Gretchen's lids.

"Barry's just ... Barry. You know?" whined Gretchen. "He flirts all the time. He's hard to resist."

"Yeah. He's a player and an ass and you did me a favor ... like I said." Sarah cleared her throat. "Is he ... is he okay?" She didn't love him anymore, but she still didn't hate him so much she'd want him shot. Not really. *Maybe just a little. Like, shot in the butt cheek or something.*

"The guy in the ambulance said he was going to be okay. They got him in the arm." She let out a very shaky sigh. "But why Barry? I mean, he's not a druggie or anything. Why would gangsters want to shoot *him?*"

"It was probably just random," said Candi, rubbing her back gently again. "Wrong place, wrong time."

She was shaking her head. "No. The police were asking us over and over why he was wearing that stupid, ugly hat and whether he had any enemies and stuff. And some little gangster guy was talking to them about it ... the hat."

Sarah's hand froze in mid-makeup-application. "What hat?"

Gretchen looked guiltily over at Candi. "The tophat he stole from Kevin."

Sarah dropped the mascara and backed up a step. "What the heck ...?" She looked over at Candi, whose face had gone nearly white. "Candi, what the fu .... dge cookie?"

"I don't know ... I mean, just before they stopped the dance, maybe like ten minutes before, Barry came over, starting trouble with Kevin, and just took his hat and ran out of the dance. Kevin wanted to go after him and pound him, but I wouldn't let him."

Sarah bent down slowly to retrieve her makeup and carefully wiped it off as she thought about what they were saying. "So some gangster-looking guy is telling the cops that the hat was somehow involved? In Barry being shot?"

"Yes," said Gretchen nodding, wiping under her nose with another towel. "That's what it seemed like."

Candi whispered. "So was Barry the target, or the guy wearing the tophat ... Kevin?"

Sarah didn't know the answer to that question, but she sure as hell was going to find out what it was. "Look up, Gretchen. I have to get this liner and mascara done so I can go figure out what's happening."

"I'll meet you out there," said Candi, running out of the bathroom.

Sarah shook her head. "Sugar Lump's gonna go kick some butt. Bad guys better look out." She pushed on Gretchen's forehead. "Tip your head back, boyfriend-stealer. I need to get this liner on right."

*****

Kevin sat in a chair in the emergency room, Candi in his lap. She was turned sideways, leaning against his chest. He could smell her shampoo and familiar perfume. It made him want to gather her closer to him. Her earlier comments about him ending up in the emergency room were kind of freaking him out a little. Sarah and Candi had just told him and Jon about a rumor that his tophat had something to do with Barry being the one shot. The concept that someone might want to shoot *him* for wearing it was blowing his mind. Candi was right. It was a stupid hat.

Kevin's eyes wandered over to the coffee machine where a guy wearing black jeans and silver-tipped cowboy boots was waiting for his cup to drop. The guy glanced over at Kevin and then looked away quickly, retrieving his drink and moving away to stand in the corner of the room, his eyes roaming around but never coming back to Kevin.

Before Kevin could consider whether a cup of coffee was a good idea or not, the smell having tempted him, a man in a suit walked over and stood in front of them. Candi sat up, looking directly at Kevin, fear in her eyes. Kevin stood, putting her on her feet and his arm around her shoulders.

"Kevin Peterson?" the man asked.

Kevin nodded.

The man held out his hand. "Agent Charles Caffey, Federal Bureau of Investigation."

Kevin shook it. The guy had a really strong grip. "Nice to meet you, sir."

"Likewise. Can you follow me, please?"

Candi's grip around his waist got tighter. Kevin tried to detach her, but she was like a spider monkey, refusing to let go.

"You can stay here, young lady."

Candi shook her head. "I'm going with him." She looked up at Kevin, tears in her eyes. "Don't you dare leave me out here."

Kevin nodded, his protective instincts going into overdrive. "She's coming. Jonathan and Sarah too." They had walked over to stand next to him, Sarah looking more tired than she should have.

"Let's go," said Mr. Caffey, his voice giving no indication of how he felt about them all sticking together. He left the waiting room and went down a hallway, leaving the emergency room area of the hospital entirely.

They all followed behind, shooting each other questioning looks but saying nothing. Candi was texting someone, probably her mother. Kevin felt slightly less stressed, knowing someone besides them and this guy knew where they were. Hopefully, whatever this guy had to say wasn't terrible news. Kevin considered why the FBI might want to talk to him, and the only thing he could come up with was the fact that Barry had taken his hat. It was stupid, but nothing else made sense. Without the rumors the girls had heard, he never would have guessed his hat could have been involved.

The man stopped in front of a door that was open, gesturing for them to enter. There were two other people in business suits inside what turned out to be a conference room with a long blonde-colored wood oval table and several brown leather chairs around it.

"Please, take a seat." He shut the door behind Sarah, the last one in.

They all sat in a row, Jonathan on one end and Kevin on the other, the girls in the middle. The suits gathered at the other end of the room, facing them.

"Do you know why we've brought you here?" asked Agent Caffey.

Kevin shook his head, his face getting instantly flushed. He felt guilty even though he had no idea what he could have possibly done.

"You were wearing a tophat to the dance earlier, is that correct?"

"Yeah. So? What's that got to do with anything?"

"Was anyone else at the dance wearing one that you're aware of?" Agent Caffey looked at each of the teens in the room individually.

They all shook their heads no.

Then Sarah spoke up. "No one has the guts to wear such a ridiculous hat." She looked over at Kevin and winked. For some reason it made the pressure on his shoulders lighten just a little.

Candi's phone buzzed. She looked around in a panic before pressing the green button. "Hello?" she whispered into the mouthpiece.

"Please put your phone away," said one of the other suits. This guy had really dark hair and a pockmarked face, and he was about four inches shorter than Agent Caffey.

Candi ignored him, which obviously pissed him off. He made as if he was going to come around the table towards her.

Kevin stood, making his intent clear with the look he shot in the agent's direction. But just in case the guy was an idiot and couldn't read body language, he elaborated. "Dude. Take one more step towards her, and you're going to be sorry."

Jonathan stood suddenly too, nodding. Kevin could see that he was shaking.

The guy put his hands up, frowning like it was no big deal, but his casual demeanor didn't reach his eyes.

Kevin sat down slowly. Jonathan tried to do the same, but his chair had swung sideways a bit. His butt hit the arm of the chair instead of the cushion, sending him down in a crooked half-fall, half-sit. Sarah leaned over and threw her arms around him, kissing him loudly on the cheek. He worked to right himself as Candi finished her call.

She sat up and said, "Our parents are on their way. They told me to tell all of you that we aren't going to answer any more questions without a lawyer."

"You can't speak for the others," said the pockmarked guy.

"I'm not talking to anyone without a lawyer," said Sarah, staring him down mutinously.

"Me, neither. I want an attorney. I'm asserting my constitutional rights to remain silent," said Jonathan, nodding firmly.

"I guess you guys will have to wait to get any answers from us, then," said Kevin, feeling extremely confident with his family next to him and on the way. "I want a lawyer too."

The third agent, a lady, rolled her eyes. "Way to go, Pete." She looked over at us. "Listen, you don't need attorneys, kids. You're not in trouble. You're not suspected of doing anything against the law. We had an appointment to meet with you tomorrow, anyway. We talked to your mother today, Candi and Jonathan. Do you remember taking Mr. Caffey's call, Candi?" This lady was obviously much nicer than the other two guys. Or at least, less intimidating.

Candi nodded. "But I'm still not talking to you until my parents get here."

The others nodded as well. Kevin took Candi's hand and squeezed it, letting her know how proud of her he was. *You can take the girl off the island, but you can't take the island out of the girl.*

The lady held up her hands in a gesture of surrender. "That's fine. We'll wait." She dropped her hands and just held her palm out in a friendly way. "Anyone want anything to eat? Chips? Coffee?"

"Oh, some chips would be awesome," said Sarah. "I'm feeling a little woozy, actually."

The lady turned to the mean guy. "Pete, please go to the machine down the hall and get some snacks for the kids. Their parents are at least twenty minutes out."

"Add a few sodas to that list, if you don't mind," said Jonathan. "Water for Sarah, though. She's not allowed to have caffeine or refined sugars."

She whacked him on the shoulder. "Hey, hard butt. I'm

allowed to have a little."

He shook his head, refusing to agree.

Kevin smiled.   He was sitting in what was essentially an interrogation room with three FBI agents, and his sister and adopted family were by his side, going on with life like this was just no big deal.   The island experience had made them all tougher, more confident. He took in a deep breath, letting it out slowly. Everything was going to be fine. They just needed to find out who hated tophats so much they'd shoot a guy wearing one.

Witnesses

FRANK PETERSON WAS STEAMING MAD. "What are you telling us, then? That someone's got it out for our kids? That's ridiculous ... they're teenagers for chrissakes!"

His wife put her hand on his arm in an effort to calm him down, but he just shrugged her off, probably more forcefully than he should have. He was the only one in the room who didn't realize it. Angie Peterson backed away, shrinking in on herself. Candi's mom reached out and put her hand on Angie's shoulder, but Angie didn't even look at her.

"Please calm down, Mr. Peterson," said Agent Caffey. "We don't have all the facts yet, but what we do know is that we have an active investigation going on that's been in process for over a year; and at this point, your kids are the only material witnesses we have who can not only identify some of the participants but who can also verify that the island they were trapped on was covered in illegal drugs." He sighed, staring from one face to another. "We need their testimony to put these guys away."

"Our appointment wasn't until tomorrow, though," said Candi's mother. "How is it that some person out there knows about our children being witnesses before we do? And they know enough to shoot at someone they think is Kevin Peterson?"

"That's ridiculous!" growled Frank. "Beyond belief! You must think we're complete idiots!" He jerked his head towards the door. "Come on, Angela. We're going. Kevin! Let's go, son."

He didn't mention Sarah, but that was probably for the best. Candi didn't relish the idea of his cruelty being advertised to the FBI anymore than it already had.

Kevin didn't move. If anything he hung on tighter to Candi's shoulders. She smiled up at him as best she could, but knew it had probably come across as more a grimace than anything else.

"I'm not done talking to these guys," said Kevin. "Dad, can you just sit down and hear them out? I really don't want someone putting a hole in my back."

Frank stared at everyone, his nostrils flaring. "Fine. You want to stay? Stay! I'm going home!" He stormed out of the room, slamming the door behind him.

An awkward silence ensued.

Then Sarah said, "Ladies and Gentleman ... Frank Peterson has left the building."

Candi snickered just a tiny bit before she caught herself. The stress from the night was causing her to lose her mind or something. Kevin leaned down and kissed her once on the top of her head, making her feel very relieved to know he wasn't mad about her kind-of laughing about his dad. Sarah looked over and winked. Jonathan was staring at his watch, probably calculating if Frank actually *had* left the building or if he were still inside somewhere.

The female FBI agent looked to their mothers. "Mrs. Peterson ... Mrs. Buckley ... we've spoken to our superiors, and it appears as if there *is* some support to the theory that someone knows we intended to approach the kids about being witnesses and are working at eliminating them or at least scaring them into not participating. That being the case, we are currently doing the paperwork to put them into protective custody ... " She lifted her hands at the obvious disapproval and worry about to be launched by the parents. "... Just until we know who is responsible, so we can take care of the problem."

"But ... that could be months. Years, even!" exclaimed Candi's mom. "They're in high school. They'll ruin their GPAs, they'll miss graduation ..." She looked to Mrs. Peterson. "Right, Angie?"

Angie nodded. "Yes. I agree. This is unacceptable."

Candace continued. "I haven't been able to reach my husband, but I know he'd agree with me."

"No, it shouldn't be that long. And we have authorization to have tutors for them, online learning, so they will be able to keep up with their classes, and there should be no effect on their GPAs at all. They'll have basic internet access just for the classes, and it will be routed through the FBIs network for total security. They may miss graduation, but there's nothing we can do about that. It would be too risky to allow them to be out in public like that."

The other two agents were nodding their agreement.

"Will we go with them?" asked Candi's mother, looking over helplessly at her two children.

"No. They will be monitored at all times by our personnel, but they will be cut off from the outside world. We will deliver recordings of them talking to you, personal messages, but that's all. No email, no phone calls, no texting ... nothing. No contact until they testify."

"And after?" asked Angie. "After they testify will they be safe?"

Agent Caffey answered. "The hope is that after the trial, they will be able to return to life as before. We will use their testimony to put the guilty parties away for a long, long time. Hopefully, forever. We should be able to add attempted murder to their already very long list of charges, based on their activities tonight."

"And what if we say no?" said Angie. "What if we don't agree to have our children subjected to this kind of treatment or even to being witnesses?"

"Then there is nothing we can do to protect them. And the fact is, they have sensitive information about the crimes committed by these drug traffickers, and the criminals know it. They will not stop until they've made sure the information cannot come out against them. It's a race to the courthouse, essentially."

Candi felt the blood drain from her face. "Oh my god ... that's just ... awful times a million." Tears sprang to her eyes. "Do we even have a choice, then?" She looked from her mother to her brother and then her friends. "We have to do this, right? I mean, we can't walk around town or school constantly waiting for a bullet to hit us."

"Actually, most of the witnesses we've lost in this case have been killed by being stabbed ... multiple times," said the pockmarked agent.

Angela gasped and then shrieked. Candi's mom put a shaking hand to her lips in silence, her eyes bright with tears.

"Pete, that wasn't necessary," said the female agent. She looked over at us. "It's true, but irrelevant. Candi is right. You really don't have a choice. You need to allow us to protect you, and the only way we can do that is if you agree to help us. You will be compensated for your time, within the rules of the federal government."

Jonathan looked up from his careful study of the tabletop. "I agree to assist you with the prosecution of the criminals in exchange for your protection for me and my sister and our friends. But I really think you should consider doing something for our parents, too."

"We might be able to fund a long vacation," said Agent Caffey. "It will take special authorization, but we're willing to give it a shot."

Kevin nodded. "I agree to those terms too." He looked down at Candi. "What about you, Gumdrop? Are you in?"

Candi thought about it and realized, there was nothing else to say. "Yeah. I'm in if you guys are." She looked over at her mother who now had tears running down her cheeks.

"I'm so sorry, sweetie," was all her mother could say before the crying overwhelmed her.

"It's not your fault, Mom," said Candi. "Life happens." She shrugged. She wished she felt as casual about the whole thing as her words implied, but all she kept imagining was some guy in a dark trench coat whipping out a knife and attacking her with it. She wished she had one of her fishing spears from the island to carry around with her.

"I agree too, if anyone cares," said Sarah sarcastically. "Can I go to the bathroom now? I'm about to lose it."

"Yes. I'll take you," said the female agent.

"Me too!" said Candi, jumping up from the table and going over to take Sarah by the hand.

"Nervous, Sugar Lump?" asked Sarah, looking as cool as a

cucumber.

"Yes. Very."

"Come on. Tell your big sister aaaallll about it," she said, as they stepped out of the door, following the agent into the softly-lit hallway.

*****

Agent Caffey was at the wheel of the large, black SUV, driving into a neighborhood Jonathan hadn't seen in a long time. Agent Booker, the lady, sat next to him. The other guy with all the acne scars, Agent Gutierrez, stayed at the hospital. The tearful mothers had been left behind, along with Jonathan's father who'd finally shown up at the end. Jonathan felt bad that his dad had missed most of the conversation and explanation, because he looked so lost and forlorn when they drove away. It was just bad luck that he'd been working late and without any phones nearby until just before they were leaving.

"Are you okay?" he asked Candi. She looked even worse than their parents had.

"Yeah," she whispered. "It's just a lot to process."

Jonathan nodded. She wasn't kidding. His brain felt like it was getting a cramp in it from trying to put all the pieces together. He knew they'd be up all night talking about this stuff. It made him a little glad that they were all in this with him, even though it also meant they were at risk. He pulled Sarah's hand over into his lap so he could stroke it gently. She had fallen asleep, her head on his shoulder. She'd probably drool on it too, but he didn't care.

"You'll only be in this place for one or two days ... three max," said Agent Booker. We just need to finish up the paperwork and arrangements to take you to the more permanent location."

"And we'll be there for how long?" asked Kevin.

"A month or so. The trial process is moving along nicely. The lawyers tell us you'll be key to the whole thing, so they'll be anxious to get you on the stand early on."

Jonathan nodded, glad it wasn't going to be that long. School would probably be over before they were finished, but that didn't matter. They still had their senior year, and more importantly, Sarah's pregnancy would still be in its early stages.

He looked down at her flat belly, trying to imagine what it would look like with a human being growing inside, getting bigger and bigger. The idea was curious and warming to him. He'd never pictured himself as a dad before, and while this was not the best timing in his life for it, he was confident he could do a good job. His dad was the best ever, so all he had to do was think to himself, *What would my dad do?* Plus, he could always Google stuff he didn't know. He'd already spent countless hours researching the hormonal issues of the pregnant female, fetal development over the months, complications, and even labor and delivery. It had two outcomes for him: one, he felt more prepared, and two, he was scared to death. So many things could go wrong, and Sarah was about to deal with the most difficult and painful things she'd ever known in her whole life. And Sarah was a handful on her best day. Sarah *pregnant* was going to be something else entirely. Jonathan was glad he had the island experience on his side. He had a feeling he was going to need it.

"Do you guys know this neighborhood?" Kevin asked, keeping his voice low so the agents wouldn't hear him over their own conversation about company picnics and softball games.

Candi shook her head no.

"I've driven through here on my scooter before, when I was

looking for some plant material for a botany project I was working on," said Jonathan. "The houses in this neighborhood have a lot of interesting things in their yards that houses don't have over in our area."

Kevin nodded, stretching his neck out to get a good look at the scenery as they drove by. "It's dark, but even so, I can tell it's a nice area. The houses here are pretty decent-sized."

"The houses on the other side of this neighborhood are *really* nice. Much bigger than these. I couldn't get near those, though, because they had walls around them."

"Why can't they put us in a house with walls around it?" asked Candi, grouchily. "Seems safer than just being out in the open."

"I think we're safer with more escape options," said Jonathan. "And we need to blend, which we wouldn't do in a very fancy neighborhood. They'd see us as not belonging right away."

"Speak for yourself, babe," said Sarah, waking up and yawning. "I could totally blend in a fancy place."

Jonathan shook his head. "As a new arrival you'd stick out, and being beautiful you'd stick out, so I'm sorry, but I have to disagree with you."

Sarah pulled Jonathan's face over to her, palm to cheek. "You always know exactly what to say to a girl, don't you?" She kissed him on his lips, making him go warm again.

"No, actually I don't ever know what to say. I think I just get lucky."

Sarah laughed, dropping her hand back to her side. "Lucky you, lucky me."

Jonathan patted her hand that still rested in his lap, happy that she was content. Sometimes she woke up from naps more cranky than when she had laid down. Tonight was a good night, which was strange considering all they'd gone through so far. Maybe Sarah functioned better when under stress. He was going to have to pay more attention to that, maybe even make a chart. The more he thought about it, the more excited he became over the potential project. He hoped they'd have a computer with Excel on it wherever they were going so he could put this all together. Maybe if he could analyze her activities and moods enough, he could calculate when they were going to change, and adjust his reactions and manage them accordingly.

"What are you cooking up there in that bean of yours?" Sarah asked him, suspicion lacing her voice.

"Oh, nothing. Just some math stuff. Statistical information, mostly."

Sarah patted his hand. "Whatever floats your boat, babe."

"Dude, you're the only one I know who does math to calm himself," said Kevin, chuckling under his breath.

"That's unfortunate, because it's quite effective. You should try it sometime. Even just reciting your multiplication tables is relaxing, and it has the side benefit of improving your math skills."

"Geez, Jonathan, you're giving me a headache just suggesting that," said Candi. "I'd rather count sheep."

"That's math," said Jonathan, cheered by the idea of his sister having the same interests as he did. "See? We agree." He turned to his sister in time to see her roll her eyes, which was something she did at him at least ten times a day. He'd actually counted them over a week's period of time, and he noticed that as the week got closer and closer to Friday she did it more often. Her biggest eye-rolling day was Friday. He'd concluded that it was the stress of school building up in the week that caused it. There was no other good explanation as far as he'd been able to determine.

Before anyone else could weigh in any more on the concept of doing math to relax, the SUV pulled up into a driveway. The house it belonged to was dark, not even a porch light on.

Jonathan frowned. It seemed to him that if you wanted a house to stay incognito, you'd use timers on the light fixtures to make them go on and off at normal hours. He looked around at the other houses and all of them had at least a porch lamp on.

"This is the place," said Agent Caffey. "Stay here in the car for a couple minutes while I do a quick sweep."

He was gone for five minutes and thirty-eight seconds before getting back into the car and driving it forward again. The garage door went up with a touch of a button, and they pulled inside, waiting for the door to go back down before getting out.

The girls slid out on one side and Kevin and Jonathan slid out the other, all of them standing now in a mostly empty garage. Jonathan looked around, taking in the empty shelves, some discarded boxes on the ground that used to hold golf balls, and dust everywhere.

"Follow me," said Agent Booker, walking up to the door that led from the garage to the interior of the house. Jonathan noticed she rested one of her hands inside her jacket, where her shoulder holster held the gun he knew was there. He swallowed hard, thinking about what that meant. Even here, in a safehouse, things weren't necessarily secure.

She was inside before he had time to consider it any further, and then he heard her talking to someone. His heart skipped a beat, thinking that a bad guy had been waiting in there and she was maybe negotiating with him; but when no shots came out of her gun and Agent Caffey just followed her in, he breathed easier. *Must be colleagues.*

Kevin was inside now, and he wasn't yelling, so finally Jonathan knew it was safe. He watched as his sister and then Sarah entered the house. He brought up the end of the line, turning around once just to make sure no one was there. All he saw were footprints in the dust.

*****

Sarah woke up. She had no idea what time it was, but outside it was still pitch dark. The FBI agents had given Sarah's phone to her parents at the hospital, explaining that the kids' location could be tracked using the chips inside, so she couldn't tell what time it was. This stupid room she was sharing with Candi didn't have an alarm clock or anything.

"Stupid friggin safehouse," she grumbled, throwing back her covers and padding over to the door. She was wearing the underthings she'd bought for the prom and a government-issue undershirt she'd found in a dresser drawer. Luckily the floors were carpeted, keeping her feet from getting too cold. She would have been pissed to not only have to get up in the middle of the night once again to go to the bathroom, but also to have to find a way to warm her feet up. She hated trying to sleep with cold feet.

She opened the bedroom door, expecting to see a man standing there, but the hallway was empty. There were four agents in the house with them - not the ones from the hospital, but new ones. Their job was to watch over the four witnesses until morning, at which point they would be relieved by even more new ones. Apparently, Agents Caffey and Booker were not house-watchers or babysitters.

Sarah sighed. Jerks were probably downstairs playing cards and drinking beers. She didn't have a lot of faith in these guys. From the minute that turd, Agent Gutierrez, had told them their last witnesses had been stabbed, she'd questioned both their professionalism and their skills at protection. She closed the door behind her as quietly as possible, making sure it latched. She didn't want Candi waking up and freaking out about an open door.

She made her way down to the bathroom and went inside, not turning on a light. She hated waking herself up all the way like that. Maybe she'd have a chance at going back to sleep if she stayed partially out of it in the dark. She sat down to do her business, her mind wandering to their days on the island. They'd been safe there for a while - no drug dealers to worry about, no guys with guns or knives out to get them. It had been pretty much perfect until those drug dealers had come along and ruined it all with their stupid pot plants. *Assholes.* She didn't bother cleaning up her language since the baby couldn't hear it inside her head.

She finished and got up to leave the bathroom. She was just about to pull open the bathroom door when she heard whispers. She was going to just step out and join the conversation, when she caught the words *"Finish them off ..."* coming from someone standing just outside the bathroom, maybe just a little down the hall nearer to her room.

Her heart dropped into her stomach, making it burn with anxiety. *Ohmygod, ohmygod, ohmygod! They're here! The murderers are here!* She wrung her hands, trying to decide what to do. She scanned the bathroom for a weapon, quickly squatting down to open the cabinet door. Using the nightlight that was plugged into the wall near the floor, she found a basket inside. The only thing even semi-lethal inside was a metal nail file. She pulled it out and held it in her fist, the point coming out of the bottom. She waited until there was no more sound and crept closer to the door, panicked she wasn't going to be able to get to whoever it was before they reached Candi or one of the others. The little Sugar Lump was sound asleep, snoring away, oblivious to the danger coming for her.

She opened the door slowly, sticking her head out inch by inch to look down the hallway. She saw a shadowy figure, standing just outside her bedroom, his hand on the door handle, turning it.

Sarah didn't know what to do. *What if it's an FBI agent just checking on us? If I attack him, he'll shoot me for sure, or maybe even Candi by mistake. But if it's a murderer and I just stand here, he'll get Candi before I can do anything about it!* Her mind was spinning with the possible outcomes, but when she saw that he was actually stepping into the room, she made her decision. The FBI agents had no reason to go into the rooms. They were just supposed to stand outside and keep watch. And since this jackwaggon was in here creeping around in the dark, she had to assume the worst.

She raced down the hallway as silently as possible, thankful the carpet was thick. She reached the door, just as he disappeared inside.

She didn't think twice, she just acted. She pushed open the door, saw the guy's back in front of her, and jumped on it. She grabbed his head and twisted it, yanking him back with her whole body, making him fall backwards. She stabbed the nail file down towards his neck, not sure if it was going to do any good, but knowing she had to do whatever she could to stop him.

He yelled like a wild man, and then Sarah heard Candi scream.

A light went on, but all Sarah could see were the stars swimming around her brain from having hit the floor so hard and having the heavy weight on top of her push all the air out of her lungs. She clung to his struggling form with all her strength, even wrapping her legs around him.

He was smallish, but wiry. He was getting up, even with Sarah still hanging onto his back. She hadn't felt the sting of a knife yet or the blazing heat of a bullet in her body, but she was sure it was still a possibility. This guy was doing nothing but fighting and no announcement of being an FBI agent left his lips. Quite the contrary, actually.

"Get off me, you fucking bitch!" he grunted out, swinging elbows out to the side, trying to catch her with one.

"Not on your life, asshole," she growled, refusing to let go.

Then the lights went out again, and her breath was muffled by a piece of cloth.

"Aaaaaahhhh! I can't breathe!" Sarah yelled. Then she felt more weight on top of her body.

"Get out, Sarah!" shouted Candi. "I've got him! Get out and help me!"

Sarah let go of her prey and squirmed and wiggled and kicked until she was free of his weight. He still struggled, but now he was trying to fight someone else off; he seemed to have temporarily lost interest in getting to Sarah.

She worked her way out from underneath him and the light came back on. Or rather, now she could see again. Candi had thrown her whole quilt over the top of the guy and had him wrapped up, at least temporarily. She was punching anything that moved, trying to slow his escape down.

"Help me!" she yelled, slowly losing the fight. He had an arm out now and had gotten a handful of her hair. She screamed in pain.

Sarah ran over to the other side of the room and grabbed the brass lamp that was sitting on the table next to her bed. She yanked the cord out of the wall and leaped over Candi's bed, stopping to lift the lamp high over her head before bringing it crashing down onto the lump under the covers.

"Ooooowwww! Jesus fucking *Christ* ... ! You're gonna pay for that you *bitch* ...!"

Sarah brought the lamp down again, cringing a little at the solid connection and the corresponding clank the lamp made.

He grunted with the last hit, and his movements slowed.

"Do it again!" yelled Candi, some of her dreadlocks still trapped in his fist.

Sarah smashed him three more times in quick succession, finally bringing his struggles to a halt.

The fist holding Candi's hair slackened, and she pulled away from him, taking the quilt off at the same time.

Both girls stood there, breathing heavily, staring down at the man who had snuck into their room.

"Well, if he wasn't ugly before, he's definitely ugly now," said Sarah, grimacing at the mess she'd made of his face. His nose was smashed to the side, and he had three big lumps - two on the side of his head near his temple. A nail file was sticking out of his collar bone area, and blood was pooling around his neck from the wound.

"Who is he?" asked Candi, gasping and panting, sounding near tears. "Why was he in here? Is he with the FBI?"

Sarah pointed to the knife on the floor nearby, one with a very jagged edge on one side and a heavy, very sharp-looking smooth edge on the other. "I'm pretty sure the FBI uses guns, not knives."

Candi's face went from bright red to white in a second, her trembling hand held to her mouth, looking like she was going to barf.

"Don't do it, Sugar Lump. We aren't done yet. First of all, we need to tie this piece of garbage up in case he wakes up. Then we have to go make sure Jonathan and Kevin are okay."

Candi made as if to run to the door. "Oh my god! Jonathan and Kevin!"

"Stop!" whisper-yelled Sarah. "We have to tie him up first! We don't want him waking up and coming after us again! Now turn on the light and lock the door so we can finish uninterrupted. He has at least one friend out there."

Candi turn around, stricken.

"I know you're worried about them!" continued Sarah. "So am I! Come on, hurry up and help me!" Sarah pulled on the cord still attached to the lamp with all her might, but it wouldn't come loose.

Candi locked the door and then was by her side in an instant with the murderous knife in her hand. She cut through the cord with one clean slice. "Wow. That was too easy. This thing is as sharp as a razor." She gulped loudly and looked at Sarah, panic in her eyes.

"Keep it together, Candi. No barfing on me or the bad guy. Not yet anyway. Grab his hands and roll him over."

Candi pulled the guy's arms above his head and dragged him free of the bed area, flipping him over onto his face and bringing his arms around his back.

Sarah stepped over, straddling him. She wrapped the cord around his wrists really tight ... so tight it made his hands go white.

"That's cutting off his circulation," said Candi, frowning with concern at his hands.

"Good. Bastien deserves it."

Candi looked up, confused. "Bastien? Is that his name? How did you know that?"

"No, that's not his name, you goof. It's my new word for B-A-S-T-A-R-D. You know I'm not supposed to swear anymore." She glanced up at Candi to get her reaction.

A small smile lit Candi's face. "He *is* a bastien isn't he?"

"Yes," said Sarah, turning back to the job at hand. "Now bend his ankles up here."

"What are you going to do with his ankles?"

"I'm hog-tying this bastien so he can just roll around up here and suffer. Maybe his hands and feet will fall off and then we'll never have to worry about him knifing us while we sleep again."

"Should I take his boots off?" Candi asked, eyeing the black cowboy boots with distaste.

"Yes. Take 'em off and thump him on the head with them while you're at it."

"Are you serious?" asked Candi, the first boot off and in her hand, the long, dirty sock soon following.

"Kind of. Not really. But only if he moves." She stopped for a minute to consider it and then nodded firmly before going back to her tying. "Yes. If he moves, beat the shizzle out of him."

Candi nodded, grabbing the other boot and sock off. "Got it. Smash him if he moves. Consider it done." She held his ankles and calves bent up behind him so Sarah could tie them together and then attach them to his tied hands. They had to cut the cord of the other lamp too to make it work, but when they were finished, he was completely immobilized.

"Geez, do his feet stink or what?" asked Candi.

"Like cat pee. Seriously, I'm ready to vom. As soon as we're done here, I'm going to barf on his head just for subjecting my unborn child to such an awful stink."

"Man, did you work on a ranch once?" asked Candi, admiring her roommate's handiwork as she waited for her to climb over the bed and around him.

"No, but I used to want to be a cowgirl, so I watched rodeos on TV all the time." Sarah reached Candi's side. "Come on. Let's go see the boys."

"Wait. One more thing." Candi grabbed the dirty sock they'd taken off one of the guy's feet and stuffed the whole thing into his mouth, using a bit of extra lamp cord to tie it in place around the back of his head. She looked up at Sarah. "Can't have him shouting for help, now can we?"

"No, we cannot," agreed Sarah, giving Candi a quick hug for her awesome idea and brave face. She seemed to have gotten over most of her panic and was now ready to kick some butt.

They turned off the overhead light and opened the door, slowly going out into the hallway, headed to the room two doors down. Sarah hoped her brother and the father of her unborn child had managed to take down their attacker, like she and Candi had theirs.

*****

Kevin was sound asleep and dreaming of the island when the overhead light went on and the girls ran into the room, shaking him and Jonathan awake. He blinked a few times, trying to orient himself, not recognizing the light fixture on the ceiling. It had weird flowers on it, and the one in his room was made of stainless steel and smoked glass. Sarah's voice began penetrating his brain.

" ... a big friggin knife, too."

Candi joined in. "But he's tied up right now on the floor, and we need to find out where all the FBI agents are and if there are anymore of these guys in the house trying to kill us."

Candi was on his bed now, leaning down for a hug. Her smell enveloped him, making him pull her to his side automatically for a couple seconds. It was her trembling that finally made it through his fog enough to get him fully alert.

He sat up and placed her down next to him on the bed, removing his legs from the covers and rubbing his head a few times. "Okay, sorry, but I was really out of it there ... can you tell me again what you just said?"

Sarah growled. "Grrrr, come on, you guys! There's a *murderer* in our bedroom! How much more information do you need?"

Jonathan and Kevin leaped out of their beds at the same time, shirtless but wearing boxer briefs, both of them shouting.

"What?!" Jonathan ran to the door, nearly tripping over his own feet, turning the lock before spinning back around to face everyone.

"Who's in your room?!" asked Kevin, ready to smash some skulls. The idea that someone had gone after his sister and girlfriend while they slept was beyond ridiculous. He pulsed his pecs a few times, getting the blood flowing into his muscles.

"Like we've already explained, three times," said a very annoyed Sarah, "I got up to pee, and as I was about to leave the bathroom, I heard voices outside the door talking about finishing us off. So I followed a guy into my room where he was about to knife Candi in her sleep."

"What happened next?" asked Jonathan in a high-pitched voice.

"We kicked his ass," she said simply, shrugging her shoulders.

"Details, Sarah. Details," said Kevin, a warning in his voice. He needed to know what they were dealing with and fast.

She sighed heavily. "I jumped on his back, Candi threw the blanket over him, and we beat him with a lamp."

"Is he ... dead?" asked Jonathan.

"No. Just tied up," said Sarah. She frowned at Jonathan. "I hope you aren't mad at us that we defended ourselves. The guy deserves to be dead."

Jonathan shook his head. "No, no ... I'm just ... glad all three of you are okay."

"Why do you care about the murderer?" asked Candi, all huffy.

"Not him, dummy. The *baby*." Jonathan rolled his eyes.

Kevin smiled. Eye-rolling was not Jonathan's thing, and it was pretty funny on him. But he had a point. Sarah had taken a big risk. Before he could scold her, Jonathan was talking again.

"You said you heard voices. As in, more than one," said Jonathan.

"Yes. Two at least."

"So where's the second guy?" asked Kevin, looking from Sarah to Candi.

They both shrugged.

"We thought he might be here, coming after you, but apparently not," said Sarah. "You guys didn't hear anything at all?"

"Not me," said Jonathan. "I was in deep R.E.M.-sleep actually. I think the stress must have gotten to me."

"Yeah. I was totally gone," said Kevin, feeling bad that he'd slept through the attempted murder of his sister and girlfriend. He walked over and hugged Candi. "Sorry, babe. I should have been there for you."

Candi squeezed him back hard, acting like she didn't want to let go when it was over. "We handled it. But we need to get out of here."

"She's right," said Jonathan. "We'll go as a group. First though, I want to see the guy who came after you two."

They all nodded their agreement, and Kevin and Jonathan moved to be first at the door.

Sarah ran over and grabbed the nearest lamp, yanking it from the wall. She walked over to Candi, who picked up the lethal knife she'd put on the dresser and cut the cord off. She wrapped the coated wire up in a tight circle and shoved it in her bra.

"Okay," whispered Kevin, "we all stick together. Give me that knife," he said, holding his hand out. Candi passed it up to him. "I'm first, then the girls, then Jon. Jon, you've got our backs." He looked at Sarah. "Give him the lamp."

She passed it over to Jon, blowing him a kiss when she was done.

They lined up at the door, one behind the other, and Kevin turned out the light, plunging them all into darkness.

*****

They stood around the body in Candi's room. He hadn't moved since they'd tied him up and she'd shoved that nasty sock in his mouth.

"I've seen this guy before," said Kevin, sounding distressed and excited at the same time. "He was at the hospital, in the emergency room!"

"What, like with the FBI?" asked Jonathan.

"No. As in, like a guy just hanging out in the waiting room. I'd remember those boots anywhere, with those silver tips. He was getting coffee right in front of me and Candi. Do you remember seeing him?" he asked her.

Candi studied the guy's bruised face and boots, cringing inwardly at the nail file sticking out of his shoulder. "No. I wasn't really paying attention to anyone else around us. Sorry." She felt useless. A murderer had totally checked them out, followed them, and almost taken them down; and he'd been standing in front of her for who knew how long. She'd been totally helpless, a feeling she hated more than anything. It reminded her of being on that lifeboat in the middle of the ocean, rogue waves tossing them all over the place and pushing them farther and farther away from safety.

Jonathan patted her on the shoulder. "None of us were thinking we were being targeted, so none of us should feel bad about not noticing anything. But that has changed. Now we *know* we're targets. And now we also know the FBI either has a leak or they aren't very good at doing their jobs ... at least in this case. So we need to start paying very close attention to our environment and be prepared for anything."

"What are you saying, babe?" asked Sarah.

"I'm saying we need to get the heck out of this house and find a place we can stay on our own. No FBI. No parents. Nobody but us."

"Are you nuts?" asked Candi, not believing her brother would be so irresponsible. "We can't do that. It's totally ... reckless."

"I agree with him," said Kevin. "It's not reckless to try and stay alive. And when the stupid FBI can't even keep us safe, then we have to take matters into our own hands."

"But ... Sarah's pregnant," Candi said lamely. "Don't we have to take that into consideration?"

"Me being pregnant doesn't change anything, other than it makes me want to be alive now more than ever. So I agree. Let's do this. Let's go finish off the last bad guy if he's still around, take what we can from here to make the trip easier, and go."

"But where will we go?" asked Candi. "And how will we live? Do you guys have any money?" She looked at each of their faces, knowing they'd each had their ATM cards taken by the FBI agents, who'd handed them all over to their parents. "Anything we could have used to get money has been confiscated so we couldn't use them and be traced. We have zero money, zero way of getting money, and zero chance of making it any farther than what's available in the gas tank outside."

"That's not exactly true," said Sarah. "We may have money here." She pointed to the guy on the floor.

"Good point," said Kevin, bending down and feeling the guy's pockets. He pulled out a wallet with about a hundred dollars cash in it and an ATM card. "I wonder what his PIN code is," he said, flipping it over and then back again.

"See if he wrote anything on a piece of paper in his wallet.

Some guys do that," said Jonathan.

Kevin searched through all the little pockets and pulled out a business card from a bank he'd never heard of. There was writing on the back. He held it up. "This might be something."

Candi took it from him and handed it to Jonathan.

Jonathan shrugged as he looked it over. "Maybe. We'll take it and try it." He put it in his pocket, adding the ATM card that Kevin handed over. "There were four agents downstairs. We need to go see if they're okay and maybe if they have any money if they're not."

"If they're okay and totally oblivious to what happened up here, what do we do then?" asked Candi, not believing for a second they were perfectly fine down there. She and Sarah had made too much noise for them not to investigate, and they should have been standing outside their doors. It made her wonder why the bad guy's partner hadn't already come to lend a hand.

"I don't know what we do," said Jonathan, sounding frazzled. "Sneak out? Steal a car? Get on a bus?"

Sarah held up her hands. "Just relax, everyone. One step at a time. First we need to go downstairs and see if anyone's there."

Candi nodded. It was the only plan that made sense. Staying here in this room made her feel like a sitting duck, begging to get shot at. Going home would only put her parents in danger. Calling the FBI would only alert whoever might be tagging them over there to what they were doing. Their lives were a total wreck, and at this point, it was just a matter of choosing the least awful option. "Fine. Let's go," she said, moving to get behind Kevin at the door.

"Okay, so eyes open for the partner of this shithead on the ground, right?" said Kevin, looking back over his shoulder.

Everyone nodded.

"Jon, grab that lamp. Girls, stay between us. I've got the knife." He held it up and nodded reassuringly at them before shutting off the light and turning the handle on the door.

Candi moved as silently as she could, keeping one hand on Kevin's back, the light weight of Sarah's on hers making her feel not more secure but like she had just that much more at risk.

*****

All four agents had been killed in different areas of the house, each with their throats slit. There was blood everywhere, indicating arteries had been severed. Only one of them looked like he'd put up much of a fight, a nearby stool turned over. Jonathan set it upright for a second and then changed his mind, placing it back where he'd found it.

As a side thought, he pulled off the undershirt he had put on upstairs before they came down and wiped the chair where he'd touched it. *Can't be too careful. What if they think we did this?* He knew it wasn't likely, but he also hadn't thought this kind of carnage would be likely either. The odds that the killer had taken out four highly-trained professional agents but had been stopped by his sister and pregnant girlfriend were too high to even calculate right now. The fact that the assassin had a partner was the only explanation that made sense; but was it possible there were *two* knife-wielding murderers after them? Jonathan shook his head, going back to the kitchen to join the others. He'd figure this all out later. Right now, he just had to get everyone to safety.

"What'd you find?" asked Kevin, breathing heavily from the stress. "Are they all gone?"

Jonathan nodded, eliciting a squeak of panic from Candi. "Yes. All of their throats were cut with a very sharp knife.

Probably either the one you're holding or one like it."

"Obviously, the other killer is long gone. He'd have already murdered us too if he were here," said Kevin.

"Maybe he's one of them," said Candi, gesturing to one of the bodies.

"Maybe," said Sarah, "but I doubt it. I heard them talking outside the bathroom, then followed that guy right to our room. That means the other guy went downstairs and either killed these four agents or left the house."

"Why didn't he come after us?" asked Kevin. "If I was a killer, that's what I'd have done."

"Maybe he wasn't a killer. Maybe he was just an informer," said Jonathan, the picture becoming clearer. "Maybe he let the guy in and had him just do a sweep of the whole downstairs, then walked him upstairs and showed him which rooms we were in."

"And he tried to kill the easiest ones first," said Candi. "Does that make sense that he'd come for Sarah and me first?"

"Who knows? What does it matter? We need to get out of here," said Sarah. "We'll have plenty of time to figure this out on the road."

"Check their pockets. Check any bags they brought. See if they have money or ATM cards we can use," said Kevin.

They fanned out, each taking a body. Jonathan could hear his sister crying and Sarah complaining angrily.

"You stupid jerk!" ranted Sarah. "Why'd you have to go and get killed like this? You've got blood all over the place, and you just left us up there to get stabbed. I don't want to die by stabbing, okay? I want to die of old age with my hot husband next to me in bed. You stupid bastien, lamefudge, jerkbag." And on and on it went.

Jonathan smiled, knowing Sarah was doing okay mentally if she had the presence of mind to be angry at the dead agent. His sister was another story. Her tender heart was taking a pummeling right now. They'd have to address that as soon as they could. Her having a nervous breakdown or a panic attack would not help their situation one bit.

"Guys, come check this out," said Kevin. "I think I struck gold."

Jonathan joined the girls in the kitchen. Kevin had a duffle bag out on the table, its zipper open. He was holding a folded-up manilla envelope in his hand.

"What's that?" asked Sarah, reaching for it.

"I'm not sure, but it looks like money to me." He opened it, peering inside. "Yep. A *lot* of money." He handed it to Jonathan. "I think we found our mole."

Sarah frowned at the bag. "Whose bag was it?"

"It belonged to that guy," said Candi, pointing to the one in the kitchen. "I saw it over his shoulder when we first got here."

"So you think someone paid him off recently, so recently he didn't bother to put it anywhere but in his bag? And then the killer slit his throat after, without taking the money back?" asked Jonathan.

"Maybe. At least, I think the guy upstairs probably paid him off and planned to take the money back when he was done. But he just didn't get that far."

A muffled thumping from upstairs silenced them completely.

Jonathan looked at everyone's face; all of them were reflecting back the fear that he felt in his heart. *The killer's awake!*

"We need to get out of here," whispered Candi, her face as

white as a ghost.

Sarah nodded hurriedly.

"We need to get dressed first," said Jonathan. "We can't run around outside in our underwear. Everyone will notice us, and we have to go everywhere incognito."

"He's right," said Kevin. "You girls stay here and write the FBI a letter, telling them what happened. In fact, write two of them and put them in different spots. If there's another mole, maybe it'll up our chances one of the good guys sees it. Jon and I will go get your dresses and our tuxes."

Candi grabbed his arm. "But what about that murderer?" she asked, her voice an octave too high.

"Good point," he said, picking up the knife in one hand and the lamp in the other. "Jon ... arm-up, dude."

Jonathan picked up a gun from the floor, examining it a little before letting it hang down at his side. "Ready."

Sarah ran over to him and hugged his neck, kissing him on the cheek. "Hurry back. We'll be right here waiting."

Jonathan nodded, following Kevin out of the room and up the stairs, the now steady thumping and banging coming from the girls' room making him want to run in the other direction as fast as his feet could take him.

*****

Kevin threw the door open, hitting the guy in the head. The murderer had somehow managed to wiggle his way several feet towards the entrance.

"Arrrrrrr!" yelled the guy on the floor, a string of probable cuss words following, but unintelligible due to the sock in his mouth.

Kevin closed the door and swung it open again hard,

knocking the guy once more. "That's for attacking my family, asshole." He pushed the door against the guy's head until it moved him far enough back to free the entrance completely. Kevin and Jonathan stepped inside, Jonathan going over to the closet to retrieve the girls' dresses and shoes from inside.

Kevin squatted down next to the guy who was still completely tied up. He hooked his finger under the wire going across the guy's cheek and pulled it down. He took the sock out of his mouth, waiting for him to stop hacking and wheezing before asking his questions. "Who sent you here? Why did you try to kill us? Why did you kill those agents?"

The guy glared malevolently at Kevin, making him want to flinch; but he held his ground. He wasn't going to let this guy intimidate him.

"You're so fucking dead, man. When I get out of here, I'm going to hunt you down and cut your fucking tongue out of your throat!"

Kevin held the knife up to the guy's nose, making him cease his struggles immediately. "No, dude. You're not. Because I'm going to call the cops and have them come arrest you for the murder of those four agents downstairs."

The guy jerked back and forth some more.

"Just tell us why you want to kill us so bad," Kevin continued.

"I don't question my contracts! I just fulfill 'em. Now let me go, and I'll agree to let you live. Otherwise, you'll be dead by tomorrow. It doesn't matter if I'm in jail, they'll just send someone else."

"Who will send someone else? *Who?*"

The guy laughed. "Oh, that's rich. You've pissed off Baskov

and you don't even know how. Stupid kids."

Jonathan stepped over, his arms full of taffeta and silk. "Baskov? That's Russian. We don't even know any Russians."

"You don't have to *know* Baskov to get on his bad side," spat the guy. "You just have to interfere in his business operations."

"What operations?" asked Kevin.

"If you don't know, it's not for me to tell you," he growled through gritted teeth.

Kevin reached out and pushed on the nail file that was sticking out of the man's shoulder.

"Aaaaaaaggggahhh! *Fuck!* That *hurts*, man! What the hell?"

"Just tell us the answer and we'll leave you alone."

"Drugs! Prostitutes! Sex slaves! Gambling! Laundering! You name it, he does it! *Fuck*, now leave me alone. I have to get out of here." He struggled against his bonds.

"You're not going anywhere," said Kevin, before reaching up to take the lamp Jonathan had set down on the nearby dresser and bringing it to hover over the guy's head.

The guy rolled his eyes. "Oh, for chrissakes, man, gimme a break."

That was the last thing they heard from him before Kevin smashed the lamp down on his temple, sending him back into la-la land.

"Wow. Was that absolutely necessary?" asked Jonathan, the dresses making rustling sounds as he moved them to his opposite arm.

"Yes. He'll get away if he has time. We need the cops to find him here first." Kevin took the guy's wallet off the dresser and pulled the driver's license out, throwing it down on the floor next to his head. He walked over and threw the wallet under the covers of the bed.

"What'd you do that for?"

He whispered, "To make sure if he gets away that he doesn't realize right away that we took you-know-what out of there." He put his finger to his lips, motioning for Jonathan not to say anything else. He wasn't sure if an unconscious person could hear and remember, but he wasn't taking any chances. In an overly loud voice, he said, "Come on. Let's go to the mall and wait for it to open. Then we can get some new clothes before we head to the Florida Keys." He banged the side of his finger to his lips and frowned at Jonathan again, praying he'd get the hint.

Jonathan looked confused for a moment, but then his expression brightened. "Yeah, okay. The mall and then the Keys. Let's go."

Kevin did a silent fist-pump in the air before joining Jonathan at the door. He took one more look at the bleeding trussed-up jackass on the floor and left him, shutting the door behind them both.

On the Road

THE SUV WAS LOADED WITH everything they'd found that might be of help. Everyone was dressed in their prom finery and had done his or her best to look presentable. Sarah had counted all the money and happily reported that they had ten thousand dollars to fund their disappearing act. She was still flipping through it in the back seat as everyone got settled in for their journey. She loved the feel of that much cash in her hands. It was a small consolation for the fact that their lives had all gone totally in the toilet, and she was feeling seriously morning sick because her stomach was empty again.

"That's all our lives were worth collectively? Ten thousand dollars?" asked Jonathan. "Well, that stinks. I would have estimated much higher, especially considering our life expectancy and the fact that those FBI agents were federal employees. The government has invested at least that much in their training. Probably much more."

"Jonathan, it's not an accurate measure of anything," said Candi, sounding very tired, "except maybe how *little* those guys value life, period."

"You have a point," said Jonathan, buckling himself into the front passenger seat, next to Kevin who was driving. "So where are we going? I only know where we're *not* going - the mall or the Keys."

Kevin attached the garage door opener that was on the kitchen counter to the car's visor. "That's right. I was thinking we could rent a cabin or something. A place out of the way and far from civilization so we would hear someone coming from far away."

"But then we wouldn't blend at all," said Sarah. "And for the record, I think using this car for more than getting money at the ATM a very bad idea. They probably have a satellite or GPS tracker on it. They'll find us before we even get out of town."

"What the hell are we going to do for a car?" asked Kevin. "I hadn't thought of that, but she's right. This car is garbage." He turned and smiled at everyone in an exaggerated fashion. "Anyone know how to steal a car?"

Candi smiled back, shaking her head.

"Yeah, right," said Sarah, snorting at the idea.

"Yes. I do," said Jonathan. "So long as it's not too new, I can hotwire it."

Everyone went silent, just staring at him.

Sarah was the first one to snap out of it. "Boyfriend, what are you talking about? You don't know how to steal a car. You've never so much as stolen a piece of gum in your whole life." She was sure of it; he'd sworn to that fact just a week prior.

"Oh, I haven't ever *stolen* a car. But I've hotwired several, just to test the online instructions I read."

Kevin chuckled, but Candi was pissed.

"What?! Whose car did you hotwire? And who was with you, so I can have Mom call their parents right now, because it had to be their idea."

"No, it was my idea. And I did it by myself." He looked at her, completely nonplussed over her threats.

"What? Why?" she asked, mystified.

"I saw it in so many movies, after a while I just had to know if it was possible. So I checked online, found some instructions, and then tried it. First on Dad's car, then Mom's, then on his friend Pike's car when he came to visit once. It totally works. They weren't lying in the movies, but they do sometimes portray it inaccurately. In a new car it's too hard, sometimes impossible without the key if it's the kind with a computer chip in it. The computer has anti-theft measures built in. So if you find me an older car, I can do it."

"Do you need anything else? Or just your mad skills?" asked Kevin, sounding like he was about to laugh.

"It would be best if I had a knife to strip some wires, some black electrical tape, and a couple screw drivers with different tips."

"I saw some of that tape in the kitchen ... in a drawer!" said Sarah, jumping out of the car to go get it.

"There were screw drivers in that duffle bag in the back," said Candi, leaving to join Sarah.

The girls got to the kitchen in a flash, Sarah wrinkling her nose at the metallic smell of all that blood that had long since congealed on the floors, walls, furniture and even ceilings. The drawer flew open at her touch, her strength much greater than she realized in her excitement. She handed the roll of black tape to Candi and took a side trip to the refrigerator, grabbing the pizza box that was inside and flipping open the top for a second to reveal half a cold pizza. She closed the box and turned it sideways, hugging it against her chest so she could also take the half-full two-liter jug of soda that was in there. Kicking the door closed with her foot, it crossed her mind that she should probably be too grossed out about the carnage around her to think of eating, but she'd either gotten used to it or her empty pregnant stomach was overruling all of her other senses.

Candi came over to assist, and together the two of them ran back to the garage, getting into the car and buckling up.

"Ready," said Sarah. "And I brought pizza and soda, too. I'm starving." She passed them each a piece, saving the biggest one for herself. *Eating-for-two privilege, cha-ching!*

"Cool," said Kevin. "Alright, so before I open this door and drive out of here with a stolen and probably thoroughly traceable car, does anyone have any thoughts or have any idea about where I should go?"

"Go somewhere that we can find an old car that we can hotwire and not be discovered for at least a day," said Jonathan.

"And go now before I lose my nerve and tell you to go to the police station," said Sarah, chomping down on a piece of pizza that tasted a little too much like cardboard.

"Maybe the police isn't such a bad idea," said Candi.

Jonathan shook his head. "No FBI, no police. If we go to the cops, they'll just turn us over to the federal government. This isn't state jurisdiction. They won't have any choice."

"Fine," said Candi, grouchily. "I suggest the airport then. There are tons of cars there, and we can leave this one there in its place."

"Yeah, but they have cameras there. They'll know it's us in the car, and they'll be able to put a search out for it too easily," said Kevin. "Try again. Come on, you guys. Think of something."

"Just drive over to the not as nice area of town. We'll just find something outside a bar maybe that'll work. We don't want to go too far or we'll give them too much time to find us," said Jonathan.

Kevin pressed the button on the opener, sending the garage door up slowly. He started the car and shifted it into drive. "Okay, then. Off we go to the ghett-o. I hope we don't get shot stealing a car from someone in the hood."

"Not the hood," said Sarah, her mouth full. "Please not the hood. Just not the fancy part of town. Four streets over from here would be good."

"Yes," said Candi nodding, "do that."

Sarah reached over and squeezed her arm. Little Sugar Lump was slowly coming out of her panic spiral, and Sarah for one was very happy about that. She hated being the only one holding it together; it was exhausting.

"You should take a nap," said Candi. "Even just a little one while we find another car. We can't have you getting sick."

Sarah smiled. "That is one of the best ideas I've heard all night. The only problem is I'm too jacked up on adrenaline to do it right now."

"Try," said Jonathan. "Even just five minutes will help you and the baby."

Her boyfriend's concern over her and their baby's health made her heart melt just a little. She lowered the pizza crust in her hand to her lap. "Okay, love monkey. I'll try." She closed her eyes, but not before she saw the disgusted look on Candi's face.

"Love monkey?" Candi said.

Sarah smiled, dozing off the second her head hit the back of the seat.

*****

Candi looked at Sarah's mouth hanging open and the drool coming out onto her shoulder, soaking the spaghetti strap of her dress. It was one of those few moments when Sarah looked innocent and harmless. She wished she had her camera so she could take a picture, thinking wasn't fair that she was the only one who was going to see it. "Oh my god, you guys, look ... she's so cute."

"Quiet, Candi, you'll wake her. She needs to sleep as much as possible," said Jonathan. "We're on the run now. This is serious." He didn't even look back.

Candi stuck her tongue out at the side of his head. "I know it's serious, Jonathan, trust me. But that doesn't mean I can't stop and smell the roses ... or smile at Sarah drooling."

"I'm not drooling," said a tired voice next to her. "I never drool."

Candi snorted. "You may want to tell that to your dress, which is now suspiciously damp near your shoulder."

"You did it," said Sarah, sitting up and swiping the back of her hand across her mouth. "You drooled on me while I was sleeping. So rude, by the way."

Candi pushed her on the arm gently, smiling at Sarah's good spirits.

"Okay, so what do you guys think of that one?" said Kevin, pointing to an older model Toyota Camry that was parked on the opposite side of the street, down about a block from a large apartment complex. "It's boring-looking, no one's around, and I think it's old enough."

"Probably gets good gas mileage, too," said Jonathan. "I'm

ready if you guys are."

"We'd better hurry," said Candi, sick to her stomach with nervousness. "The sun is going to come up soon; we don't have much darkness left."

"Which reminds me," said Jonathan. "Was there a flashlight in all that stuff we took?"

"Duffle bag," said Candi and Sarah at the exact same time. They grinned at each other.

"Who's going with me?" Jonathan asked. "It'll be faster if I have an assistant."

"Me. I'll go," said Kevin. He parked the car across the street from their intended victim, turning off the engine.

"Are we going to be charged with felonies when we get back? Stealing a car is a serious crime," said Candi, trying to block out the images of her parents' disappointed faces.

"We're running for our lives. I'm pretty sure life-saving situations equal forgiveness in the eyes of the law," said Jonathan. "Besides, at this point, I just want to *live*. I'm not so worried about a rap sheet."

"Well, maybe we should be," said Candi.

"We'll figure all that out later. I think we can all agree that we need to get out of here, and a bus or train won't work because of cameras and their easy ability to track us. Nothing is done anonymously anymore. Everyone requires IDs and everyone puts stuff into computers. We wouldn't last a day if we took public transportation anywhere out of town."

"Fine. I'll drive if we need to get away fast," Candi said, getting out of the car and waiting for Kevin to exit the front seat.

He got down off the high seat and pulled her into his arms. "Don't worry, Gumdrop. I'm going to take care of you," he said into her neck. He leaned back and kissed her deeply, letting her go after a few seconds to frame her cheeks in his big, warm hands. "You get ready to hit the gas pedal and follow us out of here, okay?"

"We're not transferring the stuff here?"

"No. We have to do it somewhere else so they won't know where we got the car we're in, right?"

"Oh. Yeah. Okay."

"Up you go," he said, gesturing to the driver's seat.

Candi climbed up and buckled in, moving the seat forward about twelve inches so her feet would reach the pedals. "Good luck, Kevin. You too, Jonathan," she said, looking over in time to catch him in an embrace with Sarah. Her heart clenched, thinking about how much more they had to lose than she or Kevin did.

Kevin shut the door, drawing a heart on the glass with his forefinger before he walked away. Candi put her finger on it and watched sadly as he went to the other side of the road.

Sarah climbed into the passenger seat and buckled in too. Jonathan shut her door and ran across the street to join Kevin. Candi watched as they looked in the windows and tried the doors. The passenger side back door was open, giving them easy access to the interior. They both climbed in and went to work. She could see flickers of the flashlight every couple seconds.

"So far, so good," said Sarah in a quiet voice, staring out the window at them.

"What do we do if we see anyone?" asked Candi, feeling like she should whisper. She didn't like the neighborhood they were in. There were a lot of seedy bars not far down the road, and the apartment building meant there were a hundred people or more who could be coming or going at any time. *This is a terrible idea.*

We're going to get caught! She made herself feel better thinking about how hard they'd be to kill sitting in a police station's jail cell.

"Honk the horn once really quick if there's a problem. And if someone comes for that car, we'll flip a quick yooey and pick the guys up. We still have the gun," she said, reaching inside the armrest and pulling it out.

"Put that away!" whisper-screeched Candi. "You want to accidentally shoot one of us?!"

Sarah frowned at her. "Pa-lease. Like I'd do that."

The gun was pointed at the ceiling when it went off, but the explosion of the bullet from the chamber made Candi go deaf in one ear. The ringing she could hear now in her brain was almost as loud as the gunshot itself. Candi's eyes nearly popped out of her head in shock, and she was struck dumb.

"Oh my god!" yelled Sarah, almost louder than the gunshot. It sounded muffled to Candi's one good ear. "I shot the car! I shot the friggin car! Are you okay?!"

Kevin was banging on the window outside, yelling, "Open up! Open it!"

Candi started the car, barely able to roll the window down, her fingers were trembling so hard. The button kept slipping away. Eventually she got it down a couple inches. "We're okay! Sarah shot the roof."

The Camry started across the street and its headlights went on. Jonathan peeled out like a maniac, nearly doing a donut in the middle of the street in his hurry to get to them. He pulled up next to the SUV, yelling, "Get in!" at Kevin through the open passenger window.

Sarah kept chanting in the background. "Oh my god, oh my

god, oh my god ..."

Candi shifted the car into drive and slammed her foot down on the accelerator, taking off in a squealing of tires towards the nearest intersection. She made a hard right, headed for the busiest street she could remember seeing. The sound of the wind whistling through the big hole in the roof of the car made her panicked brain almost believe they were being followed by a thousand wailing phantoms.

*****

Jonathan stood on the running board of the SUV, examining the hood of the car. "Well, this isn't exactly optimal, is it?" he asked, inspecting the torn metal and bits of plastic and cloth roof material that were sticking up above the car. He looked over at the others, focusing on Sarah, worried she was going to cry.

Sarah was standing off to the side, her eyebrows drawn together in a serious scowl. "I didn't mean to do it. I told you guys, it was an accident."

"Yeah, but now they're going to figure everything out. Someone's going to report that gunshot, they're going to find the SUV with the hole in it, and they'll know it was us over here taking the Camry," said Kevin, obviously angry at his sister. "Now we're going to have to steal another car!"

Jonathan shook his head, climbing down and going over to stand next to Sarah. "No, we won't. We'll just drive over to the other side of town and leave the SUV there. Hopefully, they won't connect the issues together. And we'll park it in a bad area with the keys in it. Maybe someone will just take it."

"Sounds like a plan. It's not like we have any other choice," said Kevin, climbing into the driver's seat of the SUV. "Candi, get in. Sarah, you ride with Jonathan."

Candi went along with his instructions not saying a word. She just kept putting her finger in her right ear and wiggling it around.

Jonathan opened the passenger door of the Camry that he'd left running in the gas station parking lot, holding it open for Sarah.

Kevin's window came down. "Drive the speed limit," he said. "And stick right behind us. If a cop comes up, I want him looking at your car, not this one."

Jonathan nodded, running around to the other side of the car, getting in and putting on his seat belt. "Ready?" he asked Sarah.

She just nodded, looking out the side window.

He shifted into drive and followed Kevin out onto the road, careful to use his turn signal. "Please don't be sad, Sarah. Everything's going to be fine, you'll see."

She sniffled. "But I messed up."

"No, you didn't. It's no big deal."

"We'll get caught because of me. Murdered. Our *throats* slit open!"

She was openly crying now, which made Jonathan's anxiety level go through the roof. Something about hearing that noise come out of her mouth made him want to do anything he possibly could to make it stop. "No, we are not!" he said loudly. Taking a moment to calm himself before continuing, he said, "I am going to protect you and that peanut, and we're going to be fine."

Sarah turned to him, wiping her nose with her hand. "Peanut? What peanut?"

"The peanut-shaped embryo in your uterus."

She either choked or laughed, Jonathan wasn't sure which. "Awww ... you just called our baby a peanut." She turned sideways in her seat to face him.

"Yes, I did. It really looks like one right now. I could show you a picture if we could go to a library or get online."

Sarah reached over and tickled the hair on the back of his neck. "I love you, you know. You're like my knight in shining armor."

Jonathan smiled, happy that she wasn't crying anymore, and satisfied to know she felt the same way about him as he did about her. "Well, I don't know about the knight part, but I'll take the rest of what you said."

"Tell me you love me back."

"I love you back. And the peanut, too."

Sarah leaned over and kissed him on the cheek.

"Get back in your seat. We don't want the cops pulling us over."

Sarah sat back down. "Bossy. So, where are we going?"

"I don't know. I'm just following your brother. He seems to know his way around."

"He's played rugby all over this city. He'll know where to go."

Jonathan glanced nervously in his rearview mirror, happy to see that there was no one behind him, but very unhappy to see the beginnings of a sunrise glowing on the horizon.

*****

Kevin pulled onto a street filled with houses surrounded by chainlink fences. The sun was coming up, and people would be stirring from their homes soon. Luckily it was Sunday morning, and he didn't have to worry about people getting up for work. The clock read six in the morning.

"This place makes me seriously nervous," said Candi.

"We're only going to be here for five minutes. Just relax and go to the other car as soon as we stop. I'll move the stuff over." He looked over at her, taking in her pale complexion and shaking fingers. "Did you wipe the car down? Take off all the fingerprints that you could?"

"I did my best. I think I got everything. Here's the t-shirt so you can do the things you've touched over there." She sighed as he pulled into a spot on the side of the road, in front of a house that looked abandoned. "I don't even know why we're bothering, though."

"Just to be sure we can slow down their process of finding us, that's all."

"But don't our fingerprints need to be in the system for it to matter?"

"Yeah. Maybe. I don't know. But what if someone has our fingerprints? Didn't your parents ever do one of those things at the school? You know, the free fingerprint thing?"

Candi frowned as he shut off the car. "I'm not sure. I can't remember."

"Better safe than sorry," said Kevin. "You go. I'm going to wipe this down and leave the keys here." He took her hand and pulled her over, kissing her once quickly on the lips. "See you in a minute. Don't miss me too much."

She reached up and tugged his earlobe. "Don't *you* miss *me.*"

He smiled as Candi's door shut behind her, leaving him alone in the mostly silent car. He could hear them whispering and talking in low tones behind him, through the hole in the roof.

They'd done the best they could to hide the damage from the outside, but there was no way you could miss it on the inside. The first time it rained, this car was going to get full of mildew, thanks to Sarah. He shook his head thinking about how lucky they'd gotten, with her shooting the car instead of herself or Candi. He was glad he hadn't been there. He probably would have been seriously tempted to throttle her.

He finished wiping off all the spots he thought he might have touched, and left the car, shutting the door as quietly as he could. The keys stayed in the ignition and the locks remained open. By the time he slid into the driver's seat of the Camry, everything had been transferred from the SUV into the trunk of their new ride. "Ready to hit the road?" he asked, looking at Candi next to him and then his sister and Jonathan in the back seat.

"Yep," said Jonathan.

"As ready as I'll ever be," said Sarah, leaning over to put her head on Jonathan's shoulder. She yawned wide.

Kevin shifted into drive. "Let's hit it. Tennessee, here we come."

"Tennessee?" asked Candi.

"Yep! We can get a cabin in the woods, do some fishing, take some hikes ... relax."

"If we're going to be out in the middle of nowhere, we need to have some sort of security system in place," said Jonathan. "It's the perfect place to murder a group of kids; no one would hear a thing."

"So we get some security. Or we make our own. I've been thinking about it, and I really think this is our best option." Kevin pulled out of the neighborhood and onto a main street.

"Why not a big city we can get lost in, like Atlanta?" asked Candi. "Or we could really go for the gold and drive all the way to Seattle."

"Too many people to see us on a wanted poster," said Kevin.

"Okay, small town, then," said Candi.

"Nope. We'd stick out like sore thumbs ... four teenagers just hanging out when they should be in school. We need to go off the grid."

"I guess I agree with you, but it could be because I'm exhausted and my reasoning skills are compromised," said Jonathan.

"Or, it could be because your reasoning skills are top-notch, and I'm just a genius who figured out the best plan," said Kevin, smiling in the mirror. He noticed his sister was already asleep. "Jon, better watch out. The drool monster's coming for ya."

"That's okay. She drools on me all the time now."

"I don't drool," said Sarah, her voice sounding drugged.

Candi giggled, inspiring Kevin to take her hand and pull it over to rest on his thigh. "Tennesseeeeeee, here we coooooome," he sang, making up the lyrics and the melody as he went along.

"Oh my god ... have I died and gone to hell?" asked Sarah.

Everyone laughed, including Kevin. "Don't be jealous, little sis," he said. "Not everyone can have vocal cords of a god like me."

"Thank Mount Olympus for that," she said, before letting out a small burp. "Oops. 'Scuse me. It was the peanut." A few seconds later she began snoring.

"Where did she get peanuts?" asked Candi.

Kevin waited for the answer as he pulled onto the interstate. Peanuts sounded pretty good right about now. He was so hungry anything would probably sound appetizing.

"She meant the baby. That's his nickname. Peanut."

"It's a *she*, not a he," said Candi.

"No, he's not," said Kevin. "He's a boy, and he's going to be the smartest, handsomest kid ever born ... until you and me have a kid, that is." He looked over at Candi, a little surprised at himself that he'd said that out loud, but very happy to see her grinning like a fool and very pink in the cheeks.

"Yeah, someday in about ten years," she said.

"Yeah. Exactly," he said. He squeezed her hand and she squeezed back.

"We won't know until she has an ultrasound at twenty weeks, but even then it could be wrong. I'm just picking an arbitrary gender. I don't care which it is, just that it's healthy and looks like Sarah."

"How do you know so much about that stuff?" asked Kevin.

"I cannot *believe* you just asked that question," said Candi very quietly.

Kevin smiled. She was right. What had he been thinking?

"Well, you know, I've done some research."

The car went silent.

Kevin looked at Candi and she stared back, shrugging her shoulders.

"Aaaand...?" asked Kevin. There had to be more to the story than this. There was *always* more to the story than this when Jonathan was talking.

"That's all I can say."

Candi laughed. "Why?"

"Because Sarah told me I need to learn to curb my TMI tendencies, and that if I felt the need to TMI someone, I should come TMI her instead to get it off my chest."

Kevin held up his hand, twisted around for a high five from the back seat. "Give me some skin on that, man."

Jonathan gave him a tap. "I don't want to wake Sarah."

Kevin nodded, putting his hand back on the wheel. "Good enough, dude. It's good enough for me."

*****

Sarah woke up, rubbing her neck. It had a crick in it from sitting sideways on Jonathan's boney shoulder for ... she squinted at the clock ... *I've been asleep for four hours?* "Where are we?" she asked Kevin. Everyone else was sleeping.

"About five hours out from our destination. I need to stop though and trade with someone. I'm about to fall asleep at the wheel."

"Let's go to a rest stop and get some food."

"No. No rest stops. They have cameras. We'll just get off the highway and hit a diner or something."

Sarah nudged Jonathan. "Babe. Get up. We're going to stop for breakfast. Or lunch. Or brunch. Or all three maybe, if I'm lucky." For the first time in days she wasn't feeling morning sick. She knew it was probably temporary, though. It came and went at various times during the day. She had to take advantage of sick-free moments whenever she could, especially since they seemed to be coming less and less often. "Oh, look!" said Sarah, excited. "A greasy spoon. I can smell it from here!"

All three of the other heads in the car looked over, two of them with some seriously messed-up hair.

"Wow, Candi ... Jonathan. You two need to fix that hair of yours, like soon. No way can we walk around incognito when you guys look like you just escaped from a mental institution."

Candi turned around. "Yeeeeah. You may want to check your look in the mirror before you go judging like that."

Sarah's eyes widened as she thought about the side-effects of car-sleeping on her own hair. "Oh, no. Stop the car."

"I'll stop the car in that Wal-Mart parking lot. We need to get different clothes before we let anyone see you two. Jonathan and I will go in wearing our t-shirts and pants only. They're still tuxy but not too tuxy. No way can you even get out of the car in those dresses."

"But why?" asked Candi. "We're so far from home."

"It's in the FBI's jurisdiction. Everywhere is. They could put wanted ads up all over the towns near the highways or ads on TV. All they'd have to say is they're looking for four teens in prom formal wear, and we'd be busted no matter where we went ... unless there happened to be a prom going on. Which there isn't," said Jonathan. "Just tell us what you want and what size and we'll buy it for you."

"Ha! Like we can trust you to shop for us," grumbled Sarah. She could only imagine what a full-on dork she was going to look like with either of them doing her shopping.

"We'll get you something basic, and you can go in after and get yourselves something nicer, okay?" asked Kevin. He sounded exhausted.

"Deal," said Candi. "All I need is a pair of shorts and a t-shirt."

"I'd recommend jeans," said Jonathan. "We're going to the mountains where it will still be cold at night. You want something that will work in all weather."

"I'll use the shorts for pajamas later. I can't have you buying me jeans; I need to try them on. Just get me size small gym shorts and a small t-shirt. And a pair of flip-flops."

"Make that two of each," said Sarah, preferring her clothes to fit tighter than Candi's. "Size eight for my shoes."

"Six for mine," said Candi.

"Oompa loompa," said Sarah quietly while smiling devilishly.

"Clown," said Candi back, not even looking at Sarah.

"Okay, girls. That's enough." Kevin pulled into the back end of the parking lot. "Come on, Jon. Take off your formal shirt."

Jonathan complied and the two guys left the car, wearing short-sleeved undershirts, black tux pants, and shiny black shoes.

Sarah sighed. "What do you think they're going to buy?"

"Something hideously embarrassing would be my guess."

Sarah nodded. "My thoughts exactly. If I had known my life was going to come down to this, I wouldn't have worn this disaster," she said slapping at the long, tight, formal dress she just wanted to cut off her body with a pair of scissors at this point.

"What would you have worn instead? A track suit?"

"No. A short, black cocktail dress. Preferrably Chanel. And shorter heels, too. I could have waltzed into Wal-Mart and bought an entire wardrobe for all of us in less than thirty minutes." Shopping was one of her special skills.

"Oh, right. Like a Chanel cocktail dress wouldn't stand out in Wal-Mart. You so know how to blend, Sarah."

"Thhpppbbtttt."

"Mature."

"Thhppbt."

Candi changed the subject. "I was thinking something when Jonathan was telling us about the wanted posters."

"Oh, yeah? What? How delicious that bacon smells, sizzling

across the street? Because that's what I was thinking."

"No. I was thinking that we have two problems with standing out."

"Like ..."

"Like it's not just the FBI looking for us. It's that Baskov guy, too. And I'll bet he has more money than the FBI does. What if he sends one of his hired assassins out after us? All the guy has to do is ask questions around places like this and he might get lucky and find someone who saw four kids in prom clothes when there was no prom going on. And he may have access to FBI resources since we know there was at least one mole in there. Baskov probably has more than one traitor on the payroll, don't you think? They could totally have access to the leads the FBI comes up with around the country. They're everywhere, did you know that? It's not just Washington, D.C."

Sarah listened to everything Candi said and the more she heard, the farther her heart sank down into her stomach. "Damblammit, Candi! Now I'm feeling sick again! Way to go. I was going to have bacon and sausage and ... oh, god ... shut up, Sarah ... stop talking about food." She moaned and slid down in her seat.

"I'm sorry," said Candi, sounding very contrite. She turned around backwards, gripping the headrest with both hands as she looked at Sarah. "I just didn't want to be the only one with the nightmare in my head. I actually was hoping you'd tell me I was nuts."

Sarah shook her head, rubbing her hair into a knot on the seat behind her. "No. You're not nuts. You're totally right, and *we're* totally screwed. The guys were right, too. We need serious security if we're going to be in a cabin. Like death traps and guns and ... attack dogs." She sat up, suddenly inspired by the idea of Cujo coming out and biting a bad guy's nutsack off.

"Attack dogs?" Candi laughed. "Where are we going to get an attack dog?"

"Humane society. They have tons of dogs, even some that are biters. Let's get one of those - one of the biting kind."

"I'd prefer one that didn't bite but *looked* like it could bite. Intimidation factor."

"I think an actual bite is much more intimidating than a hard look." Sarah sat up. "As soon as we get to that diner, let's look up dog adoption in their phone book. I'll bet there's one near here somewhere." She looked around the parking lot and the places beyond. "It's a pretty big town, looks like."

"I think it's a good idea. No, a great one. Not only will we rescue a dog that might get put down, it'll give us something to do so we don't get too bored. Training takes a lot of time and patience."

"Oooo, good idea. Let's make a list of all the things we can do to not be bored in the middle of nowhere." Sarah looked around the car for a piece of paper but gave up about three seconds into the process, her stomach telling her she was better off just relaxing.

"I've always wanted to learn how to knit," said Candi.

Sarah laughed. "If we get that bored, I'm just going to turn myself in."

"No, I'm serious," said Candi, smiling. "I want to make a scarf. If I get good at it, I could make you one too."

Sarah shrugged. "Whatever floats your boat. I want to paint. I've always wanted to learn how to paint landscapes and portraits." She waved her hand in front of her face, already seeing a vision of greatness. "I could create the next Mona Lisa."

Candi coughed. Or maybe she laughed, it was hard to tell. But she said nothing.

"Whatever," said Sarah, frowning at she-who-has-no-faith sitting in the front seat. "What else?"

"The guys will want to do some kind of sports thing. Well, Kevin will want to anyway; and he'll force Jonathan to do it with him."

"Baseball mitts and gloves. Playing catch is easy to do in the woods," said Sarah.

"What about archery? I think Jonathan would love that. It's all about physics and geometry ..."

"Good call," agreed Sarah. "And he could put arrows in the bad guys' hearts if they came for us." Sarah felt especially excited about that part. With a biting dog and an arrow-shooting boyfriend and brother, their odds of survival were already going up. Maybe she could learn how to launch a few herself, be a modern-day Robin Hood.

Both girls were silent for a while, Sarah busy trying to imagine what she'd do all day, every day, with no school, no phone, and no internet. "This is going to seriously suck," she said finally.

"I know. It's depressing," said Candi. "We're going to miss graduation, probably."

"And home-cooked meals, and the crowning of the prom king and queen, since they never did it at the dance. I wonder who will win with you guys gone."

"My guess is it'll be Gretchen and Barry," said Candi, curling her lip in disgust.

"Yeah. Total pity-card, though. No one will vote for them

because they deserve it," said Sarah, sniffing. *Stupid cheater and his ho-bag home-wrecker.*

"You're better off," said Candi. "Stop making that face. You're going to wrinkle permanently."

Sarah immediately straightened her expression. Those friggin wrinkles needed to stay the heck away from her. "Thank you for the reminder." She sighed. "So what else do we need to do? Now that we have the security problem figured out, we might as well solve all the rest of our problems."

Before Candi could respond, Kevin and Jonathan walked up to the car and got in, a bag in each of their hands.

"So, what'd you get us?" asked Sarah, eager to see how awful their choices were. She opened the first bag and found jeans. "We told you not to get jeans!"

Kevin snatched them out of her hands. "Those aren't for you. They're for us. You get shorts, just like you ordered."

Sarah frowned at him. "Touchy, touchy."

"I'm tired and I'm hungry, so just put your stuff on and let's go eat."

Candi pulled out a small t-shirt with a rainbow pony on the front. "What in the heck?" She held it up towards Sarah. "I think this one is yours."

"Oh, hellsbells no it's not. This one's mine," she said, pulling out a blue one still in the bag. She opened it up, but the back of it was facing her.

Candi started laughing loudly. "Oh, yeah. You're right. This one's mine. That's yours." Candi scrambled to pull her dress down and put the pink shirt on.

Sarah slowly turned it around, her face going white when she saw the front of it. "I'm not fucking wearing this."

"I thought you were going to stop cussing," said Jonathan. There was no censure in his voice, but that didn't matter.

"Did *you* buy me this nightmare?" she asked accusingly.

Jonathan's face went red. "Uhhhh ... maybe? I thought you'd like it ... think it was cute ... or not ...," he finished lamely. "Sorry. I guess I'm not good at shopping for girls."

Sarah took a very deep breath and let it out slowly, trying to find her happy place. She gave him a tight-lipped smile. "Fine. I'll wear it. But when people point fingers and laugh hysterically like Sugar Lump is right now, you'd better just be prepared to suffer my wrath."

"How about you go into the Wal Mart and buy something else?" suggested Kevin. "Wrath-suffering doesn't sound like much fun, and we already have enough shit to deal with."

The girls got into their new t-shirts and black gym shorts in record time. Thankfully, the bottoms weren't as much of a disaster as the tops were. After donning their flip-flops and doing their best to right their hair, they nearly ran to the Wal-Mart. First, they stopped off in the bathrooms, and then they started walking towards the clothing department.

A man in a pea-green t-shirt and dirty jeans stopped them before they were ten feet into their trip. He looked like he was in his thirties, his hair slicked down to the side with something gross - probably not normal gel from the looks of it and very possibly just the oil from his scalp. Sarah shuddered at the thought.

"Excuse me ...," he said, holding up a hand to make them stop.

"Yeah, what?" asked Sarah. "We need to shop, do you mind?" The guy was blocking their path and obviously thought way more of himself than he should have. He was eyeing her up and down, practically drooling. *Perv*, she thought, grimacing at the idea of this turd getting anywhere near her.

"Just relax, babe. I just wanted to ask you a question."

"What?"

"I just wanted to know if you really do?"

Sarah frowned at him, annoyed and completely confused now. "If I really do *what?*"

He gestured at her shirt. "If you really do like choo-choos."

Sarah looked down at the choo-choo train decal on her shirt, a big puff of smoke coming out of its stack, the accompanying lettering declaring to the world how she allegedly felt about locomotives. Then she looked up and gave him the most sarcastic smile she could possibly muster before answering, "Not when they look like you do, I don't." And then she stormed off in a huff. Candi followed behind, an occasional snort escaping to mix with her giggles.

*****

The girls made short work of the shopping trip. They bought not only clothes but necessities like bottled water, trail mix and antacids for Sarah's occasional stomach issues, shampoo, conditioner, soap, gel, a brush, a comb, and toothbrushes and toothpaste. Candi added knitting needles, yarn, a how-to pamphlet, a Scrabble board game and a deck of cards. Sarah found a somewhat heavy-duty archery set in the sporting good section, a couple of mitts and a baseball. Their cart was loaded.

"I cannot wait to brush my fuzzy teeth," said Candi as they walked out to the car.

"You're telling me. I can't wait to get out of this *I Love Choo-Choos* t-shirt."

Candi giggled again. She couldn't help it. Every time she

saw that silly picture of the lunatic smiling train it just killed her. She wisely decided to keep her comments to herself, though. Sarah was on a hair-trigger with her mood. She needed some food or they were all going to suffer.

"Let's go," said Sarah. "Time to eat." Sarah pulled off her blue shirt, not caring who saw her in her bra, putting on the white tee she'd bought instead. It had a cute flower design over the front, kind of surfer-girl in style. It suited her tan and highlighted hair. Candi left the pink rainbow pony shirt on, shoving the bag filled with toiletries down by her feet. "I'm starving. Breakfast?" she asked, looking over at Kevin.

He nodded, winking at her but saying nothing as he pulled out of the parking lot and onto the road leading to the diner. He looked like he was too tired to even speak at this point. Candi reached over and rubbed his upper arm. "I'll drive next, okay?"

He nodded again, putting on the turn signal to go into the restaurant's parking lot. Once there, they unbuckled.

"Should we split up?" asked Jonathan.

"What do you mean?" asked Candi, her hand on the door handle.

"I think we should eat separately. As couples. Sarah and me, and you two."

"Do you really think that's necessary?" asked Kevin.

"Maybe it's overkill, but I'd rather be safe than sorry."

Kevin shrugged. "Fine. You two go first. We'll follow in a couple minutes and sit on our own. Give us some of the cash."

Jonathan took the envelope out of the hiding spot they'd made behind the middle armrest in the back seat and handed Kevin a hundred dollar bill. After collecting the shopping change from the girls, giving him and Sarah thirty dollars to use for their breakfast, he opened the door and stepped out, coming around to get Sarah's door for her.

Once the door was shut and they were alone, Candi leaned her head on the headrest, facing Kevin. "Are you scared?"

He turned sideways and took one of her hands in his. "Nah. Just tired. My brain's a little muddy right now, so maybe I'll be scared after I've slept." He laced his fingers in hers. "Are you?"

"Yes. Very. At that house ... I've never seen so much blood ... never in my whole life. It was nothing like the movies. You could smell it, even." Her stomach churned a little with the memory of it all.

"Yeah. Pretty disgusting. And that guy was totally bad news. Zero conscience. If we had let him up, he would have killed us in a second. I can't believe you guys fought him off and were able to tie him up without our help."

Candi smiled. "You'll have to thank your sister for that. I hardly did anything. I was sleeping when he came in." Candi shuddered at the idea of ending up like those FBI agents had. It would have been not only her worst nightmare but also her parents' too.

"I think our time on the island really was good in that way - it got us fit and doing things we normally wouldn't have," said Kevin. "I mean, we stared death in the face in that lifeboat and on our way back home ... and lived to tell about it."

"Yeah, and you *literally* stared death in the face when your head went into the water right in the middle of all those sharks."

Kevin chuckled. "Yeah. Man, I was so scared I nearly pissed myself."

"Really?" Candi shook her head. "You were so cool about it. And sick. I didn't think you even knew what was going on, really."

Kevin lifted up her hand and kissed the back of it. "The first day or two was fuzzy, but after that, I remember everything. Every last detail. I never want to forget it."

They stared into each other's eyes for a long time, Candi's mind racing to the days that she mooned after him but thought there wasn't a chance in the world that he'd ever feel the same way about her.

"I thank God every day for that shipwreck," said Kevin softly.

Candi felt tears prick her eyes. "Me too." She cleared her rough throat. "Do you think we'll feel the same about this stuff ... after it's all over?"

"Let's hope so," he said, leaning forward to share a deep, passionate kiss with her.

Candi let herself get carried away with it for a little while, reveling in the heat that seeped into her bones.

"Mmmmm," he growled deep in his throat, pulling away finally. "We'd better not do that, or I'll just give up on the whole idea of eating all together."

Candi smiled. "Come on, let's go. There's a whole plate of pancakes in there with my name on it."

Kevin got out and waited for her to join him in front of the car. "Let's see," he said, draping his arm across her shoulders as they walked to the front door, "pancakes sounds good ... and sausage, and bacon, and eggs, and bagels, and a couple pastries, three pieces of pie, and ..."

"We're on a budget," said Candi, smiling to herself over her boyfriend's insatiable appetite. Her grandmother would have asked him if he had a hollow leg where he was putting it all.

"Oh. Okay, scratch the pie, then." He opened the door and followed Candi inside.

Candi tried not to look at her brother and Sarah, but it was impossible. They were smiling at each other over milkshakes and seemed so in love. She was going to have to remind them to be more chill in public. They were attracting the attention of everyone in the room. She tore her gaze away from the raw emotion she saw there and took a left, sitting along the window on the other side of the room.

Kevin dropped into the chair opposite her and picked up the menu that was waiting. "Okay ... pancakes? Get into my belly ..."

He went on to command what seemed like half the menu to join the pancakes in his stomach, and Candi just smiled as the words flowed over her. *Life sucks ... but it could suck a whole lot worse.* She couldn't imagine what a mess her head would be in right now if she didn't have her little family along with her on this horrible misadventure.

Stockpiles and Watchkeepers

JONATHAN TOOK THE FIRST DRIVING shift after they'd finished breakfast. He was about to pass the next exit when he spied a Costco sign. At the last second he made his decision and swerved off the highway, coasting down the exit ramp to the traffic signal below.

"What the heck, babe?" asked Sarah, jerked awake by the movement of the car. "Everything okay?"

"Yeah. I think we should get supplies here before we get too close to our destination." He pulled up to a stoplight near the store. "Wake the others, would you? I'd like to make a group decision on this."

Sarah leaned into the back and grabbed Candi's and Kevin's legs, shaking them awake. Jonathan watched their bodies jiggling back and forth in the mirror.

"Mmmmph ... wha ...," mumbled Candi.

Kevin just kept snoring.

"We need to take a vote. To Costco or not to Costco; that is the question," said Sarah.

Jonathan nodded. "Shakespeare. Nice."

"I know my lit-tra-ture," she said in a funny English accent.

"What?" said Candi, still obviously disoriented. "Did you say Costco? We're at Costco? Why?"

"Jonathan says we should stock up. And I for one agree with that. Fifty boxes of macaroni and cheese? Why yes, thank you very much." Sarah licked her lips. "Yummers for my tummers."

"Ugh. No *thank* you," said Candi, sitting up straighter. She rubbed her eyes a few times before nudging Kevin. "Come on, Kevin. Time to shop."

"Nooooo, I don't wanna shop anymore," he moaned, putting the back of his arm over his eyes.

The light turned green, so Jonathan pulled ahead and into the parking lot of the wholesale store. "I think we should get supplies really far from our final destination so no one recognizes us and figures out that we're staying close by. If someone sees us here and does recognize us, they'll assume we're staying in this town, so that would be good."

"Sounds smart," said Candi, sighing.

"Yeah, but someone needs to guard the car. That'll be me," said Kevin. His knee jammed into Jonathan's back as he sank lower in his seat.

"Candi and I will go in. You and Sarah sleep. I'll leave the keys. If anyone looks suspicious, just go. We'll meet you at the gas station one block that way," Jonathan said, pointing in the direction they'd just come from. "The one with the big green sign. You guys see it?"

Sarah nodded. "I see it. And I'm okay with you guys leaving me behind to nap, but if you don't come back with mac and cheese, heads are gonna roll."

"We will buy two cases, don't worry," said Jonathan. "Ready?" He looked at his sister in the back seat, concerned about the dark circles under her eyes. Maybe doing something other than worrying would perk her up. Girls liked to shop, especially at Costco.

"Yeah. Come on," she said, getting out of the back seat.

Sarah had already gotten comfortable, reclining back.

"See you soon," Jonathan said, shutting the door. He tapped on the glass. "Lock the doors." He waited until he saw the buttons go down before he left to join Candi standing at the back of the car.

"How are we going to get in? Don't they have membership cards here?"

"Yeah. I have one from the FBI guys. Took it out of his wallet. He looks enough like me he could be my dad. Hopefully, they won't check too closely."

They grabbed a cart and made it through the first barrier, the guy at the door checking to make sure that they had a card.

"One down, one to go," whispered Jonathan under his breath. "Okay, what do we need in order to fully stock this cabin?"

"Well, assuming it's furnished and has sheets and pillows and junk, we'll need just food and drinks and stuff to prepare food with, like spices and oil. Peanut butter and jelly would be good too."

"I wish it wasn't Sunday. I'd love to go into a library and do some research."

"For what?" asked Candi, adding a couple of items to the cart, one of them a recipe book.

"First, we have to find a cabin rental. Then we need to check the news, to see if the police responded to our anonymous phone call."

"And Sarah and I want to get a dog at an adoption place," added Candi.

Jonathan stopped pushing the cart. "What for?"

"Security. Plus, it'll give us something to do ... training the dog and stuff."

Jonathan nodded, considering how dogs were much better suited to guard duty in the dark than humans were. "I think that's an excellent idea. We'll research that too, then." He moved to the aisle with the giant bags of dog food and hefted one over, sliding it under the main basket. They made their way through the rest of the store, filling the cart to the top with canned and dried foods and drinks. Jonathan would have liked to add some other things, but resisted the urge to buy items that might spoil. They'd have to risk going to a somewhat local grocery store for those things. Maybe the girls could come up with a disguise so they'd be harder to identify, in case the FBI put some sort of alert out for them.

When they neared the checkout, Jonathan started to feel panicky. "Candi, you go wait at the door."

"Why? You're going to need help."

"No, I have the cart. I don't want them to see us together. We're less likely to be recognized from pictures if we're alone. They're looking for four kids, two couples, or brother and sister groups ... not single teens."

Candi went back to looking frightened. Her voice came out sounding strangled. "Fine. I'll see you outside."

Jonathan nodded, turning his attention back to navigating his heavy cart into the shortest line. The place was pretty full, and he had four people ahead of him with hundreds of items in their carts total. It was plenty of time to become quite nervous over the idea that he might be rejected at the checkout for using someone else's card. *What are the odds that this card has been reported stolen or missing? Hmmm... probably one in ten thousand or more. I'm probably good there. And what are the odds that someone in this store has seen a picture of me on the news? Factors: we are out of the county we were in when it occurred. Point in our favor. We are near the state line, so almost out of the state even. Another point in our favor. I am alone and not with three others. But I don't know if they're showing all our pictures individually or as a group, so I can't be sure whether that's in my favor or a point against ...* He continued adding and subtracting points until he got to the register, still no closer to knowing if he was about to be caught red-handed or not when he gave the cashier the card.

She looked at the name. "Grant Latimer."

Jonathan nodded.

She stared at the picture and then up at Jonathan, her eyes narrowing as she took in his features. She poked the picture on the card with her long fake nail. "This isn't you."

"No, it isn't. That's correct," said Jonathan, his face flaming. *Come up with something ... quick!* "It's my dad."

"Do you have I.D.? Something with your name on it, *Mr. Latimer.*"

Jonathan shook his head. "No, sorry, I don't. My wallet was stolen last night from my jacket, at the prom, so I have to wait until Monday to go to the DMV and get a new one."

She pursed her lips, frowning. "The name sounds familiar. Latimer. Grant Latimer. You from around here?"

"Uhhhh, no. I'm from ... out of town. Not far, though. Few miles, really." He wracked his brain for a town name from one of the many signs he'd passed while driving. "Uhhh, Billingsly?

Ever heard of it?"

She smiled. "Oh, yeah! Heck yeah! I went to high school there! Where do you go?"

Jonathan's eyes nearly fell out of his head. "Guess!" he said, not even thinking before the word flew out of his mouth. His brain was quickly calculating what the odds were that he'd picked the one town in the entire state that this woman had gone to for high school. He didn't have the exact number yet, but it was high, he knew that much.

She bit her bottom lip, nodding while looking him up and down. "Bentworth."

"No. Is that where you went?"

"Yeah. What about ... Billingsly Central?"

Jonathan smiled nervously. "Yep, that's it. Billingsly Central. That's where I go. To high school. That's the name."

"So that makes us rivals," she said, raising her eyebrows in a challenging way.

Jonathan's mouth fell open but no words could come out.

She waved at him, smiling warmly and setting the card up on her register. "I'm just messin' with ya, kid. Go ahead and start boxing your stuff up." She scanned the first item and slid it down the ramp.

Jonathan stepped to the side and concentrated on not having a heart attack or throwing up. That was the closest call he'd had since he'd been on the island, and it was enough to make him want to move to a cabin in the woods and never come back to the real world again.

*****

Kevin felt the car stop, and slowly sat up, trying to orient himself. The sounds of doors opening and shutting registered as he rubbed his face and hair. He yawned, wishing he'd gotten about eight more hours of sleep. "Where are we?" he asked, finally opening his eyes and looking around. Candi was the only one in the car with him, and Sarah and Jonathan were walking up to a small one-story building with a chainlink fence around it. He could hear dogs barking.

"We're getting a dog."

"A ... what?" Kevin wasn't sure he'd heard correctly. He squinted through the dirty windshield. "Hearts and Hands Animal Shelter." He frowned in confusion, thinking he must have missed something big. "We're at an animal shelter?"

"Yes. While you were sleeping we took a vote. We're getting a dog for protection at the cabin. We're going to teach him to be our security ... you know, to warn us when bad guys come and also maybe bite if necessary."

"Bite?"

"That was Sarah's idea, not mine. I just wanted one for alerting purposes and to help keep our minds off our situation. I'm afraid we're going to go stir crazy like that guy in that movie who was snowed in, if we don't come up with some activities."

"Like dog obedience training," said Kevin without emotion. He wasn't sure yet how he felt about the idea. Several minutes later when he saw movement out of the front windshield and figured out what he was seeing, he started laughing. "Holy crap ... is she serious?"

Candi followed his gaze. "Uhhhhh ..." She looked at Kevin. "Am I hallucinating?"

Kevin just shook his head. Leave it to his sister to do something like this. The scrappy mutt at the end of her leash was hardly what he'd call guard-dog material. More like ankle biting.

Then Jonathan came into view, and Kevin nodded. "Now *that's* what I'm talking about." A second dog was at the end of Jonathan's leash - one that looked more like what Kevin had imagined they were here for.

About five feet in front of the car, they switched leashes. Sarah bent down and started rubbing the bigger dog's chest and head, smiling like a crazy person.

"Now I'm just confused," said Candi, watching Jonathan walk his dog around a little. Kevin figured he was trying to get it to go to the bathroom or something.

Sarah came over and opened the back door. "Out, Sugar Lump. Make room for Killer."

Candi got out slowly, keeping her eyes on the white pit bull that sat next to Sarah's leg, its torn up ears and distended nipples hanging down, victims of a hard life and gravity. "What in the heck are you doing, Sarah?" she asked.

"Loading the newest member of our family in the car ... what does it look like I'm doing?"

Kevin spoke up. "It looks like you took the ugliest, sorriest excuse for a dog out of that shelter so we could use it to just *scare* the assassins away from us."

"Shush! Her ears may be a little chewed up, but she can still hear you." Sarah bent down and looked the dog in the face. "Ignore them. They haven't learned of your inner beauty yet. Nor have they seen your teeth." She looked at Kevin and Candi. "The guy told us she's a sweetheart. She was brought to the shelter by the jerk who disowned her because she refused to do anything anymore. The shelter guy told us that meant fight or whatever. She's depressed from her recent tragedy."

The dog dropped its mouth open just in that moment to pant

and maybe even smile. Kevin could have sworn he saw the edges of her mouth lift up. And *damn*, she did have some big friggin teeth.

"Does she have puppies?" asked Candi, looking warily at the dog's chest.

"Apparently, she did a few weeks back, but not anymore. The former owner killed them, right in front of her."

Candi gasped. "What?!"

Kevin felt both angry and sick at the idea.

"Yeah. The shelter guy told us. He's like, the executioner or something, and he knows all the dirt that goes on in there. He said he doesn't judge, so people who come in just tell him the craziest stuff."

Candi looked at Kevin, but he didn't know what to say to her. Jonathan's arrival and the small terrier leaping into the front seat cut off his train of thought.

"Come on, you guys, we have to go before the staff gets back." Jonathan sat down started the car by touching the exposed wires immediately.

Sarah snapped her fingers towards the back seat. "Come on, Killer. Up you go ... into the car."

The dog jumped up, sitting down in the center of the back seat like she was ready to be buckled in. She turned her head once in Kevin's direction and licked his cheek. He froze, wondering how close he'd just come to having his face bitten off.

"I'm afraid to sit by her," said Candi.

"I told you she's a sweetheart, but whatever. Sit in the front with Luke Skywalker if you prefer."

Candi said nothing, she just stepped around the open door and got into the front seat. Her hands floated up in the air, hovering over the little dog who had jumped into her lap, his tail wagging like mad.

Jonathan shifted the car into reverse. "Get in, Sarah. I don't want to get caught with these dogs."

Sarah got in and shut the door, buckling the pit bull up before taking care of herself.

"Did you *steal* these dogs?!" asked Candi, sounding slightly hysterical.

"Of course we didn't steal them," said Jonathan. "They were pardoned."

"Yeah. We rescued them from the gas chamber," said Sarah, scrubbing the pit bull's chest enthusiastically. "Poor baby was scheduled to bite the big one today."

"Actually, I think we rescued them from lethal injection, but it's the same result." The tires spun in the dirt and gravel as Jonathan took off out of the lot.

"Why the hurry, dude?" asked Kevin, still confused about what had just happened.

"The staff wasn't in, but they'll be back soon. The manager had just left. The guy who's in charge of euthanizing the dogs and cats that don't get adopted in time was the only one there."

Sarah continued the explanation when Jonathan became too distracted with the driving. "He told us they always leave when he has to do his job, but they pretend it's for other reasons, like they have to run an errand or go see the dentist. This time the manager said she had to go to the doctor. On a *Sunday*."

Jonathan picked up the rest. "So anyway, he was going to tell us to come back when the manager was in, but Sarah saw him leading Killer there on a leash and she started goo-gooing all over her, so the guy asked us if we wanted her for free, no questions asked. He said the manager would never know, and he'd just mark down that he euthanized and cremated her."

"I wasn't goo-gooing ... was I, Killer? Was I, baby? Was I, mommy of the puppies who had to go to heaven? No, I was not ... no I was not. I never goo-goo." The whole time she was talking in a squeaky high voice and rubbing the dog's head and neck. Its butt never stopped moving along with its wagging tail.

"You mean he was actually going to kill these two dogs?" asked Candi, her voice all weepy.

"Yes, he was. But he *didn't* because we came just in time. It was meant to be," said Sarah. "We got two for the price of none! A total steal!"

"The chances of us walking up and looking for an anonymous adoption just as he was coming out with the dogs to ... do the deed ... all while the manager was gone, are pretty strongly in favor of this being somehow designed. If I were a believer in destiny, I'd be swayed. As a man of science, I'm at least intrigued in the odds," said Jonathan, maneuvering the car through light traffic towards the highway. "This whole situation of us running from the FBI and avoiding trouble along the way is just one big odds calculation."

"Is there any chance we can change this one's name?" asked Kevin, rubbing the pit bull's leg gently, his heart going out to her despite her ugliness. "Killer just doesn't seem right." He couldn't avoid looking at the recent evidence of her having given birth. "She seems too ... motherly to be a killer."

"I agree," said Sarah. "The contest for naming the doggie woggie loggie is now on." She reached over and hugged the battered pit bull who sat stoically through most of it, leaning down to lick Sarah's head only once.

Kevin noticed the white beast had scars all over her body. He tried to keep his mind from wondering what and who had caused her all this pain. If they weren't so focused on staying under the radar and unseen, he might be tempted to find out the guy's address.

"What about this doggy?" asked Candi, sounding much more cheerful now. It may have had something to do with the goofy look the dog kept giving her, trying to look up at her backwards and tipping over with his efforts.

"They didn't know his name when they brought him in, so he got called Luke Skywalker."

"Ugh. Luke Skywalker," said Kevin, deciding he couldn't have come up with a dumber name if he tried.

"Two naming contests, then," said Candi, ruffling the terrier's fur, which was already pretty messed up. "I'll start. How about ... Rowdy?"

"We're naming the small one first?" asked Jonathan, driving the car onto a main road, staying in the right lane. "Okay ... how about Spock? He has really pointy ears."

"I choose Sprocket," said Sarah. "It's cuter."

"Sprocket's cool," said Kevin, getting into the game. "What about James?"

Candi laughed. "Why James?"

Kevin shrugged. "I have absolutely no idea. He just looks like a James to me."

Candi leaned down and looked the dog in the eye. "Do you like Sprocket or James better?"

He barked twice and then panted eagerly.

"I think that means he likes James better," said Kevin, warming to the little guy already. He obviously had good taste.

"Sprocket?" said Candi

The dog barked.

"James?" asked Kevin.

The dog barked again.

"Which do you like better?" Candi asked, giggling a little.

He barked twice.

"James it is," said Kevin, smiling. The contest was over as far as he was concerned. "Now what about big momma here?"

"I like Xena. She's like a warrior princess," said Sarah, draping her arm over the dog's back.

"I like that too," said Jonathan. "I was thinking Phoenix, but Xena is better."

"Phoenix is a boy's name," said Candi, twisting around to look at the dog. "I like Xena. That suits her."

Kevin shrugged. "I've already picked one name. Wouldn't be fair for me to pick both." He liked Xena for her name too. This dog was definitely a warrior, but someone had taken the fight out of her ... maybe the asshole who'd killed her babies. He watched his sister clinging to her, and thought maybe there was some kind of mother-bond between them that was tugging Sarah's heartstrings so thoroughly. Whatever the cause, he was happy to see her so content. He had a feeling they were going to need something to inspire them through the coming weeks or months. He reached up and patted the dog's head, smiling at the reward he got - a hot, soggy dog lick on his forearm.

James the terrier moved to balance himself on the center console, stretching his head out towards Xena. Kevin tensed up, wondering if James was going to be missing a head in about half a second. Before he could do anything to stop it, Xena leaned forward.

Kevin's mouth dropped open in confused but happy surprise as he watched Xena licking James' face from one side to the other. James' lids dropped to half-mast as he obviously enjoyed the bath he was getting.

"That's just ... gross," said Candi, watching the affection between the animals.

"Awww, she misses her babies," said Sarah, her eyes suspiciously shiny. "James can be her baby now."

"That's good," said Kevin, relieved there wasn't going to be a dog fight in the back seat that James would most definitely lose. "Maybe this means she's not going to eat him."

"The shelter guy said that she was never a fighter. She was a bait dog," said Jonathan.

"What's a bait dog?" asked Candi.

"The dog they use to get the other dogs to act vicious ... to give them something to practice on before they fight for real."

Candi turned around, facing out the windshield, saying nothing. Kevin could tell by her silence that she was either crying or very close to it. He reached under the dog's head and squeezed Candi's shoulder. "Let's just forget the past and think about the future, okay? She has a new name and new owners and a new life."

"And a new big bag of food in the trunk," said Jonathan, getting into the spirit. "And the guy gave me a free booklet on training the dogs, too." He leaned forward and pulled it out of his back pocket, handing it over his shoulder to Kevin.

Kevin opened it and scanned the contents. "Looks good. We can start on this as soon as we get to our place."

"Speaking of which, we need to go online somewhere and find a place to rent," said Jonathan. "The libraries are closed today, so where else can we go online? Internet cafes are kind of hard to find nowadays."

"Copy shop," said Sarah. "They let you use them for an hourly charge and some of them are open twenty-four hours."

Jonathan swerved over into the far left lane and took a hard turn across the oncoming lanes into a parking lot.

"What the hell, Jon?" asked Kevin, glad the dog hadn't decided to eat his face off for bumping into her and sending her into Sarah.

"Phone booth! We had such a hard time finding one before, I thought I should stop at the first one we saw this time."

Candi got out as soon as the car stopped and came back less than a minute later. "No phone book."

"Dinosaurs, man," said Kevin. "Phone books are extinct in those things. We're going to have to go into a business and ask for one. And I'm starving, so maybe we can kill two birds with one stone."

Jonathan drummed his fingers on the steering wheel. "Where should we go? Somewhere we can do take-out."

"Sub shop," said Kevin without thinking twice. "Twelve inches, triple meat, extra cheese. Make my order a double."

Candi shook her head. "I don't know how you can eat that much. You should be twice your size."

"Muscle burns calories. I've got lots of muscle." He flexed, and Xena turned to watch. "See that, Xena? Man muscle. People fear me."

She licked his mouth.

He grimaced and sputtered, trying to get the dog saliva off his lips.

Sarah laughed. "That's what she thinks about your

bragging. Good girl, Xena, good girl." She rubbed the dog's head behind her ears, earning herself a lick too.

"Bam. Retribution. Well done, Xena." Kevin ducked in time to save himself from another French kiss.

"There's a sub shop," said Jonathan, pulling into a plaza. "I'm going to park where they can't see us. Candi, you go in and get your and Kevin's orders. I'll come in a few minutes later and get mine and Sarah's."

"Why are we doing it that way?" asked Candi.

"So they don't see you ordering for four. If they're alerted to four teens traveling together, it might stand out. I want to be anonymous in this town as much as possible."

"Fine. You'd better let me out here, then, or they might see me getting out of the same car."

Jonathan parked down the plaza from the shop, letting Candi out on the sidewalk. "When you're done, just walk down to the far end of the plaza, and I'll pick you up when we're finished." He looked in the back seat. "Kevin, duck down."

Kevin didn't ask questions or argue. Whatever made Jonathan happy with his scheming and planning was fine with him. Jon had gotten them this far without being knifed or shot, so Kevin considered that a sign of successful leadership.

Candi shut the door and Jonathan took off, selecting a parking space a few rows down from the door of the sub place. James' eyes were glued to Candi as she walked down the sidewalk to the right of them. Kevin smiled at how forlorn the little guy looked. He was already attached.

Sarah was watching the front of the store, her arm slung casually across the white dog's back. They'd never been allowed to have a dog at their house. Their mother claimed to be allergic, but it was probably more likely that she was allergic to the messes they made. Kevin had always said when he moved out on his own, the first thing he was going to do was get a dog. He glanced over at Xena and then at James. *Well, they aren't the dogs I'd always imagined for myself, but I think they'll do.*

James turned and looked at him, barking once and panting a couple times, before going back to watching for Candi.

Yep. Definitely.

*****

Sarah drew the short straw, so she had to walk into the cell phone store and buy the prepaid phone for the group. Before going in, she removed any vestiges of makeup that might have been left after her gas station bathroom clean-up. The last piece of her disguise was a baseball hat they'd found in the duffle bag for some baseball team she'd never heard of.

Walking in, she kept her eyes on the ground, trying to be as inconspicuous as possible. She grabbed the first phone off the rack that was cheap and brought it to the counter.

"Hello. Is there anything else I can get for you?" asked the salesman.

She shook her head no.

"Would you like to buy a warranty with this? It's only five ninety-five and covers accidents for up to a full year."

"No, thanks."

"Would you like to add more minutes now? It only comes with sixty to start."

"Nope." She schooled her features to stay bland and kept her head down as much as possible without seeming weird. She just needed to pay and get out. *Pay and get out, pay and get out.*

The door dinged and something made her turn. She

probably should have just ignored it, but she couldn't. She turned her head sideways and caught the vision of a uniform out of the corner of her eye. A police officer came up to the counter and stood right next to her.

"Can I help you, officer?" asked the salesman.

"I can wait."

Sarah could feel his gaze on her and her own face flaming up in response. She wanted to run but knew it would only make the guy suspicious. *Chill out. Just relax. Pay for the phone and get the heck outta here.*

"Okay, ma'am, I just need your name and address to turn the phone on. Do you have ID?"

Sarah's mouth dropped open and for a minute, she was speechless. Then she said the next thing that came to mind. "My name is Gretchen Landin. But why do you need that stuff? This is a prepaid phone, right?"

"Yes, of course. But we use it for our marketing purposes."

"Well, count me out of that garbage. All I want is the phone."

"I hear ya on that one," said the cop. "Seems like everyone just wants a piece of us these days, doesn't it?"

Sarah just nodded. She had plenty to say on the subject but now was not the time or the place, and this was definitely not the guy to be having a conversation with no matter what it was about.

"Gretchen, you said your name is?" asked the cop.

Sarah nodded again.

"You from around here?"

Sarah sighed and turned to face him. "Am I being interrogated or what? Am I under arrest?" She used her most bitchy tone, hoping to send a very clear message - *Don't flirt with me.*

"Did you do anything you need to be arrested for?" he asked, lifting an eyebrow, completely nonplussed by her attitude.

"No," she said, turning back to the counter and pulling cash out of her pocket. "How much?" she asked the guy.

"Twenty-nine dollars and fifty six cents. Unless you want to add more minutes, I could throw in a card for another hour of talk-time for five dollars and eighty-eight cents."

"No thanks." Sarah had reached the panic point. She threw a twenty and a ten onto the counter, grabbed the bag, and left the counter for the door.

"But you forgot your change! And your receipt!"

Sarah ignored the salesman and kept on walking. She could see the police car by the front door of the store and noticed a second cop sitting inside. She put her head down and left the store, taking a left instead of going out to the Camry where everyone was waiting for her, praying they'd figure out that they should drive around and pick her up in a different spot. The last thing they needed right now was to get busted for driving a stolen car.

She walked as fast as she dared. If she ran, she just knew she'd get tackled.

"Hey! Gretchen!" came a voice from behind her. And then the sound of running footsteps and jingling chains or keys, she wasn't sure which.

Run or stop? Run or stop?! She couldn't decide at first, but since she knew she probably couldn't outrun a cop, she stopped.

The officer caught up to her, only slightly winded. "You forgot your change. What's the big hurry?" He held out his hand upside down.

She looked up at him and noticed he was giving her a funny smile.

"Why are you harassing me?" she asked.

"Take your change," he said in a calm voice.

She held out her hand, and he dropped some coins in it.

"You know, you don't have to fear law enforcement. We're here to keep people and communities safe."

"I know that." She tried really hard not to sound as pissed as she was. This guy thought he had her all figured out, and all she wanted to do was scream in his face that he was going to get her killed if he didn't leave her alone.

"Then why the anger? Why the running?"

She sighed, annoyed. "I just don't like people messing with me. Am I allowed to be a private person, or does that badge give you the authority to just get all up in my face whenever you want?"

The cop put up his hands in surrender. "No, Gretchen it doesn't. I'm just making sure you're okay. It's not about authority; it's about caring for people."

"Well, thanks for caring. I'm late for an appointment now, so if you don't mind..."

"An appointment? On Sunday?"

"Back off, Officer Feel Good."

He smiled. "Fine. I get it. You're a private person. Well, Gretchen, I hope you have a nice day, and if you ever need anything, you just give us a call." He held out his business card to her.

She was sorely tempted to grab it and rip it in half in front of him, but she didn't. She just took it and shoved it in her pocket. "Thanks. See ya." She walked down the plaza sidewalk, not looking back but tuning her hearing in as much as possible to listen for whether he was still following. She heard nothing but the passing of cars as they cruised the lot looking for parking spaces.

She kept going until the plaza ran out of sidewalk and continued walking down the main boulevard until she reached a neighborhood. She turned into the first street and stood on the corner, finally getting up the guts to see if anyone had followed her. All she saw were passing cars, none of them with cops inside, and then less than a minute later, the Camry.

She grabbed the door as soon as it came to a stop and pulled it open with a yank. "Holy shizzle, that was close!" She climbed in, patting Xena on the head and throwing the plastic bag on the floor by her feet before slamming the door shut. "Come on, let's go. But go through this neighborhood first. I need to know if that cop is following us."

"What the hell happened, Sarah?" asked Kevin, sounding angry. "What did you do in there?"

"I didn't do anything, jerk. The cop did. I was just standing there trying to buy the damn phone, and he kept talking to me and interrogating me. I finally just told him to back off."

"Oh boy," said Candi.

Sarah pushed the back of the seat. "Shut up, Sugar Lump. You probably would have collapsed in tears if he'd come after you like he did me."

"He wouldn't have done that to me," said Candi. "He would have ignored me like all guys do."

Kevin snorted. "Right. Tell that to Jason."

"Listen, guys," said Jonathan, "now's not the time to get into disagreements. I think we're fine. No one is behind us and we've taken about five turns now, so I'm going to get back out onto the main road."

"What did he give you? We saw him on the sidewalk doing something," asked Candi.

"He gave me my change from the phone and his business card." Sarah fished it out of her pocket. "Here." She handed it up to Candi.

"Officer Douglas Betts. It has his cell phone and work phone on it."

"Throw it out," said Sarah. "I would have done it already, but I didn't want him to see me and start bugging me again. He's all mister taking-care-of-the-community-guy, and I guess I'm the troubled youth he's going to rescue."

"Well, technically speaking, we are troubled youth. He has good instincts," said Jonathan. "Just put it in the ashtray. Who knows when we'll need to speak to someone in law enforcement. It could come in handy someday."

Candi slid open the compartment and put it inside. "You came out with a bag. Did you get a phone?"

"Yep," sighed Sarah. "The trip wasn't a complete waste. I did get a phone and kept my identity a secret. Mostly."

"Mostly? Uh-oh. What's that mean?" asked Kevin.

"He asked me for my name, and I panicked."

"What'd you say?" asked Kevin in his menacing tone.

"I told him it was Gretchen Landin."

"What'd you do that for?!" exploded Kevin.

"Because he pressured me!" Sarah yelled back. "Get off my friggin back, okay? I did the best I could." Sarah wanted to stay mad, but instead, she started bawling. "He was asking me questions and that cop was standing behind me and everyone was just waiting for me to say something ..."

Xena turned to Sarah and began licking her face and arms, anything she could reach. She even whined a little.

"Kevin, don't talk to Sarah like that," said Jonathan sternly. "She did a good job, and none of us can say what we would have done in her shoes. Everyone needs to just stay calm and be respectful."

Sarah sniffed loudly, wishing she had a tissue.

"Damn, Jon. You're going to make a great dad," said Kevin.

"That was straight out of our dad's toolkit, I can promise you that," said Candi. "I can't tell you how many times we heard that growing up."

Sarah smiled. The idea of her kids getting a dad like Candi and Jonathan had made her happy. Six months ago it would have horrified her. It was funny how much her perspective had changed. She moved her hand to her belly, rubbing it absently. All this introspection was cool, but the hormones were a serious bitch.

Candi twisted in her seat, reaching through the center area to pat Sarah's leg. "Don't cry, Sarah. You did great, and we're fine. We're safe. Kevin's sorry." Candi shot him a look.

Kevin sighed heavily. "Yeah. Sorry. Just ignore me. I'm stressed."

"We all are," said Jonathan. "And I'd like to say it's going to get better; I just saw a copy shop back there and I'm going to turn around so we can go online and find a place to stay."

He flipped a u-turn and pulled into the shopping plaza's parking lot, stopping in a space that was surrounded by other cars. There was a baby toy store in the same plaza, so it was packed even late on a Sunday. "Who's going in this time?" he asked.

"Not me," said Sarah. *No friggin way am I going through that again.* She put her head back on the seat and closed her eyes. "Wake me up when we get to our final destination."

*****

Candi and Jonathan sat at the computer, surfing an online classifieds site to find owners that had rentals of furnished cabins in the Tennessee mountains. They were the only ones in the glassed-off room so they made phone calls while they were at it. They struck gold about twenty minutes into the process.

Candi hung up the phone, a huge grin splitting her face. "That one is available for the entire summer. It's perfect!"

"What'd the owner say about it?"

"She said that it's really isolated and that's why it's so cheap. She didn't say cheap, actually, she said *affordable.* The owners used to use it themselves during the summers, but they're elderly now and their kids live too far away to enjoy it."

"And they take cash?"

"Yes, she said they'd take cash as long as we paid up front for the whole thing."

"So how much?"

"Fifteen hundred for a month, three thousand for two months, four thousand for three months."

"Is she going to require identification?"

"You heard me tell her we lost everything in a fire. She said not to worry about it, that I sounded trustworthy over the phone."

"That's incredibly naive," said Jonathan, frowning. "Maybe it's a scam."

"She sounded really old and very sweet. I don't think someone that old would scam someone."

"Well, she got the ad online. She must be somewhat sophisticated."

"She said her grandson did it for her from wherever he lives. He used an old photograph from when he used to go there with his parents." Candi leaned over and pointed to the pictures online. "Look how adorable it is. And it has two bedrooms, a bathroom, a kitchen, and a living room. The porch is just a bonus. It's perfect."

Jonathan nodded. "So how are we meeting up with her?"

"I wrote down the directions here. She said there's this small grocery store in this nearby town where everyone gets their groceries if they don't want to go into the city. Here's the address."

Jonathan checked an online map to find it, printing a copy out to take with them. "I guess we're all set, then. I figure it'll take us four hours to get there."

"Good. So we just have to find a place to sleep tonight, and we'll leave early in the morning to meet her at ten o'clock."

"Perfect," said Jonathan, logging off. "That went easier than I expected."

"Getting through eight phone calls and rejections isn't what I'd call easy," said Candi, standing and stretching her back in a couple directions. "Man, I'm going to be glad to sleep in a real bed tonight. We're getting a motel room, right?"

"Yes. I think we should, for Sarah if nothing else. I'm personally looking forward to a shower. I've been perspiring like crazy."

"Speaking of showers and washing hair ... I was thinking of cutting mine."

"To make the dreads shorter?" asked Jonathan, walking with

Candi to the counter so they could pay for their time used.

"No, to cut them off entirely."

"Your hair will be really short."

"Yeah, I know. But not totally. I can cut the dreads off at like the four-inch point and then un-dred them. I'm just tired of the heaviness from them, you know? And they really make me stick out. Let's face it ... there aren't a lot of teenagers in Tennessee with dreadlocks."

"You're right. I think it's a good idea. You'd better ask Sarah though, before you do it." Jonathan paid the bill and walked to the door, folding the map he'd printed on the way and sticking it in his back pocket.

"Sarah's not in charge of my hair," Candi said, following behind him and rolling her eyes at how whipped her brother was.

"Technically, she isn't, you're right. But she thinks she is, which in her current condition is a thing we should factor into our decisions."

"*Pfft*. Like her being pregnant means we all have to change our lives? I don't think so. As long as her health isn't at risk, I'm not considering it at all."

"Do what you want. It's your funeral," said Jonathan, walking up to the car.

Candi got in next to him in a huff.

"What's wrong? Are we screwed?" asked Kevin from the back, pulling himself forward using Jonathan's headrest.

"No, actually, we found a spot. Candi's just upset about a suggestion I made." Jonathan started the car. He glanced back in his mirror to make sure Sarah was still sleeping. She was out like a light, and Xena was sleeping with her head in Sarah's lap.

"What was it?" asked Kevin.

"Nothing important." Candi turned so she could look at Kevin's expression. "What do you think about me cutting my hair?"

He shrugged. "I don't care. You'll be hot no matter what."

Candi smiled. "That's nice to know."

"Sarah might not be too thrilled about it, though," he added.

Candi rolled her eyes again and turned around. "Sarah's not the boss of me."

"Nope. You're right. Do what you want."

He was agreeing too easily. She pulled down her visor and looked at his reflection, seeing a devious smile there. "What are you so happy about, troublemaker?"

"I'm just looking forward to the fireworks."

Candi pushed the visor back up. "As if," she mumbled under her breath. *It's my stupid hair. I can do whatever I want with it.* "I'll be right back," she said, getting out of the car on impulse before Jonathan could pull out of the parking space and jogging over to the drugstore that was next to the copy shop. She ignored the yelling out the window coming from Kevin and Jonathan.

Candi quickly cruised the aisles looking for scissors and hair dye. *I'm not just going to cut it; I'm going red, too.* She'd always wondered what she'd look like as a redhead, and nobody was going to stop her from doing whatever the heck she wanted with her hair. She studied the color swatches on the shelves and the boxes, finally picking one that looked like a deep reddish-brown. She bought two boxes, not sure how much of the dye it would take to get her blonde hair the right shade.

The cashier rang up her purchases without a word, more worried about the text message waiting for her on her phone than customer service. Candi paid with cash and left the store with her plastic bag swinging at her hip. She was proud of herself, taking her destiny and safety into her own hands. No one would be able to identify her when she was done. No more blonde-haired girl with dreadlocks for the police or FBI to track down. When she saw this old lady who owned the cabin, she was going to be a short-haired, normal-looking redhead.

*****

Jonathan was afraid to wake Sarah up. He'd heard Candi in the bathroom banging around for a while, but she'd been quiet for way too long. Then a few cusswords came out from behind the door.

Xena lifted her head off her paw once, but then went back to sleep. The smaller dog, James, had taken up a position just outside the bathroom door, practically leaning on it in his desire to be near Candi.

Kevin and Sarah were both sound asleep on separate beds. Kevin had checked them into the sleeziest motel room Jonathan had ever seen, using his charm on the heavily made-up woman at the desk to avoid having to give his identification. It was an hourly rental type place, so it probably hadn't taken much to convince her.

As soon as he laid eyes on the room, Jonathan knew they'd be sleeping with all kinds of bacteria and maybe even lice or bed bugs. He'd insisted on spraying the entire room down with a can of disinfectant he purchased in the store down the street before allowing Sarah to go inside, and he did a thorough check of the mattress for bugs. The windows were open now to let some of the smell out. Even with the disinfectant soaked into every crevice of the room, the rancid odor of old cigarette smoke and nicotine would never leave; they were just going to have to deal with it for one night.

Jonathan walked up to the bathroom door and tapped on it lightly. "Are you okay in there?"

"No, I'm not, thank you very much," came Candi's annoyed voice from inside.

"Anything I can do to help?"

"Yeah." The door flew open. "You can go get a razor to shave my head with."

Jonathan stood there, staring at the girl who was supposed to be his sister. He blinked several times to clear his retinas of the misinformation they were sending through his optic nerve to his brain.

"Stop blinking at me like that and *say* something."

"Uhhh ... uhhhh ... that is such an ... interesting color. It reminds me of Mars."

"Eerrrrrhhh!" yelled Candi, slamming the door in his face.

"I like the color of Mars," said Jonathan to the particle board that was inches from his nose now. "Kind of a reddish-orangish-brownish."

"What's going on?" mumbled Sarah from the bed.

Jonathan strolled over, in no hurry to unleash the fury that would be Sarah realizing Candi had taken hair matters into her own hands.

Sarah sat up, running her fingers under her eyes. "I heard Candi yelling. Is she mad about something?"

"Maybe," said Jonathan, sitting down and taking Sarah's exposed foot in his lap. She liked massages. He was thinking maybe she wouldn't go so bananas over his sister's hair if she had nice happy feet to walk around on.

Sarah squinted at him. "What are you hiding?"

He widened his eyes trying to look innocent. "Who? Me? Nothing. Nothing at all. I'm just sitting her rubbing your feet with zero ulterior motives."

Sarah pushed him off and stood up. "Liar liar pants too long in the dryer and now they're squeezing your hacky sack. What's Sugar Lump hiding from me?" She walked over to the bathroom, knocking on the door with a knuckle. "Hey! Sugar Lump! Let me in."

"No! Go away!"

"No can do, Scooby Doo. Open it, or I'll have one of my bouncers take it down."

"I can't," came a weepy voice from inside.

"What do you mean you can't? Is it broken?"

"No. There's nothing wrong with the door."

"What is it then? Come on ... pregnant lady's gotta pee."

"Go in the sink."

Sarah laughed. "I'm not going to pee in the sink. Seriously, what's wrong with you?" Sarah looked over at Jonathan and ran her finger in a circle around her ear.

Jonathan shook his head. His sister wasn't crazy, but her hair sure looked it.

"It's my hair."

"What's wrong with your hair? I can help you, just let me in."

"There's no helping this horror show. It's over. I'm going to have to shave it down to nothing."

"You've got five seconds, Sugar Lump."

Jonathan could tell Sarah was serious now. Apparently, so could Candi, because the door creaked open slowly. And as more and more of Candi was revealed, the more shocked Sarah's expression became.

Sarah said in an awed voice, "Holy Mexican jumping beans, what in the hellsbells did you do to your hair?"

"I cut it. And I dyed it *Midsummer Night's Dream Red.*"

Sarah just shook her head. "Oh, no you did not, young lady. You massacred it, and dyed it *bleeding carrot red.*" She grabbed Candi's arm and pulled her out to face the big mirror. She talked to the reflection of them both. "All my hard work. Hours of dreading, of fixing, styling, slaving over a hot head of frizzy hair ... and now *this.*"

"I know!" wailed Candi. "I'm so ugly, Kevin's going to break up with me as soon as he sees me!" She dropped her face into her hands, crying for real now.

Kevin sat up, looking around, disoriented. "What? Who's ugly?"

Jonathan said nothing. He just pointed.

Kevin scooted forward on the bed so he could see what Jonathan was gesturing at. A second later, he snorted.

Candi whipped around, dropping her hands to her sides. "Don't *laugh!*" she screeched.

Kevin broke out into loud guffaws, rolling over sideways on the bed and falling onto the floor when he ran out of mattress.

Candi shrieked in frustration and ran back into the bathroom, shutting and locking the door behind her.

"Hey! I have to pee!" yelled Sarah, banging on the door.

Candi yanked the door open, grabbed Sarah's arm, and pulled her inside, shutting the door behind both of them.

Jonathan could hear echoing voices from within. Candi was whining and moaning, and Sarah was first trying to sooth her and then just yelling at her to shut up and stop complaining. He smiled to himself. Sarah's particular brand of tough love was usually quite effective. He had no doubt that she'd fix Candi's hair as much as it was fixable at this point. He looked down at Kevin who was wiping the tears from his eyes as he crawled back up on the bed.

"Are you going to break up with her?" Jonathan asked, worried about his sister dealing with a broken heart along with all this other stress.

Kevin frowned at him and laughed once before answering. "Are you kidding? Hell no, I'm not going to dump her. She looks like Strawberry Shortcake. Do you have any idea how much of a crush I had on that stupid character when I was a little kid?" He sighed as he flopped back onto the bed. "My mom had these dolls in plastic containers in her closet from when she was younger, and one of them had this reddish pink hair that smelled like strawberries. I thought she was so pretty when I was, like, five or whatever."

"I'd say Candi's hair is more rusty red than pink."

"Meh. Rusty red ... pink ... it's all the same to me. Hilarious and cute." He swiveled his head to look at Jonathan. "Dude, she could shave her head bald, and I'd still want to be with her, you know?"

"Yeah. I know." Jonathan had the same emotional ties to Sarah.

"I never felt that way about a girl before. I used to like a girl *just* for that stuff - looks and shit. Now," he shrugged, "doesn't seem like it even matters." He pointed at Jonathan. "Don't tell her I said that, though. I don't want her to let herself go or anything."

"But I thought you said it didn't matter what she looked like."

"Dude, it's not about looks. It's about personal pride. I need to be with the Candi who feels good about herself, proud, confident ... you know? I don't want some depressed mopey girl for a girlfriend."

"Oh, okay ... I see what you mean. So as long as she's confident, she can be ugly."

"Did Kevin just say I'm ugly?" whispered Candi from the open doorway. Jonathan could hear the sounds of Sarah using the bathroom in the background.

"Close the door, would ya?!" Sarah yelled.

"No! Kevin didn't say that!" said Jonathan in a panic.

"Then why did you say that?!"

"Way to go, Jon," admonished Kevin, jumping off the bed to join Candi. "Babe, I didn't say that. I said, *if* you were ugly I'd still want you to be my girlfriend."

"Liar! You said I'm ugly!" she yelled, going back into the bathroom and locking it before Kevin could get there to cut her off. He tripped over the dog in his efforts and stumbled to the floor just outside the door.

He looked over at Jonathan after reaching up and unsuccessfully trying the handle. "Way to go, genius."

"What? What'd I do?" Jonathan sat on the edge of the bed, feeling like a fish out of water. This sensation was nothing new when it came to either of those girls, but it was still frustrating.

He shook his head after watching Kevin try to cajole his way into the bathroom and the heart of his sister for five straight minutes with no success. "This is totally not my fault," mumbled Jonathan to himself as he pulled back the covers and climbed into the bed that Sarah had vacated.

He fell asleep before Kevin got into the bathroom. His

dreams were filled with pink-haired aliens from Mars and angry girlfriends threatening to shave his head.

Home Sweet Home

KEVIN WAS THE FIRST ONE awake. He took the dogs out for a walk, relieved to find they were both housebroken and that there was no dog crap to clean up in the room - not that it would have mattered in that place. The smell probably would have blended right in.

He got back in time to take a hot shower before everyone got up. When he was done he put his dirty clothes back on and went out into the room to join the others. He used every ounce of willpower not to bust a gut at Candi's hair when she sat up.

She eyed him carefully. "I can see you laughing inside your head, Kevin."

He sat down on the edge of the bed and pulled her into his arms. "Listen, Gumdrop. Sarah fixed it up nice. You look cute, so stop worrying."

"That extra box of dye helped, but I'm still a long way from being fixed. I look like that Shirley Temple girl."

"I have no idea who you're talking about, but she must be hot because I know you are." He laid a loud, juicy kiss on her unresponsive lips. "Better pucker up, Gumdrop, or I'm gonna have to tackle you and force you to kiss me back."

She smiled hesitantly. "Are you being serious? Do you really think it's not awful?"

He stood and pulled her to her feet. "I really think it's not awful, I promise. It's all good. Now hurry up and get ready. We need to go if we're going to eat and get there on time to pay that lady."

"What time is it?" groaned Sarah from the other bed.

"Five. Get up. There's an IHOP down the street, and I can already smell the pancakes and sausage and bacon and pies and milkshakes ..."

Sarah jumped out of bed and raced to the bathroom faster than he'd ever seen her move. When he heard the sounds of vomiting coming from around the corner he knew why. "Oh boy. Sorry about that." He grabbed the leashes off the dresser and hooked the dogs up again. "I'm going to wait outside. See you guys in five. Don't forget the money."

He escaped as fast as he could without being rude about it. He loved his sister and all, but that morning sickness was just plain gross. Someday if his wife ever had a kid, he'd be there for her; but until then, he was going to leave the managing of Sarah to Jonathan. He was much better-suited to it anyway. The science behind it gave him all kinds of stuff to think about and calculate. The kid was only happy when he was reciting factoids, and this pregnancy was a bottomless well of data for him.

Kevin stood on the sidewalk absently watching the dogs goof around and the early-morning traffic using the road. A police car cruising by slowly caught his attention, the cop behind the wheel staring at him for a few long seconds. It made Kevin wish he'd stayed inside the room. He tried to turn to the side casually so he wouldn't be so recognizable. After waiting for the car to pass, he walked over and stuck his head inside the door to the room. "Let's go," he said loudly, seeing only Candi standing in between the beds, brushing her teeth. "There are cops cruising around, and one of them just looked at me."

Less than a minute later they were all piling into the car in a panic, the dogs jumping in along with them. "Are we going to the IHOP?" Candi asked from the driver's seat, scooting it forward so she could reach the pedals.

Sarah groaned.

"No. Go to a McDs or something, the drive-through. We can't afford to sit around where we'll be seen," said Kevin. Seeing that cop staring at him had freaked him out. He just wanted to get to that cabin and settle in, and the first thing he was going to do was train the big dog to kick some ass. Hopefully that assbag owner who'd had her before hadn't beaten her protective instincts out of her along with everything else.

"Should we go through with all of us in the car?" asked Candi.

"Yes, I think we'll be okay, said Jonathan. "Fast food establishments are usually staffed by teenagers, and that's the age group with the fewest amount of viewers of the news. I think we should just get to the cabin as soon as possible."

Kevin held up his fist for a bump which Jonathan returned in confusion.

Candi pulled out onto the road and went two blocks before locating their breakfast stop. They asked for a few extra empty sacks which Sarah ended up using as barf bags in response to the smells from the greasy food. Candi gulped down her breakfast burritos as fast as she could.

"I'm sorry, Sarah," said Jonathan. "When we stop for lunch,

we'll eat outside the car."

Kevin glanced back to see her waving weakly at them from her spot in the passenger seat, her head resting on the open window frame. "Don't worry about it. I'm feeling better. I just wish I had a cracker or something."

"Fry?" asked Kevin, holding up a limp strip of potato in between the front seats.

Sarah took it out of his hand and ate it. "Thanks. That's good."

"If you can't keep food down we're going to have to bring you to a hospital," Jonathan said worriedly.

"I'll be fine. It's just really bad in the morning. The problem is I feel like I'm sick because I have an empty stomach, but at the same time, all that food just smells so disgusting I can't imagine eating it."

"So you're basically screwed," said Kevin. "If you can eat fries, though, we can get more."

"She needs a balanced diet," said Jonathan.

"Yeah, but if all she can eat is fries, I'm buying her fries. It won't kill her for a few weeks to be on a potato diet."

"We don't need to figure this out now," said Candi, diplomatically. "We just need to get settled. I'll bet once we have a routine and a normal bed to sleep in, everything will be just fine. I bought a recipe book, so we're all set with home-cooked meals."

"Assuming someone knows how to use the thing," said Sarah, the wind out the window taking away some of the volume from her words.

"I know how to cook. My mom's been teaching me and Jonathan for years."

"Good. Maybe you can teach me."

"Yeah," said Kevin in a soft voice. "Please. Or she may do the Russian guy's job for him by poisoning us all." Kevin hunched over, leaning forward to try and escape the punishment he knew was coming.

Sarah pulled her head in the window and reached forward to flick her brother on the back of the ear, missing and hitting just air. "I'm nauseous, not deaf, idiot." She sat back, putting her face to the window again.

Kevin stayed leaning forward for the next five minutes until they were back on the highway and Sarah was asleep. He never could tell when she was going to start feeling better again, and she never forgot a missed ear flick. He was safer staying out of reach while she was conscious.

*****

"I'm totally starving," said Sarah.

"I thought you were sick," said Candi, looking at her in the rearview mirror.

"Whatever morning sickness I had before has now been replaced with a gigantic hole in my stomach that needs food in it, stat. Pull into that rest stop, Sugar Lump."

"But Kevin said no rest stops before."

"I don't give flying fudge brownie what Kevin said, I have to get some food. I'll go in and out really quick - like lightning fast, I promise."

Candi looked at the sleeping forms of her brother and boyfriend, deciding that she could deal with their anger if she had to. If Sarah didn't eat some real food and fast she was probably going to get sick all over again, and *that* wouldn't be good for anyone.

"Okay," said Candi, putting on the turn signal. "I'm going to park way over here behind this big truck. You put your hair in a pony tail, and put that hat on and these sunglasses." She took the FBI-issue pair off her face and handed them back to Sarah. "Don't talk to anyone, and don't make eye contact. Keep your head down and hurry up. If I see anyone like a cop taking you out in handcuffs or whatever, I'm going to leave you behind, you got it?"

Sarah nodded, looking like she wasn't sure whether she should laugh or cry at Candi's orders. But she put on her brave face and nodded, apparently deciding doing neither was her best option. She got out of the car wearing the disguise Candi had suggested, walking with her head down to the rest stop building entrance.

True to her word, Sarah got back much faster than Candi expected, and no one was leading her out in handcuffs. Candi watched her through the windshield of the truck next to them, just barely able to make out her slim form as she made her way back past the smashed bugs and other gross stuff on the glass that stood between them. Sarah had a fast-food bag in her hand and kept her head down all the way back to the car. She opened the door and got in, slamming it shut quickly behind her. "Let's go," she said breathlessly.

"What'd you get?" asked Kevin, waking up from his nap.

"Fries."

"Jonathan's going to be pissed."

"Too bad." Sarah dove her hand into the bag and came out with three fries, cramming them all in her mouth at the same time. "Heeve buff gonna haffa beal wiff it."

"What are we doing? Where are we?" asked Jonathan.

Candi put the car into reverse and began backing out of their spot. "We had to make an emergency stop. Sorry."

"Wait! Don't go yet!" said Jonathan.

Candi stopped. "What?"

"Pull back in!" he said, gripping Candi's headrest and yelling right in her ear.

"Chill, Jonathan, geez," she said, shifting the car into drive and going forward. "What's the big deal?"

"Sorry for yelling. What I'm thinking is that they won't have cameras out this far, and the way you've parked - good job by the way - isn't visible from up there. So if there's a longer wait between when they see her leave, they'll assume she's in another car that goes by, not this one."

"I don't get it," said Candi.

"I do," said Kevin. "If the camera caught Sarah, and the cops want to know what car she got into, they'll guess that it would be the next car coming by or one coming by in the next couple minutes. So we need to wait here for longer than that."

"How much longer?" asked Candi, swallowing the lump in her throat as a police car cruised by behind them. The officers inside weren't looking at the Camry, but just seeing them nearby was making her feel sick.

"Ten minutes."

"But ... lots of people go to a rest stop and sit in their cars, just to relax or take a quick nap," said Candi, worried she'd really blown it by listening to Sarah and coming in here.

"Not kids on the run. Not kids who have alternate drivers who can take over when the other one is tired," said Jonathan.

Candi shut off the engine.

"I can't believe you thought all that out," said Kevin, shaking his head slowly. "You were asleep when she started to leave."

"Don't be too impressed. I thought of all this before, when the girls wanted to go into a rest stop earlier. It just stuck in my head as I played out the various scenarios."

"You play out scenarios in your head?" asked Kevin. "For real, dude?"

"Oh, yeah. All the time. I learned from playing chess. You always need to try and predict what the other player is going to do several moves ahead."

Kevin smiled vaguely. "That's an expression ... I'm several moves ahead of you."

"Exactly. It comes from chess. We need to stay at least three moves ahead of law enforcement in order to stay safe until the trial. If they get within one move of us, we will lose. They have too many resources at their disposal for us to succeed at remaining invisible in that situation."

"So how do we stay three moves ahead?" asked Sarah.

"For one, we cannot be careless, like you were by coming here. And we can all change our appearances. Or those who can, should. Candi already did that, so she's helping us. People are looking for a blonde girl with dreadlocks, not Shirley Temple. Kevin, you could make your hair dark, and you'd blend better. My hair won't go blonde without looking fake, so I'm afraid I'm stuck how I am. Sarah, you could cut your hair, but using dye isn't a good idea when you're pregnant. I've read some documentation that suggests that it could be unhealthy, all those chemicals, and I'd rather err on the side of caution."

"I'm not dying my hair anyway," said Sarah. "I had it highlighted before I knew I was pregnant, and I'm not going to ruin that on the very slight, off-chance that it might help."

"Oh, that's brilliant," said Candi. "You'll sacrifice our lives for your hair. Nice."

"Shut up, Shirley! I didn't say I wouldn't do *anything*. I don't mind cutting it. A little." She looked at the guys one at a time, pointing with her thumb at Candi. "But I'm not going as short as Shirley, here."

"Stop calling me Shirley!" Candi couldn't believe Sarah was being so casual about the whole thing. They were hiding from the law - the law that could be trying to kill them right along with some Russian mafia guy - and Sarah was worried about her stupid hair.

"Girls, girls ... no fighting," said Kevin in a calming voice. "I know hair is a sensitive subject, so let's just drop it. Move on to the next thing, Jon. What else can we do?"

"Leave false trails elsewhere, create distractions, stay off the radar, keep to ourselves, be vigilant, have an escape plan in case anyone gets close. There's a lot we can do. They have eyes everywhere, thanks to the public that always wants to help find kids. We have to always be aware that someone looking at us could be the one who turns us in."

Candi slouched down in her seat, noticing a man in a track suit nearby, gazing off into the distance. *Maybe he's just trying to seem casual or something.* She looked to her right and noticed a lady sitting in her car a few rows down. *Is she looking at us? She's on her phone! Is she calling the police?!* Candi started the car again.

"What are you doing? It's not time to go yet," said Jonathan.

"I'm going. That lady's on the phone, and she's making me nervous." Candi looked behind her as they started to reverse out of the parking spot and had to slam on the brakes to keep from hitting the car that was barreling past. It was a police car with its lights on.

The car rocked with the sudden stop. Candi thought she was going to barf in her lap, she was so freaked out. For a split-second, she was sure the cop car was just going to stop and block her in, but it continued on, allowing her to breathe again.

"Time to go," said Jonathan. "Go, Candi. And don't speed. Sarah, lie down - put your head in my lap."

Candi watched Sarah's head go by the rearview mirror as Candi backed out of the space, very carefully now since she was completely freaked out about getting into a traffic accident. One wrong move and they'd be done.

As they pulled out of the parking lot and back onto the highway, Candi tried not to look at the three police cars that had converged on a dark SUV, not unlike the one they'd abandoned before taking the Camry. Candi swallowed the bile that rose up to burn her throat. *Just keep going and don't stop until you're at a cabin in the woods, surrounded by trees and wind and nothing else.*

*****

The french fries Sarah had eaten did the trick. She didn't feel sick for the first time in days. She watched the scenery go by, smiling at all the beautiful trees and lush landscape that appeared as they got closer to their destination.

"What are you so happy about?" grouched Candi from the front seat.

Kevin had taken over the driving again, while the poor Shirley Temple wannabe was looking at her pitiful hair in the small mirror on the back of her visor. She was using the reflection to give Sarah the evil-eye.

"I was just thinking that it's really pretty out here. I could get used to this."

Candi sighed, pushing the visor back up before looking

around. "It is nice. I just wish we were here for a real vacation and not running from someone trying to kill us." James thumped his tail rhythmically on the emergency brake handle, happy with whatever Candi was doing to his head. She looked down with a smile, giggling when he jumped up to lick her chin. Her expression quickly went back to one of concern.

Sarah stroked the giant head of Xena, pit bull doggie warrior. The dog's butt was half on the seat and half on Jonathan. "Yeah. The murderous villains part sucks, but the rest of the trip has been pretty decent. I mean, you even got a new hairdo." She smiled, thrilled at being able to tease Candi and be out of her reach at the same time.

"This dog is a space hog," said Jonathan, trying once more to nudge Xena over. She ignored his efforts, merely twitching an eyebrow and snuffling a couple times before going back to sleep. Sarah's touch seemed to mesmerize her. She'd been quiet the entire ride so far.

"Hush, Barfy Barbie," said Candi to Sarah. "My hair issue is only temporary, but soon you're going to be a big roly-poly, so I'd watch it if I were you. Karma is a you-know-what."

Sarah narrowed her eyes at her friend. "Me? Fat? No way. Never gonna happen."

"Chances are you'll gain between twenty-five and fifty-five pounds," said Jonathan.

Sarah stared at him aghast as Candi laughed. She leaned forward to tweak Candi's hair while she shot death glares at her boyfriend. When she finally recovered enough to speak, she said, "Like hell I will." *Fifty-five pounds? He must be smoking something.*

He shrugged. "It's a simple fact. You can't fight nature."

"Oh, yes I can," said Sarah, sitting back against the seat,

giving up on messing with Candi's hair in favor of scowling out the window. The landscape that had so thrilled her earlier now looked ugly. *Stupid grass. Stupid fat trees. Stupid fat flowers.*

"It won't be so bad, Sarah," said Candi, sounding chagrined. "You'll probably be one of those lucky girls who just has a tiny little bump and then pops out the baby like no big deal."

Sarah was surprised Candi was being so nice, considering how much Sarah had been teasing her about her horrible hair. It took some of the wind out of Sarah's angry sails. "Whatever. Even if I do gain some weight, and I'm not saying that's going to happen, I'll work my butt off after and be back to normal in a week. No problem."

Jonathan cleared his throat and opened is mouth to say something, but Sarah shot her hand out and clapped it over his lips. She stared straight ahead, growling, "Don't. Say. A word. Or I am going to eat your stupid TMI face off."

"Daaaamn," said Kevin, whistling in respect. "I heard about mother instincts and everything, but that's off the hook, sister." His barely controlled snorts had her seeing red.

"Say one more thing, and see what happens to you, *Kevin*. I'm not kidding."

He lifted up a hand and waved it. "I'm done. I surrender. Don't eat my face off, please."

Sarah shook her head at everyone - they were all laughing at her brother's antics. *Idiots.* "You guys have no clue, you know that? You're just running away from some bad guys. I'm not only running away from ugly-butt assassins, one of whom I had to nearly kill, thanks to sleeping beauty over there, but I'm also growing a life inside me *and* protecting both of us from being murdered, the whole time sick as crap *and* starving at the same time. I'd like to see you do it."

The car went silent.

"I'm sorry, Sarah," said Candi. "We're being insensitive, and I know that's not cool."

"Yeah, sorry. Lost my head there for a second," added Kevin, sounding sincere.

"I have the utmost respect for what you're doing and going through for us and our child, Sarah. I want you to know that. And it would be very easy for you to succumb to the pressures put on us by this situation we're in and the effects of the hormones you have swamping your system right now, so I just hope the levity that everyone is providing can be something useful to help ease your stress."

Sarah frowned at him. "A word to the wise ... you may want to keep your so-called *levity* about my weight to yourselves."

"Noted," said Jonathan, pressing his lips together and nodding.

Sarah reached over and took his hand in hers, knowing he was just trying to help in his own awkward way. "You guys are forgiven. For now, anyway."

"The queen has spoken," said Candi, turning to grin at her, taking the sting out of her words.

"Exactly," said Sarah, nodding very regally at her subjects.

"Hey, there's the sign for the town," said Kevin. "Where do I go from here? Should I get off at this exit?" He turned to look at the traffic behind them, his finger poised on the small lever for the turn signal.

"Yes," said Jonathan, grabbing some papers from behind his seat that were sitting on the shelf under the back window. "Follow the signs to the main part of town, and then pull into the first fast food place you see."

Kevin followed Jonathan's directions, and five minutes later they were sitting in the parking lot of a burger place. Sarah looked around, thinking they were probably at the only restaurant of this kind in the whole town, since it was so small and very old-school quaint - hardly a place where a bunch of junk food places could make it. Her mother probably would have labeled it very pedestrian, but Sarah liked it. It had an old soul. She smiled, thinking about the idea of raising a child here. *Not that I'll be here that long.*

"Happy?" asked Jonathan, squeezing her hand and pulling her out of her thoughts.

She nodded, not trusting herself to speak. For some reason she felt like crying, and it made absolutely no sense, which only served to piss her off at herself. She should have been crying earlier when everyone was talking about her getting fat. Now she wanted to cry because she was finally feeling some hope. *Pregnancy sucks.*

"So what are we going to do next?" asked Candi.

"Well, you're the one who looks the least like our pictures, and you're the one who spoke to the owner," said Jonathan, "so I think you should be the one to go talk to her again and give her the money. We'll all just wait at this restaurant, and you can come get us once you have the key."

"What if she wants to drive me to the place? Should I just go and leave you here?" Candi sounded very nervous, and her eyes looked huge in her pale face.

Jonathan shook his head. "No, just tell her to give you directions because you have to do some grocery shopping first. Then when you're sure she won't see you, come get us. If you have to act like you're going to the store first, do it."

"Okay ... but don't blame me if things don't go according to plan."

"We'll be here whenever you're done," said Kevin, leaning over to kiss her on the cheek. "Take whatever time you need. We've all had some sleep and food, and we'll be right here by the fries if Big Momma back there gets hungry."

Sarah leaned forward and flicked him on the ear.

"Ouch! Son of a ..." He glared at Sarah, his anger turning immediately to joy when he saw how annoyed she was. He winked at her which only made her madder.

"Kevin, stop," said Candi, opening up her door. "Come on, let's do this before I wimp out."

Everyone exited the car, Jonathan taking James' leash and Kevin taking Xena's. The dogs stood quietly next to the humans' legs, watching their faces for clues of what they were doing or where they were going.

Sarah got a strong urge to eat another bag of fries when the smell of the restaurant's cooking hit her nose. A tiny voice in the back of her head told her that fries for every meal was the surest way to grow a fat butt, but she didn't care. Her appetite was so hit-or-miss these days, she had to take advantage of it when it was on *hit*.

"Let's go, boys," she said, grabbing Jonathan's hand and nearly dragging him to the door.

"Do you need any money?" Candi asked as they walked away, leaving her by the car.

"Nope. Got some," said Kevin, waving at her.

Sarah pushed him in the back to get him walking again. "Come on, Romeo. Time for fries."

"Time to feed the baby again?" he asked.

"Mmm hmmm," said Sarah, hoping it was the baby ingesting all those fry calories and not her.

"Give me the leashes," said Jonathan, holding out his hand. "I'll keep the dogs out here. Just get me a meal deal. Hamburger and a bottle of water."

"You got it," said Kevin, giving him the thicker leash. "Xena, protect your master. I'll be back in a few."

Sarah bent down to pat the dog and give her a quick hug before disappearing inside. She had to force herself to not run up to the counter. The crunchy, salty goodness of the fries was calling out to her by name.

*****

Candi pulled into the designated meeting spot, drumming her fingers nervously on the wheel as she scanned the area, searching for an old lady in a dark green sedan. Her heart nearly stopped beating when a police car went by at a leisurely pace. *Is it my imagination or are there cop cars everywhere out here?* She'd never noticed them before when their job was to protect and serve. Now that their job was to find her and bring her in not only to testify against drug dealers and the Russian mafia, but for stealing a car too, their patrol vehicles had a certain menacing quality to them they'd never had before.

A tapping on the glass near her left ear made her jump and squeak with fright. An older lady stood at the window, smiling to reveal the perfectly white teeth and pretty pink gums of her dentures.

Candi turned the crank to lower the window.

"Are you Cathy?" the woman asked. Candi nodded, almost forgetting she'd used that fake name over the phone. She felt her face go red with the disaster she'd come close to causing by saying, *Hi, my name's Candi!*

"I'm Agnes. Why don't you come sit down inside for a few minutes and have a cup of coffee with me while we work out the arrangements?"

Candi nodded, not trusting herself to speak. She was feeling very shaky about this whole thing. She had never been good at lying to adults and could probably count on one hand the attempts she'd made in her lifetime. She opened the door and stepped out. The duffel bag was over her shoulder, now empty except for the money; all she could think about was getting attacked and having all that cash taken in a mugging. The stress of being responsible for it felt like it was going to give her a heart attack.

"Did you have very far to travel?" asked Agnes, walking up to the door of a diner.

"Oh, yes. I came from ... California." She had tried to think of a place as far away from the truth as possible, but the second it was out of her mouth, she realized her mistake.

Agnes looked at her and frowned. "I thought you said you were from Colorado."

Candi grimaced, not even sure at this point what she'd said in that copy shop but knowing it was critical that Agnes trust her. *Recovery! Quick!* "I guess it's possible I said that. I spent a month in Colorado with my friend on my way, but I started out in California. Where I was going to school. As a journalism student."

Agnes smiled, apparently happy with Candi's explanation. "Oh, isn't that nice. What a beautiful place, Colorado. What town were you in?"

Candi only knew the names of two cities in the state, so she picked the one that she'd memorized as the capitol in geography class. "Denver."

"The mile-high city. Don't you find it difficult in the winter?"

"Uh ... yeah. It's cold there."

"And dry too. I went when I was younger; and boy, oh boy, did I have trouble with my breathing. I prefer the lower altitudes myself." Agnes opened the door and gestured for Candi to go in front of her. "Let's sit just over there by the window, shall we? I like to watch the people walking by. I'm a busybody, or so my husband likes to say. Old coot never did appreciate a good people-watching exercise."

Candi smiled, despite her stress over the whole situation. "I used to do that at the mall all the time with my brother." She stopped talking immediately, realizing she could really get into a lot of trouble by telling this woman too much about herself. *What if she asks me the name of the mall? Just shut up, Candi. Be polite, but don't make friends.*

They sat down and the waitress came immediately to take their order for coffee. Candi wasn't much of a coffee person, but she ordered one anyway so she wouldn't give her new landlord any reason to think she wasn't just your average college girl in need of a vacation cabin.

"So, you said you're a journalism major, eh? That sounds exciting. What are you going to write at the cabin? A novel?"

"Uhhh ... yeah, that's my plan. I have an outline, but you know ... it's hard to do anything serious in a dormitory with other college students around. They're always noisy and having parties ..." Candi had quickly tried to imagine what a dorm would be like, and that was the best description she could come up with.

"And you had a fire in the dormitories? That's terrible!"

"Oh, no, the fire wasn't at the school. It was at my friend's house ... where I had a lot of my stuff ... where I was trying to stay and do my writing. So I figured that was an omen that I just needed to get away, far away from school." Candi started to sweat, the lameness of her lies freaking her out.

"Well, you sure managed to do that. You went to the other side of the country! Seems like you could have found something closer to home." Agnes was studying her closely, taking a sip of the coffee that had just been poured by the waitress.

Candi nodded, putting two creamers and three teaspoons of sugar into her cup. "Yes, well, my story takes places on the East Coast, so I thought maybe it would seem more genuine if I was here writing it." She shrugged, knowing her reasoning sounded lame. *Who drives across the country just to rent a cabin in the woods for writing?*

"I think it's romantic," said Agnes, a faraway look in her eyes. "I always wanted to write a novel." Her gaze came back to Candi. "What's the book about? Or am I not allowed to know?" Her eyes sparkled and she winked, wrapping her hands around her cup as she waited for Candi's answer.

"It's a secret," said Candi, praying the woman wouldn't press for more details. The only story she could think about right now was a horror story that involved killers chasing teenagers across the country to stop them from testifying in a murder and drug trial.

"Well, when it's published, you need to let me know so I can purchase a copy and read it."

Candi smiled nervously. "I will." She felt really bad for

lying. This lady seemed really nice.

"Forgive me for saying so," said Agnes, leaning in a little, "but you seem so young to be in college."

"Well, I am. I mean, I'm eighteen, but I started when I was ... younger."

"Ah," she said nodding, "you're ahead in your classes. I knew you were intelligent. I could tell even over the phone."

Candi blushed. "Thank you."

"I suppose you want to get this business taken care of so you can settle in, eh?" Agnes pulled a sheaf of papers out of her large handbag. "I have a little contract right here that I found on the Internet, and a receipt I can write out for you. Oh, and the keys." She slid a small keyring across the counter. "There are two keys there; both of them open the front and back doors. And I'll keep a set for myself, but you don't need to worry. I won't be bothering you while you're there." She laid the papers down on the table and put on a pair of reading glasses. "Here we are," she said, pushing one towards Candi. "One copy of the rental contract for you and one for me. We'll sign both of them, and then that'll be that."

Candi lifted the paper up from the table, pretending to read it. She caught most of what it said but had no idea what a lot of it meant legally. She just prayed she wasn't getting ripped off. Agnes seemed like such a nice person, Candi didn't feel like she should worry. There were other things more important to stress about.

Agnes sat with a pen poised above the rental contract. "Are you going to be staying in the cabin alone?"

Candi's mind raced. *Should I be honest? Lie? Half-lie?* "To start, yes. My brother might come visit." *Oh, crap! Why did I say brother?* "I mean my cousin." *Oh, crap! That sounded so stupid! Why did I do that?*

Agnes looked up over her glasses, an eyebrow raised. "Is he your brother, your cousin ... or maybe your boyfriend?"

Candi frowned. "What? Oh, no! *Ew,* gross. I mean, no. We're related, so that would be ... yuck. No. He's like a brother but a cousin, you know? Like, we're really close." Candi so wanted to slap her own face right now.

Agnes smiled, her eyes crinkling at the corners. "Oh, yes, I understand. Sorry. I was confused for a moment there." She waved her hand carelessly as she looked back at the papers. "You'll be out in the middle of nowhere, so having guests is not a problem. I just want to be sure the property isn't damaged. You understand." She looked up and after receiving a furious nodding from Candi, before turning her attention back to writing. "Cathy ... what did you say your last name was?"

"Cathy Redwood. Redwood is my last name." Candi wanted to shrivel up and die. *Redwood? What the hell is wrong with me? Where did that come from?* Candi's eyes strayed over to the red-stained wood of the chairs just next to their table. *Real slick, Candi. Smooth.*

"Oh, what a lovely name! You must adore it." She leaned in and whispered conspiratorially. "I married into mine." She grimaced before putting her hand up to her mouth to shield it from others who might be listening, and whispered, *"Guckenberger."*

Candi smiled and then laughed, realizing the woman was serious. "Guckenberger?" she whispered back. "For real?"

Agnes nodded sadly. "Yes. And I've spawned all manner of other Guckenbergers - four sons, and each of them have two sons apiece." She waved her hand out in front of her slowly. "Guckenbergers as far as the eye can see."

Candi had to cover her mouth to keep the laughter from getting away from her. She was so stressed out, this little bit of light-hearted banter was threatening to turn her into a raving loon.

Agnes turned the document around that she'd been writing on. "Here. You fill in the rest. I'll sign the one you have, and then we'll trade." She drummed her fingers on the table lightly. "Oh, and there's TV out there - cable - but I have to turn it back on. I'll try and get that done today."

Candi nodded, taking the form and trying not to laugh at the name *Cathy Redwood* staring up at her. She filled in a fake address in California, using the zip code Jonathan had forced her to memorize when they were on the computer in the copy shop. Thank goodness he'd thought of that detail, otherwise, she'd be sitting here right now trying to think what number to start with. The idea of being busted by such a small, seemingly inconsequential detail instantly sobered her up. One wrong move and they could all be dead. And maybe nice people like Agnes would end up as collateral damage, too. She swallowed hard, the coffee burning in her stomach like acid. *I've got to get out of here before I blow it.*

Candi hurriedly scrawled her fake signature across the paper, almost choking when the *t* in Cathy looked more like a *d*.

Agnes didn't seem to notice anything was amiss. She signed her name with a flourish, her penmanship reminding Candi of her grandmother's. Each letter was so easy to read, perfectly slanted and uniform in size. Her own was a mess of directions and hardly legible.

"And now for the fun part ... the money," said Agnes, putting her copy of the contract back into her purse.

Candi reached into the duffle bag and found the envelope. She kept it inside the bag as she extracted the small pile of bills that Jonathan had counted four different times. "Here you go," she said, placing it on the table between them. "I'd like the cabin for one month to start, but maybe I could extend it a month if necessary? I don't need to be back to school until September, so ..." she shrugged, not knowing what else to say.

"Sure. I have the listing up on that Internet site, but I haven't received any calls for July or August yet. If I do, I'll call you, and you can let me know if you want to stay. I'll give you first right of refusal, how's that?" She picked up the money and carefully counted it on the seat next to her, using her purse to screen it from the view of anyone standing out on the sidewalk who might be looking in the window at them.

"That's fine," said Candi, hoping they wouldn't need to stay much longer than the rest of May and June.

"Oh, and I forgot to ask you," said Agnes, putting the money in her purse. "Do you have any pets? I didn't see any in your car, but I thought I'd ask just to be sure. Maybe you have a cat or something in a carrier I didn't notice."

"Ummm ... yes?"

Agnes smiled. "Are you asking me or telling me?"

"Telling you. I actually have dogs. Two."

Agnes frowned. "Where are they? Surely I didn't miss two dogs in your car."

Candi panicked. Her cover was blown. She'd gone and ruined everything right at the end of the deal, and the lady already had her money! *Think, Candi, think! Where are the dogs?!*

"The dogs are at the groomers."

"Oh, really? We have a groomer in town?"

"It's just a lady I found online," said Candi in a rush. "She's not a professional or anything. I just wanted to be sure they were clean and sparkling for the cabin so they didn't mess anything up. They're very well-behaved, I promise; I just feel more comfortable having some watchdogs around. Especially out in the woods." Candi's face was burning red, and she was less than a minute away from vomiting out of fear and panic. She wondered if it would be possible to race from the dining area to the bathroom without looking mentally unbalanced.

Agnes stood, waving her hand nonchalantly. "Don't worry about it. We Guckenbergers are huge dog lovers. That cabin just wouldn't be the same without a mutt running around in it and diving into the lake. Just make sure you keep them in at night. There are some small bears and mountain lions that like to wander around the area, and dogs get them treed sometimes. That just upsets them and causes a ruckus - not to mention it'll scare the living daylights out of you to hear one of them being unhappy."

Candi's mouth fell open as she watched Agnes hitch her bag up onto her shoulder.

"You've got the keys and your copy of the contract and your receipt." She smiled, huffing out a satisfied breath. "So! Is there anything else you need?"

"Directions?" Candi said, barely above a whisper, still fixated on the bears and mountain lions thing.

"Oh, silly me! Of course you do!" She reached into her bag and pulled out a piece of paper covered in perfect, script handwriting. "Here you go, dear. Just follow these directions

carefully, and you'll be there in no time. Twenty minutes, tops."
She patted Candi on the shoulder. "It was nice meeting you,
Cathy. You have my phone number on the paper there. I have
yours on the contract. Just call me if you have any trouble at all.
I'm going to be late for bridge club, so I have to go now. Toodle-
loo!"

Candi's eyes followed her disappearing form as Agnes
weaved through the tables and then out the front door. "Toodle-
loo," she said weakly. *Bears? Wildcats? What have we gotten
ourselves into?*

*****

Jonathan was the navigator and Kevin was the driver. After
making only one wrong turn, they ended up on a dirt road full of
potholes that Jonathan was sure was the right one. "Just keep
going; follow this road. The directions say it goes on for a mile
back into the woods."

"Ugh, I feel sick," said Sarah from the back seat. "Can I get
out and walk?"

Kevin stopped. "I don't mind if you do. I can drive slow
while you come behind us."

"I'll go with you," said Candi, opening her door.

The two girls and the dogs tumbled out, all of them seeming
very relieved to be out in the fresh air. Jonathan was glad they
were getting a chance to exercise. Being stuffed up in the car with
the two somewhat odiferous dogs couldn't be good for the health
of a pregnant girl. He glanced back at Sarah and was relieved to
see a smile on her face for a change. She'd been really grouchy
the last fifteen miles.

"Thank God," said Kevin, grinning. "Those dogs stink, and if
I had to be stuck in the car with Sarah another five minutes I

might have just thrown her out myself."

"You don't mean that," said Jonathan, back to staring out the front windshield again, his eyes scanning back and forth for signs of the wildlife Candi had warned them about.

"If you're looking for bears and mountain lions, you can forget it."

"I know. I just thought maybe I'd see some signs of them being there."

"Like bear shit? I hear they do shit in the woods." Kevin chuckled at his own lame humor.

"No, I'm not looking for bear scat. I was thinking more like scratch marks on trees or the smell of cat urine." He sniffed the air coming in from the window experimentally.

Kevin laughed loudly, until tears came to his eyes, and he kept at it for the rest of the bumpy ride to the cabin. It was only when he caught the first glimpse of its dark wood exterior that he sobered up and got serious. "Is that it?" he asked.

"It must be," said Jonathan. "But it doesn't look exactly like the photos, does it?"

"No. It looks ... older."

"Yes ... but definitely serviceable. It'll be perfect. Park over there, in front of that shed thing. Maybe it'll be big enough to put the car in. I'd like to try to hide it if we can, just in case the police come out here."

Jonathan was out of the front seat as soon as the car was safely stopped. He jogged over to meet the girls, taking Xena's leash from Sarah so she could walk unencumbered. Her earlier enthusiasm about being out of the car seemed to have been replaced by a general feeling of malaise. "You okay? You look a little ... green."

She reached out and took his hand, one second before leaning over and vomiting into the weeds at her feet.

"I'll take that as a no."

Candi came over and took the dog from Jonathan, which he was really grateful for since Xena seemed a little too interested in possibly cleaning up Sarah's mess. He put his arm around Sarah and helped her stand upright, walking her carefully towards the house.

"This Peanut better be really cute, that's all I have to say," said Sarah, wiping her mouth off with the back of her hand.

"How can she not be? She's going to look exactly like you," said Jonathan.

Sarah sighed shakily. "If I didn't have barf breath, I'd totally make out with you right now, babe."

Jonathan tried to smile. "I'll take a raincheck on that if you don't mind."

She reached over and patted his cheek, a little harder than he would have liked. "You got it."

They got to the front porch just behind Candi. She had the keys out and was trying to prop open the rickety screen door, hold onto the dogs, and fit the key into the lock. The keys dropped twice before Jonathan rescued them from the porch floor and took care of it himself. He pushed the door open and stepped back so the girls could go in first. He knew Sarah would want to lie down on a couch as soon as possible.

"Holy crud balls," said Sarah, "this place hasn't been cleaned in ..."

"... Ten years," finished Candi. She waved her hand in front of her face. "What is that smell?"

"It's musty something," said Sarah, sneezing twice before

stepping back out onto the porch. "Someone needs to dust this place before I go in. It's not good for the baby."

Candi put her hands on her hips. "What? *Dust?*"

"Yeah," said Sarah, waving her hand in her face. "Dust, smells, bacteria. The place is probably full of it. I'll just rest out here while you guys clean it up." She turned. "Oh, look! There's a hammock. Wake me when you're done." She stepped off the porch and headed out to the two trees with the ropes slung between them.

Jonathan looked at his sister and saw the storm brewing in her eyes. He went over and touched her arm to distract her, a technique he'd learned from his mom doing it to him at least five times a day. "Hey, just let her go. She doesn't feel good." He leaned in towards her ear. "And she's pretty terrible at cleaning anyway."

"I heard that, Jonathan!" Sarah yelled from the trees as she tried to balance long enough to lie down.

Candi snorted when Sarah flipped herself out of the hammock and fell on her butt in the dirt. "You're right, Jonathan. Come on. Let's go buff this place up. I'm sure it won't take long at all."

"Yo! Hey, come check this out," said Kevin. He was standing in front of the shed.

"You go. I'll start on the house," said Candi, leaving Jonathan on the porch.

Jonathan walked over to join Kevin at the open shed door in front of the car. "What's in there," he asked, waiting for his eyes to adjust to the change in light.

"A canoe and a rowboat. If we can get them out of there we could fit the car in, I'm pretty sure. Plus, we could use them on the lake, right?" Kevin looked around the side of the shed. "Assuming there is a lake here somewhere."

Jonathan shrugged. "I don't see why not. Come on, I'll help you. Just be careful about rusty parts. I'm up to date on my tetanus immunizations, but I'm not sure if you are."

"Me neither. Probably not. I can't remember the last time I had one."

"Dammit!" yelled Sarah.

Jonathan looked around the side of the shed, watching Sarah pick herself up off the ground again. "If you're worried about dust and bacteria, you might want to stop lying in the dirt!" he yelled.

"Shut up, Jonathan!"

"Okay!" he said, going back to helping Kevin. "She never likes it when I give her suggestions."

"Dude ...," said Kevin, laughing, " ... oh, man. You kill me."

"I don't see why. I'm not trying to kill you. I just think if she's worried about cleaning the house, the last thing she should be doing is sitting on the ground. There are probably bird droppings and worm casings and who knows what else there just on the surface."

"You should tell her that," said Kevin.

"Really?" Jonathan turned, considering doing just that.

"No, dude, no. I'm messing with you. Just keep your head down and your mouth shut. The less you say, the better off you are. Haven't you learned *anything* after living with her?" He grabbed the edge of the canoe and lifted it off the hooks that were hanging it from the ceiling.

Jonathan grabbed the other end, walking out backwards. "Yeah. I guess I have. Like for one, she doesn't always make a lot of sense, but she seems to feel better after yelling about stuff."

"Who are you talking about?!" came a loud voice from behind Jonathan, making him spin around so fast he had no time to orient himself. His head hit the side of the canoe, and it was lights out. The darkness closed in immediately.

*****

Kevin moved the canoe out of the shed and put it on the ground next to the car before going in and checking on Jonathan. The guy had fallen to the ground in a pile after walking right into the side of the boat. If it hadn't knocked him out, Kevin would have been laughing his ass off. It was like watching one of those old black and white movies of the three guys who were always bonking each other over the head and stuff.

"Dude. Jon. Come on, time to wake up and help me move the boats." Kevin had seen guys get knocked out in rugby games several times. He knew there was nothing to worry about when Jonathan started coming back within seconds of falling down.

Jonathan's eyes opened, fluttering a few times before finally looking normal. "What happened?"

"You got the crap scared out of you by my sister and hit your head. Get up and help me with this other boat."

Jonathan stood, stepping up on one foot and then the other with his arms out, testing his balance. He looked like a deranged bird. "Maybe I have a concussion."

"Probably not. Come on."

"Maybe I should relax for a minute just to be sure."

"Are you dizzy?"

"No."

"Disoriented? In pain? Nauseated?"

"No."

"Then shut up and help me move the damn boat. We need to get the car in here."

Jonathan stepped over to the bow. "Tell me when to lift," he grumbled.

"Go."

The two hefted the boat up first to waist-level and then over their heads, using hands on either side to steady it as they walked out of the shed with it above them.

"Where are we going?" grunted Jonathan.

"To the lake."

"Which way is that?!"

"I don't know! Past the trees near Sarah, probably."

They moved as fast as they could, but didn't make it much past the hammock before they had to stop and put it down.

"Damn, that thing's heavier than it looks. Maybe we can drag it," said Kevin, eyeing its bulky form.

"Not now, though. Later," said Jonathan, out of breath.

"Man, you are out of shape," laughed Kevin, punching Jonathan on the upper arm as he walked by. "Don't worry. I'll get you back in the groove. Morning calisthenics start at oh-six-hundred tomorrow morning." Kevin grinned like a fool, rubbing his hands together over the idea of having his exercise crew back online. He'd missed their routine from the island. Somehow, working out alone or with the guys on the rugby team had never been quite as much fun. He liked getting reluctant participants to enjoy themselves; it was like a personal challenge or something.

"I'm not sure about the oh-six-hundred part of that plan," said Jonathan, rubbing his shoulder as he caught up to Kevin, "but I do like the idea of improving my cardiovascular performance. Ever since Sarah moved in, I kind of quit running, and I can totally feel it."

"You'd better not be blaming me for that," came her voice through the trees.

"I'm not," said Jonathan, hastily walking over to join her at the hammock. "Not exactly. I mean, the reason I don't run now is I'm too busy with you, but that's not your fault. It's my choice."

"You can do both - be my sister's slave and exercise. You don't need to sacrifice." Kevin shook his head at his friend. Poor kid didn't have a chance with Sarah on one side and him on the other.

"Speaking of slaves ...," said Candi, standing at the door looking out towards them, "... Kevin could you come in here? I need help with something."

Kevin looked at Jonathan and his sister who were now standing in front of each other, Jonathan peering down into her face, probably to check her pupil dilation or something.

"She probably needs my muscles." Kevin flexed for effect.

"Exactly. Come move this furniture for me," said Candi

Kevin frowned, and his sister laughed. "See you later, muscle man," she said.

"Shut up," he responded, walking slowly over to the house. He had to move furniture for his mother all the time. She was never happy for longer than a week or so with the way things were arranged. It was one of his least favorite things to do, not because it was hard but because it seemed like a colossal waste of time. No one cared where the damn side tables or armchairs were except her.

He walked into the cabin and was immediately struck by how neglected it was. The pictures Jonathan had printed from the online ad had shown it as a homey place, filled with knickknacks, a fire in the woodstove, and pictures on the walls. Now it was just a shell with some lame furniture in it and dust covering everything.

"Can you move this couch with me?" said Candi. "I think it'll be better over here in front of the television."

Kevin eyed the old set with suspicion. "Does that thing even work?"

"She said it did. I think she was going to get the cable turned on today or something."

"Yeah, right." *I'll believe that when I see it.* It was going to be a serious pain in the butt if they had zero access to the outside world. Television was a bare minimum as far as he was concerned. How else would they know about the trial or whether they were being hunted by the FBI?

Kevin moved the couch and three chairs around to several different spots until Candi declared herself satisfied. She may have quit early on account of him kissing her every time she got near, but he wasn't complaining. More soft lips and less lifting was fine with him. Her goofy hair probably should have been like a cold shower keeping him at bay, but for some reason it was having the opposite effect. At this point she probably could have shaved her head bald, and he'd still want to see her naked. His eyes roamed the room as he held her against him. "Where are the bedrooms in this place? You should probably bring me to ours so I can move some furniture in there, too."

Candi pulled away. "Are we going to be roomies?"

"Of course." He frowned. "What? Did you think you were going to sleep with Sarah?"

Candi looked horrified. "No. Please. Don't make me."

Kevin grinned. "I'll think about it. Maybe you'll have to

convince me, you know, to be your roommate."

Candi got a wily expression on her face. "Follow me." She dragged him across the room to a set of stairs that led up to a closed-off loft. They climbed to the top and stood at the entrance of the open space. There in the middle of it was a double bed.

"You want to snuggle with Jonathan on that?" she asked.

Kevin snorted. "Hell no."

"Good. I guess I can consider you convinced, then."

Kevin scooped her up into his arms. "Not so fast, young lady."

She squealed as he ran to the bed and threw her down on it, preparing to jump on after her. But his plans were foiled when her weight hit the mattress and the whole thing collapsed, a big poof of dust flying up into the air to surround her.

"Ack! Gack! Kah!" choked and wheezed Candi. "Get me off of here!" she yelled, holding out her hands.

Kevin couldn't stop laughing.

"Shut up, you big oaf," she said, standing finally and trying to wipe all the dust off of her body. "This place is a giant pile of dirt! And now you broke the bed. We're going to have to pay for that, you know."

She was so mad, and her hair was sticking out all over the place, making her look like a deranged clown. He couldn't keep the smile off his face. "Come here, you lunatic," he said, pulling her close again.

"You're the lunatic," she said into his chest, her arms going around his waist, "throwing me on the bed like that."

"What can I say? That new hairstyle of yours brings out the caveman in me."

She pinched his butt hard.

"Ow! Hey! Watch it, Shirley."

She pulled back and put her finger up in his face. *"Don't* call me Shirley, or I'm going to do very bad things to you."

He wiggled his eyebrows at her. "Oh, reeeeallly? Hmmmm, sounds interesting." He leaned down to kiss her neck, but was stopped short by her defensive maneuver.

"Wet willy!" she squealed before pushing him away and running down the stairs.

Kevin sighed heavily as he pulled the edge of his shirt up and used it to wipe out his now very wet ear canal. "Payback's a bitch, Shirley!" he shouted down the stairs. "You'd better run far and fast!"

The only response he could hear was a very loud and pronounced raspberry.

*****

Sarah got bored with the hammock and watching Jonathan try to wrestle the rowboat through the trees. She wandered over to the trunk of the car and started pulling food out. She opened boxes and bags, snacking as she walked to the cabin. "Mmmm, cheese puffs. I looooove me some cheese puffs." Her fingertips quickly turned orange, and she savored every last speck of the terrible stuff as she licked it off. Jonathan would have a fit if he saw her eating this crap, but she totally didn't care. It was deeerishus.

"You can just put that stuff on the counter," said Candi. "I'll arrange the pantry later." Her head was stuck in a cabinet where she was busy pulling out pots and pans of all different sizes.

Sarah put the bag and the big plastic jar of nuts she'd been holding down on the dirty tile countertop. She ran her finger over its surface, cringing at the dust and residue that came off. She went over to the sink to rinse it and jumped back when a loud groan came out, followed by the sink sputtering and vomiting out yellow water.

"What the hell!" She slowly backed into the family room, afraid to go near it.

"It's nothing," said Candi, coming over and turning the water on harder. "Just let the water run until it's clear."

"But ... it's *yellow*. What is that? Lake water? Toilet water?"

"No, it's just from the pipes. It's normal in old houses that sit and don't get used."

"Pfft. Sha. Right." *Yellow water might be normal in your world, but it's not in mine.*

The water did start to go clear pretty quickly, but Sarah didn't trust it. Jonathan was going to have to do something about this. Yellow water couldn't possibly be good for the Peanut. They had a case of bottled water, but it wasn't going to last very long.

"Go get the rest of the food so I can put this pantry together and figure out what's for dinner," ordered Candi.

Sarah walked out of the kitchen, deliberately going very slowly. "Bossy cow." After digging around in the trunk, she was halfway from the car to the cabin with two small things in her hands when she heard the guys yelling back in the trees. She dropped the things on the ground and ran, Candi right on her heels.

"What is it?" Candi asked breathlessly, as they ran past branches covered in leaves.

"How the heck do I know?" responded Sarah, getting a stitch in her side from the sudden, intense exercise. She knew she was close to the guys when she heard Kevin whoop again.

The reason for his excitement and joy became clear when they rounded a bend in the path and came out from the edge of the trees. Huge evergreens ringed a body of water that was too small to be called a lake. It was more like a pond, but it had a dock; and the rowboat and canoe were now tied to it, bobbing on the small waves the guys were making. Both Jonathan and Kevin were in the water.

"Come on in!" yelled Kevin, splashing towards the girls. "The water's great!"

Sarah noticed his pile of clothes on the dock. "Are you naked in there?"

"No, I'm in my shorts. Come on! It's awesome!"

"The water is quite refreshing. Join us!" said Jonathan. He flipped onto his back and floated with his arms and legs spread wide. "This is nice. Can you hear me? I can't really hear myself. Hello? The water's in my ears."

Sarah rolled her eyes. Jonathan had done the same thing in the ocean when they were practicing holding their breath. It made her wonder if she could still do it for as long as she had before. She'd gotten pretty good, but none of them were able to match Kevin's stamina.

Jonathan disappeared below the surface as if he'd been yanked down by a lake monster, making Sarah's breath catch in her throat. But when Jonathan came up sputtering and Kevin appeared a moment later, laughing his butt off, she started breathing again. *Idiots.* She was sorely tempted to join them but wasn't interested one bit in Kevin messing with her.

"Are you going in?" asked Candi.

"No. I'll put my feet in, maybe, but I'm not in the mood to deal with Kevin. He's on the warpath."

They both watched as Jonathan tried to escape Kevin's clutches, but failed. He couldn't get away fast enough and was pulled back into Kevin's range by the ankles. He yelled once, his scream getting cut off when Kevin pushed the top of his head below the surface.

Sarah was about to yell at her brother about harassing poor Jonathan, when a big arm came up out of the water from behind Kevin and put him in a choke hold. Kevin disappeared underwater with Jonathan rising up over him, yelling, "Ah-haaaa!! Take that, butthead!"

The next ten minutes were a battle back and forth between the two idiots, both of them trying to drown the other and claim superiority. Eventually they gave up, doggy paddling over to the dock because they'd run out of energy to do anything else. Candi helped drag Kevin out onto the dock and he helped Jonathan up after him. They all laid on the sun-faded and slightly warped wood surface, the boys breathing heavily.

Sarah walked over and sat down, dipping her feet into the water. *Wow, that does feel nice.*

Candi sat up and scooted to the edge of the dock next to Sarah, putting her feet in too. "Ooooh, that is scrumptious. As soon as I'm done with the cleaning, I'm coming out here for a swim."

"It'll be too dark. That place is a mess."

"It would go faster if I had help," she hinted.

Sarah sniffed, totally unconvinced. "Maybe. Ask Kevin to help. He's a neat freak. You should see his room at home."

"Cleaning's woman's work," said Kevin, snickering.

Sarah raised an eyebrow. "Someone wants to die, apparently." She twisted around to see what Candi was going to do.

Candi got up and went over to her boyfriend, putting her

foot on his chest. "You want to try that again, mister?"

He grabbed her ankle. "Cleaning is woman's work." He ran his hand up her leg, probably intending to tweak her butt, but Candi was too fast for him.

She grabbed his arm and yanked back as hard as she could, effectively flipping him over onto his stomach.

"Hey!" he yelled, sounding surprised.

She twisted his arm around behind him and yanked his hand up high towards his head, going down on her knee in the middle of his back, pressing it into his spine. "One more time for good measure."

"Oh, shit ... no! I give, I give!"

"Say, *cleaning is men's work.*"

"Never!" he yelled, grunting as he tried to move, but stopping every time the pain hit him.

"Say it or the arm goes!" Candi was grinning evilly down at him.

"You got three seconds to get off me, Shirley, or you're going down." He put his free arm slowly up under his chest, and Sarah knew exactly what his plan was - but Candi didn't because she was sitting at the wrong angle to see it. Sarah said not a word, smiling as she waited for the inevitable.

"Cleaning is men's work! Say it!"

"Three!"

"Say it!"

"Two!"

"I'm not kidding!"

"One!"

Kevin launched himself up and to the side, a kamikaze dive into the water with Candi on his back.

The look on her face was classic. Shock, surprise, anger ... Sarah was immediately seized with hysterical laughter, watching them go over in almost slow motion.

Candi struggled around in the pond, either trying to brain Kevin or hug him, Sarah wasn't sure. All she could see was a lot of bubbles and churning water. Her stomach hurt from the laughing.

"You think that's funny?" asked Jonathan, getting up off the dock and slowly coming towards her.

"Yeah, I do," Sarah answered, more focused on Candi's struggles than her boyfriend.

"A poor defenseless girl being forced into the water?" Jonathan stopped when he was in front of her.

"Move, you're blocking my view."

"Make me," he said.

Sarah frowned, looking up at him. The sun was so bright behind him, it was impossible to see his face. "Say what?"

"You heard me. Make me move."

She loved the challenge in his voice and couldn't help herself from rising to the occasion. She reached out and slapped him on the calf. "Move it or lose it, bud." She half expected him to just do it without a fuss.

"No hitting." He didn't move an inch.

She pulled a couple of hairs out of his leg. "How about that? Is that allowed?"

He reached down and grabbed her under her arms, lifting her high in the air. "No. Leg-hair pulling is definitely *not* allowed."

"Jonathan!" she screeched. "Put me down! Right this second!"

"Okaaaay, whatever you say," he said gleefully, just before launching her through the air and into the water.

The shock of the cool water hitting her body took her breath away for a second. And the exhilaration of her normally very compliant and non-aggressive boyfriend being the reason for it made her want to attack him - both with anger and passion. She came to the surface ready to let him have it. "Jonathan!" she screamed, looking around for him. "I'm going to kill you, you idiot! Where are you?"

All she could see was the dock.

"Jonathan? Where are you?" She spun around, but he wasn't behind her. The surface of the water only moved because of her. "I'm not kidding, Jonathan. Where are ..."

The rest of her sentence was cut off when something unseen grabbed her by the ankles and pulled her completely under the water.

*****

Candi and Kevin climbed up onto the dock in time to see Sarah surfacing next to a laughing Jonathan.

"You stupid jerk!" she yelled, splashing him in the face. "You scared the crap out of me! I thought a sea monster was eating me!"

"A sea monster?" he laughed. "We're nearly eight hundred miles from the nearest salt water. There's no access from this pond to the ocean."

"Shut up, turd-for-brains, you know what I meant. Arrrghh!" She swung her arms out widely, trying to drown him above water with her splashing.

Jonathan swam over to her, heedless of his own safety, wrapping his arms around his seriously cranky girlfriend.

"He's brave," said Kevin, softly. "I wouldn't go near that pond monster if it were me."

Candi giggled. "Me neither. Let's get out of here." As she waited for Kevin to gather his clothes, she watched her brother convince Sarah to give him a kiss and forgive him for trying to cool her off. Candi couldn't help but feel all warm inside at the love they shared for each other, even though they seemed to be no better matched as a couple right now than they had been before they'd really met - before the cruise had wrecked their lives and thrown them together.

Kevin took her by the hand and led her to the cabin. "What's for dinner, chef?"

"Something from a can. I can't cook in a dirty kitchen. I'll work on cleaning it tonight with help from you guys, and then tomorrow I can get serious about making good food."

"What'd I tell you about cleaning?" asked Kevin, laughter in his voice.

"That you'll do as much of it as I tell you to do because you fear the consequences?"

"Exactly." He pulled her to his side, squeezing her close. "And now, in exchange for the cleaning I know you're going to force me to do all night against my will, I'm going to require that you take a shower."

"No need to require it; I was going to do that anyway."

"With me."

"Yeah, right," said Candi, her face getting warm over the idea of seeing him naked. She hadn't been with him in that way since they'd been marooned on an island together - and then only once. She'd had a vague idea that maybe he'd been planning some sort of sexy event for after the prom, but she hadn't let herself think too much about it; and then of course it had all become a moot point.

"I'm serious." They stepped up onto the porch, and Kevin stopped her from going inside, turning her so that they were face to face. He leaned down and kissed her thoroughly, now making the rest of her go warm.

As his lips moved against hers and his tongue invaded her mouth, a shower with him in it was sounding more and more like a good idea; and then when he reached down and squeezed her rear end, pushing their hips together, she decided it was a perfect plan. "Okay," she said against his mouth, "but no sex."

Kevin smiled devilishly, pulling away. "We'll negotiate that in just a couple minutes. I'll meet you in there." He jumped down the entire staircase to the ground and jogged over to the trunk of the car.

Candi went into the cabin, headed for the bathroom at top speed, nervous about what was going to happen. She wondered if he was going to get not only the soap and shampoo they'd purchased, but also the monster-sized box of condoms that Jonathan had insisted on putting in the cart. *"One teen pregnancy is more than enough, thank you very much,"* he'd said at the time. Candi colored all over again with the memory, as she stripped off her wet clothes and stepped into the steaming shower.

Settling In

JONATHAN AND SARAH DEBATED THE idea of sleeping outside on their first night to avoid the dust and other things that might be lurking unseen in the cabin, but the lure of a semi-comfortable mattress won out in the end. Jonathan did his best to go outside and shake out all the sheets and blankets, trying to remove as much dust as possible, but they still spent a few minutes sneezing before finally falling into a deep sleep. He woke up the next morning feeling somewhat refreshed but totally determined to make sure their second night in that room would be more pleasant. Sarah was much more fun to be around when she'd had a good night's sleep.

Jonathan crept out of the room as the first rays of the sun were coming into the windows. He found Candi and Kevin busy cleaning out the cupboards in the kitchen. "What's going on, guys?"

Kevin's voice came out muffled, his head buried in a cabinet. "Candi refuses to make me pancakes until this place is clean." He came out of the small space and faced Jonathan. "This is slave labor. Blackmail. Tell her to feed me."

"Jonathan, grab that cloth and clean out those three

cupboards over there," said Candi, pointing to the other side of the kitchen, near the sink.

Jonathan sighed. "Yes ma'am."

"Oh, come on!" complained Kevin. "Just like that, you cave?"

"You caved. Why can't I cave?" asked Jonathan, opening the first cabinet, dismayed to find bits of stuck-on grossness in the bottom of it. There was even a mouse trap that hadn't done anyone any good, long since having gone off without snaring anything. He pulled it out gingerly, telling himself he was going to have to thoroughly disinfect not only the cabinet but his hands and arms when he was done.

Kevin smacked his towel on the ground with a snap. "I caved because your sister has the power of the pootie over me. What's your excuse?"

Jonathan heard the distinct sound of a head being slapped.

"Ow! What the heck was that for? Did you see that, Jon? Physical violence. Add physical violence and intimidation to the charges against this woman."

"I'm going to add pit bull attack to the list too, if you don't shut up and finish your work," she promised. "I swear, you could have been done already if you'd just cleaned instead of complained."

"Ha! Xena's too busy snoring and farting over there to bite me."

"Yeah, well, I'm not. Get cleaning."

"Oh, hey now ... *you* biting me? Now that's a different story." Kevin's head went back into the cabinet. "That sounds interesting. I'm cleaning now! Look! I'm cleaning!"

Jonathan smiled as he returned to his work, scrubbing away at the stains. He couldn't imagine being stranded with anyone else out here in the middle of nowhere besides them. The irony that they were going through nearly the same type of isolation as they had when their cruise ship went down was just overwhelming. He knew that if he told this story to anyone who didn't know their history, they'd never believe it. The calculations of the odds of all of this happening again were too complicated right now. His mind kept straying back to his conversation with Kevin about chess moves and staying ahead of the game with these bad guys who were probably after them. It gave him an idea.

He pulled his head out of the now mostly-clean cabinet. "Hey, guys? I just thought of something."

"What?" asked Candi.

"I know. Let me guess ...," said Kevin. "You've discovered the theory of relativity."

"No, the theories of general relativity and special relativity were already introduced by Albert Einstein. But technically, he didn't *discover* these ideas, since they always existed and were never hidden, per se. He just made the ideas clear for the first time."

"Whatever, dude. What did you want to tell us?" asked Kevin.

"Oh ... yeah." Jonathan paused for a moment to gather his thoughts before continuing. "I wanted to say that I think I know how we can get some messages to our parents without being figured out."

Kevin got up off the floor and stood up, jogging in place. "Talk to me, Goose." He shadow boxed a few punches, backing up so he wouldn't hit Candi.

"Who's Goose?" asked Jonathan.

Kevin sighed, halting his running and rubbing his stomach. "Talk to me, *Jon*. And hurry up. Candi was just about to make me some pancakes."

"Not until you finish!" she insisted, hands on her hips.

Kevin pointed down to his cabinet. "I finished, harpy! Look!" He ducked out of her way, coming over to join Jonathan as she inspected. "Tell us your grand plan, dude."

Jonathan stood up. "I have a couple friends who play online chess. There's a chat room we all go in and discuss the games and stuff. I know I can get in there and talk to them in chess code and have them pass messages. We used to do it all the time."

"You used to do *what* all the time?" asked Candi, finished with checking Kevin's work.

"Talk about people in code, making it seem like we were talking about games. It was fun."

"Sounds complicated," said Candi. "I've looked over your shoulder before at all those codes."

"Sounds badass, you mean," said Kevin. "But how are you going to do it without a computer or Internet?"

"We'll have to go to a library or copy shop. Somewhere not too close. But I think we could do it in just one town over and not worry too much. I can go through a proxy server and surf anonymously. That should cover the most basic level of staying hidden. And then my friend Stephen can talk to my dad, pass on the code in person so they won't track where anything came from or who's responsible. Even if they hacked into Stephen's computer, they'd never know it's some kind of code unless he tells them, which he never would."

"Your dad speaks chess code?" asked Kevin, now finally going still, not out of breath at all despite his random kitchen exercises.

"Sure. He's a great chess player. He taught me almost everything I know."

"Until the day you beat him and started teaching him," said Candi, a note of pride in her voice.

"It's true, I have taught him some strategies, but not nearly as many as he's taught me. Anyway, we just need to get to a computer, and I can do it. I just need you guys to tell me what message you want to send out. It can't be a like a word-for-word thing ... just general ideas."

Sarah came out of the bedroom and shuffled into the bathroom without saying anything.

"It's alive," whispered Kevin.

Jonathan's eyes bugged out. "Shhh! You want her to hear you?"

Kevin made spooky gestures with his hands. "Beware the kraken!" he whispered in a high-pitched voice.

The toilet flushed and Sarah emerged. "You'd better shut your trap, or I'll release the kraken all over your sorry butt."

Kevin stared at the ceiling, pantomiming an innocent whistle.

"So what kind of diabolical plans are you cooking up in here, boyfriend?" she asked Jonathan, slapping him lightly on the cheek as she walked by. She turned on the faucet and stared at the stream of water with suspicion. "It's clear today. Does that mean it's not toxic?"

"Here," said Jonathan, handing her a water bottle that was half-full. "Drink this. We'll work on the drinking water later. Right now we're discussing passing messages to our families using a chat room I've frequented for chess club."

"Oh, good," she said, shutting off the water and taking the bottle from Jonathan. "I need you to send my mom a message to cancel my hair appointment for next week." She took a big swig, burping cutely when she was done.

"Sarah, we're not passing non-critical messages about your hair," said Candi.

"It's not non-critical, okay? It's *very* critical. Lorenz will refuse to book me again if I no-show, and I don't plan on being up here in no-man's land forever."

Jonathan patted her shoulder. "I'm sure your mom has already taken care of that. We just need to let them know we're okay and that we plan to come back for the trial. Unless you guys have anything to add, that's what I'll tell them."

"Is that such a good idea? The trial part, I mean," asked Kevin. "If I was the bad guy, I'd be waiting on the courthouse steps for us to show up and then - *BLAM*." He mimicked shooting a rifle with a big kickback.

"Oh, that's nice. Thanks for the visual, Kev," said Sarah, rolling her eyes.

"He's right. They're killers. Don't forget what that guy did in that house," said Candi.

"Like I'll ever forget that as long as I live," said Sarah, her voice suddenly gruff. "All that blood ... those poor people with their eyes just staring out at nothing ..."

Jonathan put his hand on Sarah's arm, trying to pull her out of her trance. "Hey ... we don't need to talk about that right now. Let's get this discussion about the messages we want to send figured out first."

"I think we *should* talk about what happened," said Candi, her eyes haunted. "I'm afraid ignoring it will make my nightmares worse."

Kevin put his arm across her shoulders. "You don't need to have nightmares. I'm sleeping right next to you, babe, keeping you safe."

"You slept through us being attacked last time," said Sarah, her voice heavy with disdain. "I think I'd rather be prepared to kick some you-know-what on my own and not have to rely on you guys. No offense."

"You will be prepared. That's the plan," said Jonathan, looking at each of them in turn. "We need to train like we never have before. What we did on the island is nothing compared to what we have to do now. Before, we just did stuff to keep from being bored. Here, we're fighting for our lives. Hired, vicious assassins could come for us at any time. Who knows ... maybe we were followed here and they're just waiting for the perfect moment. Or maybe tomorrow they'll find the trail of clues we left and get here the day after. We need to assume the worst and prepare for it."

"Are you *trying* to make me freak out, Jonathan? Is that your goal?" asked a nearly hysterical Sarah.

"No!" said Jonathan, getting frustrated with all the crazy emotions, going up and down and up again. "My goal is to be realistic and get you to understand that this isn't about camping or fun and games! This is about survival!"

"Jesus, Jon. Lighten up, already," said Kevin, running his fingers through his hair. "We'll train, we'll do all that stuff, yeah. But I don't think it's a good idea to constantly be thinking about being shot or stabbed. We'll go nuts up here if we do that. Let's just be smart about things."

"Yeah ... don't forget, we have the dogs," said Candi, not

sounding very confident about the idea.

"And we can set traps and alarms out in the woods," said Sarah. "If someone comes to take me out, I'm not going to go easy. Screw that."

Jonathan nodded, pleased to see his family being strong and determined. They were going to need those qualities to face what was coming; he was sure of it. "Okay, then. Tell me what you want me to say in the message, and I'll get working on crafting the code."

"I'll make pancakes while we put it together," said Candi, walking over to the cabinet she'd designated as the pantry.

"I'll set the table," said Sarah, pulling out drawers until she found the one with silverware.

"And I'll prepare to eat everything you put on the table," said Kevin.

"No, you go walk the dogs," said Candi. "Make sure they poo somewhere we won't step in it."

Kevin grumbled something about being demoted to dog-poo-manager, but Jonathan blocked most of it out. He had to figure out the best way to tell his friend and fellow chess-club member that the King, Queen, and their rooks were holding the line, but ready to make sacrifices of their pawns as soon as today.

*****

Kevin went outside with Xena and James, his only thought at first being how much he wished he was back in the halls of his high school, his cute girlfriend Candi tucked under his arm, and his rugby buddies around him cracking jokes. Life pretty much sucked right now, in his estimation. Instead of enjoying his summer with his friends, he was out in the wilderness with two furry shit-machines and a bossy chick who'd taken over his girlfriend's body telling him where to let them take a crap. If that assassin were here right now, he'd punch him in the face before shooting him, just for ruining the end of his junior year.

Xena did her business and then came over, sitting directly in front of him. She seemed as if she were waiting for something.

"What?" he asked, looking at her face. The battle scars there and on her chest, legs, back, and ears made her appear vicious. He knew she was a sweetheart, though. In the couple days they'd been together, she'd never so much as growled, even when nipped by James in play and stepped on a few times by him.

Her tongue lolled out to the side as she panted.

"Why are you looking at me like that?"

She whined once and dropped down into a prone position on her stomach and elbows, still staring up at him.

"Roll over," said Kevin, just for the hell of it.

He never expected her to do it, but she flipped over once and then jumped to her feet before sitting back down on her haunches.

"Down," said Kevin, experimentally, his heart rate picking up.

She lowered herself again.

"Play dead."

She tilted her head.

Kevin held up a finger in the shape of a gun, thinking maybe she'd do the trick with a prop.

She immediately stopped panting and closed her mouth, standing up on all four legs and widening the space between them. A low growl came rumbling up from her chest as she watched his finger closely. The tail that had been swishing back and forth was sticking straight out in the back and raised a little.

Kevin felt his heart go - ka *thump* - really hard behind his ribs before it started a new frantic rhythm, trying to manage the shot of adrenaline that had just entered his system.

"Okaaaaay, doggie ..." He lowered his hand very slowly and immediately stopped making it look like a gun. "I'm just going to step away, and you're going to stay right there and not eat my face off ..."

As soon as his hand went down, the growling stopped and the panting started again. Kevin nearly pissed his pants when the sides of her mouth went up into a smile and she sat down.

He wasn't sure what possessed him to do it, but something in his crazy mind had to see if it was a fluke or not. He put his hand back into the shape of a pistol and lifted it up once more.

The unholy cacophony of angry growls and barks that erupted from the white demon of death with teeth so big they couldn't possibly fit in her mouth made him turn and run for his life.

He raced through the trees blindly, leaves and limbs smacking him in the face. He prayed she wasn't behind him and hoped beyond all hope that he would get to the house before she took him down by the achilles tendon.

Holy shit! I'm going down! I'm gonna die by pit bull attack! With pain!

"Get the gun! Get the gun!" he screamed, crashing through the branches and leaves he'd easily pushed aside earlier trying to find a safe place for the dogs to take a shit.

He got within view of the cabin and saw everyone standing out on the porch, all of them innocent to the tragedy unfolding. He waved his arms frantically. "Run! Run! Get back in the house! The dog's gone crazy! Shoot her! Shoot her!"

His pace only slowed when he noticed Candi laughing and pointing at something behind him.

When Sarah bent over double in hysterics, he stopped completely.

"What the fuck, man?!" he shouted, barely able to breathe, his heart was pounding so fast. He rested his hands on his hips as he gulped in huge volumes of air, looking from them to the spot where was certain he'd see death on four legs, ten boob bags hanging down to the ground between them just to mock him with their seeming innocence.

Even Jonathan was smiling now. "I can see why you'd want us to shoot her. She does look terrifying."

Kevin spun around completely. The stupid dog was behind him on her back, lying on the ground with her legs up in the air, curving her stupid baggy-boobed torso into the shape of a comma and pawing at the air.

Basically, she was begging for a tummy scratch.

"Oh, for cryin' out loud, Xena, *come on!* You just tried to *kill* me, you asshole."

Candi guffawed even louder at that. "You can't ... *ha-ha-ha* ... you can't ..." Her breath was coming in gasps. "You can't call ... *ha-ha-ha-ha* ... Xena an asshole!" She collapsed with Sarah onto the porch floor, and Xena jumped up, running over to join them with her tail wagging like mad the whole time.

Kevin shook his head. "That fucking dog was going to kill me, I swear to God."

"What did you do to make her want to kill you?" asked Jonathan.

"I pointed a finger gun at her."

"What's a finger gun?" he asked innocently, making Kevin

feel even more like an idiot.

The girls were busy laughing, and Jonathan was standing there waiting for a stupid explanation that made no sense. The combined effect equaled a level of humiliation that caused Kevin to blow a gasket and lose all control of his common sense.

"You want to know what a finger gun is, Jon?!" he yelled. "I'll show ya! *This* is a finger gun!" He held up his finger and thumb. "Hey! Xena! Check this out!" He jacked his fingers back three times, pretending like he was actually shooting it, yelling the sound effects. "Pop! Pop! Pop!"

And then he screamed like a girl on fire when the dog spun around and came for him, snarling.

*****

Candi went instantly sober when she saw Xena take off after her totally stupid boyfriend. She acted on instinct more than anything else, yelling, "Xena! No! Heel!"

The dog skidded to a stop in the dirt just feet away from Kevin, its legs splayed out for balance. Her sides heaved with the deep breaths and growls that were still coming out of her low-slung jaw.

"Come! Heel!" yelled Candi, desperately trying to put as much authority into her commands as possible.

Xena stared at Kevin for two more seconds before turning and jogging back to Candi, stopping at her right leg. She turned to face the same direction as Candi, sitting down on her haunches with her head held high and proud.

"Daaaaaaang," said Sarah, backing up a couple steps to stand behind Jonathan. "That dog is scary obedient."

"Or just fucking *scary!*" screamed Kevin. He hadn't moved a muscle the entire time. He just stood in place as if frozen.

"Well, I guess it's safe to say she's not a fan of the finger gun," said Jonathan.

"I'd hate to see what she'd do if you pointed a real gun at her," said Candi, bending down to pet her behind the ears. "Good girl to come and heel. Good girl. Please don't eat my stupid boyfriend, even if he does point little boy finger guns in your face. He shouldn't have to die for being a fool."

"Hey! How about a little understanding over here! I almost died, you know. *With pain.*"

"You probably would have sustained a pretty serious injury, but I'm not sure you would have died," said Jonathan, going down the stairs to join Kevin in the yard. "I think you'd better call her to you and make peace, though. I don't want there to be any bad vibes with her and you out here. She's a pretty powerful canine. If she decides to lock those jaws on someone I'm not sure how we'd get her to open them without hurting her."

"No shit, Sherlock." Kevin bent down on one knee, putting his hands up in the air in front of him with fingers splayed, making it perfectly clear they weren't shaped like guns anymore. "Come here, Xena."

Candi nudged Xena with her knee, and the dog obeyed, ambling down the stairs and trotting over to join Kevin. Candi was seriously impressed with Kevin's nerve. He didn't look nearly as afraid as she would have been in his shoes.

"Sit," he said, when she got close.

She sat down, panting with her tongue out.

Kevin leaned forward and patted her on the head. "Good girl. Good girl to attack guys with guns."

Candi smiled, really glad Kevin got the situation so clearly and wasn't holding what Xena had done against her. Especially since she was like a gift from the heavens. Somehow they'd managed to get not only a free dog, but one that had come complete with the instinct or training to attack a guy with a weapon pointed at her. Candi didn't know if she had it in herself to train a dog to do that, but she sure wasn't going to disregard its value. She laughed as she watched Xena roll over onto her back begging for a scratching, and Kevin trying to comply without actually touching any of her boobs. No matter where he put his hand, there was another one in the way.

"Man, when are these things gonna dry up and go away?" His hand kept popping up and moving out of the way as she wiggled around.

"They're already smaller than they were," said Sarah, going down to join Kevin.

"Coulda fooled me," he said, standing up and rubbing his hands off on his new jeans. "So, pancakes? I hope?"

Candi waved him in. "Yes, I have pancakes for you, but they're probably cold by now."

Kevin jogged over and took the stairs two at a time. "Just show me to the stack, and I'll take care of the rest."

They went inside, and Candi watched him descend on the plate of pancakes, practically inhaling them, stopping only to add more syrup and take gulps of water from a nearby bottle.

"Just seeing him eat makes me sick to my stomach," said Sarah from the doorway.

"Don't watch," said Jonathan. "Come with me to find some firewood."

"Firewood?" Sarah said, following him back out the door. "What do we need firewood for? It's summertime."

"Just humor me, would you?"

Candi listened to their voices fading off in the distance, no longer able to hear what they were saying.

"These ... are awesome," said Kevin, waving his fork at the dogs who were sitting just at his feet, hoping he'd drop something. "No! No pancakes for dogs. I'm eating every last crumb. Maybe if you hadn't tried to kill me, I might have given you a bite, but no deal now."

"Don't be mean. She was being a good girl today." Candi bent down and rubbed both dogs' heads. Then she stood and put more dry dog food in the two bowls that were on the floor. "Here you go, Xena and James. Doggy pancakes. Get 'em while they're hot."

The dogs happily complied, not seeming to care that they were getting kibble and not the sugary sweetness that was filling Kevin's bottomless pit of a stomach.

"Girl, all I can say is you can cook. Even my mom can't do these."

"I just used pancake mix; don't get too excited."

"Whatever. It's better than the restaurant. I could eat another stack." He gave her the look he knew had powerful heart-melting properties.

"Don't look at me like that. If I make you another one, there won't be any for another day."

"Fine," he said, dropping the sexy eyes. "Got any eggs? Sausage?"

"Now you're just fantasizing out loud. You know we don't have any of that stuff. We have to go to a real grocery store. Maybe we can do a run today."

"I was thinking about that. I couldn't decide if we should risk doing a bunch of stuff all at once right away like grocery shopping, Internet search, and all that ... or wait and do a bunch of stuff like a week from now, or just do little things here and there."

"I know. I was trying to figure that out, too. I'm so worried a cop is going to check the license plates of the car and find out it's stolen. If that happens, any of us in the car will be done. Like arrested and then killed ... dead. We can't risk that. But we can't stay out here without fresh food, so at some point we have to go in."

"The solution is to have a car or vehicle that isn't stolen."

"Yeah," said Candi, bitterly. "All we need is another ten thousand dollars so we can buy one, and we'll be all set."

"We don't need that much. Maybe a grand."

"A car that's worth a grand isn't going to run."

"Maybe not a car, but a motorcycle or even a scooter would."

Candi thought about that for a minute before responding. "Jonathan has a scooter at home, and he uses it to go everywhere. It gets great gas mileage, too."

"Exactly. And we don't all need to go places together - just one at a time to the store and stuff. And we have that duffle bag, so we could put groceries in it, no problem. A trunk is just optional."

Candi smiled, walking over and hugging Kevin hard before letting him go. "I think you just came up with the perfect solution. Low expense, only one person is seen at a time, and it can get in and out of places that cars can't."

He reached over and smacked her butt before taking his last bite of pancakes, talking the whole time. "Which would come in handy if we were being chased by a dude in a car."

"How much money do we have left?" Candi asked, unable to

remember what they'd spent.

"Not sure." He put his fork down, using his fingers to calculate. "Hmmm ... let's see ... we paid fifteen hundred for the cabin, so that dropped us to eighty-five hundred. We've spent about three hundred more on clothes and our food run. Maybe another fifty on other food. That leaves ... what? Eighty-one fifty or so?"

"Ha, I can't do math in my head like that. But I think no matter what, we could spare a thousand for transportation. The question is, what do we do about driver licenses and stuff like that?"

"Pray we don't get pulled over. And if we do, refuse to give our names until after the trial is over. We'll either get a ticket and the bike will get towed, or worst case, we'll be in jail as John or Jane Does; but we won't get ourselves killed by a mole, and that's the most important thing."

"But what if someone recognized us at the police station?"

"First of all, we tell them we're eighteen, so they won't think we're kids and runaways and look through those missing persons files or whatever. And we should tell them we're from another state, like California or something, so they're thinking we're from really far away. We're already two states over. I doubt very highly we're going to be on the national news, so why would they even know about us being on the run?"

"I'm not sure if I could just lie and lie and lie like that and not totally give in and tell them everything. Besides, not telling them would make them look harder, don't you think?"

Kevin abandoned the scraping of the last drop of syrup onto his fork and stepped over to stand in front of Candi, holding onto her upper arms and staring intensely into her eyes. "Listen,

Gumdrop ... you would have to lie. Lie your ass off. If by some weird fluke you get caught, you *cannot* under *any* circumstances, tell them who you are. It would be as good as just walking up to the assassin and giving him your throat. They. Will. *Kill* you. Do you get that?" He shook her gently for effect. "I can't have you dying on me. I'd never ever get over that. Do you understand what I'm saying?"

Candi nodded, fully sobered by the idea of being murdered or knowing that Kevin or Sarah or Jonathan would be, merely because she or one of them had given up their names. She knew exactly what Kevin was trying to say. They'd been through too much to not be together anymore or to have to try and survive this crazy world alone. "I get it. I understand. Mum's the word. If I'm ever caught, I'll tell them my name is Cathy Redwood and I'm from California."

Kevin nodded at first, but his agreement quickly morphed into a frown. "Cathy Redwood?" He laughed, letting go of her arms to go back to his syrup-scraping. "Oh, yeah, they'll totally buy that one. Good plan. I'm going to tell them my name is Sponge Bob Square Pants. First name SpongeBob, last name Squarepants. From Pineapple, California."

Candi play-smacked him. "Shut up. It's the name I used for this rental, and she totally went for it."

"Yeah, well, she was a hundred years old, so she doesn't count. I think you'd better come up with something else. Don't even use the same initials, like C for Candi."

"Okay, fine. I'll work on it, Spongebob."

Kevin grinned as he tipped his head down towards her, looking for a kiss. "How about a hike out into the deep dark forest, miz Redwood?"

Candi backed away. "Who are you now, first name Bigbad, last name Wolf? No, thanks. I have cleaning to do."

"Cleaning, smeaning. We have plenty of time to clean. Let's go have some fun."

Candi sauntered back towards him as sexily as she knew how. "I'll tell you what. How about ... you help me clean for an hour ... and then I'll run through the woods with you afterwards for an hour. Deal?"

Kevin grabbed her into a bear hug. "You drive a hard bargain, but I'm not afraid of you *or* your cleaning rags. It's a deal."

Candi fell into a deep kiss with him, only managing to pull herself out of it when she heard Jonathan and Sarah coming back. She turned to face the door, but then yelped a second later when the tip of a wet rag snapped against her butt cheek. "Hey!"

Kevin stood behind her, acting like he was busy cleaning off the counter. "What? What's the matter?"

"Nothing," she said, walking casually over to the other counter to grab the rag that was sitting on its edge. "Nothing at all ..."

Kevin saw her coming and took off running out of the cabin. Candi and James followed hot on his heels - Candi whooping out her war cry and James barking his fool terrier head off. Jonathan and Sarah just stood to the side with Xena at their feet, giving the crazy ones room to get by.

*****

Sarah stared at the food on her plate that just didn't look or smell appetizing, even though she knew normally she'd love it. Macaroni and cheese had been her guilty pleasure since she was old enough to eat solid food - or so her mother had always quipped when she would plop a big gooey spoonful of it down on a lunch plate for her.

Candi hadn't done anything wrong when she cooked it; it looked fine. But the smell was about to send Sarah into the bathroom. She buried her nose in her water glass, inhaling the non-smell of the clear liquid in an effort to calm her stomach. Whoever had named this kind of nausea morning sickness was a real jerk. A better name would have been *all-day-sickness*.

"I think it's a great idea," said Jonathan. "I'm in favor of either the scooter or motorcycle. I'm kind of partial to scooters in my normal life, but I'm might actually prefer a motorcycle for our current situation."

"Why?" asked Sarah, her face still in her glass. She was just going to keep using it like a gas mask for as long as it worked like one.

"Scooters are more rare in the United States, first of all. Did you know that of all the developed countries, we have the lowest per capita ownership of these eco-friendly forms of transportation? It's shameful, really. Anyway, we'd stick out using one. And they're not as fast, so if we ever had to engage in evasive maneuvers, we'd be better off with more horsepower."

"Motorcycles are more expensive, though," said Candi. "And I'd be nervous about riding one."

"I'll teach ya," said Kevin, shoveling another scoop of pasta into his mouth. "It's easy." A noodle dropped from his mouth back to his plate.

Sarah had to look away. She was getting angry at him for being so carefree about satisfying his hunger and for being such a slob about it. There was nothing she'd like more than to eat like he was doing right now, enjoying every bite of that gooey, buttery-tasting cheesy mess, but for some really stupid reason Jonathan had tried to explain to her, everything smelled like something rotten and totally unappetizing now.

"I think we could find something for around a thousand dollars, maybe a little more. And if we get an older model, it could be easy to fix or not very expensive to repair, at least," said Jonathan. "The question is, how do we find it?"

"We've gotta go online," said Kevin. "One or two of us have to go to the grocery store, too."

"And we need a budget," said Candi. "This money isn't going to last forever. Plus, we need to keep money aside for another month of rental if it comes to that."

Sarah raised her finger. "I can do the budget."

Everyone at the table looked at each other, saying nothing.

"What? You think I can't?"

"You spend a minimum of three hundred dollars anytime you shop," said Candi.

"No, I don't."

"I've seen you, Sarah. Yes, you do."

"Okay, fine ... so I have done that in the past. But not every time; and when I did, there was no need for a budget. Now there is." She shot warning looks at everyone. "I'm doing it, so just keep your comments to yourself. You'll see." She was going to show these dorks who could make a budget and stick to it. Just because she had taste and liked to spend money, it didn't mean she couldn't simplify and live with the bare essentials. "Just tell me what you like to eat and what you can't live without, and I'll make it happen."

Jonathan patted her hand. "I can't wait to see it."

"Me too," said Kevin, barely concealing his grin behind the

hand holding his fork. "What's it gonna have on it? Manicures and pedicures? Those sound like essentials to me."

Sarah threw her wadded-up paper towel napkin at him. "Shut up. And don't bother putting beer on the list because that's definitely non-essential."

"Hey, now ...," said Kevin, pointing at her.

"I agree with Sarah," said Jonathan. "No alcohol. No soda. Just water ... and fresh juice for Sarah."

"No soda, even? Come on, don't you think you're taking this a little to the extreme?" asked Kevin.

"No, not at all. We can't get jobs to earn more money. This is all we have, and that's barring any emergencies. What if one of us gets hurt? We need transportation back to the trial, and we'll need money not just for that but for staying hidden up until the day we testify."

"Fine," grumbled Kevin. "I'm going to stay out of it. Just give me food a few times a day, and I won't say anything else."

"Yes, you will," said Sarah. "You'll complain and whine and make us all want to kick your butt. But I, for one, won't be listening."

Kevin looked over at Candi, but she shook her head. "Me neither. We all have to sacrifice. If I can't have a soda or a candy bar until the trial, then you're just going to have to suck it up too. No beer."

"You guys think I care about beer that much? I don't at all. I could care less about that. But soda? Can't we even get the generic stuff? It's less than a buck."

"I'll let you know," said Sarah, serenely. "I'll have the budget completed by tomorrow after breakfast. I suggest we shop immediately afterwards."

Jonathan looked around the table. "Do we all agree with the basic plan, then? We're going to shop for a motorcycle and get some groceries?"

Everyone nodded.

"This means someone's going out in the car to do that stuff. Who's going?" asked Sarah.

"Candi should go. She looks the least like any picture of her," said Jonathan.

"I'll go with her," said Kevin.

"No, I think it should be Sarah," said Jonathan. "She can disguise herself much better than you or I can. All she has to do is be without makeup and put her hair up, and she'll look much different than her pictures."

"Are you saying I'm ugly with my hair up?"

Jonathan's eyes widened in alarm. "No. No way. Not at all. You're beautiful with your hair up. You just look different."

"Stop fishing for compliments," said Candi smirking at her.

"I'm not. Just clarifying." Sarah was more than happy with Jonathan's explanation. He was pretty much incapable of lying to her. That was another reason she was going to make this trip tomorrow, even though she would have preferred hiding out of sight in the cabin and resting her poor stomach - Jonathan, if caught, would probably totally implicate himself and everyone else, getting them all unintentionally killed. *No.* If there was lying to be done, it was she who was going to have to do it. Even Sugar Lump was a possible problem. The lies could probably actually come out of her mouth, but whether they'd be convincing or not was a whole other issue.

"Okay, so Sarah and I will go into town with her shopping list and buy some groceries and then go online somewhere. But do you expect us to find a motorcycle and bring it back, too? Because I'm pretty sure that's not going to happen."

"Oh. That is a problem, isn't it?" asked Jonathan, frowning.

"You could do it," said Kevin. "I'll give you a lesson in the morning."

"Isn't that going to be a little difficult, seeing as how we don't have one to practice with?" asked Candi, sounding as skeptical as Sarah felt about the whole thing.

"It'll be a challenge, but I'm up for it." Kevin leaned his chair back and rubbed his stomach. "Man, I'm full. What's on TV tonight?"

"Maybe nothing," said Candi. "I'm not sure if the owner got the cable turned on or not."

Kevin pushed his chair back. "No better time than the present to check, then."

"You're not going anywhere until the dishes are done and the kitchen cleaned," she warned.

Kevin froze in the middle of standing up. "Uhhh ... excuse me? What was that? Come again?"

Candi stood, taking her plate over to the kitchen sink. "You heard me. Girls make the dinner, guys clean it up."

Kevin snorted. "Yeah, right."

Sarah stood too. "Free ride's over, bro. Start cleaning."

"But ... this place doesn't even have a friggin dishwasher!" Kevin sputtered, looking at Jonathan for support. "Come on, man. Are you gonna put up with this?"

Jonathan shrugged. "What's there to put up with? We ate the meal. I don't see why they should have to prepare it and clean up after everyone. It seems fair to share the workload."

Kevin let out an annoyed burst of air. "Whatever, dude. You're so friggin whipped I don't know why I even bother asking you anything anymore." He grabbed his plate and utensils and stormed over to the kitchen. "I hope you don't expect me to do a good job. I've never done dishes in my life."

"Well," said Candi, coming up behind him and draping a dish towel over his shoulder, "it's about time you learned, then, isn't it?"

He dropped the dishes in the sink and grabbed the towel off his shoulder, turning it into a makeshift whip so fast, Candi never saw it coming.

"Youch!" she screeched after the crack of it hitting her butt had her automatically running for the stairs. "Get away from me!" She flew up to the second floor and shut herself into the bedroom. "Go do your work, dish wench!" she yelled from behind the door. Her voice was muffled but clear enough that Kevin heard the insult just fine.

"Dish wench? Oh, man ... you are so going down when I get my hands on you." He walked back down the stairs and into the kitchen, flipping the faucet on high and banging things around in the sink.

Sarah and Jonathan watched from off to the side. "Do you think I should show him how to do the dishes?" whispered Jonathan.

"I think you should *supervise*. But whatever you do, don't let him con you into doing the work for him."

"Oh, I won't," assured Jonathan. "I'll just give him some tips on the proper temperature of the water and the importance of removing all possible bacteria using enough soap and proper scrubbing technique." He moved away, intent on his new role as kitchen supervisor.

"You do that, babe," said Sarah, already laughing inside at the feathers Jonathan was going to ruffle with her formerly highly-coddled, now lowly dish-wench of a brother.

She left them to their task and climbed the stairs to join Candi, finding her on her back on the bed, staring at the ceiling. She joined her, lying on her side, facing her friend. "Whatchya thinkin' about?"

"Oh, nothing. Just the idea of driving a death machine that I have no idea how to operate, the images of being pulled over, arrested, interrogated, transported back home, and then finally murdered by having my neck slit ... Like I said ... nothing much."

Sarah reached out and pressed her forefinger into the middle of Candi's forehead and left it there.

"What in the heck are you doing?" asked Candi, not moving.

"I'm not sure. It seemed like a good idea at the time."

"Well ... strangely enough, it's taking my mind off my impending doom and now focusing it on your insanity." She moved her eyes as far to the right as possible. "Thanks. I think."

Sarah removed her finger. "You're welcome. But for the record, I don't think you need to worry about it so much."

Candi turned her head to look at Sarah. "Oh yeah? Why? Are you psychic now in addition to being pregnant?"

"No. I'm just playing the odds, as Jonathan likes to say. I mean, we're in the middle of some shit ... I mean, *crap* town, out in the woods where no one will ever see or hear us. We're going to make a single trip in that car, and then we'll be done with it until it's time to go. The chances of us getting pulled over in it are very slim. I've driven my car around for over a year ... almost two ... and I've never been pulled over even once."

"Yeah, but your car wasn't stolen."

"No, but that doesn't mean anything. As long as you obey the laws and don't do anything stupid, they won't even bother checking the license plate. Do you know how many Toyota Camry's there are on the road?"

"No."

"Well, Jonathan enlightened me. There are a lot. So it's not like the cops just run plates randomly through their computer. They do that when they pull you over if you can't produce a registration that makes any sense. Just don't get pulled over, and you'll be fine."

"What if we do? What's the plan?"

"Well ..." Sarah thought about it for a second, letting her mind wander over to that horrific scenario she'd avoided thinking about, specifically because it really had no good ending. "Hmmm ... I guess we try to run for it. Chances are there will only be one cop, so one of us will get away. The other just has to keep her mouth shut."

"It won't work. I've run it through my head a million times. Say we get pulled over. Say I get caught."

"So far that makes sense," said Sarah. "I'm much faster than you, so you will be the one who gets caught."

"No, you're not; but whatever. Say I get caught ..."

"I'll race you."

"Sarah, shut up. You're not faster than me and you're interrupting."

"I'm just saying. Let's race. I'll bet I beat you."

Candi frowned hard. "Fine. We'll race tomorrow, and I'll show everyone how slow you are. But back to the real issue, which is not racing but death by assassination. So ... say I get caught. I say nothing, but they run the plates on the car in the computer and find out it's from our area. Then they report some girl has this stolen car and there was another girl in the car with her, they send them pictures of me, maybe of you too, and *bam*. We're done. They say, *Ship her back, she's a wanted felon*, and then I'm done. Dead. Probably hung in the jail, making it look like a suicide." Tears were shining in her eyes. "I don't want to be a fake teen suicide ... or a real one for that matter."

Sarah reached over and pressed her finger into Candi's forehead again. "You're not going to be a teen suicide. If you get caught we'll just ... bust you out of jail or whatever."

Candi laughed bitterly. "That only works in the movies, Sarah. It's not going to work in real life."

"How about this, though ... if you got caught and told them you were only fifteen, they wouldn't be able to put you in jail, right? You'd have to go into a juvenile place."

"Yeah, so?"

"So, maybe those are easy to escape from."

"Right. They make prisons for kids who like to run away easy to get away from."

Sarah frowned. "Oh, yeah. That doesn't make much sense, does it?"

"No," sighed Candi, "but I appreciate the effort."

"Well, you know ... we have a gun. If someone tries to take you, we could just hold them up and make them let you go."

Candi pushed her shoulder. "Don't you even think about doing something that stupid! Could you imagine? You'd get shot for sure. Cops are allowed to shoot to kill and they have training, Sarah. They practice hitting targets in the heart. Do not even talk about that stupid gun. We should bury the damn thing."

"Heck no, we should not! If that killer shows up, I'm going to shoot his ass *and* his heart. That gun could save our lives one day."

"Fine. I won't bury the gun. But we're not bringing it tomorrow."

Sarah didn't reply because she wasn't sure she agreed.

"Sarah, I'm serious. Say it. No guns."

"No guns ... " *... out in the open where you can see it.*

"Are your fingers crossed behind your back?" Candi asked.

"Why so suspicious?"

"Because you never go down this easy."

"You know me too well, Sugar Lump. It's getting annoying."

Candi reached over and pushed her forefinger into the middle of Sarah's forehead. "Don't frown. It's giving you wrinkles."

"Are you serious?" asked Sarah, sitting up, wishing she had a mirror in bed with her to check.

Candi laughed, rolling over again onto her back. "No, I'm not serious." She yawned. "Wake me up for TV."

"Wake yourself up," said Sarah, rolling over onto her other side. "I'm taking a little dessert nap." The vision of herself waving a gun around at a police officer who was trying to take her friend into juvie was the last thing she remembered before falling into a heavy slumber.

*****

Candi pulled out onto the main road, making sure to use her turn signals. "We're almost there, and believe it or not, I haven't had a heart attack yet."

"See? I told you it was no big deal," said Sarah. "We just need to get in and out, no big."

"No big. Right." Candi was scanning the street in front of her, looking for cop cars that might be coming for them at any minute.

"Pull into that plaza," ordered Sarah. "There's a grocery store and a copy shop. Double score."

Candi did as she was told, making a perfect turn, signaling ahead, and all the while keeping her eyes peeled for officers of the law.

"I'll do the shopping, you do the Internet searching," said Sarah.

"No, we need to stick together. Let's do the Internet search first."

"Why not shop first?"

"Because, the food will spoil if we find someone and have to go through all the time to get the buying done."

"Good point. Okay, lead on, then. To the copy shop."

Candi turned off the car and grabbed the duffle bag from the back seat. It didn't have all the money in it - just enough to pay for the groceries and a cheap motorcycle. She tried to ignore the twisting her stomach did every time she imagined riding one of those things. Jonathan's scooter was one thing, but a real motorcycle that could go fast enough to be on the highway? That was a whole different animal.

They walked to the copy shop, both of them keeping their heads down and going as fast as they could without looking crazy. Candi had to battle to keep from grabbing Sarah's hand and running. She was terrified of being out in public now; she felt watched and hunted by some unseen monster. Being prey totally sucked.

They walked in the door and Candi was immediately on her

guard.   This place was much smaller and not nearly as anonymous as the other one. Her eyes scanned the room to take inventory of the situation. *Three copy machines, one computer, two employees staring at us.* Candi cleared her throat without thinking, trying to clear the blockage that felt like it was in there cutting off her air.

Sarah seemed totally unconcerned. She walked up to the counter and said in a voice that was way too loud for Candi's liking, "Do you have a computer we could use to go online?"

The guy gestured to the corner of the room where the single desktop machine sat humming away. "Right over there. It's twenty bucks for a half hour."

"Wow, that's pretty steep," she said. "How about ten?"

Candi rushed over the few remaining steps to the register and took Sarah by the elbow. "Never mind. Twenty's fine." She dragged her away from the bemused employees, wishing she could just yell at her right now and not have to worry about being arrested for disturbing the peace or whatever.

"What's the problem?" asked Sarah, pulling her arm out of Candi's grip. "I was just trying to negotiate a little. We have a budget you know."

Candi whispered furiously near her ear, barely containing her frustration. "Yeah! And we also don't want to call attention to ourselves! How many people come in here and try to negotiate the freaking online fees, do you think?"

Sarah's face remained impassive.

"Exactly. None," Candi said in a calmer voice. "So what you just did is memorialize our trip into town and into this plaza for those two guys. Thanks for that, Sarah. If I get my throat slit, I'm blaming you."

Sarah pinched her hard on the arm as she sat down in the chair in front of the computer.

"Don't do that!" Candi growled in Sarah's ear, sitting down next to her using a nearby chair that she pulled over. She reached over and pinched Sarah's leg.

Sarah jabbed Candi in the ribs with her elbow before reaching up to log on using the username and password printed on a small strip of paper stuck to the front of the computer.

Candi elbowed her back and jerked the keyboard over. "I'm surfing. You just sit there and try not to get us killed." Out of the corner of her eye, Candi saw Sarah's finger coming at her. "If you put that stupid finger on my forehead, I'm going to break it."

The finger slowly withdrew. "Man, oh man, the stress is seriously getting to you, Sugar Lump. You should let me press your valve. You'll feel much better, I promise."

Candi stopped in mid-Google, turning to face Sarah. "What are you talking about?"

"Your valve." Her gaze shifted up to Candi's forehead. "The one in the middle of your head up there. It lets off the steam when I push on it."

Candi shook her head in disbelief. "Where on earth did you get that idea?"

Sarah shrugged. "I just happened on it one day when I was really sick. I kept pressing there because I just couldn't deal with the sickness, and it went away, like magic. It worked for you last night, you can't deny it."

"*Pfft.* That didn't do anything other than confuse me."

"Yeah, well confusion, steam valve ... it works." Her finger started to come up again. "Just let me press it once."

Candi snatched Sarah's finger and squeezed it. "I'll totally do it to you, Sarah. I'll break your finger right off. I'm like an inch away from totally losing my cool right now. Don't tempt me."

Sarah pulled back again. "Fine. But don't come crying to me asking me to de-steamify you later."

Candi shook her head. "This pregnancy is making you totally looney." She went back to searching the website with all the motorcycle listings, taking a few deep breaths to try and center her anger. It wasn't like her to get this freaked out, even when it was life or death situations. "Help me find our bike."

She heard nothing more from Sarah as she fell into research mode, clicking on photos and reading descriptions. She checked over fifteen listings, but nothing felt right to her. The bikes were either too big or too fast-looking. Nothing was just a plain motorcycle, nondescript, and not over three thousand dollars.

Candi didn't even notice that Sarah was gone until she sat down again and bumped into her arm, sending her mouse-click awry. "Hey, watch it, klutz."

A white index card hit the keyboard, blocking Candi's fingers from doing their next search. She took her hand from the mouse and picked it up. "What's this?"

"Our motorcycle."

"What do you mean, *our motorcycle?*" The index card had a description of a motorcycle for sale for two thousand dollars, and the photograph showed the bike she'd been searching for online and not been able to find. She smiled. "Hey, this is nice."

"Yeah. It was on that bulletin board over there," said Sarah, gesturing towards the back of the store.

"Should we call this person?" asked Candi, gesturing towards the name. "Mike." Her heart rate picked up at the idea of contacting a person while on the run. So much risk ...

"I already did."

"What?" Candi was confused.

"I said, I already called him. Geez, what's your problem? You're acting like you're on drugs or something."

Candi shook her head. "I'm fine. I'm just ... I guess I thought you were sitting next to me this whole time. And I've been looking for something for ..." she checked the clock on the computer, "...for twenty minutes, and I haven't found anything."

"Yeah, well, I decided to take a look around since you were being boring. Oh, and I haven't even told you the best part yet."

Candi logged off and swiveled in her seat to face Sarah. "What's that?"

"He's selling two helmets as part of the deal."

Candi grinned again, for the first time feeling a little lighter in the chest area. "That is awesome news. I hadn't even thought of that part. Did you ask him why he's selling?"

"He said his wife just had a baby, and she told him he's not allowed to take risks like riding motorcycles anymore."

"Are you worried about that? I mean, with being pregnant?"

"Yes. But I'm more worried about being killed by a crazy Russian mafia assassin, so I'll just pick the less dangerous thing."

"And that would be the motorcycle," said Candi in full agreement.

"Exactly. So let's go do our shopping. I told him to meet us here in a half hour."

"Perfect." Candi felt like singing, everything was going so well. "Do you have our shopping list?"

"Do bears go poo in the woods?"

Candi stood, smiling. "I assume they do. I've never caught

one in a port-a-potty."

Sarah took her by the hand and led her over to the front desk so they could pay for their online time.

Candi was just about to crack a joke about what bears use for toilet paper, when the words froze in her throat. She squeezed Sarah's hand so hard, Sarah yanked it out of her grasp and started to complain. But one look at Candi's face had her turning around to see what was sending her into such a panic.

A police car had pulled up to the curb and parked, and the officer behind the wheel was getting out. Sarah turned to face Candi, her complexion now very pale. Candi looked back at the clerk, hurriedly passing him a twenty-dollar bill, sweat popping out on her upper lip as she waited for him to get her change together. He couldn't do the math in his head, and he hadn't put the correct amount that she'd given him into his keyboard, so he was trying to figure everything out.

"The change is like two bucks, it's no big deal if it's not exact," said Candi, trying to keep herself from sneaking glances towards the door. She nearly peed herself when the bell hanging on the door jingled, signaling the entrance of a customer. *Please don't let him come over here! Please please please!*

"Hello, Brandon," said a voice from the door.

The clerk looked up and smiled. "Hello, Officer Amalong. How are you today?"

"Fine, I'm fine. How's business?"

"Pretty good. Just sold some online time to these ladies."

Candi heard footsteps coming up behind her.

"Hello," said Sarah, sounding totally self-assured - maybe even a little cocky.

Candi's face burned with fear and embarrassment. She was

afraid she was going to throw up right there on the counter.

"Hello. You girls from out of town?"

"Yep," said Sarah. "Out of town. Waaay out of town. Just passing through. Had to check emails."

"Good. I was a little concerned when I drove by and saw you two in here. I thought I had some truants on my hands."

Candi tried to laugh, but it came out more like a strangled squeak.

Sarah nudged her hard. "Nope. We're not in school at the moment. We're on break."

"What kind of break happens in the last month of school?" asked the clerk, frowning at Candi and Sarah alternately.

Sarah continued to speak to the cop when she answered. "We go to private school, so our year doesn't end until the end of June. It's not really the very end of the year for us, where we're from. Which isn't here."

Candi held her hand out for the change that still hadn't come.

The clerk stared at her for a second before jerking his attention back to his task and tapping away at a calculator he had near the register. He finally reached inside the drawer after what seemed like forever to pull out her one dollar and eighty-five cents. Candi wished she'd just walked away from it earlier like she'd been tempted to do, before that cop had seen them. Trying to guess what would look suspicious and what wouldn't was making her crazy.

"Where would that be now, this place that makes you stay in school for half the summer?" asked the police officer, sounding like he felt sorry for them.

Candi had to turn around now; she had no more excuse to

keep her back to him. She faced him, forcing herself to look him in the eye. She could feel the heat rising up her neck to her ears and cheeks.

"California," said Sarah. "San Francisco. It's a boarding school, so we're roommates. Anyway, it was nice meeting you, Officer. It's a great town you have here. Too bad we can't stay, but we have some groceries to buy, and then we have to get on the road. Time to get back home before school starts again."

"You're driving all the way across the country? Just the two of you?"

"Yep. We're adventurous. We do this stuff all the time." Sarah grabbed Candi's hand and pulled her past the officer who stood with his thumbs in his belt.

Candi couldn't help but drop her gaze to stare at the gun and club that rested at his hips. She nearly fainted when she looked up again and saw the expression on his face. He didn't look convinced at all anymore, and he was staring at them like he was trying to place them from somewhere. Candi wasn't sure if she was imagining his suspicion or not, and she didn't trust herself to speak, so she just gave him a lame wave and let Sarah drag her from the store. She resisted the urge to run back to the car and peel out of the lot back to their cabin.

"Holy shit, was that guy a nosy asshole or what?" asked Sarah.

"You're cussing," said Candi, now finally realizing how scared Sarah was.

"Hell yes, I'm cussing! *Shit*, we almost got totally busted in there! I'm not sure if we should shop or run at this point!"

Candi took in a few deep breaths. It wasn't working to calm her racing heart like she'd wanted it to. "Press the button," she said, looking at Sarah sideways as her legs churned out strides she hoped looked natural to the cop who she knew was watching them leave.

Sarah reached over without breaking stride and smacked Candi in the forehead. "There. Button pressed. Now what?"

Candi couldn't help but laugh through her shock. "Remind me not to ask for any of your nutty pregnancy therapy ever again." She switched back into life-saving mode, not allowing herself the luxury of humor. "I think we should just go into the grocery store, shop fast, and get the hell out of here. Screw the motorcycle idea."

"Okay. Fine. I'll call the guy and tell him we'll do it another time." She pulled the phone out of her back pocket and dialed. Candi took her by the elbow to lead her into the store. She grabbed a cart and pushed it up to the first aisle, letting Sarah go once she was done dialing and could follow along without bumping into anything.

Sarah hung up the phone after a few long seconds. "He's not answering." Out of her pocket came her shopping list. "Here are the essentials. Just get this stuff and nothing else. It should cost no more than thirty bucks."

Candi didn't argue, she just turboed her way through the aisles, filling the cart about a quarter of the way with fresh fruit and vegetables, cheese, pastas and rice, and then some eggs and meats.

"We'll freeze some of this stuff to make it last longer. This should be good for a week."

"A week? Kevin could eat all this in a day. Two, tops."

"Hence the pasta and rice. He's just going to have to step away from so much meat until we can get back to our normal lives."

The cell phone rang.

"Who is it?" said Candi, instantly in a panic all over again.

Sarah pulled the phone out of her pocket and hit the green button. "Hello? Oh ... hey, Mike. Yeah, I'm here. Where are you? ... Okay, I'll be right there." Sarah hung up. "He's on the north side of the plaza. I'm going to go over there and do this. You finish with the groceries and meet me at the car." She unzipped the duffle bag and took out a pile of bills, folding them and shoving them into her pocket.

"You're going to buy the motorcycle *now?*" asked Candi, freaking out. "I thought we decided to wait!"

"But he's here, and it's perfect! Nothing's changed, Candi ... we still need the transportation. So just finish shopping, buy the stuff, pack it into the duffle bag, and meet me at the car. Go!" She pushed Candi on the back and sent her towards the checkout line. There were two people in the one she'd chosen, so Candi just stood there, gripping onto the cart like it was her lifeline, watching Sarah weave her way past the shoppers and displays towards the exit.

Passing her on the way in was the police officer from the copy shop. Candi wasn't sure Sarah had seen him, but he'd definitely seen her. He turned to watch her go, and then continued into the store, his eyes scanning the whole front area. Candi backed up quickly, getting out of line and turning to run down the aisle towards the back of the store. She was pretty sure he hadn't seen her, and she was going to do whatever she could to make sure he didn't.

*****

Sarah spotted the bike right away. The guy was standing next to it, using a cloth to buff the gas tank.

"Hey," she said, walking up. "You're Mike, right?"

"Yes. And you're ... Beulah?"

"Yeah. Beulah Mayberry. Nice to meet you." She held out her hand and shook his with a strong grip.

"You don't look like a Beulah," he said, studying her face.

"Yeah, well, I am one. So, what's the deal?" she asked, gesturing towards the bike. "It run?"

"Heck yeah, it runs. Like a dream."

"Why are you selling it so cheap?"

He smiled bitterly. "To save my marriage. This thing has to be gone, like, today or my old lady's gonna make me sleep in the garage."

"Damn. She sounds mad."

"Yeah, well, she asked me to get rid of it months ago, and I just couldn't do it. She finally put her foot down and you know ... with the economy and everything, I just haven't been able to find anyone."

"I'll give you fifteen hundred for it."

He frowned, looking pissed. "Two grand is a steal for this bike."

"Yeah, maybe. But it's all I've got." Sarah pulled the money out of her pocket. "Take it or leave it." She looked over her shoulder at the cop car that was still parked by the copy shop. *Asshole followed us to the store. What's his friggin problem, anyway?*

"You in some kind of hurry?" he asked, tucking the polishing cloth into his back pocket. He couldn't seem to take his eyes off the money.

"Yeah, you could say that. The bike's a surprise."

"It's not for you?"

"No. It's for my ... dad. Yeah, he's been wanting a bike like this forever. He said he had one when he was younger and really misses it. He'll take really good care of it, I promise. I've been saving for a year for this, waiting for the perfect bike to come along." She decided to really lay it on thick, knowing he was close to caving. "It's his birthday tomorrow. I can't believe how lucky I was to find your ad today. It's like a dream come true."

The guy sighed heavily. "Fine. I'll take your offer. But only because of your dad. I need to be sure it's going to go to someone who's going to love it like I do."

Sarah held the money out, but didn't let it go when he put his hand on it. "It includes those two helmets, right?" She gestured to the one hanging from the handle bar and the one strapped to the back with bungee cords.

"Yep."

"And the title signed over right now, too, right?"

"Of course. You're gonna have to go over to the DMV and get it put into your name, though. I'm not going to do that."

"Fine," said Sarah, thanking her lucky stars he wasn't going to do that or anything of the sort. There was no way this bike was getting registered in her *or* Beulah's name. "Are you going to need a ride or something?" she asked, looking around. He'd ridden the bike over, and she didn't see any partner around to give him a lift.

He reached into a small bag that was hooked to the back of the bike's seat, taking out some papers. He shuffled through them, pulling a light blue one on heavy stock from the middle. "Here's the title. And nah, don't worry about it. My wife gets off work in less than an hour, so she can pick me up here."

"She works weird hours," Sarah said, taking the document

from him and waiting for him to get a pen from his bag. She handed him the money which he put in his shirt pocket, and he took the title back, signing his name at the bottom. She didn't bother putting her name or Beulah's on it. *Better to remain as anonymous as possible.*

"Yeah, she does. She's a nurse. Here's the registration, too, by the way. You'll need to show that to the DMV so they can put it in your name."

Sarah took the paper from his hand, moving closer to the bike. "I'm just going to put all that stuff back in here," she said, folding all the official documents in half and closing the waterproof bag over them, making sure not to catch anything in the zipper.

He took the money out of his pocket and counted it. When he was done he put it back and asked, "Do you know how to ride?"

Sarah took the helmet off the handle and pushed it down over her head. It was tight, and the thick cushioning inside pressed uncomfortably against her ponytail. She reached back and pulled the elastic around her hair out, breathing a sigh of relief over how much better it felt. Her head was super heavy now, but it was safely encased in all this space-age plastic and foam. "Yeah, I know how to ride. Kind of. Give me a quick lesson if you want." Sarah gripped the handles and swung her leg over the seat, straddling the bike and sitting down gingerly. She realized immediately that it was a *lot* bigger than Jonathan's scooter. Her heart rate picked up as she straightened the heavy machine out and felt the weight of it beneath her.

He frowned. "Yeah, okay ... so that's your accelerator there." He pointed to the right handle. "And that's your clutch," he said, pointing to the left handle brake thingy. "Brake is over there. You shift the gear by pressing with your foot there. It's basically like a manual transmission in a car."

"You mean like a car with a clutch?"

"Yeah. Manual. As opposed to automatic. You *do* have your driver's license, right?"

"Yes, of course I do. I got it. So first gear, second gear, third gear ..."

"Yeah, you have to just get a feel for the different gears, when to shift, when to downshift. You'll stall if you don't go down fast enough, just like a car."

Sarah turned the key in the ignition. Nothing happened. She frowned, not sure what the heck was going on. "It's not working. It's broken."

Mike stepped closer to the front of the motorcycle. "Are you sure you've driven a bike before? It's not the easiest thing in the world to do, you know."

"Yeah, I'm sure. It's just been a while. I'm used to ... something smaller than this." Jonathan's scooter started with a little red button by the handle. She was scanning for something red all over the place and couldn't see it.

Mike sighed. "Alright. Just turn the key like you did, and then press this button." He reached over and pressed a gray button, the engine turning over a few times before catching. Mike put his hand over hers on the right handle bar and twisted it back a few times, giving the engine some gas and making it roar with life.

"Whoa ... that's loud," said Sarah, her heart racing right along with the horses that wanted to break free from their reins and race this motorcycle across the parking lot.

"Yeah. It's not as bad as a Harley, but people will hear you coming. Anyway, when you're ready to go, just ease off on the clutch here ... and twist the handle here. The bike will pull forward pretty fast if you give it too much gas, and it's easy to lose control, so be careful." He backed away, leaving Sarah alone.

"So I just turn my right hand and let out the clutch in my left?" she shouted.

"Yeah! But put up the kickstand first!" he shouted over the roar of the engine she kept revving.

She couldn't help it - it was addicting, hearing that sound. She leaned down, the helmet so heavy it made her feel like her head was just going to roll right off her shoulders. The visor or bottom part of the helmet made it difficult to see the ground just under her. "How do I do that?!" she yelled.

Mike walked over and tapped his foot on the black metal stick by her left foot and it popped back into place. "Good luck, Beulah. Take care of my baby."

"Don't worry, Mike. I got it under control. My dad's gonna be thrilled." Sarah twisted the handle, letting the engine roar to life again, and slowly, slowly let up on the clutch. She squealed with delight and fear as the bike began to crawl forward, the revving of the engine getting louder and louder as she twisted it back more in her excitement.

"Too much power!" yelled Mike. "Too much! Let it go!"

Sarah barely heard him, letting the clutch out even more. Then it slipped in her sweaty fingers and popped out the rest of the way, throwing the bike forward. She nearly flipped off the back, her legs flying up involuntarily, her death grip on the handlebars keeping her just barely in her seat. She recovered her balance in time to realize she was headed right for the plaza sidewalk and a pole that held up the overhanging part of the roof.

"Aaahhhh!" she screamed, trying to keep the wiggling, swaying bike that seemed to have a mind of its own from collapsing and sending her into a death slide across the pavement.

By some miracle, it straightened up, and her right hand lost its grip on the handle, letting the accelerator go back to its neutral position. The engine immediately stopped racing the bike forward and stalled, allowing her to coast to a very ungraceful stop about six inches from the edge of the sidewalk.

Mike came running over, a big grin on his face. "Not bad, Beulah!" He clapped her hard on the back. "My wife totally wrecked it the first time she tried it. That was the first time that also ended up being the *last* time she ever rode it."

"Thanks," said Sarah, weakly, wondering why she hadn't peed her pants. She looked down just to be sure she hadn't.

"No prob. Hey, thanks for the cash. I hope your dad's happy with it."

"I'm sure he will be," said Sarah, her heart slowly getting back to its normal rhythm. She reached up a shaking hand and pressed the ignition button, making sure to pull the clutch in first. The engine started right up, rumbling and humming, in a way calling her and daring her to try again.

She gritted her teeth and flared her nostrils, psyching herself up for what had to happen. "I. Can. Do this," she chanted to herself, now seeing the bike as a living breathing thing ... challenging her to try and take it under her control.

She pressed her lips together in concentration and twisted the handle a little, easing up on the clutch and holding her legs out stiffly to the side. The bike pulled smoothly forward, only wavering the tiniest bit. She turned the handles so she could stay in the parking lot and not kill any pedestrians, letting the slow speed take her around to point back towards the car where she was supposed to meet Candi. Her legs relaxed, and she pulled them in to rest on the small black rubber-covered pegs.

She smiled at her newly discovered skills, as she cruised confidently through the lot towards their meeting point at the Camry. She shifted as smooth as silk and let out a whoop of joy over it. For the first time in her life, she totally got why guys were so nuts over motorcycles.

Her joy was short-lived, however. As she drew near the car, she looked up towards the store hoping to see Candi coming out. Her friend was at the door now, the duffle bag full and on her back. Everything seemed perfect until Sarah noticed who else was there.

The police officer who'd been harassing them in the copy shop was standing at her side, one hand resting on the butt of his gun and the other on the end of his nightstick. "Oh, fuck me," she whispered to herself. *Now what the hell are we going to do?*

Close Call

CANDI STOOD AT THE ENTRANCE to the grocery store in full-on, level-ten panic-mode. Her whole body was shaking with nerves, and she had to keep coughing just to keep her throat open. She refused to look at the cop who'd followed her out, knowing if she saw his suspicious eyes she'd probably start crying. She was super close to bawling as it was, and he hadn't done anything except stand in line with her and ask her a bunch of questions about what she'd been doing in town and where she lived.

"I'll walk you to your car. Can I carry that for you?" he asked, gesturing to the duffle bag she'd slung across her back.

"No, thanks. I'm walking. No car."

"But I thought you said you were driving back home today. You must have a car somewhere."

"Yeah, we do. But not here. We walked here. From where we're staying."

"Oh. Where are you staying? At a hotel?"

Candi breathed out a loud sigh. "No. Not at a hotel." She searched the lot for Sarah, but couldn't see her. There were too many cars blocking her view. She could hear what sounded like a motorcycle somewhere, but she had no idea if it was Sarah out there or just someone else who couldn't help her get out of this mess.

"So where are you staying then?"

Candi tried to think of a lie, but they just weren't coming anymore. She'd pulled all kinds of facts about San Francisco out of her butt to answer his earlier questions, garbage based on stuff she'd seen in movies, but she was totally tapped out now. Her lying reservoir was dry.

She turned to face him, angry that he'd pushed her to this point. "What difference does it make? I mean, *really?"*

He stared at her, his head jerking back a little in surprise. "No difference. I was just curious."

"Yeah, well, your *curiosity* is starting to feel like an interrogation. Do you mind?" Candi was shaking so bad her voice was coming out all funny.

He shifted his weight to rest on his right leg. "No, I don't mind. But it seems you do."

Candi frowned at him, channeling as much pissed-off-Sarah-Peterson vibe as she could into her body. Her voice sounded stronger now. "Yeah. As a matter of fact, I *do* mind. I'm allowed to walk around a town as a tourist and buy some stupid groceries without being harassed by local law enforcement, aren't I?"

He nodded slowly. "In most cases, yes. But in some cases, no."

"Like what kind of cases?" she asked, shooting for distain and arrogance in her tone, but not sure if she'd pulled it off or not. Mostly she just felt terrified.

"Well, if you're a minor and you're supposed to be in school, that's a problem. If you're a runaway, that's also a problem."

She snorted. *"Pfft.* Yeah, right. Whatever. Just ... whatever. Leave me alone. I'm busy, and I'm not doing anything wrong. I'm an American citizen, and I have a right to do what I want and not be bothered with a million questions."

He opened his mouth to say something else, but the roar of a nearby motorcycle cut him off.

Candi didn't know whether to cry with joy or fall into hysterics with the fear that overcame her when Sarah pulled up alongside them riding a big, black, and very loud motorcycle. If it hadn't been for her friend's ridiculous Wal-Mart shorts, Candi wouldn't have even recognized her with that helmet on. She looked like a giant, skinny bug.

"Ready to go?!" yelled Sarah, flipping up her visor and then reaching behind her to wrestle the other helmet off the back.

Candi nodded, feeling numb to the bone. She decided neither crying nor hysterics were going to work now. She just had to go into robo-mode and block out all ideas of fear or pain until they were far, far away. She'd fall apart completely when it was safe to do it.

She took the helmet from Sarah and pulled it down over her head, her shaking fingers unable to get the buckle under her chin right. She gave up trying to fix it and adjusted the duffle bag on her back so it was as centered as possible. Steadying herself on one leg, she swung the other over, climbing onto the back of the bike and sliding forward until she was pressed up against Sarah's back. She wrapped her arms around Sarah's middle, put her foot up on the pegs Sarah had pulled down with her toes, and nodded. "Let's go."

Sarah looked at the police officer who was still standing on the sidewalk, now with a slightly stunned look on his face. "See ya later, Officer Feel Good." She smacked her visor down and roared away from the curb. The bike swayed enough to elicit a scream of terror from Candi's mouth before it finally straightened out. Sarah weaved it smoothly through the lanes of parked cars to the road that awaited just beyond the plaza.

"Is he following us?" screeched Candi, her hands in fists as they squeezed Sarah's shirt for all they were worth.

"He can try," said Sarah, twisting her right hand backwards and sending the bike lurching out into traffic. She was headed in the opposite direction they needed to be going in to get back to the cabin. "But he won't be able to catch us."

Candi squeezed her eyes shut and gripped Sarah's abdomen as tight as she could without taking her friend's breath away. The wind was buffeting her body, and the constant roaring of the engine filled her ears, but the only thing she could think to do was pray. Words she hadn't spoken since the second grade in Sunday school came flooding into her mind: *Our Father, who art in heaven, hallowed be they name ...*

*****

Jonathan heard the drone of a motor off in the distance. He was working with the dogs on basic obedience commands, learning in pretty short order that Xena was highly-trained and that James really wasn't at all. He'd spent over an hour trying to get James to focus on the commands for sit and stay. Jonathan hadn't done this kind of work in a long time, but he didn't recall it being this difficult before.

As soon as James realized Jonathan's attention was diverted by the approaching engine, he took off running towards the sound, barking.

Jonathan sighed. *So much for stealth.*

Kevin came walking out of the woods, holding a bow and a quiver of arrows. He'd been practicing for hours, working on just hitting the target at all. Archery was a lot more difficult than it seemed in the movies. Jonathan had tried but eventually gave up in favor of training the dogs.

"That them, you think?" he asked.

"Yeah. But I only hear the motorcycle and not the car. Maybe Candi pulled ahead."

The vision of the girls appeared from around the corner. "Or maybe there is no car anymore," said Kevin, watching as the black motorcycle with two riders entered the weed-filled yard that surrounded the house and eventually came to a stop at the bottom of the stairs. The driver shut off the engine and pulled off her helmet, letting it dangle from her fingers at her side. The passenger climbed off the bike and then fell down in the weeds at her feet, unmoving. The duffle bag sat on her back, looking as if it had just tackled her and taken her out.

Kevin leaped down the stairs in one huge step, Jonathan right on his heels.

"Sarah!" Jonathan shouted at his girlfriend, who sat straddling the machine with a big smile on her face. She hooked the helmet strap over the handle bar and ran her fingers through her hair.

"Candi, what's wrong?" asked Kevin, concern making him sound angry. He reached her side and gently rolled her over onto her back, pushing the duffle bag off to the ground nearby. She was shuddering on the ground, as if having small seizures. "What'd you do?" he growled at his sister before pulling Candi up by the armpits to get her to stand.

"I didn't do anything. She's just having a panic attack or

something." Sarah swung her leg off the bike and pushed the kickstand down. She held onto the handles and tested the strength of the stand a little before letting go. When she seemed assured it wouldn't fall, she released her grip and turned to face Jonathan, her face practically glowing with happiness.

"Where's the car?" asked Jonathan, stunned to say the least. He wasn't able to compute exactly what was happening yet; he needed more facts.

"The car is in the grocery store parking lot where it probably needs to stay. We had to outrun a cop to get back here un-arrested."

"What?" asked Jonathan, his voice going up a higher level than normal.

Kevin was trying to get Candi's helmet off, but she wasn't helping so it seemed to be stuck.

"I *said* we had to outrun a cop. It was no big deal, though. He totally ate our dust."

"Help me get this off of her," said Kevin, speaking loudly to be heard over Candi's weird moaning.

Before Jonathan could comply, Sarah walked over with her finger held out. "All you have to do is press her release valve."

Sarah hadn't even closed half the distance between them before Candi had gripped the side of her helmet, pushed it off her head, and dropped it to the ground. "Touch me with that finger, and I'll punch your lights out!" screeched Candi, putting her fists up like she was ready to fight.

"Hey, hey, heeyyyy," said Kevin, pulling her up against his body, "what's going on here?"

Candi started bawling into his chest, her arms falling limply to her sides.

Sarah turned, smiling again. "See? I told you she was fine." She walked over to join Jonathan.

"She doesn't look fine to me," said Jonathan, frowning at his sister who was now being carried up the porch steps to the cabin.

Sarah took his hand and laced her fingers through his. "Trust me. She just had a little bit of a close-call with this nosy cop who made her tell like a hundred lies, and it finally just broke her. I got there just in time to keep her from spilling the beans."

Sarah walked, dragging him over to the bike. "See what we got? Nice, right? Fifteen hundred bucks. It's worth at least twice that, maybe more. The title and registration are in that bag there."

Jonathan nodded, a little numb right now over the mixed-up facts zipping around in his brain trying to connect themselves to each other into a cohesive story. Sarah let go of his hand to pick up the duffle bag. She handed it to him, and he was surprised to see how heavy it was.

"Those are the groceries. There's some meat in there and there *were* some eggs, but they're probably broken now thanks to Candi's breakdown." Sarah sighed loudly. "Total bummer, right? I was so looking forward to an omelette."

Jonathan followed her quietly into the cabin, trying to unzip the bag as they went. "So what exactly happened with the car? Did you get pulled over?" When he reached the kitchen he set the groceries gently down on the counter.

"No. It's just parked in the lot; but the cop that was dogging us is probably going to figure out it's ours and stolen before we can get back to it. I'll bet it's the only one in the whole stupid lot with out-of-state plates on it."

Jonathan didn't know quite what to say, so he started unpacking the duffle bag. Sarah helped him in companionable silence. Jonathan examined each item as he put it down. He saw nothing wrong with anything there; Sarah had done a good job with the budget as far as he was concerned. "Lots of pasta and rice. Good idea."

"Thanks," said Sarah, leaning over to kiss him on the cheek. "I did the list. Candi stuck to the budget perfectly."

"And you found a motorcycle that seems to run fine, for a great price." Jonathan nodded in respect. "I guess the mission was mostly a success."

"Yep. We just kind of screwed up the car thing, but that's better than not getting the motorcycle or getting arrested."

"Sure. Maybe."

Sarah smacked him on the arm. "Hey!"

Jonathan rubbed it to get the sting to go away. "Well, I am a little concerned ... not only with Candi's obvious issues, but also with that car being left there. I really think we need to go back and get it before the police officer figures out it's stolen. If he connects that car to you two, I really doubt that we'll be able to live here for very long without being caught."

Sarah frowned. "He *was* overly persistent, actually. The guy was a total donkey butt, following us around and asking all kinds of questions about where we were from and what we were doing there."

"I need to talk to Kevin. Will you put these things away for us?"

Sarah patted his cheek. "Sure, babe. No problem." As he walked away, he heard her opening a box of crackers that he knew she used to calm her stomach. A glance back told him Xena was going to wait at her feet, hoping for some crumbs to drop.

Jonathan climbed the stairs to the loft bedroom, James at his heels. He knocked lightly, waiting until Kevin told him to come in before entering. He found Candi in bed with Kevin spooning her. She sniffed when Jonathan walked over, but at least she wasn't crying or moaning anymore.

"Hi," Jonathan said, sitting down on the edge of the bed nearest his sister. "How are you feeling?"

"Like crap, thank you very much."

"Shhhh, you're fine," urged Kevin, "just a little freaked out, which is understandable." He squeezed her three times fast. "Come on, babe, you're fine. You made it back here, mission accomplished, and you did it without our help. You're amazing."

"No, we aren't amazing. We left the stupid car there and had to outrun a police officer who was suspicious of us from the minute he saw us. He's not going to give up until he finds us, and this town is too friggin small to hide in for longer than a couple days."

Jonathan felt a small spark of fear over their situation. He had to do something to fix it so he could concentrate on other things. "I'm not exactly sure what happened, but I'm thinking that Kevin and I need to go into town right now and see what we can do about getting the car back."

"I agree," said Kevin, sitting up.

Candi's hand shot out and grabbed his wrist. "Don't leave me."

Kevin leaned down and kissed her cheek. "I'll be back soon. Just take a nap. I think you're exhausted."

"I'm too sick to take a nap. Sick to my stomach."

"Jesus, I hope you're not pregnant too," said Kevin, stark fear flashing across his face.

Candi slapped him on the arm. "I'm not pregnant, idiot. I'm

just freaked out, okay?"

Kevin put his hand on his chest. "Thank all the holy things in this world. One morning-sick chick is about all I can handle." He patted her leg before getting out of the bed. "Rest until your stomach feels better, have some lunch, and by then we'll be back."

"Did you hide the hotwiring job we did when you parked the car?" asked Jonathan.

"Yes, of course I did."

"Okay. Don't get offended, I was just asking."

Candi sat up, her funny hair sticking out in all directions. Jonathan schooled his features to look normal. He knew if she looked at her hair right now or knew that it looked like this, she'd probably go right over the edge.

"The car is parked just a few spaces from the front door of the market. I'm not sure if that cop will go back there or if he's even still there. It's not like he chased us out of the lot or anything. We left him standing on the sidewalk. And Sarah did the smart thing - she left going in the wrong direction to throw him off. She got back in the right direction by taking some side roads, so if he followed us at all, he's probably going in the wrong direction."

Jonathan nodded, proud of his girlfriend's evasive maneuvers. She was really good at thinking on her feet. He hoped their child inherited whatever gene in her DNA sequence that was responsible for that type of brain development. "Ready?" he asked Kevin, patting his sister's arm a couple times before walking to the door.

"Yep. I just gotta take a leak first. Meet you outside."

Jonathan nodded, walking down to the kitchen where he found all the food still out on the counter and Sarah happily munching away on crackers. There were crumbs all over the counter. He cleared his throat, wondering how he could say what he needed to without getting her mad.

"Don't even open that mouth of yours," she said, spraying some crumbs out of her mouth onto the table. "I know exactly what you're thinking. Don't worry about it. I'll clean up my mess before Sugar Lump gets out of bed."

"Will you put away the groceries too?"

"Yes, yes, yes..." She waved him away. "Go save our butts. I'll take care of the groceries and the shivering hunk of nerves in the other room."

Jonathan walked over and kissed Sarah on the head. "Be gentle with her, okay? I think she's really scared."

"I'm more the tough love type," said Sarah, sounding grouchy now.

"I know. And usually that works. But this time, I'm not sure it's the best course of action."

"Just go get the car. Everything's going to be fine as long as you get back without being caught." She stood, brushing crumbs off her lips and puckering them up for a kiss.

Jonathan complied, resisting the urge to pull her close for a more thorough coupling. She always knew how to get his engine revving.

The sound of a real engine growling caught his attention. "I think we have to go now."

"Be safe," she said, smacking him on the butt before letting him go.

"I will. You too. Maybe keep the dogs inside while we're gone."

Sarah nodded, whistling so James would come in from the

porch. Xena was still standing at her feet. Jonathan turned on his way down the stairs, happy to see both dogs on either side of Sarah, inside the screen door. If nothing else, he knew James would bark like a mad dog if anyone came anywhere near the cabin.

*****

Kevin had only ridden a motorcycle once before, so he was no expert on the machines or anything. But he didn't need to be, to know he was taking one sweet ride on this bike that the girls had bought. It purred like a big cat and had incredible power. He'd goofed around a couple times on Jonathan's girly scooter for fun, but it had nothing on this beast. He smiled at the scenery going by in a blur. Jonathan was yelling at the side of his head, and he had to strain to hear him through the thick helmet.

"I think you should stop down the road from the plaza! I'll walk to the car. I'm going to leave in the wrong direction like Sarah did. You follow on the bike and make sure no one is following the car, okay?"

Kevin nodded. "Yeah! Good plan! Take some neighborhood streets! It'll be harder for someone to follow you and not be noticed in there!"

"Okay! Better pull over soon!"

They had reached the main part of town and Kevin could see the sign announcing the entrance to the plaza not far ahead. He pulled into a gas station and looked down at the gas gauge. He stopped at the pumps, shutting down the engine.

Jonathan got off the bike and took the helmet from his head. He studied the back of the bike for a minute before messing with some elastic straps back there that would secure his safety gear. "Are you going to get some gas?" he asked when he was done.

"Yeah. Might as well. It's pretty low."

"You have money?"

"Yep. I got it covered. So you're going to go down there and get the car and take off that direction, right?" Kevin nodded towards the opposite side of the plaza.

"Yes. I'll go in a store of the plaza first and watch the car for a few minutes to be sure it's safe to go up to it. If it looks like it's all clear, I'll get in and start it up and drive out."

"I'll follow you like two blocks back. If I see anyone following you, I'll try and do something to get them off you and onto me; then I'll lose 'em."

Jonathan frowned. "Are you sure that's a good idea?"

"You have a better one?"

"Well, if someone's following me - which I'll assume that would be a police officer because I don't know who else would follow me - perhaps I'm better off just getting out of the car and running."

"Nah, man. If you do that, they'll have the car and probably figure out we're here. We've blown too much of our wad on the rental of that cabin. We can't afford to leave it and find another place. We'd have to stay in a friggin abandoned building or something, and Sarah won't be good there."

"No," agreed Jonathan. "I wouldn't want her in a place like that. Candi either. There could be asbestos dust and rats carrying bacteria and who knows what else."

"Exactly. So if you're followed, I'm gonna come by and do what I can to get in between you and the cop and give you a chance to get away."

"Okay. And if that fails, I'm going to jump out of the car and hope you can swing by in time to pick me up. If not, I'll walk back to the cabin."

"That's a long walk, man."

"Yes, but it's manageable. I have my Wal-Mart running shoes on. I can jog most of the way."

"Good. We have a plan. And if nothing else works, if everything just goes in the crapper, say what the fuck and just go for it."

Jonathan nodded absently and started jogging away. Kevin walked towards the store so he could pre-pay for his gas. Before he got to the door, Jonathan turned and yelled, "What exactly does that mean?!"

Kevin laughed. "Whatever you want it to mean!" He shook his head at Jonathan's expression. The dude was going to try and figure that out the entire way back to the car - maybe even all the way back to the cabin. He hoped it wasn't going to distract him from what they needed to get done.

*****

Jonathan stood in the thrift shop near the window, keeping an eye on the car. He was holding a small elephant, turning it over and over in his hand, when a lady came up to him.

"Are you interested in purchasing that? It's only a dollar. All of our profits go to charity."

Jonathan looked away from the car. "Uhhh ... yeah." He pulled a dollar out of his pocket and handed it to her.

"Stay right there, and I'll get you a receipt."

"Oh, I don't need one. That's okay." He shoved the little porcelain figurine into his pocket, turning back to the parking lot. So far there'd been no activity out there, other than shoppers coming and going. *Might as well get this over with.* He looked back at the lady who was standing behind the cash register, ringing up his purchase. He waved goodbye when she looked over, and she smiled in return. *Nice people in this town. I hope she doesn't think I was going to rob the store.* His behavior was pretty suspicious. He was glad to be leaving and doing something to fix their situation.

He counted his steps as he walked around the plaza sidewalk. At first he was just going to make a bee-line to the car, knowing the shortest distance between two points was a straight line. But on a whim he decided to go a more circuitous route. It was less obvious that way. As he reached the door of the grocery store, he was preparing to leave the sidewalk when he glanced at the glass entrance and noticed a police officer standing inside. Jonathan might have just ignored him and continued on his mission, except for one thing: he was just standing there, staring out into the parking lot. Jonathan's blood ran cold. *It has to be the guy that Sarah was talking about.* He wasn't looking at the Camry right now, but he was definitely looking for something.

Jonathan didn't know what to do. He could try and wait him out, but he didn't look like he was going anywhere anytime soon. And Kevin wasn't there to help him put together a plan. He needed more time to analyze the situation and come up with a solution. And the first step was to stop standing there in one spot staring at the guy. He forced his feet to move in the one direction they didn't want to go - towards the police officer.

He entered the store, barely sparing the man a glance. He took a hand basket from a stack, not five feet from the guy's back. The officer glanced at him and nodded briefly in greeting before returning to staring out the window.

Jonathan walked away, headed for the aisle farthest on the left, his mind churning out idea after idea. *Hostage situation? No, absolutely not. Do not involve innocent strangers. Leave the car? No.*

He's definitely looking out into that lot for a reason. I don't know for sure if he knows the Camry belongs to the girls. Maybe he's not even looking for them or anything else. Maybe he's just bored. Maybe he's doing security for the store. But no matter what, I have to get the car out of there. If there's a chance he hasn't run the plates and hasn't figured out it's stolen, I can't give him time to do that. What I need is a distraction.

Jonathan put together a plan based on his last coherent thought, racing through the aisles as fast as he could without calling too much attention to himself. *Paper towels and diapers ... check!* He held the two packages together as closely as possible, hoping if there were any cameras that they would only see one item in his hands.

He entered the hardware aisle, relieved to see he was alone - at least for now. Scanning the ceiling above him, he didn't see any cameras that could identify him in this aisle. He figured the store probably had them somewhere; it seemed like everyone did these days. But at least none of them would catch him doing this deed.

He put the paper towels down on the ground, tucking the diapers under his arm. He reached over and took a bottle of lighter fluid off the shelf, opening it quickly and spraying several ounces of its contents all over the paper towel package. A group of lighters was hanging from a hook display on the aisle, so he quickly pulled one down, tore the packaging open, and flicked the lighter on. He leaned down and touched the flame to a splattering of the fluid on the ground, and it immediately caught fire.

He didn't stick around to see what was going to happen. He raced to the end of the aisle and then casually turned the corner, going down three aisles before turning back the other direction, headed towards the cash registers. He pulled a random can of something off the shelf and proceeded to the nearest line. Luckily it was empty. He tried not to scream with the pent-up anxiety that was making his heart race and his sweat glands go into overdrive, but it was nearly impossible. He tapped his foot on the floor over and over to try and give himself some sort of pressure relief. The lady who was scanning his two items looked at him funny.

Jonathan smiled. "I have a baby."

She raised an eyebrow.

"At home. It's not just mine. It's my girlfriend's too."

She gave him a smile that didn't reach her eyes. "That's nice. That'll be fourteen dollars and eighty-two cents."

Jonathan's eyes widened. "Wow. Those are expensive."

She said nothing, just waited for him to pay.

He handed her a twenty-dollar bill, wondering when someone was going to discover the burning mass of plastic and paper towels he'd left behind.

Just as she was counting out his change, someone screamed. "Fire!"

He'd been expecting something like that, but it still made him jump in fright.

"What?" said the lady, frowning, looking out into the store, her hand frozen over her open register drawer.

"There's a fire over here in the hardware aisle!" yelled a lady. "Fire! Fire!"

A couple of men who'd been standing at the customer service desk left their posts and ran in the direction of the yelling.

Jonathan grabbed his bag and headed towards the exit.

"Wait! You forgot your change!"

"There's a fire! I need to evacuate!" he yelled back, wanting to run, but making himself walk fast instead. The police officer who'd been standing at the door ran past him as he approached. As soon as he was gone, Jonathan ran for the parking lot.

He didn't bother to look if anyone was watching or coming for him. He opened the door, and threw the diapers into the front passenger seat. After getting in, he pulled out the ignition assembly that Candi had placed back in its spot to make it more difficult to see that it had been taken apart. He reached inside the small hole on the steering column and pulled out the two wires that had been secured together with the black electrical tape. Taking out the third wire, he touched the tip of it to the others that had just a very small metal end exposed.

The engine tried to turn over once, twice, and then finally on the third attempt roared to life. Jonathan quickly attached his seatbelt, put the car into reverse, and started to back out. He yelped when a car came zooming past him, slamming on the brakes. It seemed like everyone who'd been in the store was deciding to leave at the exact same time. It was a mass exodus from the plaza. He had to wait for two more cars to go past before he could back out. He looked in his rearview mirror as he pulled out, noticing the police officer running out and over to his car that was parked at the curb about twenty yards away from the entrance.

*****

Kevin watched in confusion as a whole bunch of cars started pulling out of the plaza parking lot. In the last fifteen minutes he'd watched as one or maybe two would leave and then be replaced by another one coming in; but now it was crazy. And they weren't just exiting leisurely, either. They were zooming out of there like they were running from a terrorist.

The distant wailing of a siren came to his ear.

What the hell? Before Kevin could put everything together, the Camry came out of the parking lot, hot on the tail of an SUV in front of it. He watched as Jonathan made a hard left and then a right as he swerved out into traffic and around a slower moving vehicle.

Kevin started the bike and pushed down his visor, signaling his entrance into traffic. He needed to go now if he was going to be able to tail him effectively. For some reason, Jonathan was driving like an idiot; and if he kept it up, he was going to get so far ahead Kevin would lose him.

As he pulled the motorcycle out into the right lane, it became suddenly clear why Jonathan was in such a hurry. A cop car came out of the plaza going in the same direction Jonathan had. His lights weren't on, but he sure looked determined. He weaved around the same cars that had been holding Jonathan back.

"Oh, shit, dude ... you're being followed." Kevin wished he had a phone to call Jon or text him with. He twisted the right handle back and gave the bike more gas. *Time to get busy.* He changed lanes left then right and then left again, getting closer and closer to the back of the police car that was most definitely trailing Jonathan.

*****

Jonathan checked his rearview mirror and almost had what felt like a stroke when he saw the marked law enforcement vehicle about three car-lengths back. "Oh, crud. What do I do now?" He was about to look away when a quick flash of movement caught his eye. *Kevin.*

Jonathan kept going in the direction that would take him

farther and farther away from the cabin and the girls. No matter what, he couldn't let them get caught with him and Kevin. If he could help it, he'd make sure Kevin didn't get caught either. Not all of them had to sacrifice to save the others. Maybe it could be just him. He sped up, preparing to turn into a neighborhood that he prayed would have a way out and not leave him stuck in a cul-de-sac.

*****

Jonathan was pulling ahead. Kevin prayed he was reading the kid's mind and knew exactly what he was going to do. *That's right, Jon. Get in that neighborhood and lose the cop. I'll be right behind you.* A plan was forming in Kevin's head as he accelerated forward, getting closer and closer to the cop car.

Jonathan turned into the neighborhood, right on cue. A few seconds behind him, the police officer pulled in, too. Kevin raced ahead, passing three cars and cutting the last one off to join Jonathan and his pursuer. He didn't think the police officer had noticed. His eyes never even went to his rearview mirror to see who was behind him. He was obviously too intent on what was in front of him.

Two blocks up ahead, Jonathan went left. Kevin nailed the accelerator, taking the left turn one block ahead of the one Jon had taken, temporarily abandoning his pursuit of the cop car. He pushed the bike to the limit, going so fast it made his stomach turn with crazed butterflies.

He didn't even stop at the stop sign; he just leaned the bike hard to the right until it was nearly to the ground, racing to beat Jonathan to the next intersection.

He got there at exactly the same time as Jonathan and nodded once at his friend's shocked expression. As soon as

Jonathan was through the intersection of the four-way stop, Kevin took a left, pulling in behind him. His rearview mirror revealed the police officer coming to a stop at the sign. "Go, Jonathan, go!" he yelled, knowing Jonathan couldn't hear him, but praying he'd figure out what the plan was anyway. He slowed way down, forcing the police officer who'd come up behind him to do the same.

*****

It took Jonathan a minute to figure out what the heck Kevin was doing, but as soon as he saw him slow down and become a barrier between himself and the police officer, he knew what he had to do. He accelerated, taking one quick turn and then another, until there was enough space between them that he could take a chance at evading the officer.

He pulled out into busy traffic and raced across all four lanes to enter a neighborhood on the other side of the main road. He was into it and turning right before the police car even made it to the turn that would take him over to the busy road. Jonathan made three more turns and then pulled the car back out onto the main road, headed in the direction of the cabin. He had to take the chance and just get the heck out of town before the cop came cruising around and accidentally caught up to him again. Hopefully, the guy would go in the other direction, the one they'd been going in each time he'd seen them.

Jonathan checked his rearview mirror over and over again, desperately hoping to see Kevin, but there was nothing but nondescript civilian cars there. Eventually, he made it out of town and was only minutes from the cabin.

The whole time he was driving his mind was racing through every scenario he could imagine of what might have happened.

Kevin was driving a much faster vehicle than Jonathan was, and he should have caught up by now.

Jonathan's throat burned, and he had to keep swiping at his eyes, as he considered the outcome of Kevin having been arrested and brought to jail. Jonathan knew the chances of Kevin holding out and keeping his identity secret were slim. And that meant only one thing: Kevin was going to be killed, and probably within the next forty-eight hours.

*****

Kevin could see that the cop behind him was frustrated. His head bobbed left and right as he tried to keep an eye on the Camry. Luckily, Jonathan had done his part and had sped ahead. With Kevin running interference, Jon had a decent chance of getting out of this mess - but only if the cop didn't throw on his lights and go around Kevin. The situation reminded him of rugby. Jonathan had the ball and this cop was on the other team, trying to tackle him. Kevin had to do whatever it took to keep his opponent clear and give Jonathan a chance to make it to the in-goal area so he could get the Try and the points for it - freedom, in this case.

Jonathan turned out of sight, and soon after, the cop put on his lights.

Kevin ignored him, swerving out to the left a little when the police officer tried to go around him. *Go, Jon, go!* yelled Kevin in his head. He couldn't see the Camry anymore, but it couldn't be that far ahead yet. There hadn't been enough time. Once more, the cop tried to go around, and Kevin swung out. He turned his head back a few times, trying to give the guy the impression he was nervous. *Just a few more seconds. Come on, Jon, come on, dude! Put the pedal to the metal and get the hell out of here!*

A loud warning siren blasted out behind him and then shut

off. Kevin turned again to look over his shoulder and slowed even more, acting like he was looking for a place to pull over.

Another siren blast came, followed by a voice over a speaker. "Pull your motorcycle over to the right and shut off your engine. Remain seated on the bike."

Kevin complied, knowing he'd done everything he could to get Jonathan to safety. His heart was hammering in his chest as if he'd actually run all those miles he'd just driven, on a rugby field. He felt both triumphant and scared to death. The fact that this could be the beginning of the end of his life was freaking him out. His survival instinct was humming, telling him he wasn't ready to die. He wasn't ready to just follow the hangman to the gallows. He had to think of a way out of this. Whatever it took, he was going to do it.

The police officer sat in his car, talking on the radio to someone. After a couple of minutes that felt more like an hour, he got out of the car with a small clipboard in his hand. Kevin waited, flexing his hands over and over on the handles, trying to work off the nervous energy that had his muscles jumping.

"Good afternoon," said the cop, drawing up next to him.

Kevin nodded. "Afternoon."

"Do you know why I pulled you over?"

"Uh, no. I wasn't speeding, I know that. And I used my turn-signals."

"Yes, you are correct. But you were impeding the flow of traffic to begin with, and then when I signaled to go around you, you blocked my progress. Now, why would you do that?"

"I don't know what you're talking about, officer." Kevin was making stuff up as he went along. The officer's statements were giving him just the tiniest bit of hope that he might get out of this.

"I was just driving along, and then all of a sudden you were tailgating me. It kind of freaked me out, if you want to know the truth."

"You swerved out to block me," said the officer, now sounding irritated.

"No, I didn't. I looked over my shoulder to see who was on my tail, possibly going to knock me off my bike, and I realized it was you back there. Then I got a little freaked out that a cop was there trying to run me over."

"License and registration, please."

Fuck me. "Can I get off the bike to get it for you? It's in my bag."

"Go ahead. Take your helmet off, too."

Kevin took the helmet off and put it on the back of the bike, balancing it so he could grab it if necessary. He unzipped the pouch he'd gone through thoroughly while he was waiting at the gas station and pulled out the papers inside. "Here's the registration." He handed it over and then dug through the bag some more. He felt around in his back pocket and mimed a very upset expression. "Shit, man. I left my wallet at home."

The officer lifted an eyebrow. "You left your wallet at home? Does that mean you have no license?"

"No, man. It means I have a license, but I left it at home."

"Give me your full name."

Kevin smiled. "Mike. Michael Hart. Do you need my address? I can give that to you now too if you want."

"Yeah, go ahead." The cop stood ready with his pen poised above his clipboard.

"One-one-zero Maple Drive. It's in town here." He gave the officer the zip code and then coughed, trying to hide the satisfaction he was experiencing from knowing that he'd done the right thing by memorizing that stuff off the registration. At the time he'd thought he was being overly paranoid. He should have known his instinct to expect the worst would be right on target.

"Stay here. I'll be back in a few minutes."

Kevin nodded. He watched the officer go back to his car, and after a minute or so, got back on the motorcycle. The cop was going to run the registration, but hopefully that wouldn't cause any problems. It was the license issue that had Kevin freaking out. He didn't know what the cop's computer could do from his car - maybe nothing, maybe everything. But there was no point worrying about any of it until the officer made a move. Kevin knew he needed to keep as calm as possible so he would have the energy he needed to do what needed to be done.

He took the helmet and held it in his lap. It was in pretty good shape, obviously never having been in an accident. One hand stroked its shiny surface, while the other reached up to adjust the handles of the bike a little so he could watch the officer in his mirrors. The guy was talking on his radio and then writing some stuff down.

After a while, the officer got out of the car and came walking over. "Son ... we have a little problem. You want to step over to my vehicle with me for a minute?"

Kevin's heart stopped beating for a few seconds, and the blood drained from his face. He shrugged to act all nonchalant while the rest of his body tried to get back to functioning again. *Heartbeat re-engaged.* He got off the bike and put the helmet on the seat. "Sure," he said, his voice sounding gruff. *What is it? It's the license thing; I know it is. I should have just taken off. Dammit!*

The officer leaned into his car and pulled his laptop out a

little so it was hovering on a platform over his seat. "You see this picture?" He pointed to the screen where the image of a driver's license was sitting, blown up to super-size.

"Yeah."

"That's not you."

"Yeah, I can see that. So?" *Stay calm. Stay cool. Act like he's the idiot.*

The officer looked at him and frowned. "It's supposed to be you."

"Says who?"

"Says the Department of Motor Vehicles, that's who."

"What? I don't get it." *Frown. Look confused. Look innocent!*

The officer gestured angrily at the screen. "That's your driver license, but that's not you!"

"Dude, it's *not* my driver's license. Anyone can see that. The picture is of some other guy I've never seen before." Kevin shook his head. "Is this some kind of joke?" He paused and then smiled hugely. "Oh ... wait ... I get it. You're punking me, aren't you?" He looked around as if searching for hidden cameras. Kevin raised his voice, yelling out to the nearby houses. "Alright, assholes ... you can come out now! You got me! I fell for it!" Kevin looked back at the cop, still smiling big. "Those guys are such dicks. I can't believe they got you to go along with it. Did they pay you, or what?"

"Mister Hart, this is not a joke, and you're not being punked. Please go back to your vehicle and wait for me. I need to make some calls and get to the bottom of this."

Kevin shrugged. "Yeah, sure. Whatever you say." He looked around and yelled out one more time to make it look as convincing as possible. "Fuck you, Barry! Kiss my ass, Bill!"

When he reached the bike he got on it, acting casual, keeping the helmet in his lap. He watched as the cop got into his car and put a cell phone to his head.

What the hell should I do? Take off? Wait and see what happens? He decided pretty quickly that waiting would be a bad idea. The guy was going to call for backup or maybe even call this guy Mike's house, and then he'd be screwed. That left only one solution. He had to go for it.

He took one last look in his rearview mirror and made his decision. He lifted the helmet up to his head, slammed it down, turned the key in the ignition, and pressed the gray button. He was shooting off like a rocket and halfway into his first turn before the cop even realized what was happening.

Kevin leaned into every turn like he was on a racetrack. In and out of neighborhoods, over curbs and yards, he did everything he could to shorten his path to freedom and put as much distance between himself and the friggin persistent-as-hell cop behind him. He cut through residential and business areas, even hiding for a while behind some warehouses. Eventually he found his way back out onto a main road and left town, going in the opposite direction of the cabin. He had to shut down any chance they'd see him and track him to his family. It was his only option.

*****

Sarah came running out of the cabin as soon as she heard the car. She was so relieved to see Jonathan getting out of the driver's seat, she nearly cried. Her relief turned to worry as soon as she caught a glimpse of his expression.

"What happened?! Where's Kevin?!" she shouted from the stairs.

"I'm not sure. Help me get the car into the shed."

Sarah ran over and helped Jonathan open the doors. She held the one that didn't hang straight to keep it open until he'd pulled the car all the way in. As soon as he was out, they both closed the shed up again, securing the doors with a turn of the handle.

"Come inside. I'll tell you what I know," Jonathan said, his voice without emotion. It made Sarah's queasiness come back full-force.

They went into Candi's room and woke her up. Her hair was a complete mess and her voice was hoarse, but as soon as she heard Kevin hadn't made it back she woke right up, grabbing onto Jonathan's hands. "What happened? Tell me!"

Jonathan pulled himself out of her grip and held up his hands in a calming gesture. "I will. Just relax so I can think it all through. It was a little confusing."

He related the story of the grocery store distraction and Kevin coming to his rescue. Finishing, he said, "So I got away and came here after going through a bunch of neighborhood streets, just making sure I was really alone. But Kevin got left behind, and I don't know whether he tried to outrun the guy or if he's still trying to keep him away from me ... or worse."

"Didn't you guys have a plan?" asked Sarah.

"Yeah, you always have a plan," said Candi. "Always. You would never do anything like that without one."

Jonathan's face turned a little pink. "Yeah, well, we had a plan. I believe it was called a Just-Say-What-The-Fuck plan."

Candi's nose flared. "Don't tell me ... let me guess. That was Kevin's idea, right?"

"Yes, how did you know?"

Candi just shook her head, angry for some reason.

"Are you mad at me?" he asked.

"Yes, of course I am! And at him, too!"

"Why? We did everything we could to do the right thing. It's just that the police officer who latched himself onto you was very persistent with me, too. He waited at that grocery store all that time you were gone. Why would he do that?"

"Maybe he had a hunch," said Sarah. "Cops get those, you know. It's not just in the movies. I guess we're just lucky he didn't call in a bunch of his friends to help him out. Kevin at least has a chance against just one guy."

"You think so?" asked Candi, sounding on the verge of tears.

"Of course," assured Sarah. "Come on, you know Kevin. Would he just walk into some cop's arms and give up?"

Candi shook her head. Jonathan did the same.

"Right. So we just keep doing what we're doing, and hopefully he'll get his butt back here in a little while."

"And if he doesn't?" asked Candi, her voice sounding annoyingly pitiful.

"Well, I guess we have confidence that he's not an idiot and that he's strong, and he won't give up his name or anything and get sent back home. He'll be safe in jail. Probably safer than we will be sitting out here."

Candi nodded. She didn't look very convinced, but at least she wasn't doing that crazy moaning thing she had been earlier.

"He has the motorcycle," said Jonathan. "I'm sorry we lost it, even if it's only temporarily until he gets back."

"Hey, crap happens," said Sarah, shrugging. "We have enough food to last for at least a week. Maybe more, since Kevin isn't here. We'll be fine. Maybe next time we want to shop we should go the other direction to another town, though."

"How can you be so cold about this?" asked Candi, scowling at Sarah. "Don't you worry about Kevin, about how he's feeling and what's going to happen?" Her voice had a bit of a shriek to it.

Sarah glared at her, pissed Candi would even suggest such a thing about her feelings towards her own twin brother. "I'm not *cold*, Candi. I'm confident. I know my brother. He can handle anything. *You* of all people should know that about him." She threw up her hands and let them slap her thighs when they came down. "For crap's sake ... he punches hammerheads when they come near our boat! He gets cut open by propellers and just keeps pushing through! He can hold his breath underwater longer and run faster than any of us!" She grabbed Candi's shoulders and shook her once. "You just need to stop all that crying and poor-me bullcrap and think positive for a change. Your whiney-baby act is getting seriously old." She let go of Candi - kind of flinging her away lightly - and stepped back, folding her arms over her chest. There was a challenge in her eyes, and she was hoping Candi would take her up on it. The little crybaby needed something to get mad about to wake up her courage and independence. Sarah knew it was in there somewhere.

Candi was the girl who'd fed all of them when they were stranded. She'd taken a bullet and just handled it, even when her stupid boyfriend had crapped all over her. The real Candi needed to stand up and be strong again, or Sarah was going to knock her out; and she wasn't going to feel one bit sorry about it either if she did. Wimps were seriously annoying.

It was so quiet after Sarah's little speech, they could hear

James scratching himself in the other room, his small back paw thumping the ground rhythmically while the opposite one worked on the fur under his chin.

Candi cleared her throat, blinking a couple times before standing straighter. "You're right. I'm sorry for being such a big baby. If anyone can get out of this mess, it's Kevin. I shouldn't have doubted him."

Sarah yanked Candi's little body into a hug, talking over her shoulder. "See? Things are better already. Now I don't have to kick your butt. And you know what?" She pushed Candi away from her and looked her in the eye. "Kevin's Just-Say-What-The-Fuck Plans always work. *Always.*"

"They do?" asked Candi in her pitiful voice again. But then she straightened and said it once more in a confident, strong tone. "They do?"

"Yes. Definitely. So let's focus on getting ready and cleaning and whatever else we can do to get your mind off this. We'll have some dinner, watch some TV or play a card game, and then go to bed. Maybe he'll get here in the next hour or so, and we'll all just laugh about this. Or maybe it'll be in the middle of the night or tomorrow or next week. Whatever. He's going to be okay." Sarah refused to consider any other alternative, knowing it was only this unwavering confidence in his infallibility that was keeping her from turning into a complete mess of unbalanced emotion.

Jonathan nodded. "We have preparations to make in the event we're discovered, and idle minds will be our enemies right now. Worry and anxiety could make solid reasoning an impossibility, and we need to be sharp and on our toes at all times." Jonathan cast a glance down at the pit bull who was lying on the ground nearby, her head resting on her paws. James came walking into the room as if on cue. "I'm going to go work with the dogs and see what I can do about setting up some early warning systems around the cabin. What are you two going to do?"

"We're going to make dinner and clean up. Come back in an hour to eat."

Jonathan nodded, leaning over to grab a quick kiss from his girlfriend's soft lips. He left the two girls together, whistling for the dogs to join him as he walked out the door.

*****

Jonathan spent several minutes walking the perimeter of the cabin with the dogs, talking to them as he went.

"I think if we get a warning about someone coming from this far out it should be enough time to mobilize and be prepared." He crouched down and pointed to the dirt road that was about fifty feet in front of them and then to the cabin, looking at each dog in turn. "See, we don't want anyone getting close to the cabin without us knowing. Stranger danger, do you understand?"

Xena just stared at him as if she were trying really hard to understand. James tilted his head once looking confused for a few seconds before something off to the side caught his attention. He ran over and chased whatever it was through the leaves, disappearing into the trees.

Jonathan shook his head as he reached out and patted Xena on the head. "I'm afraid you're our only hope, Xena. James unfortunately has a pretty serious case of attention deficit disorder. Maybe you're in better shape because you're a mom. You have to be more serious and mature when you're a parent. I think that has a calming effect."

Jonathan was struck by Xena's kind eyes. She just looked at

him as if offering him comfort. At least that was what it felt like, especially when she stepped over and licked his chin a couple times. He rubbed her neck on both sides, digging his fingers into her short fur to make sure to give her a good scratch, too. "Yes, you're a good momma. Just like Sarah's going to be. Strong and loyal and protective. And tough when she needs to be. That's you too, isn't it, Xena? Isn't it, girl?"

She responded enthusiastically, her tail wagging rapidly, moving her hind quarters right along with it. Jonathan patted her one more time before standing. "The question is ... what kind of early warning system would work out here? Let's go into that shed and see what we can find in there to help us." He left the wooded area he'd been traipsing around in and went back to the shed, opening the handle and stepping inside.

The walls were lined with hooks that had all manner of tools and other things hanging from them. There was a dirty workbench in the back against the far wall, and on it were boxes and bins that looked long-forgotten. Squeezing past the side of the car, he made his way to the first dusty box. Inside were stacks of magazines.

"Well, this is no help for anything except maybe keeping the girls busy or starting fires with." He shoved it aside and pulled another box closer. This one was full of metal parts. He took a few rusted things out and studied them. Some he couldn't identify, and others he knew to be things he might find in small motors or even kitchen appliances. Other boxes revealed much of the same thing, all of their contents rusted and none of them usable as any parts for any type of operating machine.

He pushed the last bin back into place on the bench and studied the walls. There were several coils of rope and twine hanging there, an extension cord, a rake, an axe, a saw and a shovel. All of the tools were really old and in need of maintenance. Jonathan climbed over the car to get to the axe and took it down along with the saw. He hefted the chopping tool up, staring at it closely and testing its weight and balance. "At least we can get some firewood prepared if nothing else," said Jonathan to the two dogs who were sitting just outside the entrance of the shed now. James came inside for a few seconds in response to Jonathan's voice, but then ran out again soon after, disappearing around the side of the door.

Jonathan walked back to the house with a tool in each hand, looking out towards the dirt road driveway, wishing it didn't make him feel so empty and scared to not see Kevin driving up on that motorcycle. It was getting dark, and Jonathan strongly suspected that if Kevin could get back, he would have already. Jonathan didn't believe in praying to any deity for help in times of need, but he sure was going to work whatever bit of math and science he knew of into whatever formulas he could come up with to make himself feel better about Kevin's chances of survival. He couldn't bear the thought of losing his best friend and future brother-in-law - which is what Kevin would be someday if Jonathan ever got up the nerve to convince Sarah to marry him.

Safehouse

CANDI LAY ON HER BACK in bed alone, tears dripping silently down her temples and into her hair and ears. Last night Kevin had been in bed with her, and she'd enjoyed it; but she hadn't really fully appreciated how lucky she was to have him there until now. Now that he was gone.

Sarah had been so positive all evening that he'd show, Candi had almost expected him to drive up the dirt road and announce himself before dinner. But then dinner came and went, and then several games of cards were played, before she finally had to admit to herself that no matter how positive they were, Kevin wasn't going to come back. At least not tonight. There was no reason for him to stay gone this long unless there was a good reason, like he'd been arrested.

Candi's mind wandered to the day he'd finally spoken to her in the lunchroom, after they'd returned from the island where they'd been marooned together for so long - days and weeks that had been scary, thrilling, satisfying, and life-changing, all at the same time. He'd avoided her for weeks after returning, looking as if he'd fallen right back into his normal life, the one that hadn't included her or Jonathan. She'd nearly died from the neglect and broken heart. And then he'd been there on bended knee, begging for her forgiveness.

He told her about how scared he'd been when she was shot in the boat - how terrified he was to think he was going to lose her to the grim reaper. He explained how his life had changed, and she realized, listening to him talk, that it had been one of those massive, fundamental shifts in his whole perspective that he'd experienced - maybe more devastating for him than hers or Jonathan's, or maybe even Sarah's had been. Their time together had caused him to question every single thing about himself: his morals, his lifestyle, his friends, his goals, his past, and even his future. What used to seem so important to him had suddenly become empty and disgusting. What he used to blow off or worse, disdain, had become the center of his universe and his reason for being. He told Candi that falling in love with her and then seeing her almost taken from this world had caused something to short-circuit in his brain. So he'd drowned the pain and confusion with familiarity, submersing himself in his old life, trying to get back some control.

She'd accepted his reasons and excuses only because he'd been so sincere; and it hadn't hurt that he'd made such public declarations of his love for her in front of the whole school. But it was only now that she fully appreciated what he'd said. Right now, she'd give anything for some control over her life. It felt like this crazy Russian mobster was maneuvering them around like puppets on strings, as they lived every moment expecting one of his henchmen to come sneaking up with a knife in his hand.

James barking madly at the front door cut off her train of thought like an assassin's blade had just sliced right through it. She jumped out of bed, racing to the door. *Kevin!*

Jonathan was already at the bottom of the stairs, his arm held out to stop her.

She pushed on it, intent on running right past him, but he refused to let her by. He leaned in and whispered in her ear, "Get in the room with Sarah. Lock the door. We don't know who it is yet."

"But I hear the motorcycle!" she nearly screeched.

"You hear *a* motorcycle. Get in the room!"

Candi's heart plummeted. He was right. She ran into the downstairs room and slammed the door behind her.

Sarah was sitting up in bed. The light coming in the window from the moon outlined her sleepy form. "What's up?" she asked drowsily.

"A motorcycle's coming up the road. Jonathan told me to come in here and wait with you. He's going to see if it's Kevin."

"Of course it's Kevin," said Sarah, lying back down. "Does he think a killer's going to ride up making a bunch of noise and announce his arrival? Hey, kids, I'm here to murder you! Wake up!" She snorted once and then quieted down. Candi heard the deep breathing that told her Sarah had already gone back to sleep.

She stood at the door, wanting to be as sure as Sarah that everything was okay so she could run out and welcome Kevin with the fiercest hug she was capable of giving; but Jonathan was right. It was better to be safe than sorry. No one said the bad guys were always going to come with knives. Maybe the next one would be riding a motorcycle and carrying an automatic rifle or handguns strapped inside of his jacket. Anything was possible, and she had to be prepared for that.

The creepy sensation of being a mafia-manipulated puppet slithered over her body again, making her feel like the strings being pulled were slowly moving themselves into position to hang her with an invisible noose. She had to breathe long and deep to move past the feeling of being strangled with fear.

*****

Kevin used the flickering headlamp and the memory he had of the road to lead him back to the cabin. It had been one hell of a long friggin day, and he was exhausted. *Just another hundred yards to go and I'll be home.* The idea of home being a place he barely knew, temporary, a hideout from people like the one who'd dogged him for the last ten hours - either in reality or in his mind - would have been unbearable if it hadn't been for the people waiting there for him. Not only was it his twin sister, carrying his future niece or nephew in her belly, but his best friend Jon, and his girlfriend - Candi - the girl who'd turned his entire world upside down, shaken him out, and put him in a whole other universe filled with love and loyalty like he'd never known before. He'd thought that the true love crap and soul-mates thing was just in the movies, but his feelings for Candi had taught him differently. And he was damn sure not going to lose it if he had anything to say about it. He'd already come close once during their escape from the island. He was still working every day to convince her he should be forgiven for his three weeks of temporary insanity.

The first thing he saw was James, who came tearing out of the darkness to bark at his wheels. "Hey, buddy! James, it's me! Good dog! Good dog to come out here and kick my ass."

James' growl went from vicious to happy, his short sharp barks replacing the hair-raising growly ones he'd used on his approach.

Xena came running out of the cabin as Kevin got closer, his

headlight illuminating her boobs swinging from side to side under her legs. She didn't growl or bark, she just got close enough to trot next to the bike. Kevin could tell she was withholding judgment until he stopped. Clearly, it would only be when he fully identified himself and was accepted by one of the cabin's occupants that he'd be safe to get off the bike, as far as she was concerned. His heart swelled with gratitude for this ugly dog's adoption of the people he loved. Her tattered ears and beaten body took on a new beauty for him in that moment. She was a survivor, and with girls like her on their team, maybe they could be survivors too.

He drew up to the bottom of the stairs, Jonathan coming down to greet him. Kevin shut off the engine and pulled off the sweaty helmet, accepting the embrace his friend offered. They stayed in that position, hugging each other for a few seconds, each of them patting the other hard on the back as they finished and pulled apart.

"Glad you're back, Kevin. You freaked us out being gone so long."

"Where are the girls?"

"I made them stay locked up in Sarah's room, just in case."

Kevin nodded, angry at the idea of a murderer coming after his family while he was gone. He looked down at the pit bull. "Do I pass, Xena? Can I get off the bike and come inside?" He held his hand down for her to check out. She sniffed at him, trotted around the bike once, and then came back and licked his hand. When she was finished with her approval process, she left him to run up the stairs and go inside the cabin.

"I guess that's an affirmative," said Jonathan, taking Kevin's helmet from him. "Come on in. Candi's been having a rough time. You should go see her."

Kevin's throat closed up, thinking about how he must have put her through the wringer being gone so long. He got off the bike, pulling the keys out and handing them to Jonathan who was standing by silently. "Take care of these, would ya?" Kevin was shaking, either from the evening cold or his nerves, he wasn't sure. He'd driven maybe a hundred miles today, getting away from the town and hiding in places he was sure no one would ever look. He tried to be visible in the next town over, letting several police officers see him driving out of town, headed away even farther from the cabin than he already was. And then he'd backtracked, avoiding being seen as much as he could. Anytime he thought a cop might have seen him, he turned around and made sure they saw him going the other way.

It was exhausting because of the effort, but also because the whole time he was doing it, he had no idea if it was helping or hurting them. There'd been no one to bounce ideas off of or share in the responsibility. He used to pride himself in going his own way and being the leader of everything he did. Today he learned that he much preferred the team approach and letting other people who might be more analytical help make the decisions. It was just another reminder for him of how much Jonathan and Candi Buckley had changed his life for the better.

He strode across the wood floor to the door leading to Jonathan and Sarah's room, tapping on the wood. "Candi, it's me. Open up."

The door flew open, and he was immediately tackled by a spider monkey of a girlfriend. It threw him back a few paces, but he steadied himself quickly and gripped onto her as tightly as she did to him.

"Don't you ever do that to me again," she cried into his neck.

"I promise ... I won't," he said, crying a little into hers.

*****

They ate a breakfast of oatmeal together at the table. Candi and Kevin's chairs were touching. They hadn't let each other out of their sight since Kevin had come back last night.

"Thanks, Kevin," said Jonathan. "I know what you did yesterday was difficult and stressful, but I have to think it had some positive benefit. At the very least, you were seen over in that other town by a few cops, so if any of them put together all the pieces of us being together, they'll hopefully assume we're staying somewhere over there and not here."

"Yeah, well, you're welcome; but it's highly possible I was just running from my own shadow. I mean, yeah, I took off on that cop when he was in the middle of busting me, so I'm sure I'm a wanted man now. But all those other cops I thought I saw? Who knows. Maybe they were so busy eating donuts they never even noticed me. I just had to be sure I wasn't leading anyone back here, you know?" He shoved a big scoop of oat cereal into his mouth.

Sarah nodded, waving her spoon at him. "I get it. Totally. You did the right thing. I just wish you'd had a phone so you could have called us and told us what was going on."

"One phone isn't enough," agreed Candi. "Next time we go into a town, we need to buy a second one. I don't know why we didn't before. I mean, we should all have one."

"Too expensive," said Jonathan, shaking his head. "Plus, there would be a big problem if any of us were ever taken into custody. They'd confiscate the phone, trace the numbers it had called before, which would be all of our numbers, and then pinpoint the location of the other phones using satellite technology. We'd be found within an hour."

"Oh," said Candi, sounding deflated. "That would be bad."

"So, one phone it is," said Kevin, leaning back in his chair and rubbing his full stomach. "And whoever gets caught with the phone has to eat the chip inside before anyone can get to it."

Sarah laughed. "What are you talking about?"

"The little chip thing under the battery. Pull it out and eat it. It's the only way."

Candi frowned at him. "The only way to what? I'm not eating that plastic chip."

"Yeah, you've got to. It's the only way to keep them from tracing our steps."

"But we haven't called anyone from here, so we're safe," said Jonathan. "But, you bring up a good point. Where's the phone?"

Sarah pointed to the kitchen. "In that drawer over there."

Jonathan got up and went to the drawer, taking out the only thing linking them to the outside world.

Sarah watched as he pulled the back cover off, took the battery out, and removed the chip underneath. "What'd you do that for?" she asked.

"As long as the phone isn't sending power to this chip, they can't trace it to find us."

"I'm lost," said Candi, sighing loudly. "What'd I miss? Apparently I haven't watched enough spy movies or whatever."

Jonathan came back to the table with all the phone parts in his hand, looking at everyone as he calmly explained. "If they figure out where we went after we left the FBI's safehouse, it will be fairly easy to trace our steps to the cell phone place. If they get there, they could find out what cell phone we bought and what the chip identifier is, and then it's just a simple matter of putting that information into a tracking program. If the chip is live and sending a signal, they'll be able to latch onto it and determine our location. I'm not sure how accurate the location is - maybe it's only to a few-mile radius. But it could be within feet."

"Great. So we have a phone, but we can't use it," said Candi, disgusted.

"It's for emergencies only. And I suggest that we don't use it from here when we do. Only from that other town."

Sarah stood up and went into the kitchen, opening up cabinets.

"What are you doing?" asked Kevin.

"Looking for something ... this," Sarah said, grabbing the small plastic container she'd put away yesterday when she and Candi had been cleaning to get their minds off Kevin being missing. She carried it over to Jonathan and set it down on the table. "Put all the parts in here and then put it back in the drawer. That way if we ever need it, it'll be easy to find and put together."

Jonathan put everything in the container and sealed it up tight. He stared at it for a long time, making Sarah smile.

"What are you thinking right now, babe? That hamster in your head is out of breath."

Jonathan looked up in confusion. "What hamster?"

"The one that runs on a treadmill in your brain, keeping it powered with hamster energy for all that analyzing you're always doing."

"Hamster energy. Hmmm ... an interesting concept. I wonder how much energy they could generate running on a wheel in an average amount of hours a day."

Sarah stood, picking up her empty bowl and his. "Sounds

like a really fun experiment for a much different day. Or not. Speaking of which, what are we doing today?"

"Security detail," said Jonathan firmly as he stood, the box full of telephone pieces in hand. "We have to get this place ready for intruders. I drew up all of the plans last night."

"Where are they?" asked Kevin, moving to the sink to do the dishes. "I'd like to check 'em out."

"They're in my head," said Jonathan.

Sarah leaned over and kissed him on the cheek, taking the sugar off the table so she could put it away in the kitchen. "Of course they are."

"Just read it to me out of your superbrain, then," said Kevin, sudsing up the sponge. "It'll help keep my mind off this woman's work."

The sound of a wet rag snapping on his arm echoed in the room, followed shortly by a very girl-sounding scream. "Aaach! *Shit!* ... Candi! I'm gonna get you back for that, you little punk."

"No, you're not," said Sarah, coming up to stand next to her little red-headed friend. "You have to go through me, first. And you deserved it for that comment."

Kevin looked over his shoulder and shot them both a glare, but they just laughed at him.

Candi held up her hand for a high-five and Sarah happily obliged, declaring, "Kickin' butt and takin' names."

"Taking names but not prisoners," added Candi, smiling and looking like her old self - or at least, her island self, which was the very best version of Candi as far as Sarah was concerned.

"Is it safe for me to come over there?" asked Jonathan. "I'd be happy to help with the dishes, but I'm not really a big fan of the wet-towel-in-the-locker-room game."

"You have a free pass," said Sarah, waving him over. "You know your place in the man-woman hierarchy, so you have nothing to fear."

Jonathan raised an eyebrow as he walked over cautiously, setting the box down on the counter. "I'm afraid to ask, but my curiosity won't let me sleep tonight if I don't." He picked up a dry towel and took the rinsed dish that Kevin handed to him so he could wipe it down. "Please educate me on this concept of man-woman hierarchy. Is that from sociology class? I don't remember it."

"Gender equality in chores. There's no such thing as women's work or men's work. But there are some things we might be more suited to than you, and in those cases, we have veto power."

"Ha! And what areas would those be?" asked Kevin. "Dish washing and toilet cleaning?" He looked at Jonathan and winked. "See? Told ya. Woman's work."

SNAP!

Kevin threw his sponge down. "Dammit, Sarah! I told you ..." He spun around, but stopped when he saw his sister and Candi.

"Take one more step and you're going down," said Candi, twirling the towel in a slow circle below her hand.

"You cracked my ass, Gumdrop?" He almost looked happy about it.

Candi smiled proudly. "You're damn straight I did. And I'll do it again if I have to." She gestured to the sink. "Get back to your washing, boy. We did the cooking, you do the cleaning. Those are the rules."

Kevin smiled devilishly. "You are *so* going down later when

I'm done here."

Candi smiled back, just as evilly as he had. "I look forward to seeing you try."

Sarah leaned over and took the towel from Candi's hand. "Give me that before you get into anymore trouble." She pointed at Kevin. "Seriously, hurry up and finish. We have other work to do, and we need your man-muscles to do it."

Kevin flexed a couple times, sighing with self-love. "Yep, that's what it all comes down to eventually." He went back to soaping the dishes. "You're all about the woman-power until you need some raw man-power. Then you're all back to the helpless chick who needs a real guy to bail her out. Where would they be without us, Jon?"

CRACK!

"God*damn* it!" Kevin yelled, spinning to face the girls. "Sarah!"

Sarah didn't stick around to see if he'd come after her. She sprinted to her bedroom and locked the door behind her, bending over with the giggles that were attacking her as she pictured the look on his stupid face again.

*****

Jonathan stood in the shed, handing out boxes. "Take these and pull out anything that's metal and not too heavy."

Candi was digging through the first box that Kevin had put on the ground next to her. "How heavy is too heavy?" she asked.

"Well, I don't have the exact weight calculated. I could do that if you want me to."

"No, please don't," said Kevin. "Just give us a ballpark. Heavy like this?" he asked, holding up what looked like an old car alternator. "Or is this also too heavy?" he held up an old rusty fork.

"Yes, the first item is too heavy, but the fork isn't. It's perfect, actually."

"What are we going to do with all this junk?" asked Sarah, picking gingerly through the box nearest her.

"We're going to string them up together and attach them to a rope of some sort. We'll put the rope up at the areas leading to the house, and anytime someone steps on it or runs into it, it'll make the items bang together and create noise."

"Like old forks hitting each other?" asked Candi, holding up the fork and looking a little unconvinced.

"Yes. A very strange noise for the woods, so hopefully one that would alert us to the arrival of an intruder."

Kevin held up several metal parts that were unidentifiable. "Yeah, and they can double as some kind of art stuff. You know, like those gardens where people hang crap they've welded together in the trees and call it genius."

"That would be kind of handy, actually, to have it seem like art," said Sarah, creating a small pile of usable items on the ground next to her box. "In case that lady who owns the place comes by. She might decide she doesn't want to rent to us anymore if she thinks we're nut cases."

"Better she thinks we're terrible artists," said Candi, smiling. "Makes sense to me."

Jonathan supervised the gathering of items and then left the girls to the boxes, working with Kevin at stringing the main lines across several areas leading to the cabin. Kevin was a great worker until he got hungry. Then he was easily distracted and tended to complain.

They were back at the shed again, pulling out more ropes and pieces of twine when Kevin started whining again. "Is it lunchtime yet? I'm starving. And don't even think about feeding me plain noodles, either. I need some meat to fuel all these muscles that are getting a workout."

"Hold your horses. We're going to go make you lunch *with* meat in just a minute," said Sarah. "We just need to put this last piece together." She was tying some fishing line into several knots, to make sure her fork, spoon, and old wrench noise-maker wouldn't fall apart.

Candi stood and took the end of the clear string, holding it up for their inspection. Several metal parts attached to it bumped into each other making a clanking sound.

"Perfect," said Jonathan, smiling. "Just what I was looking for. Give it to Kevin. I'll take this one, and we'll go put up our first operational alarm."

"And we'll go make lunch," said Candi, brushing off her pants before offering her hand to Sarah. "Come on, pregnant lady. Let's go do this."

Sarah stood with Candi's help, her hand on her stomach. "I'm not so sure about lunch."

For the first time today, Jonathan noticed her face was pale. "Why don't you go lie down?" he suggested.

She nodded. "I think I will." She left the area, not waiting for Candi.

"Is she okay?" Candi asked, looking to Jonathan for his diagnosis.

"I think so. She's got another month of feeling like this from what I read. Maybe a little less. We'll just have to wait and see."

Candi nodded. "Okay. I won't worry, then. See you guys

soon."

Jonathan signaled to Kevin, and they both walked out to the first line they'd strung across the main driveway.

"So, how is this going to work, exactly?" asked Kevin, following Jonathan's lead.

"That line we hung just there by the road is connected to another one we tied to the house. The tree branches we used will give them the support needed to keep tension on the lines. I need you to go hang that noise-maker to the rope attached near my bedroom window. Once you've got it on, signal me so I can test the tension. It has to be loose enough to send the vibration through the rope and create enough motion to jiggle the noise maker. It works on the concept of a basic wave, like we learned in physics class. I could use some trigonometry functions to get the ideal tension, but I don't think that's necessary."

"Yeah. Me neither," said Kevin, sounding bored. "I'll be right back."

Jonathan waited until he heard Kevin whistle. Walking over to the rope that was strung up about six inches from the driveway's surface, he approached it from the direction of the main road. He stepped on it, simulating the action of a car tire rolling over the top of it. He might have heard a slight tinkling sound off in the distance, but he wasn't sure.

"That's good!" yelled Kevin.

"Maybe," said Jonathan, speaking softly to James who'd come to sit nearby. "I can't really tell from here, though." He traipsed through the woods and over to the cabin, the dog right behind him. When he got to where Kevin could hear him, he said, "You go back there and step on the rope. I need to see if I can hear it from inside."

Kevin jogged out of sight, and Jonathan ran into the cabin so he could be in place before Kevin started his part of the experiment.

Candi watched him run in with alarm. "What's wrong?" asked Candi from the kitchen.

"Nothing," he said, not stopping to explain. He threw open the downstairs bedroom door and jumped onto the bed, lying on his back and simulating his sleeping posture.

Sarah sat up in bed. "Is it nap time for you too?"

"Shhhh," said Jonathan, lifting his finger to his lips briefly before letting it drop to his side. He focused on being calm and quiet, just like he was at night with Sarah at his side. He opened one eye to peek at her, unable to stop himself.

She had her arms crossed over her chest. "What's going on?"

"Shhhh!" He said louder this time, wishing she would be quiet so he could complete his experiment properly. He lifted his head and gave her a serious look.

Candi came into the room to stand beside Sarah. "What's he doing in bed?"

She dropped her hands to the bed and shrugged. "You've got me."

"Would you two *please be quiet?!*" Jonathan yelled.

A sudden muffled jangling near the window made all of them look over.

"What was that?" asked Candi.

Jonathan smiled, sitting up and scooting off the bed and going over to stand at the window. "That was our alarm system. That's what we'll hear if someone comes up the road in a car or motorcycle, or if they walk up it and don't see the string, which they might not in the day but definitely wouldn't when it's dark."

"Nice," said Sarah. "Are you done then?"

"Heck no. We have to put these all over the place. We can't assume anyone coming here with bad intentions is just going to come up the driveway. If they're smart, they'll come from the back or side of the house. We have to set up all approaches with warning devices."

"Maybe we should eat lunch first," said Candi, coming over and patting him on the shoulder.

Jonathan nodded absently, his mind generating visions of the different points of entry into the perimeter of the cabin. His brain took those positions and calculated their approximate distances from the house, comparing them to the length of rope he knew they had left and the number of noise makers available. He was going to have to be very precise if he wanted to be able to cover all their bases.

Sarah got up and took him by the hand, leading him out into the main room and over to the table. She pulled out his chair and pointed. "Sit. Calculate. Analyze. We'll bring you your food."

Jonathan just nodded, his brain too busy with the variables to focus on putting together the words necessary to formulate a proper response.

*****

For the next week, Jonathan and Kevin busied themselves with securing the area around the cabin, and Candi and Sarah worked on training the dogs. All of them practiced their archery on and off, Candi being the one with the best aim by far.

At first Candi had to guilt Sarah into participating with the dog training, but after they enjoyed their first successes with the dogs, she didn't have to say anything anymore. Sarah was a natural at convincing the dogs what they should do, especially

James. The fact that she could get that mutt to do anything but chase his own tail was some sort of miracle in itself, but she'd gone even way beyond that.

"How did you get him to do that?" asked Candi, watching James run over and pick up the item Sarah had pointed to. No matter what it was, he'd grab it and bring it back.

"It's all about incentive. Use the right one with James, and he'll be putty in your hands."

"I've used treats and praise and everything else, and the only thing I can get him to do is sit and stay for about five seconds."

"You have to use the force of your gaze. He's watching you to see how serious you are. You're not serious enough."

"Xena thinks I'm serious." Candi reached down and tickled the belly of the white dog at her feet. Her chest was flat again, which made it a lot easier to give her a decent rub.

"Xena's easy. She lives to please you. James is more complicated. He has other interests besides just making humans happy."

"James isn't complicated. He's a hyper goofball who can't focus on any one thing for longer than five seconds."

"Whatever. He's good practice for me. Maybe the Peanut's going to be hyper; you never know. Kevin was when he was little."

"Not Jonathan. My parents say he'd sit in a corner of a room and play with his toys all by himself for hours not bothering anyone."

"Why does that not surprise me?" asked Sarah, wryly. "He must have livened up when you came along, though."

"Nope. When I was born, he just sat next to me and talked to me while he played."

"And what did you do?"

"My parents said I just watched him like a hawk, like I was memorizing his every move."

"Or you were looking at him thinking, *'What the hell is this kid's problem? Why isn't he raising hell like every other boy out there?'*"

Candi smiled. "Maybe. He's always been different than other boys."

Sarah smiled with self-satisfaction. "And that's what makes him perfect for me. I'm an original, so it's only natural that I be with another one-of-a-kind."

"You sure are," said Candi. Sarah would get no argument from her on that.

"I know you're mocking me, but I'm ignoring you. See, I'm more mature than you are. That's because I'm a mom."

"Whatever, *mom*. Help me with this command." Candi had been trying to get Xena to go on alert, but she wasn't sure what technique she could use to simulate a bad guy coming without actually having someone play the role.

"I still think you should get Kevin to tie some blankets on his arms and let her attack him for practice," said Sarah.

"You're nuts. She'll tear him apart. We can't risk him actually getting hurt."

"Whatever you say," sighed Sarah. "You're the boss." She looked over at James. "Fetch!" She pointed to a broken lawn chair someone had pulled out from under the porch.

Candi laughed. "He can't fetch that; it's five times his size."

James ran over and stopped in front of the chair. He turned to look at Sarah who merely nodded. The dog dipped his head down and grabbed the metal leg with his teeth and started dragging it through the grass.

Candi fell into hysterics, watching him struggle with it and then go nuts over the chair getting stuck on a bump. He yanked and pulled and twisted all over the place until he got it free, not giving up until the stupid thing was sitting at Sarah's feet.

"Good boy, Jamesie, good boy!" Sarah squealed, rubbing his little ears and feeding him something from her pocket.

Candi's eyes narrowed. "What did you just give him?"

"What are you talking about?" asked Sarah innocently. "I didn't give him anything."

"Yes, you did. You are so busted; I totally saw you." Candi walked over and held out her hand. "Come on ... hand it over."

Sarah sighed heavily before reaching into her pocket. She pulled something small and red out, putting it in Candi's palm.

"Gummy bears? You're giving him *gummy bears?*"

"Yeah. So?" She shrugged. "He likes 'em."

Candi laughed again, a little less enthusiastically. "I'm not sure if I should be mad at you for cheating or worried that James is going to have some sort of diabetic attack."

"He's fine," she scoffed. "He's been eating them for two weeks without a problem."

"But I thought you said you needed gummy bears to settle your stomach." Candi put her hands on her hips, now thinking they'd all been conned.

"I did, but then they stopped working, so they were just sitting there getting stale. And one day I dropped one, and James went nuts for it, so I figured I might as well give it a shot."

"And all this time you'd been letting me call you the dog whisperer. Unbelievable," said Candi, feigning outrage.

"Well, I *am* awesome at this, gummy bears or not."

Candi patted her on the back, giving up on being mad over a few fruity snacks. "Yes, you are. I'm only kidding. But those gummy bears remind me ... we need to get more food. We're almost completely out. And Kevin's going to kill us if we don't get him some eggs and meat soon."

"I know. He was whining again this morning about his muscle mass shrinking or something."

"Yeah. He had a nightmare that the guys in the computer club beat him up after school. He's doing extra pushups and sprints now to try and counteract a possible future geek ambush."

Sarah snorted. "That'll be the day."

The girls walked towards the cabin, stepping over the various ropes and clear fishing line strings that criss-crossed the different pathways on their route. Anyone who didn't know where the traps were would make a lot of noise trying to get close; Jonathan and Kevin had made sure of that.

When Sarah and Candi arrived at the cabin, the two guys were standing on the porch, bath towels in hand.

"What are you doing?" asked Candi.

"Going for a swim," said Kevin. "All of us. Come on."

"We have to make lunch and go into town today," said Sarah. "We don't have time to play around."

"Hell yes, we do," said Kevin, jumping down the whole staircase in one leap. "We've been working our asses off all week. Today we're going to chill out. We can shop later. Come on." He grabbed Candi by the elbow and led her through the trees. Both of them avoided tripping over the ropes on the way.

"But what about lunch?" she asked.

"We handled it. Jon's got that covered," said Kevin mysteriously.

They reached the small rickety dock that stretched out over a small portion of the lake. "Come on. Strip down. I don't have all day." He lifted an eyebrow at her, giving her a lecherous look.

"Hands to yourself, mister," she said, before lifting up her t-shirt and taking it off, dropping her shorts right after. Swimming in her underwear the first time had been weird. Now after doing it almost once a day for the past week, it felt totally natural. She jumped in the water as Jonathan and Sarah were walking up. James hit the water next to her, sending a small spray up into her face. She sputtered and spit it out, reaching over to push him away.

"Hey, watch the splashing, ya goofy dog," said Kevin, making waves to push the dog back towards the shore.

James had invented a game where he'd run as fast as his little legs could take him down the dock, launch himself into the water like a superhero canine, and then doggy paddle back to the shore so he could do it all over again. He always did it when they were in the water too, so there was no peaceful floating or zen moments for the humans when James was around.

Xena came to the dock and laid down on the end of it, her eyes open and moving around, tracking them in the water silently. She completely ignored the terrier who'd jump over her whenever she was in his flight path towards the lake, preferring to laze in the sun instead of exercise in the water. She'd go in if begged and cajoled, but mostly she was a land lubber.

Sarah stripped down and lowered herself slowly into the water. Candi smiled at the tiny little bump she thought she could see forming above her friend's panty line. She'd lost so much weight with the morning sickness, it made it easier to see. Maybe it was just Candi's imagination, but it was cute anyway.

"We need to talk about going to get more food," said Jonathan. He jumped into the lake in between Kevin and Candi, splashing both of them with his cannonball move. Bursting up out of the water, he whipped his head left and then right. "How was that one?"

"Awesome," said Kevin, not sounding very impressed as he wiped his face off and blew water out of his nostrils. "You threw half the lake up my nose and pretty much blinded me, too."

"I've been working on it. I think I have the perfect altitude, weight, and surface tension formula figured out."

"I think you do, too," said Candi, blinking hard to clear her eyes. They were going to be red for sure.

"I think I've got *my* formula all figured out too," said Kevin, doing a single breast-stroke in Jonathan's direction.

"Oh, yeah?" asked Jonathan, all excited. "Tell me about it."

Kevin stroked a little closer. "Okay, sure. See, if you take a certain amount of downward pressure and assert it against a non-stationary and buoyant item, you can force it in the opposite direction ... sometimes pretty fast."

Jonathan frowned. "Yeah. That's just basic Newton's law stuff. The acceleration of a body is parallel and directly proportional to the net force acting on the body, and is inversely proportional to the mass of the body. You know the formula, right? F equals MA."

"Actually, I used a different formula," said Kevin, now treading water right next to Jonathan.

"Really? I wasn't aware there was another one."

"Oh yeah, dude. It's KM plus JH equals JD."

Jonathan frowned. "That's not standard scientific notation."

"Sure it is. Let me explain it to you. It goes like this: Kevin's

Muscle pushed down on Jonathan's Head equals Jonathan being Dunked." He pulled his hand up out of the water and slapped it down on top of Jonathan's skull, leaping up out of the water with a big kick to force Jonathan down. The last thing Candi saw was Jonathan's eyes bugging out of his head just before they disappeared below the surface.

"Oh, no you don't," said Sarah, swimming up behind Kevin and grabbing him in a headlock. "Here's my formula," she grunted out, hanging on for dear life. "Sarah's headlock on Kevin's head equals Kevin swallowing pond water." She pulled him backwards and then swam over the top of him, shoving him down undernearth her. She smiled triumphantly at Candi. "Who says I suck at math?" Her head disappeared beneath the surface a split-second later as she was pulled down from below by the victim of her equation.

Jonathan came up sputtering and looked around. "Where'd he go?"

"He's busy drowning his sister right now," said Candi, having swum out of range, pointing over to the disturbance in the water about ten feet away. "Over there."

Jonathan and Candi waited in silence for the other two to surface. When Kevin and Sarah came up they had a short splashing war before Sarah got tired and played the pregnancy card to get away.

"Stop! I'm sick. Leave me alone. You're going to hurt the baby."

"You just totally surrendered. Did you hear that?" Kevin asked Candi and Jonathan. "She surrendered. I win. I'm the champion." Kevin held up his arms in victory turning to acknowledge the legions of imaginary fans who were apparently standing around the lake admiring his prowess.

"Can we talk about shopping now? And other stuff?" asked Jonathan.

Something in his tone made Candi stop moving for a second. She had to quickly start kicking again to stay above the surface. "Other stuff? What other stuff?"

"Contacting our families."

Everyone swam over until they were in a circle. James even tried to join them, but he was quickly pushed away by anyone he came near since he tended to scratch them with his claws when he tried to climb onto their shoulders.

"What's up?" asked Kevin. "Your super-computer brain's been busy, I take it?"

"Well, I don't know about super computer, but I have been thinking some things through. We've been gone long enough that news of our departure and the trial should be pretty well-disseminated. And early attempts at finding us have been fruitless, obviously. So maybe we should risk seeing what the local law enforcement or FBI knows and maybe getting a message through to our parents at least."

"Using your friend and the chess code stuff?" asked Sarah.

"I was thinking we could try two different avenues. See which one yields the best results."

"You want to run an experiment in the middle of all this?" asked Candi. "Come on, Jonathan. I appreciate the science and everything, but it's a risk already."

"No, I know that. But there's another benefit too, in addition to having more chances of getting our messages delivered. First, we make sure we can get a message through both avenues. Then, when the time comes, we can use one of our messengers to deliver false messages. And he or she won't even know they're false, so they'll be very convincing."

Sarah lifted up her hand and pointed a finger at herself. "Short bus. Tired. Take it down a few notches, babe."

Jonathan took her by the hand and dragged her over to the dock, putting her fingers on the wood above their heads. "Here. Hold this while I explain."

She nodded her gratitude.

Jonathan waited until Candi and Kevin had gotten closer before continuing. "So what I was thinking is that we contact two people who have zero connection to one another. Like one of my friends and one of yours, Kevin. And we feed them the same info."

"Why?" asked Kevin. "And besides, we have a lot of the same friends now."

"Just because. And not all of our friends are the same. Just listen, and I'll explain the rest." He readjusted his hold on the dock and continued. "We give the same messages to the two resources. Later, when we're ready to make an appearance, we feed false information to one of them and make sure it's publicized a lot, so the bad guys will have a fake trail to follow. We feed the correct info to the other and make sure it's kept a secret."

"Okay. I guess I kind of get it," said Kevin, "but I still don't know why we need two people. Why not just tell one guy everything and also tell him what's fake, what's not, and stuff like that?"

"Because ... someone will figure out where the info is coming from eventually, and they'll start hacking into his life to learn the rest and try to track us down."

"So we feed the false info to the guy who's easiest to hack?" asked Kevin.

"Exactly. That would be your friend," said Jonathan. "My friend will be the one we use for our actual real plans."

"Maybe your friend is the hackable one," said Kevin, sounding offended. "I'll bet they can't keep secrets longer than a day."

"I don't think so," said Jonathan.

"Stop arguing," said Candi, bored already with the subject of whose friends were more trustworthy. "Who did you have in mind, Jonathan? To be the messengers, I mean."

"I was thinking already of my friend Stephen, who I mentioned before. And for Kevin's friends, I'm not sure. Who do you know that could be circumspect and careful about who he talked to and revealed things to?"

Sarah shook her head. *"No one* in our group fits that description."

Kevin frowned at her. "Maybe. Maybe not."

"Come on, Kevin," said Sarah, admonishing him. "You know what I mean. They *live* on that gossip crap. There's no way any of them could keep a secret. Could you picture it with Gretchen? Barry? Brandon? Charlie? ... No way."

"Jason could do it," said Candi, softly. "He's trustworthy, and he'd never sell us out."

No one said anything for a few seconds. The silence got awkward.

"The dude's too involved in your life as it is," said Kevin grouchily.

"Don't be like that, Kevin," said Candi. "He's a really nice guy."

"Yeah, and he wants to get in your pants, so forgive me if I'm not all that excited about him being your knight in shining armor."

Candi splashed water into his face. "Shut up, you jerk. You have no idea what you're talking about."

"Not cool, Kev," said Sarah.

"What?!" he said angrily. "You know it's true. The guy's chasing after her all over the place. He's lucky I don't take him out onto the rugby field and pound him."

Candi stuck her finger in Kevin's face. "No, *you're* lucky that doesn't happen. Because if you *ever* did something neanderthal like that, I'd never speak to you again."

He grabbed her finger and pulled her close. "Yes, you would." He smiled at her, trying to use his charm to diffuse the situation.

Candi put her hands on his chest, pushing him away. "No, I would not. I don't like you acting like that, especially towards him. He's my friend, and he's been very nice to me. Even when *some* people weren't."

Kevin stopped trying to hug her, surrender in his tone. "Okay, okay ... fine. I won't pound the twerp. But regardless, you know I'm right. He's hot for you."

"Well, I'm not hot for him, so let it go."

Kevin leaned in for a kiss, but Candi dunked herself under the water to avoid it. She didn't want to encourage either his jealousy or his idea that he could just give her a quick kiss or hug and make everything go away. Life wasn't that simple, and her emotions weren't that easy to just turn on and off. She came back up for air a few feet away to hear Jonathan say, " ... and I think she's the best one to go. Either her or me."

"Who's the best one? For what?"

"You. To go shopping today."

"Me? Why me?" she said, her voice going weak. The idea of driving that beast of a motorcycle scared her, and the thought of being chased by a police officer on it was enough to make her want to throw up.

"If they're looking for the motorcycle, they're looking for a big guy to be driving it. If they see your tiny form on it, maybe they'll just ignore you."

"But they'll still see the license plate number," she argued.

"You just have to make sure they don't get behind you," said Jonathan simply.

"Oh, *that's* easy. Just be watching behind me and in front of me at the same time, all while trying to remember how to drive the stupid bike. No problem."

"You can practice before you go," said Kevin, sidling up to her again. She let him this time. "I'll help you." He put one arm around her, the other holding onto the dock.

She loved the feel of his body up against hers, and it calmed her the smallest bit. She stopped paddling and held onto his muscular arm. "I'm scared."

"You'll be fine, Sugar Lump," said Sarah, patting her wetly on the head. "We'll give you a list and you just need to get in and get out."

"Well, she also has to send a couple messages online," said Jonathan. "But you can do that at the library. That's a safe place to be. You can park the bike in the back, and no one will see it. I'll give you the address of a proxy server you can use to surf anonymously."

"I don't even know what that means," whined Candi,

wishing there was another way to do all this. It wasn't that she wanted someone else to go instead of her; if she had to choose anyone, she'd choose herself to save her family. But that didn't stop her from wishing none of it was necessary.

"It's very simple. I'll explain later."

"When should she go?" asked Kevin, squeezing Candi tighter for a second before letting her go.

"As soon as possible," said Jonathan. "Cops eat lunch just like everyone else. I think she'd be in better shape if she was driving around when the lunch crowd is busy or getting out. Too early in the morning and the library won't be open. Too late and she risks getting lost in the dark."

Candi reached up to the dock and pulled herself out of the water. "Fine. Let's get this over with so I can go back to bed and hide under the covers for the next week or two." Somehow just facing the fear and working fast to finish the task made her feel stronger. *At least I know what's going to happen. I'll either get caught, arrested, sent back home and murdered, or I'll make it there and back without a problem. That's better than not knowing anything.* She swallowed hard as she gathered up her clothes and walked back to the cabin, forcing the tears to stay out of sight.

*****

Kevin showed Candi how to drive the motorcycle, making sure she understood not only how the gears worked but also how to operate it at high speeds as safely as possible.

"You have to lean into the turns," he repeated for the third time.

"But I'll fall over!" she complained, staring at the bike with stark fear.

"No, you won't. It's total physics. And if I were Jonathan, I could describe it all to you in massive detail, but since I'm just me, I'll tell you that you won't fall off and the bike won't tip over either. You'll see when you try it. We can't do it here, though. The road is too short, too bumpy, and too straight."

"I'm not going to do that ... lean into the turns at high speeds. I'm not even going to *go* high speeds."

"You might have to, so it's better to be prepared and know than to be unprepared and freak out."

Candi put her hand up on Kevin's shoulder. "Trust me ... if I end up in a situation where I have to go fast, I'm *going* to be freaking out, regardless of how well you prepare me."

Kevin embraced her, wanting so badly to make her fear go away. He'd even take it into himself and suffer it for her if he could; but the best he could do now was to try and convince her she was going to be okay. He knew she was strong enough to do this, or he'd never let her even try. "Babe, you're going to be just fine. You'll be totally badass on this bike. Plus, you're pretty hot on it, too."

Candi pushed away, play-hitting him on the chest. "I can't believe you're making a move on me at a time like this."

Kevin gave her the smile that he knew she couldn't resist. "At a time like what? There's never a bad time for me to make a move on you as far as I'm concerned."

"When I'm about to be captured and tortured ... that's a bad time."

Kevin's heart seized up a little before he got a handle on it. "That's not going to happen to you, Gumdrop." He stood back a little and ran his fingers through his hair, unable to totally ignore the visions of that assassin on the ground in her bedroom at the supposed safehouse. *Why didn't I kill that asshole when I had the chance?* Kevin knew the answer to his own question: he was not a murderer. But that didn't stop him from wishing the guy coming for them was gone from this earth. The idea of him going after little Candi was unthinkable. He'd go insane if something like that happened.

Jonathan came walking over, a folded piece of paper in his hand.

"What's up, dude?" asked Kevin.

"I have the messages for Candi to send. After you do this, destroy the paper. Burning it is the best way. Here's a lighter," he said, handing over a small, blue disposable one.

"Why are we going all spy novel on this thing?" asked Candi, taking the lighter and putting it in her front pocket. "Why can't I just throw the paper away or keep it?"

"Because, if you're being followed, the person will watch you throw it out and take it after you walk away. If you get captured, they'll take it as part of their intake procedure. Either way, our contacts will be compromised. We can't afford that."

"Won't the library computer be able to tell everyone what she did and who she contacted? Aren't we already taking massive risks?"

"I've included instructions on how to make sure she's not only surfing anonymously through a proxy but also how to disable any keystroke logging software. I assume they're using PCs, but in the event they have Macs, here are the alternate instructions." Jonathan pointed to different blocks of text on the paper.

"You've written a book," said Candi, sounding annoyed.

"No, I haven't. A book would be much longer. There are

only about five hundred and fifty words here, more or less. See? Not even short-story length." He pointed to a smaller block of single-spaced text. "Here's the message you have to send, and here's Stephen's contact info. I assume you have Jason's?" He looked up and received an answering nod. "Good. So send this message to both of them, but only after you've done steps one through five right here. Got it? Don't forget to create a new email account. That's on step three."

Candi looked at the paper along with Kevin for half a minute before answering. "Yeah. I get it."

"Now ... after you follow all these instructions and finish sending the messages, I need you to go online and just surf amusement parks in California."

"Why?" asked Kevin, now completely confused.

"We want to create a false trail in the event my safeguards don't work. It's just a contingency plan on one hand ... make them think we're leaving the area to go have fun far away. And on the other hand, it will give Candi time to wait for a response from either or both of the contacts. You can see in the message that we've asked them for information. Chances are they won't know much, but you never can tell until you ask. If one of them happens to be by their computer or on their smartphone, they can answer right away. I assume they will if at all possible, based on the nature of our situation."

"Shouldn't I surf for info on the trial or the dead FBI agents?"

"No. Don't do that."

"Why? Aren't you even curious?" asked Kevin. "Man, you're like Ice Cold Jonathan Buckley or something."

"No, I'm not ice cold at all. I'm just as nervous as you are. And of course I'm curious. But there are algorithms the FBI can run that pull up IP addresses of people who do searches on certain stories or sites. Most people around here will ignore that news, so the library will show up as a hot spot. We can't afford to clue them in on where we are that way, so we need to depend on our contacts to tell us that stuff. I would like to assume the proxy surfing would shield us from this possibility, but I can't be sure that will happen. I'm trying to cover all our bases with as little work as possible. Candi is not an expert in computers, and the library network could be quite sophisticated."

"Oh," said Candi after Jonathan was finally done talking. "For a minute there I was thinking there might be one positive thing to this trip ... that I could find out what was going on. I guess that hope is totally lost now."

Kevin rubbed her upper arm. "Babe, don't forget ... you're getting food, too. That's good stuff, right?"

She frowned and sighed. "I guess. I'm not as excited about it as I know you are."

"I'll tell you what. You bring me back some white bread and cheddar slices, and I'll make you one of Kevin Peterson's world-famous grilled cheese special sandwiches, okay?"

"Are they good? Because I like grilled cheese, but I'm kind of picky."

"The best. Poems have been written about my grilled cheese. I could open a grilled cheese stand, and it would be busy every day of the week, all year long. Even on Christmas."

Candi smiled. "Okay, then. I'll get you the cheese and bread and you can impress me with your skills."

"And butter," he said, pointing at her so she'd understand the importance. "Don't forget the real butter. None of that margarine crap; it has to be genuine."

"Real butter. Gotcha."

"And if you're a fan of tomatoes, get one of those too," he said. "The beefsteak kind. They go good with it."

"I am a fan, so I'll get one or two. I know Jonathan likes them too."

"Sarah does too, I think. Well, when she's not pregnant, anyway."

"So you understand all of the directions?" asked Jonathan.

Candi nodded, looking scared all over again.

"Time to go, Gumdrop," said Kevin, gesturing to the bike. "You can do this. We'll be waiting."

Candi walked around the bike and climbed on board, putting the helmet on before standing the bike upright. She lifted the visor. "Tell Sarah I said I'll see her later."

"Okay, I'll tell her," said Jonathan, nodding.

"And tell her ... tell her if I don't make it ... that I was really looking forward to being an aunt and that I'll just be a guardian angel instead if I have to."

Kevin's voice caught in his throat, and he found himself unable to respond. The idea of someone killing the girl he loved had him furious.

"Smile, Kevin," she said. "I won't go down easy." She put the visor in place and started the bike, taking off in the perfectly smooth maneuver Kevin had taught her just thirty minutes before.

He watched as she disappeared down the dirt road, James running after her for a few yards before giving up and trotting back.

"She's going to be okay, right, Jon?" he asked, his voice rough with emotion.

"Yes. The odds are high that she will accomplish her mission and return to us safely. The odds are slightly lower that she'll return without having divulged our location to anyone, but we have to take the bet that she can do this if we're going to get out of this alive."

Kevin didn't know whether to be grateful for Jonathan's accuracy and honesty or angry about it, so he said nothing, walking back to the cabin as his mind cooked up the hundred ways his girlfriend could be caught by some very bad, bad guys.

Intruders

AFTER HER POST-LUNCH NAP which lasted a wonderful two hours, Sarah got busy finishing up the cleaning of the kitchen. She was almost finished when she heard a weird sound outside. It barely registered until James began barking. Then suddenly it took her full attention. Her hand froze over the stovetop, the wet sponge going cold as she hesitated, listening for the sound again.

"Jonathan?" she called out. He'd taken off with Kevin somewhere, and she couldn't recall where they'd said they were going. This pregnancy-brain thing was making her crazy. She felt like she had dementia or something. She had to keep writing herself notes to remember things.

The sound came again, and as its import registered, her heart froze in her chest. She could hear the weird pounding as her organ started up again, the beats irregular and hurried. *Forks and spoons banging against each other ... the alarm! Someone's coming!*

She couldn't figure out which alarm had rung, though. Jonathan had told her time and time again, if this one rings, someone's coming from the back door. If this other one rings, they're coming from the front. If that other one did, it was from the side ... and so on and so forth. All of it was blending together into one big, fat, information overload.

Sarah dropped the sponge and spun around, looking for the dogs. Both of them were gone. She could hear James barking outside somewhere, and it wasn't his usual bark. It sounded more frantic or crazy. Xena was nowhere to be seen, and her deep bark wasn't present at all that Sarah could tell.

She rushed over to the drawer where they kept the gun, but it was empty. "Dammit!" she whispered out into the room. "Where is that friggin thing?" She opened all the drawers nearby as fast as she could, but the gun was obviously somewhere else.

The last drawer she touched had all the knives in it. She took out the most lethal one she could find, hoping she was just being paranoid. She backed up towards the sink area and crouched down behind the island in the middle of the kitchen so she wouldn't be seen from the front door. *Please don't let it be a murderer! Please just let it be my stupid brother or boyfriend!*

A knock came at the screen door.

Sarah sat completely still, squeezing the knife in her hand. *Jonathan or Kevin wouldn't knock.* Sweat broke out on her upper lip. *But neither would a killer ... would he?*

Another knock came, louder this time. "Hello? Is anyone home?" A man's voice.

Sarah stood. It was a stranger for sure, but he sounded friendly; and he wasn't busting the door down or sneaking in a window, which was definitely a good sign.

She took a few cautious steps towards the door, hiding the knife behind her back. "Who is it?" she called out when she was still too far to the side to see who was standing on the porch.

"It's Jack. Jack Guckenberger. The owner? I'm just here to check in with you and see how things are going."

Sarah remembered the name from Candi telling them about the lady who owned the place. No matter how pregnant she was, she could never forget a name like that. This guy sounded younger than how Candi had described the lady, but the woman had mentioned something about having kids and grandkids. This guy at the door was probably a son or something.

Sarah put the knife down on the counter as she passed by the last part of it and stopped in front of the screen door.

The man was standing there in khaki pants and a polo shirt. His hair was neatly cut, combed, and gelled - he could have been on the cover of a magazine featuring expensive, well-made clothing for the entire family. His smile was dental-ad bright, but didn't quite reach his eyes. For some stupid reason, it caused Sarah to not want to open the door.

"Hello," she said, not smiling.

"Oh, hey there," he responded, blinding her with another fake smile. "Didn't see you there. Do you mind if I come in?" He took a tentative step forward, fully expecting an affirmative answer.

Sarah battled with herself. She didn't want to be rude, but his creepy smile was getting to her. And where was James? She tried to look around him but didn't see the dog anywhere. He'd been barking like crazy earlier and then he'd just stopped. *Maybe he's with Jonathan and Kevin. Maybe they're just outside.* She realized the guy was waiting for an answer, so she cleared her throat, trying to earn herself more time to answer. *Be rude and protect myself or be polite and risk it?*

Almost eighteen years of discipline and manners hammered into her by her parents finally won out. She reached over and unlatched the screen. "Come on in. My name's Gretchen, by the way." Sarah forced herself not to grimace over her choice of name. It had come flying out of her mouth before she could think too hard about it.

Maybe she was just imagining it, but she could have sworn the guy had frowned when she said it. Fear and paranoia had her automatically backing away from him as he entered, moving closer towards the knife she'd left on the counter.

"So, where are the rest of them?" he asked, looking around the room. He shut the door behind him, locking it.

The clicking sound made Sarah sick to her stomach - it had never seemed so menacing before, so permanent. She frowned, trying to calm her racing heart. "Rest of them what?"

He smiled, but there was no humor or happiness to it. "Rest of *whom*, not what. You know who I'm talking about."

Adrenaline shot into Sarah's bloodstream. The suspicious smile and too-perfect looks had quickly taken on a sinister quality. "I have no idea who you're talking about, but I think it's time you leave. I don't mean to be rude, but I came out here for privacy, and I was told we ... I ... wouldn't be disturbed." *Dammit! And I was doing so well!*

His smile disappeared completely. "Cut the shit, Sarah. You came out here to hide, but guess what? You lose because I found you." He took a step towards her.

She moved back to the counter quickly and picked up the knife, whipping it out to point it at him. "Come any closer to me and I'll slice you wide open, you sonofabitch!"

He held up his hands in surrender, lowering one of them to his lower back. When his hand came back out, Sarah blanched.

"Put the knife down, Sarah. I don't want to have to shoot you before it's time. Do you understand?"

Sarah nodded numbly, setting the knife down on the counter without making a sound. Her mind was going a million miles an hour, trying to figure out what had happened, what was going to happen, and what she could do to stop it. But nothing was coming to her. All she could picture was a frightening, black void of pain and fear. It threatened to overwhelm her, bringing the all-consuming nausea with it.

"I'm going to throw up," she said, her voice trembling.

"No, you're not. Go sit down at the table," he ordered, gesturing with his gun.

Sarah shook her head, and then turned to run for the sink. She grabbed the edge of it and heaved several times, sure she was going to be shot in the back, but just as certain she didn't want to die in a pool of her own vomit.

When she was done, she turned on the water and rinsed out her mouth, spitting it back into the sink. Candi was for sure going to want to disinfect that whole area now. *Assuming Candi is still alive and that we're not all dead.* The thought was more than sobering. Sarah swallowed the bile that wanted to come up to join the rest of it and stood up straight. Facing her captor, she lifted her chin. "Who are you? Why are you here?"

"Who I am is not important. And I think you know why I'm here. Go sit."

Sarah considered arguing, but since he had the gun pointed at her and there was nothing to distract him with, she decided her best bet was to just go along with whatever he wanted. At least for now.

She tried to take the seat nearest the wall, but he stopped her.

"No. That one, not that one."

"But ..."

"Just take the fucking seat and don't argue. I really have no problem putting a bullet in you right now."

Sarah sat down with her back to the room. It was freaking her out to have him behind her, not able to see anything he was doing. She heard movement and then him talking, but not to her.

"Yeah, it's me. I've got one of them. I think it's Sarah." There was a pause and then, "Hey, you ... you're Sarah, right?"

"No, I told you ... I'm Gretchen, asshole." She decided to shelve her commitment to not swear anymore. These were desperate times.

The guy went back to what Sarah assumed was a phone call. "Yeah, it's Sarah. The bitch is mouthy." He was silent for a few seconds before continuing. "No, I haven't done anything yet. We might need her to call the others or something, so I'll wait until they're all here." Another hesitation came, and then, "Good. I'll wait here. What do you want me to do when we have all of them?"

Sarah listened as hard as she possibly could for the answer to the bad man's question, but she couldn't catch what the person on the other end of the line was saying. The voice was too tiny to make out any words. She was hoping not to hear two syllables: *Kill them*. There were definitely more than two coming out of the phone, but they could have been anything. *Like, kill them and bury the bodies.* Her hands shook as she put them out in front of her on the table, pretending to examine her fingernails while her mind went into overdrive, trying to come up with a plan of escape.

*****

Xena was sitting at Jonathan's feet as he stood on tiptoes, trying to get the line for one of his noisemakers hooked higher up in the tree. A couple of them had gotten too loose during the night, losing the tension they needed to be effective.

The dog growled, and Jonathan froze. She never did that for no reason - that was James' penchant. It was only when Xena felt threatened that they heard her make those scary sounds. She'd done it at Kevin when he'd been stupid enough to kind of bait her, but that was it.

Jonathan turned around, but saw no one. "Kevin?" he called out. "Is that you?"

Xena growled again, the deep timbre sending shivers up Jonathan's spine.

"Kevin, if that's you, you should announce yourself. I won't be able to stop Xena if she comes after you."

A voice came out from behind some trees - one Jonathan didn't recognize. "Call your dog off, or I'll shoot her."

Jonathan dropped down into a crouch, putting an arm over Xena's shoulders. He had no idea who this person was, but he probably had a weapon and sounded confident enough about using it. "Xena, no. Calm down, girl. Calm down." Jonathan took several deep breaths, using the oxygen to fill his lungs and brain, getting his body ready to mobilize if necessary.

A man wearing jeans and a black t-shirt came out into the open.

I know that man! Jonathan schooled his features to remain bland. He didn't know if it was critical that this man not realize he'd been recognized, but Jonathan decided it was better to have as many cards up his sleeve as possible. He studied the man's face and demeanor. *He'd been standing in the emergency room at the hospital, when we were there to check on Barry.* Jonathan's head spun with the ramifications. They'd been followed, first there and now here. *What does it mean?* Jonathan was short all the variables and insights he needed to figure out exactly what was going on. *Pay attention to everything he says and does. There are clues to be gathered.*

"Come on," said the stranger. "We're going back to the house." He didn't have any weapons out or showing; he just gestured with his hand.

Jonathan quickly decided his best bet was to just do what the man said, at least until he had a better idea about what kind of defenses he might have or what the man's plan was. He made a move as if to walk that way, but Xena's growl stopped him.

"I told you to shut the damn dog up."

"I did, sir. I mean, I tried to. But she seems to have a mind of her own." Jonathan was afraid to move now, but more because the dog was acting like she wasn't going to let him go without a fight. He wasn't even sure whose side she was on right now or if she was maybe suffering from a form of confusion. Obviously, she saw the guy as a threat, but beyond that, Jonathan had no idea what was going through her canine gray matter.

"Tell her to shut the hell up and go!" The man was obviously getting angry, fully expecting Jonathan to just jump and follow his orders without question or hesitation.

Jonathan looked down, trying to make his voice sound confident and very alpha male. "Xena! No! Down! I'm going to the cabin. Heel." He moved one step forward, and she growled again, this time a snort coming out on her inhale. She definitely meant it - Jonathan was not permitted to go anywhere as far as she was concerned.

The guy reached behind him and pulled a knife out of somewhere. "Last chance. Go or she dies first, then you."

He doesn't have a gun or he would have used it already! He can't hurt me if I keep the proper distance between us! Jonathan calculated his odds of success against the odds of getting stabbed if he stuck around, and made the only rational decision. He spun around and took off running. He sprinted as if his life depended on it. And it did. He was sure of it. There was no chance in the world that this person was here to just visit or threaten. His job was to exterminate, and Jonathan was his target. So were his sister, friend, and the mother of his child. But in order to save them, he had to save himself first.

Xena kept pace with him, no longer growling. The two of them leaped over branches and divets in the ground, trying to put as much distance between themselves and the man, running in the opposite direction of the cabin. Jonathan knew if he didn't turn soon, he was going to end up at the pond. He put his head down and channeled all his available energy into his legs. The thousands of miles he'd run in his life had prepared him for this one moment, and he wasn't going to let it end with being caught.

Crashing sounds coming from behind them told Jonathan he was being pursued, but the lack of any gunshots let him know his assumption had been correct. *No gun! I have a chance!*

*****

Kevin was staring up at one of the noisemakers hanging from one of their lines, waiting for Jonathan to finish fixing it.

He turned and looked out in the direction of the driveway. He couldn't see it from here, but his ears were tuned in for the sounds of the motorcycle approaching. Candi should be back anytime, assuming all went well at the library and grocery store.

James was barking like a fool off in the distance, making him wish he was close enough to throw something at him. That dog was a serious pest sometimes. Good thing he was so smart with the fetching stuff. Kevin's goal when they got back to the real world was to have Sarah teach him how to fetch cans of soda from the fridge. Now *that* was a useful skill for a dog to have.

The crunch of dry leaves behind him was the only clue he had that he was no longer alone in that section of the woods. He turned around to greet Jonathan, wondering why he didn't just yell that he was finished. He caught a flash of yellow teeth and a bad mustache in his field of vision, but had no time to connect the idea of a stranger sneaking around out in the woods and the threat to his safety before a sharp pain blossomed across his temple and the lights went out. He slid into a deep, unconscious sleep, his brain short circuiting the entire way down.

*****

Sarah stood when the door to the cabin opened, ready to scream out a warning, but slowly sat down again when she realized it wasn't one of her family there. She remained twisted around so she could watch the two killers interact.

"What's up?" asked her captor of the second man.

"Found one of them out in the woods. Big guy. Knocked his ass out. He'll be dead to the world for the rest of the day, at least. No way could he get up from that. Maybe I already killed him. *Crack!*" He laughed, proud of himself.

"What about that fucking barking dog?"

"Same. Down for the count." The second man walked into the kitchen and opened the fridge, reaching in and taking out a bottle of water.

"You should've just killed it."

Sarah gasped at their callousness, but the second man didn't even acknowledge her presence. And now he was just taking their stuff as if he owned it and talking about hurting her family.

She scowled at him. He was *so* going down if she had anything to say about it. She prayed he was wrong about Kevin. He was way tougher than anyone realized; he'd proven that enough times on the rugby field.

"I was going to, but then I saw that other guy and didn't have time to take care of it. It's just a friggin mutt anyway. Worst it could do is bite your ankle."

"Where's Jimmy?" asked the gunman.

"I dunno. I haven't seen him. He's out there somewhere taking care of that other kid. Where's the fourth one?" asked the second guy.

"Not here. Ask her where she is," the gunman said, pointing in Sarah's direction.

Sarah turned back around, refusing to acknowledge them now. They'd get nothing from her. She heard the sounds of his shoes crossing the room and then the chair next to her being pulled out. Refusing to look over, she stared at her fingernails, acting as if her manicure was way more important.

"Where's the other girl?" came the voice of the second man.

Sarah said nothing.

"I got your friend out there in the woods who's dead asleep with a big lump on his head. I got no problem going back out there and finishing him off with this," he said, placing a huge and very lethal-looking hunting knife on the tabletop. "So tell us ... where's the other girl?"

"Shouldn't you have a Russian accent?" Sarah asked.

The guy gave her a half smile. Maybe it was meant to be something nice, but all it did was make Sarah's stomach contents curdle.

"So you wanna play, huh? That's fine." He stood. "I'll be

right back. I'm gonna go cut that guy's ear off and bring it in here for her."

Sarah stood up and screamed, "No! Don't do that! I'll tell you where she is!" *What's the harm? She's far away, and Kevin will never forgive me if I let them cut off his body parts. Hell, I'll never forgive me if I let that happen.*

He walked back, slowly, as if he'd much rather be out dismembering her brother. When he got to the table, he faced her, standing much too closely for her comfort. "You don't wanna play anymore?" He lifted his knife up and brought it slowly to her chin, stopping when the point was just barely touching it. "That's too bad. I was looking forward to playing a little game with you."

She tipped her head back as far as she could to avoid being cut, but she felt the sting of his blade as it dug into her skin anyway. A warm trickle of blood came to the surface and bled down her neck in a slow stream.

"Leave her alone," said the guy on the other side of the room. "We need her alive, at least for now."

The knife left Sarah's face and she tipped her head back down, resisting the urge to punch the guy in the nose and kick him in the balls.

He turned his head and scowled at his partner. "You don't give me orders, Jack."

"No, you're right. I'm just repeating the orders of the guy who does. So leave her alone and get the information from her so we can get the hell out of here. If we found them, so can the others; and I don't want to be anywhere near here if that happens."

Sarah could hear her pulse in her ears. *Who are the others?*

More assholes with knives and guns or the police? She had a feeling asking would be fruitless, but she tried anyway. "Who are the others? The FBI?"

"Shut up, bitch. And tell me where that other little whore is, before I go remove parts of your sleeping friend out there."

Sarah swallowed the insult that was on the tip of her tongue. "She's in town. She left hours ago. We don't expect her back until ... tomorrow."

"Bullshit. She wouldn't leave you guys for a whole day." He looked over at the guy with the gun. "She probably went in for supplies. Their fridge is empty. She'll be back probably any minute."

"Good. We'll just wait for her then. Once we have them all together, we'll figure out what they know and then take care of the problem."

"Take care of the problem?" asked Sarah, unable to keep the fear from running her mouth. "Does that mean what I think it means?"

The guy sat down again next to her and laughed quietly, using the tip of his knife to carve some letters into the top of the table. "It means, pretty girl, that you are going to take a little nap. A dirt nap."

"Shut up, asshole. You're not going to help the situation by getting them all wired up."

The man in front of Sarah shrugged. "I don't give a fuck about helping the situation. I came here to do a job, and I'm going to do it. Simple as that. Like it or not. That's life." He smiled at her, revealing uneven, grungy, yellow teeth.

Sarah cringed at his disgusting face and horrific promises. She could almost hear Jonathan's words in her head, telling her their odds of survival had just gone down, knowing that the man in front of her was insane. He didn't just kill for money; he enjoyed it. He probably had a collection of body parts at his house. The blood drained from her face again as she realized she was probably staring into the eyes of the man who would take her life from her. And the life of her unborn child.

"Where the fuck is Jimmy?" asked the guy with the gun, distracting Sarah from her mother's instinct that had started to bloom across her chest, making her heart beat double-time. "That asshole should have been back by now."

"Want me to go look for him?" asked the guy with the knife, abandoning his carving job and standing.

"Yeah. Go find him and bring him back here. And tell him if he's fucking with that kid, he's going to answer to me."

"I doubt that's gonna do anything to scare him," said the guy as he walked out the door.

"Well, it better!" yelled the gunman at his partner's retreating form. "I speak for Baskov, you know!"

"Yeah, yeah!" came the faint response.

Sarah heard nothing for a few seconds and then just the gunman acting frustrated.

"Fuck! Goddamn asshole *idiots*. Why do I always get stuck with the degenerates?"

"I find it highly amusing that you don't include yourself in that group," said Sarah, feeling just a tiny measure of safety over the fact that he'd kept the other guy from hurting her brother. And he had chosen a gun for his weapon, which told her that he preferred to kill from a distance and move on. It struck her as slightly less psychotic than the hunting knife that was big and sharp enough to kill a grizzly bear. She glanced down at the table and read the name carved into it with the lunatic's blade: *Zed*.

"Shut up, you stupid bitch. You have no idea what you're talking about." His cultured tone disappeared. Maybe it was the stress doing it, but now he sounded like a guy faking being a man with a nice haircut and clothing.

"Are you going to let Zed kill us?" Sarah asked, wondering if he'd bite.

"How'd you know his name? I didn't use it once." He walked over to stand next to her on her right side, the opposite one from where Zed had been sitting.

Sarah slid her arm over on the table, covering up the carving as casually as possible. "Oh, we know about all of you. Jimmy, Zed, you ... Jack. The FBI told us to expect you and to set off the silent alarm as soon as you showed up." Sarah was busy pulling false information out of some secret dark recess of her brain that may have existed as a result of watching too many action films with Kevin at the helm of the remote.

"You don't have a silent alarm to the FBI. Do you think I'm a complete idiot? They'd have agents here if they knew where you were or that you were being followed."

Sarah shook her head. "Nope. This is how they decided to let it play out. They knew you'd be watching us and would see them if they were here. Plus, they're not far, so like I said ... they'll be here any minute."

As if on cue, footsteps came running up the porch stairs and the front door burst open.

*****

Candi was flush with the success she'd had at the library and grocery store, and in a huge hurry to get back and share the news with the others. Jason and Stephen had both answered her emails, and the information they'd given her had lit a fire under her butt. Things were happening, and they needed to make some decisions.

She pulled off the main road and onto the dirt road, but she hadn't gone far before she came upon a car parked over on the shoulder. She pulled up next to it and peered in the windows. It was a nondescript sedan, reminding her of a typical rental car. There was nothing inside it but a single manila folder lying on the front seat. Something that looked like a photograph was sticking partway out of the top.

Candi's blood pressure zoomed up. Something felt very wrong about a car being out here at all. *Why would someone stop so far from the house and the main road?* All of the answers that came to her were bad. She shut off the motorcycle and put the kickstand down, making sure it was going to stay up before she let go of the handles and walked around to the other side of the car.

She tried the front passenger door and found it unlocked. Reaching in with a shaking hand, she took the folder off the front seat and opened it up. She stopped breathing for a few seconds when she saw the first item.

It was her driver license picture. Her heartbeat roared in her ears as she paged through the other papers inside. Each of their DMV photos was there, printed in color. A couple other papers were with them, one of them a copy of a receipt from a cell phone store, another a printout of a map of the area with several Xs in outlying areas. One of those markings was directly over the spot where their cabin was located.

Candi shut the folder quickly and threw it back down on the seat. Pushing the door almost closed, she focused on not making a sound. She didn't want to make any more noise than necessary, now that she knew someone was here specifically to find them - someone who'd been searching lots of other cabins in the area, probably for the last week.

She rushed back to the motorcycle, standing it straight and pushing it with all her strength over to the other side of the road. She got it as far back into the trees as she could before abandoning it there, putting the keys in her pocket while hoping like hell she wouldn't have to get it out of there in a hurry later.

As she walked down the edge of the road, she thought about all the time and effort they'd put into setting up their warning systems and training the dogs for security, wondering if had been well-spent or wasted.

When she came upon the still form of James lying in the middle of the road, she thought she had her answer. Tears welled up in her eyes as she rushed to his side.

*****

Kevin moaned. Someone had hardcore tackled him on the rugby field. It was even possible he'd been slammed into an un-padded football field goal pole in the in-goal endzone area, the way his head felt. He tried to sit up, but the earth was spinning too much.

"Holy shit," he moaned again. "What the hell?" He looked down at his hands, realizing for the first time that there were leaves under him and not turf. "Where am I?" He lifted his head, blinking his eyes several times to get his vision cleared up. When things finally came into focus, he realized he wasn't on the rugby field; he was in the woods somewhere.

And then the memories came flooding back: prom, the tophat, gunshots, Barry in the ER, the FBI, an assassin, running away, getting this cabin, setting up security for ... He sighed and then punched the ground with a tight fist. "Fuck!" The bad guys had gotten through somehow, and he'd been lying on the ground passed out for who knew how long. He had to get up and find the others. Maybe it wouldn't be too late.

He struggled to his feet, battling nausea and intense dizziness. He held onto a nearby tree as his thoughts cleared and left him with the most amazingly awful headache he'd ever experienced. He took a few tentative steps forward, knowing that he probably looked like a drunkard, but not caring at all. His family was at risk, and he had to get to them, no matter what.

Ten feet into his trek he had to stop and vomit. The pain in his head was overwhelming, and the spinning was making him feel sea sick. He hadn't felt this bad since he'd been on that lifeboat in the middle of the ocean.

He continued on, trying like hell to stay quiet; but no matter how high he tried to lift his feet, they still made too much noise shuffling in the leaves and grasses. He fell twice before he reached the road.

"Left or right?" he asked out into the air around him. He couldn't tell were the cabin was in relation to where he was standing, and the dizziness that wouldn't go away wasn't making it any easier.

"Kevin?"

He rubbed his ears, not sure if he had imagined the sound of Candi's voice or not. There was a ringing there that accompanied the dizziness, making it difficult to get things straight in his mind. "Candi?"

"Kevin!" came her yelled whisper. "Where are you?!"

"Here," he said weakly, the idea of shouting making him want to throw up again.

Candi appeared around the corner to his right, her face way too pale and her hair sticking out in all directions. Sarah was going to be really upset when she saw it. Heck, so was Candi. He was wondering if he should say anything or just keep quiet about it. It probably wasn't important. Something was important, but he couldn't remember what it was. His head was hurting too much to concentrate.

Candi reached his side and hugged him hard. Kevin swallowed with effort, trying to keep from barfing on her head.

"Oh my god, I thought you were dead!" she cried.

"Dead?" he asked, wondering what she was talking about. "Why would I be dead?"

"Because! Someone's here to kill us!" She stared up at him and frowned. "I think. What's wrong with you?"

Kevin rubbed his head, wincing at the big bump his hand ran over in the back of his scalp. "Someone hit the shit out of me. I have a huge lump back here." He touched it again, more gingerly this time. It hurt like hell.

Candi reached up and touched the back of his head, her eyes going wide. "Holy crap, Kevin! It's as big as an egg!"

"Yeah. Hurts as big as an egg too."

"Lean down so I can see it," she commanded.

Kevin tried, but it made him fall a little to the side. He barely caught himself before going down again.

"You have a concussion, don't you?" she asked.

"Not sure. Maybe. Hold on a sec." He held up a finger for a couple seconds, then leaned over to the side and threw up again. He stood up straight and wiped his mouth off with the back of his hand. "Yeah. Maybe I do. Sorry about that."

Candi took him by the upper arms and pushed him back

into the woods.

"Where are we going?" he asked, not really caring at this point. He was just glad to have her at his side again and safe. All he needed to do now was take a little nap and he'd feel all better.

"You're going to stay here where no one will see you while I go find out what's happening at the cabin." She pushed on his shoulder, forcing him to bend his knees. "Sit! And don't get up."

Kevin slid down the tree she'd leaned him against, only cringing a little at the burning sensation it made as it scraped the skin on his back.

"Stay here. I'll be right back with James."

"Okay," said Kevin, sighing because sitting made the dizziness not as bad. And man, was he tired.

A little while later he was jarred awake by Candi's approach. She was carrying a dirty carpet in her arms.

"Watch him while I'm gone, and don't fall asleep," she commanded.

"Who?"

She set the carpet down in his lap. And now that it was closer, he could see it wasn't a carpet; it was a dog. *James.* "Hey, little guy. What's up? Taking a nap?" Kevin jiggled his left arm in an attempt to wake him up. "Yo, sleepy head. Time to get up and bite someone."

"He got hit too, just like you. I'm not sure how badly he's hurt, but he's breathing and his neck seemed fine, which is why I moved him. Just hold him until I get back, okay?"

"Okay," breathed out Kevin, closing his eyes. "I'll wait right here."

A shuffling sound following by an awful blazing pain at the back of his head had his eyelids flying open and his mind much sharper.

"Don't fall asleep, I said!" she whisper-screeched at him, her face only inches from his own.

"What the hell'd you just do?" Kevin asked pitifully, reaching behind his head.

"I pushed on your lump to wake you up. You cannot fall asleep, do you understand me? You could go into a coma or something."

Kevin stared at her, speechless.

"Don't you look at me like that!" she yelled. She dropped her voice, tears now in her eyes. "I had to do it to wake you up! I can't carry you if you go to sleep and don't wake up. And the others are in trouble, so I need you to be able to go on your own, do you understand?"

Kevin nodded.

"Anytime you feel yourself falling asleep, push on your lump."

He scowled. "Hell no, I'm not going to do that! Are you nuts?"

"Do it!" she yelled, slapping his face hard.

Kevin's head spun again once and then seemed to right itself. He stared at the sweet little gumdrop who he'd fallen in love with - the one who'd been scared and crying for half the trip. Right now she looked like she was about to go all Rambo on someone's ass, and he was a little frightened ... for them.

"Okay, okay, I'll stay awake. Geez. No need for physical violence." He pulled his arm out from under James' back and rubbed his jaw. "Nice left hook by the way."

"Thanks. Good. Now, I have to go. Stay quiet. Don't let anyone know you're here. If James wakes up, keep him with you." She stood. "I'm counting on you, Kevin. Don't let me down."

Kevin nodded, wincing only a little at the pain. It did have the effect of waking him up more. "Gotcha. Be careful, would ya?"

She leaned down and kissed him on the forehead. "I will. Wish me luck."

Before he could get the words of his response out, she was sprinting out of the forest. He quickly lost sight of her through the trees.

*****

Jonathan got to the lake with a big headstart. He panicked, not knowing what to do. He could keep running through the forest, his stamina such that he could probably go for hours without slowing; but he knew that eventually the guy would give up and go after his family - the ones who couldn't run like he could.

He spied the dock and made a split-second decision. It was reckless and completely un-reasoned, but there was no time to reconsider his instinctual thought process. He ran down the length of sun-faded wood planks and slipped into the water at the end of it.

Xena stopped at the edge and watched him go under, turning and dropping down onto her haunches to face the woods, once he was fully submerged. Jonathan could see her form just above him, wavering with the ripples he'd created in the water. He focused on breathing slowly and calmly, trying to keep the water from being disturbed and sending out signals showing exactly where he was.

He couldn't hear anything under the water, and he was almost out of breath, when he saw Xena's tail come out straight and then her hind end get closer to the edge of the dock.

He's here! He's coming!

Jonathan wasn't sure at first if he should stay underwater and swim away, surface and attack, or try and hide under the dock. But when he heard Xena's muted growling through the water, he surfaced, deciding that he'd rather face the danger and deal with the consequences than just wait for it to reach down and get him.

He came out of the water as smoothly and quietly as possible, the first thing he heard upon surfacing the frenzied growls of Xena. Whoever was upsetting her was close. There was no questioning the tone of her warning. One more step and whoever it was would be toast.

Jonathan couldn't wait any longer. He peeked up over the edge of the dock.

Standing just a few feet in front of his dog was the attacker, his knife out and held pointed in Xena's direction.

"Come on, you fucking mutt! Come on over here and get a taste!"

Jonathan reached up and touched Xena's ankle, praying she wouldn't swing around and bite him, but wanting her to know he was there. For some reason the idea of her protecting him and possibly sacrificing herself for him was more than he could bear. They'd gotten the dogs for protection, but now when faced with using them for that purpose, he felt very guilty - as if he'd valued his own human life more than her canine one, when she was just as valid a creature as he was. She'd suffered in her life and come out loving and protective to mere kids, even after having her own children murdered. He was ashamed to know that he had a lot to learn from a dog about how to treat others.

"Xena, back down. It's okay, girl. Just go back to the cabin."

She ignored him completely, her eyes never leaving the knife in the guy's hand; and as a result, she was more prepared for the guy's move than Jonathan was.

One minute the killer was standing there, and the next he was lunging for the dog, knife out and ready to slice and dice.

Xena moved so quickly, it was hard for Jonathan to put all the pieces together about what happened. The knife looked like it had met its mark, but then the guy was falling forward, faster than he seemed to want to, yelling.

The knife dropped to the dock, but his hand stayed on the dog. He rolled onto his side, coming to rest with his back to Jonathan's face. Whatever focus the killer might have had previously on getting Jonathan into custody had been completely taken over by his instinctual drive to save his hand from being torn from his body.

Jonathan used the distraction to his advantage. He grabbed the guy by the hair and pulled him back as hard as he could, using the leverage of his feet against the dock's support piling to extend the man's head out over the water.

The man screamed, now facing threats from two fronts. He struggled against Jonathan's pull, but his efforts weren't very effective. Jonathan held tight, despite being jerked around by the force of Xena's attack. She had the guy's wrist in her jaws, and she wasn't letting go for anything.

"She's tearing my hand off!" screeched the man. "Get her off me! She's taking my hand off!"

Normally, Jonathan would have helped him out, maybe even putting himself between the furry killing machine and her victim, but in this case he knew it was the man or him. If he helped him escape the dog's attack, the man would turn around and use the knife on both of them. He'd come here to kill and that's what he would do if given the chance. Jonathan couldn't allow that, so he just held on, refusing to help, refusing to let go. Just like Xena.

Something warm hit Jonathan in the face. At first he didn't know what it was, but then when he saw the arc of red liquid flying through the air, he knew. *Arterial spray. Xena's hit an artery. He's going to bleed to death.* The idea of a human being dying in his arms was too much. Jonathan let him go, intending to climb out of the water and hold him at bay with the knife, giving the man a chance to staunch the bloodflow.

But he underestimated the man's will to live.

The killer sprang up, the dog hanging from his mutilated arm.

He grabbed the knife off the dock in his other hand, raising it up to shoulder level.

Jonathan leaped out of the water and grabbed the man's ankle, but he was too late.

The knife came down hard and fast, burying itself in Xena's shoulder.

She growled anew, but didn't let go of his arm.

Jonathan was sure he was next for a knifing. He half-crawled and half-threw himself the remaining distance towards the man, bowling him over sideways. The dog went right along with him, her legs no longer working.

Blood sprayed everywhere, covering the dog's face and shoulders in a gruesome veil of red. Jonathan slipped on it, trying to gain purchase so he could end the mayhem once and for all. He fell over the man's legs, and his face landed very near Xena's.

It was the look in her eye that did it for him.

Patience. Dedication. Love. Loyalty. Death coming for her.

Jonathan grabbed the hilt of the knife and eased it out of her shoulder before lifting it high and plunging it down into the man's chest.

Gurgling sounds came from the killer's throat, but Jonathan ignored them, knowing the man was no longer a threat to him. He kneeled on shaky legs and leaned down to gather Xena in his arms. "Let him go, Xena. *Release.* We need to get you to the doctor."

Her jaws finally unlocked. Jonathan's stomach turned over at the hand that fell limply to the dock, almost completely severed from the man's forearm.

He struggled to his feet, the nearly seventy pound dog almost bringing him back to his knees several times as he made his way back to the cabin as quickly and as quietly as he could. With every step, Xena's blood ran down his arms to drip into the layers of dead leaves beneath them.

*****

Jack the kidnapper and probably soon-to-be murderer had been pacing the floor when the door flew open and Jonathan came running in, blood all over him and the dog he carried in his arms.

"Stop right there!" Jack yelled, holding out his gun.

Sarah saw him pointing the weapon at her boyfriend and lost her mind. She leaped up out of the chair and ran for him, intent on stopping him but with zero plan for how she was going to do it.

Jack saw her coming and swung the gun over at her. "Stop!" he yelled, just before she reached him.

She tackled him at the same moment that the gun went off.

Blinding pain seared her shoulder, but she ignored it in favor of ending the loser underneath her. They'd hit the wall behind him, giving her the perfect set-up to knee him in the balls. And knee him in the balls she did, as hard as she possibly could.

The gun fell from his limp fingers and was immediately snatched up by Jonathan.

The guy took Sarah down with him as he fell, his hands latching onto her shirt as he went nearly comatose with the pain.

She struggled to get him off, punching him in the face twice using her good arm before his hands finally came loose. The satisfying crunch of his nose breaking made the bleeding mess of her shoulder just slightly less awful.

"You've been shot!" yelled Jonathan, his voice going up an octave in his panic. "Oh my god, you've been shot!"

"Shoot him," gasped Sarah, rolling away from the killer and kicking him hard on her way. "Shoot him in the balls!"

"No, I'm not going to shoot him! I have to get you to the hospital!" He leaned down and pulled her away from the guy, dragging her over to the dog's side. "Stay here with Xena. She's injured too. I'm going to get the car." He put the gun in her hand and pointed it with her at the guy still writhing on the floor. "Only shoot if he comes after you, okay?"

Sarah nodded vaguely, looking first at the slimeball in front of her and then at the dog next to her, who was obviously suffering. Xena grunted whenever she tried to move and was whining at a barely discernible volume.

"It's okay, Xena," said Sarah, her voice sounding groggy to her own ears. "We're going to be fine. Jonathan's going to fix us up, you'll see. He's a total genius. I promise."

The gun sagged a little, so she let it rest on her leg. She had cramps down low in her belly that reminded her of period pain.

The warmth spreading out from her shoulder was a weird contrast to the cold that was taking over her body. She began to shiver.

The man in front of her moved, acting as if he were going to crawl in her direction.

She tried to lift the gun, but it was so heavy. "Stay over there or I'm going to blow you away, you sonofabitch."

He kept coming and Sarah began to panic. The dog growled and whined, struggling to move closer to Sarah.

"Don't move, asshole," Sarah begged, crying at the pain in her shoulder and the valiant attempts by her dog to help her. "I'm going to fucking shoot you, you idiot."

He kept coming, getting up on his hands and knees to cover the rest of the distance. He reached her foot and put his hand on it.

Sarah screamed, lifting the gun and pointing it at him. "Get off me, you *fuck!*" she howled, just before she pulled the trigger.

*****

Candi saw Jonathan tearing out of the cabin and racing towards the shed.

"Jonathan!" she yelled, jogging now in response to his obvious panic. "What are you doing?! Why are you soaking wet?"

"Getting the car! Sarah's been shot and Xena's been stabbed! Go help her!" He yanked the shed door open as Candi raced by. "Direct pressure on their wounds!" came a muffled yell from inside.

Candi made it to the cabin so fast, she didn't even notice her feet touching the ground or the fact that Jonathan hadn't answered all her questions. She took the stairs two at a time and burst through the door just as the sound of a gun went off, partially deafening her.

A man who'd been in front of Sarah fell back from the force of the bullet hitting him in the chest. He landed near the bedroom door, one of his arms twisted behind him.

Candi was shocked into immobility for a few seconds before she could gather her wits enough to continue on into the cabin.

"Sarah!" she yelled, getting over her shock enough to speak.

Sarah turned and looked at her, her complexion dead white. "Oh. Hey, Candi. What're you doing here?" And then she passed out, her head falling back and hitting the floor with a solid thunk.

Candi screamed and ran over to her, hovering over her friend's still form. She wasn't sure what she should first, do there were so many things wrong with this picture in front of her.

Xena's whining caught her attention, and she noticed immediately that the dog wasn't in any better shape than Sarah was. Both of them were covered in blood, and Xena was just seconds away from going into la-la land too. Her eyes had a faraway look to them, but she was crawling towards Sarah and made it far enough to rest her head on the girl's chest before she closed her lids too, letting out one long sigh as she lapsed into unconsciousness.

"Nooooo!" screamed Candi, standing there and wringing her hands. "Jonathan! Help me!"

No help came, and she knew she had to do something. She dropped to her knees, scrambling over to Xena so she could lift her head gently off Sarah's body and place it carefully on the ground. She was bawling as she worked and talked.

"I'm sorry, baby! I'm so sorry! Please forgive me. I have to get Sarah out first. She's carrying a baby in her tummy." She went back to her friend, staring at her white face. "Oh my god, oh my god ... *Sarah!* Don't you die on me, you brat!" She stood up halfway and leaned over, taking Sarah and dragging her through the door and out onto the porch by the material of her shirt, almost pulling it completely over her head in her hurry. "Noooo, dammit! Don't you die, you stuck up, self-centered jerk! Don't you dare! If you die, I'll *kill* you!"

Candi ran back into the house to get a kitchen towel, racing back out to put it on Sarah's shoulder. She left it there to go inside again when she heard the Camry roaring to life and driving up to the front of the house.

Xena lay on the floor, her eyes still closed. Candi rushed over and stood above her, straddling her prone form. "Okay, Xena. Now, don't bite me. I'm sorry if this hurts." She put her hands under the dogs front armpits and lifted her enough to drag her. She walked forward two steps at a time, using her lower back muscles to heave the dog towards the door between steps, inch-by-inch. The dog's limp legs just bumped along the floorboards behind her.

The door burst open and Jonathan strode in. "You go hold the towel on Sarah's shoulder. I'll get Xena." He scooped her up like she weighed nothing, and Candi stood up to go hold the door open for him. She followed Jonathan out to the porch and dropped to her knees by Sarah as he went down the stairs and loaded the dog in the back seat. She pressed down hard on the towel against Sarah's bleeding shoulder, trying not to freak out about all the blood that was already soaking through it.

When Jonathan was done, he came back for Sarah, picking her up like a baby in his arms, water dripping from his wet pants onto the porch at his feet. "How long has she been unconscious?"

"I don't know," wept Candi. "A couple minutes? Five? I have no idea!" Time had stood still. She had no concept of it or of reality in general. All of this was too unreal and awful to be happening.

"Don't worry about it." He reached the front passenger seat and waited for Candi to open it before putting Sarah inside. He leaned over to buckle her in before coming out again. "Where's Kevin?"

"Up the road. Just go," said Candi, breathless from the stress and the worry and the crying. She jumped into the back of the car, lifting Xena's head so she could cradle it in her lap in the center of the backseat.

Jonathan got in and buckled up, reversing so fast and yanking the wheel so hard to the right he made the car spin out to point in the right direction. Slamming the gears into drive, he pressed the accelerator to the floor, making the car shoot out diagonally at first and then down the path leading to the dirt road.

Seconds later they were barreling towards Kevin.

"Stop here!" yelled Candi. "He's over there in the trees with James. James got hit too. Both of them were hit."

"Stay put," said Jonathan, putting the car in park and getting out. He was only gone for less than a minute before he came out with Kevin walking next to him but hanging onto his shoulder for support. Kevin held James in one arm. The dog was awake now but definitely missing his usual energy.

Kevin got in next to Candi, shoving her over in his hurry to get inside and shut the door.

"Hey, what happened to Sarah?" he asked. "Jonathan's too freaked out to talk."

"She was shot by the jerk in the house."

Jonathan got into the front seat, slamming the car into gear and flooring the gas pedal. "Hang on. I'm going to break the speed limit." The car roared around the corner nearest the main road, sending gravel and dirt flying.

Kevin held onto the handle above the window. "I think you mean the sound barrier."

"Sarah and Xena have lost a lot of blood. We have to get them to the hospital or ..." Jonathan choked on the last part of his sentence.

Candi leaned forward and patted his soggy shoulder, his fear making her gain better control of herself. She couldn't fall apart when they needed her so much. "She's going to be fine. We all are. Just relax and get us there in one piece."

Candi was distressed to see the rental car missing as they drove by, the one with the folder in it. That meant the killers would still be out there, maybe even waiting for them at the hospital. But she'd worry about that when the time came. Right now, she just needed to pray that they were all going to survive the attack they'd just suffered. Later they could worry about how they were going to get through the next few days without being murdered.

Trials and Tribulations

KEVIN MASSAGED HIS SORE SHOULDER. He'd carried that little dog for what seemed like hours until someone at the hospital had finally felt sorry for him and taken the mutt off his hands, promising to watch him carefully while Kevin waited for his sister to get out of surgery. He was surprised they even let him in with the dog in the first place, but he figured it was probably the fact that they looked like they'd just barely survived a bombing or something that had caused the hospital staff to bend the rules. The veterinarian someone had called for them later had arrived two hours ago and taken Xena to her office for surgery and James for observation. He had her business card in his back pocket.

Candi came over and sat down next to him, handing him a cup of coffee in a styrofoam cup.

"Thanks," he said, nudging her affectionately before taking a big sip. He looked around as the cup rested on his lips. The stares of the strangers around them had ceased to bother him as of about three hours ago. Their bloody clothes were quite a sight, so he could hardly blame them. He'd stare too if he saw three kids who looked like they'd gone on a killing spree.

Kevin leaned over and tapped Jonathan's knee, gesturing for him to take the cup. "Come on, man. You have to drink something."

Jonathan just shook his head, saying nothing.

"Listen ... she's going to be okay. I know she is. She's too mean to do anything else." Kevin ignored the lump that rose up in his throat. He refused to go weak on his sister now. Candi and Jonathan all needed him to be strong and positive.

"Kevin's right. She's going to be fine," agreed Candi.

"I'm not just worried about her," said Jonathan, his voice ragged with emotion. "The baby ..." He dropped his head into his hands and sobbed quietly.

Candi rushed over, crouching down in front of her brother and taking him in her arms as much as she could. She was crying now too. "Jon, please don't cry. Everything's going to be okay. You know Sarah. She's strong and stubborn and totally protective of the baby. She'll pull through. They both will."

Kevin was glad Candi didn't say what he'd been thinking - that someday they could have another child if this one didn't make it. It was a natural thing to consider, but definitely the wrong thing to say. If he had to choose one or the other, he'd choose that his sister survive, no question; but hopefully, they wouldn't have to.

Kevin reached over and rubbed Jonathan's back, patting it hard a few times, at a loss for what to say to him. The guy was completely overcome with worry and sadness, and Kevin didn't consider himself that great with words on a good day. Physical stuff was more his thing.

Candi and Jonathan were so wrapped up in their misery, neither of them noticed the man who stopped in front of them.

Kevin was immediately on alert, and not because he thought the guy was an assassin, but because he was wearing a uniform.

"Hello," he said to Kevin, glancing at Candi on the ground and Jonathan in front of her.

"Hello," said Kevin. Candi and Jonathan looked at him for a second but ignored him, immediately going back to their own private world of misery.

"Can I talk to you for a minute, please?"

Kevin stood. "You can talk to me. Not them."

The officer raised an eyebrow but didn't argue. Motioning for Kevin to follow him, he walked away from the waiting area and into a nearby hallway. Kevin stopped when they got to a point where he'd no longer be able to see the Buckleys. "This is as far as I go."

The officer stopped and walked back to stand in front of him. "This is good enough. My name is Officer Baker with the local police department. Can you tell me your name?"

"No."

The cop's posture signaled that he didn't like being given this particular answer. "And why's that?"

"Because I have the right to be who I am without having to tell you, that's why. I haven't done anything wrong.

"You're with the young girl in surgery from a gunshot wound, correct? A nurse directed me to you."

"Yes, that's my sister. My twin sister."

"How'd she suffer the wound?"

"Some guy shot her, but not me."

"I need to fill out a report, and since you're a witness, I need to have your name."

"Who said I was a witness? I didn't say that. I know my

sister didn't."

"Oh ... well, I suppose I assumed it since you're the one who brought her in here."

Kevin crossed his arms over his chest. "You assumed wrong. Can I go now?"

"Of course. You're free to go whenever you want. But I'd appreciate it if you'd choose to stay and talk to me."

The officer's expression softened, and Kevin couldn't help but feel a little bit bad about evading his questions. But he had to hang tough for the safety of his family. This guy was a direct line to the FBI which was a direct line to their killers. He couldn't take the chance.

"I'm concerned about your sister. She's been seriously wounded, and that means either there's a person out there I need to apprehend and put behind bars, or there's someone out there who at the very least needs a lesson in gun safety. Either way, I'd like to be involved. The State wants me to be involved, yes, but this is personal too."

Kevin frowned. "How so? You don't even know us."

"No, I don't. But I had a younger brother who was killed by gunfire, and so I take these kinds of situations to heart." He cast his eyes down, clearing his throat a couple times.

"How old was he?" asked Kevin, unable to help himself. He was picturing losing Sarah, and it was killing him to even imagine it.

The officer's voice was rough. "He was seventeen. I was nineteen. He and a friend were playing with our father's gun when it went off."

Kevin's heart went out to the guy. "Man, I'm sorry. That really sucks."

"Yes. Thanks." He lifted his head to look at Kevin again. "So you can see why I'd want to help out here. Every time I see a young person with this kind of injury, I need to be involved ... for my brother."

Kevin searched the guy's face but could detect nothing but honesty and genuine caring there. Either he was a really good actor with a heart of stone trying to trick Kevin into trusting him so he could kill him later, or he was just a good cop trying to make a difference. Kevin wasn't sure if he should take the gamble and believe in the good cop angle, and with so much to lose, he wasn't in a position to make the decision alone.

"Listen, man ... I know you're just trying to help here. I can see that. But I've got my sister in surgery, and she's pregnant; I've got my girlfriend and her brother in there - and he's the baby's father ... it's just too much for me right now to be talking to you. You get where I'm coming from? I really need to get back there with them, so I'll see you." He held out his hand. "Sorry about your brother. I'm glad you're doing what you're doing to try and fix things with the world."

The officer took Kevin's hand and shook it firmly, reaching into his breast pocket with his free hand. "Take my card. It's got my cell phone number on it. If you ever want to talk or just ... whatever. Give me a call. I answer twenty-four seven."

Kevin took it and read the name. "William Baker."

"That's me," he said, holding onto his belt with two hands. "Call anytime. Seriously."

"Will do, man. Thanks." Kevin walked back to the emergency room, resisting the urge to turn and see if the guy was watching him.

*****

Jonathan looked up as Kevin approached, shivering a little from the cold air on his damp clothes. He'd seen him talking to the police officer in the nearby hallway and was relieved to see him returning so soon and not looking too distressed. Obviously he was concerned about his sister like they all were, but he didn't appear to be worried about being arrested too.

"What did he want?" asked Jonathan, his voice scratchy and hoarse. He twitched around a little on purpose, trying to warm himself up. His clothes were taking forever to dry out, and he could smell his damp sneakers without even bending over. It wasn't very pleasant.

"He wanted to talk to me about what happened to Sarah."

Candi stood and went back to her seat on the other side of Kevin. "What'd he say?" she whispered.

"He told me he wanted to help."

"Help with what?" asked Jonathan. He couldn't imagine how anyone but the surgeons could help them now. Everyone else was just going to get them killed.

"Help with the gun safety issue we're having."

"That's an interesting way to put our problem," said Candi, sarcastically.

"He assumed she was hurt by someone playing with guns. I guess we don't look like the type of people that get shot by criminals. Whatever. I told him we were too upset to worry about it right now and that I didn't do anything wrong."

"He gave you something," said Jonathan.

"Yeah. His card." Kevin pulled it out of his back pocket and held it in front of him so they could all see it. "He was a nice guy. I think he really cared and wanted to help. He told me about his younger brother who got killed when he was goofing around with a gun."

"That's terrible. I mean, that his brother was killed," said Candi.

Jonathan's heart spasmed, thinking about someone young being killed with a gun. Maybe that would be Sarah. He felt the tears coming again and turned away from the others, standing when it wasn't enough to keep them from spilling over. "I'm going to take a walk outside. I'll be back in a couple minutes."

"Want me to go with you?" asked Candi.

"No. I need to be alone for a little while. Just ... I'll be right back." He left without another word, needing to put some space between himself and the people he loved. It was too much, all this emotion and pain and worry. It was closing in on him, making him feel powerless and suffocated and overwhelmed. All he needed was some fresh air to help him gain his perspective again. At least, that's what he hoped would happen.

His shoes made squeaking sounds on the hospital's acrylic flooring with every step. *Squeak, squeak, squeak,* he went down the hallways, turning the last corner that would lead him out the doors of the emergency room.

He stopped short when he saw the police cars outside. There were three of them and a tow truck in the middle. It was hooking up their Camry and loading it to be taken away.

Jonathan's brain went into overdrive. *Why are they towing the car? It's not in a tow zone. It was in a legally designated space. Someone must have run the plates. It's the only explanation. Now they know the thief is probably in the building.* He made a u-turn and walked as fast as he could back to the surgery waiting area. *Squeak-squeak-squeak-squeak!* He ran when he thought no one would see him.

He got to the waiting area and made a beeline right for Candi and Kevin, sitting down next to Candi which put her in the middle. He spoke in hushed tones. "We have to leave!"

Kevin looked at him like he was crazy. "Leave? What are you talking about? We can't leave. Why would you say that?"

"There are three police cars outside, and they're towing our car away. They'll know the thief is in here!"

Candi looked around, fear etching lines into her forehead. "How will they know it's us?"

"Yeah, this hospital is huge," agreed Kevin. "There have to be hundreds of people here."

"Yes, but who comes to the hospital and parks in the emergency room parking lot? People who just had emergencies, that's who. All they have to do is talk to the nurses at the intake window and they'll be able to describe all of us perfectly. And Sarah's a virtual captive in there right now."

Candi grabbed each of their arms, squeezing until it made Jonathan catch his breath with the pain; but he didn't tell her to stop. He understood her panic, and the sensation she was giving him was waking him up out of the numbing fog his brain had been in.

"Babe, I'd like to keep the skin *on* my arm," said Kevin peeling her hand off and putting it onto his leg instead. "Come on, we just need to come up with a plan. We've made it this far, I'm not going to give up and just get arrested for stealing a car at this point."

Jonathan pushed his fingers against his temples, trying to block out the extraneous sounds and emotions that roiled around inside him and distracted his mind from being able to analyze the situation. "I just need to think!" he said, frustrated.

Someone patted his back, but his eyes were closed so he couldn't see who. *Probably Candi. Small hand.* Even this was too distracting. He dropped his hands to his lap and sighed. "I'm too stressed to think straight. I'm sorry, you guys. I'm falling apart under the pressure." He lowered his head. "I'm so disappointed in myself. I don't know why I thought I'd be a good father." Tears came to his eyes once more. He smiled bitterly at how easy they were flowing today. *I'm such a coward.*

Kevin stood all of a sudden, grabbing Jonathan by the shirt and hauling him to his feet. "Dude, say that one more time and I'm going to just punch you right in the face."

Jonathan's jaw dropped open as he stared at Kevin's serious expression. "Why?"

"What do you mean, *why?* You're my sister's boyfriend and the father of her kid! If you want that privilege you need to man the hell up! Sarah doesn't need a fucking wuss for a man in her life. She needs a *real* man. A fucking cowboy who doesn't fall apart when the shit gets difficult. I thought you were the guy for the job, but maybe I was wrong."

Jonathan smiled sheepishly, warmed to his soul that Kevin would care enough about his sister to feel so protective. It was exactly how he felt about her. Seeing Kevin being so strong inspired him. "I guess I should cowboy-up, then."

"Yeah. Whatever. Just grow some balls before I have to get ugly on your ass."

Candi stood and slapped Kevin's hands off her brother's shirt. "Okay, now that we have the testosterone show out of the way ... what's our plan?"

Jonathan shrugged, pulling his shirt back down. "I'm open to suggestions. I think my brain-computer is rebooting right now.

Analysis function not available, it's telling me." He smiled at his own amazing tech-humor. He was the only one, though. He contented himself with the knowledge that Sarah would have smiled at his joke, and he refused to let that make him sad. *Time to cowboy-up*. Sarah was going to be fine, and the most difficult thing he was going to have to manage later would be convincing her that the scar didn't make her hideous, which is exactly what she'd been moaning about as they'd wheeled her away to surgery hours earlier.

Kevin pulled the business card out of his back pocket. "I say we call this guy. Maybe he can help."

"What's the difference between talking to him and being arrested by cops we haven't met?" asked Candi. "Either way, we're going to jail and then we'll be dead. Game over."

"Maybe not. Maybe this guy has other ideas that might work for us. I really got a good vibe from him. I think he's the real deal ... like a good cop."

"But like Jonathan said ... the FBI has jurisdiction," countered Candi. "He'll just turn us over to them."

"I know, but maybe there's something else he can do. If they know our story and they know about the mole, maybe there's something *someone* can do. It's not like everyone in the FBI is bad. There's just a couple. We just need to hook up with the good ones."

"The problem is, we don't know who's good and who's not. How would anyone know?" asked Jonathan.

"I don't know!" said Kevin, clearly frustrated. "But I just don't see how we're going to get out of this! That cop who had Candi cornered at the grocery store knows that car. He was watching to see who was in it, and he followed it. I'm sure he put a report out on it, and that's how they found it so easily. Everyone in the damn force is probably looking for it ... and now us! We have to be proactive."

"By now they know the car is from our town," added Jonathan, his mind finally kicking into gear.

"Exactly. That's what I'm trying to say here. That car is a direct line to us. It's not going to take an investigative genius to put the pieces together." He looked around and dropped his voice to a whisper. "We're sitting ducks."

Jonathan stood. "Come on. Let's go hide."

Candi jumped up next to him. "Where?" She grabbed his arm, squeezing it again.

"Follow me," said Kevin, leading them over to the hallway where he'd stood with Officer Baker. He pulled open a door a little farther down from where they'd stood, revealing a storage room of some sort. "Wait here." He pushed Jonathan and Candi in.

"Where are you going?" asked Candi, freaking out.

"To a phone. I have to call this guy and tell him to meet us over here."

No one said anything for a few seconds. They just stared at each other, all of them near the edge of hysteria in their own way. Kevin was in bulldozer mode, ready to tackle anything that moved or disagreed with him. Candi was scared and using her nails on any available skin surface. Jonathan knew he himself was pale and losing his train of thought way too easily. "Okay," he said, finally. "We'll wait here for ten minutes, no longer. After that, we're leaving and hiding somewhere else, far from this area of the hospital. And if we can't get in to see Sarah, we'll just go back to the cabin on foot."

"That'll take a whole day!" said Candi.

"We have to do whatever it takes to survive," argued Jonathan, not unkindly. "I want to see Sarah, but she'll be safe here without us around to alert anyone coming through the waiting areas to our presence. And we all agreed that if one of us got caught, the rest would let him or her go. Sarah can't move for days after a surgery like this, probably more. She's not going back to that cabin anytime soon, if ever." Jonathan forced the tears away. *Cowboy-up. You can fall apart emotionally later when no one's around and no one's counting on you.*

"I agree. I'll see you in less than ten," said Kevin, kissing Candi quickly on the lips once before leaving them alone in the closet.

It was suddenly quiet as the door clicked closed. Jonathan turned his back to it and leaned against the fake wood, sliding down to rest on his rear end.

Candi slowly lowered herself to a sitting position in front of him. She stared at him for a long time before finally speaking. "Are you scared?" Her voice came out flat, no room in the small space for any echoes.

"Yes. Very much."

"Me too."

"It's normal ... to be frightened at a time like this. I'd be worried about our mental health if we weren't."

"But we've lived through so much, with the lifeboat and the island and everything. Shouldn't we be more calm and collected?"

"We've dealt with plenty of adversity before, but that doesn't make us immune. When our lives are threatened, which they are right now, chemicals in our bodies are manufactured and released into our systems to help us survive. It's a real miracle of science. I wish I had more time to think about it and study it right now, actually."

"Yeah. Not the time for TMI, though. Stay with me, okay?"

Jonathan frowned, confused. "I'm not going anywhere. We stick together."

"I don't mean physically. I'm talking mentally."

Jonathan nodded. "Yeah, I'll stay here with you. Sorry about earlier. The stress of worrying about Sarah and ... Peanut ... was getting to me."

Candi patted his knee. "I know. It's natural. But I'm a wimp, and I need you to keep me from freaking too hard."

"You're not weak; you're strong. I admire your ability to stay calm and be able to make well-reasoned decisions when dealing with these conflicts. I could learn a lot from you."

Candi laughed. "Oh, Jonathan ... you are so funny sometimes."

"What? What'd I say?"

Candi didn't have time to answer before someone was pushing on the door, trying to get in. Jonathan was ready to force it closed when Kevin's voice came through the crack.

"Let me in. It's me."

*****

Candi scrambled to her feet, her eyes widening in fear as the door opened wider. Kevin was standing next to a police officer with a very serious expression on his face. Candi's heart sank. This man did not look ready to help them; he looked fully prepared to hand them over to the people who wanted to end their lives. She felt judged before she'd even been able to open her mouth and give her side of the story.

"Come on," said Kevin. "We need to get out of here."

Jonathan stepped out without a word.

Candi hesitated, not so willing to just walk into certain death.

"He's cool, Candi. Let's go." Kevin reached in and took her by the hand, pulling her out. The warmth of his skin and sure attitude calmed her considerably. She knew he'd fight as long and as hard as he could to keep her safe. It gave her courage to face what was coming.

"Follow me," said the man, walking away. "There's a place we can talk without being interrupted."

He led them through a maze of hallways and doors, passing nurses' desks, administrative offices and room after room of patients, equipment, and supplies. He finally stopped at a nondescript door with a blank nameplate outside it on the wall. He turned the handle and pushed the heavy-looking door open, gesturing for them to go in ahead of him.

Kevin put his arm out to keep any of them from entering. "After you, Officer," he said.

The police officer lifted an eyebrow in question, but went in without arguing. Kevin followed, waiting for the others to get inside before shutting the door and turning the lock.

"Please, have a seat," said Officer Baker, pointing to the chairs that circled a conference table. There was a whiteboard at one end of the small room and a small table with a coffee machine on it at the other. Cups, spoons, sugar and powdered creamer sat next to the machine. A water dispenser stood on the floor just beside the cups.

Candi walked over and got some water for herself, Jonathan, and Kevin before finding a chair on the opposite side of the table from the man. Kevin and Jonathan were already seated, leaving her a spot between them. She sat down, feeling only a small amount of security over being in this room next to her two guys. It was too much like a trap to feel comfortable in.

"You called me and told me you had something to discuss. I'm all ears."

"Whatever we say ... can it be used against us?" asked Jonathan. "Like in a court of law?"

"Technically, if I ask you a question right now and you answer it, no. I haven't read you your Miranda rights. If you just volunteer information, then yes, it could be."

"Okay, then, you ask us a question and we'll answer it," said Jonathan, nodding at Kevin and Candi.

Kevin nodded back. Candi looked between the two of them before answering the obvious question. "How do we know you're telling us the truth?"

The officer blinked once before answering. "I guess you don't. The police dramas on TV get the process wrong a lot of the time, so you've probably seen it done differently. But on my honor as a police officer, I am telling you that's the truth and I have no intention of arresting you. At least not at this point. And if I change my mind about that, I will read you your Miranda rights and you will be entitled to an attorney before answering any other questions."

Candi nodded. Something about him was trustworthy, maybe because he could have just arrested Kevin out in the hallway and he hadn't. Kevin was right; this guy seemed genuinely caring.

"I'll ask the first question, and any of you can respond. First, why are you here in the hospital?"

"My sister was shot by a man with a gun. A man who wanted to kill all of us," said Kevin.

Candi measured the police officer's response by his expression and body language. He remained impassive, nonjudgmental.

"And why did this man want to kill you? Was he robbing you?"

"No. He was hired to kill all of us. By a Russian guy named Boskerov."

"Baskov," corrected Jonathan. "His name is Baskov, and he's responsible for a lot of organized crime in the area we're from."

"And where are you from?"

"South of here. And East," said Candi in a hurry, cutting off answers from the guys. She wasn't sure she was ready to divulge that information yet.

The officer stared at her for a second before nodding once. "Okay, and why would an alleged crime boss want to kill four teenagers who look ... well-mannered and taken care of?"

"We witnessed something we shouldn't have while we were ... out of town. And we were being approached by the FBI to testify against him. The same day, before we could meet with them, someone tried to kill one of us," said Kevin. "Me, specifically."

"And what happened?"

"They shot a friend of mine who looked like me."

"How did he look like you?"

"He was wearing my tophat."

"You were wearing a tophat?" The officer looked confused. "Why would you do that?"

"I asked him the same thing," said Jonathan.

"Me too," said Candi, sneaking a glance at her boyfriend and giving him a little smile. It had seemed so fun and carefree at the time - such a big change from right now. She'd give anything for that stupid tophat to be the biggest worry in her life.

The officer sighed deeply, leaning forward in his chair, his hands folded together. "Explain, please."

"We were at the prom. I wore the tophat because it was cool as hell. And then my friend stole it and went outside and got shot. Later that night in the hospital we were approached by the FBI and put in a safehouse. They told us some guy said the shooter was looking for a guy in a tophat. That night while we were supposed to be sleeping, a guy came in and killed everyone."

"A guy." The officer sounded like he didn't believe Kevin.

"Yes. A guy. He had greasy black hair, and he used a big friggin knife."

"And how do you know who did it? And you said he killed everyone? Who did he kill?"

Candi jumped in. "We know because he came for us after he killed the FBI agents, and we jumped him."

"How did you manage to survive when trained FBI agents didn't?" His tone was clear. He didn't believe them at all.

"We're trained too," said Candi proudly. "Maybe not in the traditional sense, but we're a lot more physically fit than your average teen."

The officer raised an eyebrow again. "Explain?"

Jonathan sighed. "Sir, we really don't have time to tell you everything. Honestly, there are people looking for us, and we have to do what we can to stay hidden. Our lives depend on it."

Officer Baker put his hands flat on the table, looking at each of them with a very serious expression. "I can help you if you have good reason to stay hidden and you haven't broken the law."

Candi shifted in her seat, knowing that was going to be a problem. She opened her mouth to speak, but Kevin beat her to it.

"Short version: This past Spring, we were on a cruise together. We ended up on a lifeboat and then out on a deserted island. Or so we thought. After a month or whatever, we found a whole drug operation going on there, and ended up escaping using one of the drug-runner's boats. The FBI needs us to testify to what we saw there and identify the men who were involved."

Officer Baker sat back in his chair suddenly, a look of shock passing across his features. "Wait a minute ... you're ... you're those kids who were on that cruise from Miami!"

All three of them nodded.

"I read about you online, on the news!"

"Yes. That's us. And now we're running for our lives. We did steal a car to get away, we admit that," said Kevin.

"But that was to save our lives, so I'm pretty sure there's some sort of ... rule that we can't be in too much trouble," added Jonathan.

The officer was shaking his head. "I can't believe it. This is all so fantastic."

"I don't think it's very fantastic," said Candi, frowning at his casual response. "I think it's pretty sucky, actually."

"No, not fantastic as in great ... fantastic as in unbelievable. Literally, not to be believed."

"I can see as how you'd feel that way, sir, but it's true," said Jonathan. "All of it, one hundred percent."

"Why didn't you just go to the police?" the officer asked, his voice full of professional passion. "That's what we're here for! We could have helped you avoid all this." He leaned in towards them again, gesturing with his hands. "You kids have really stressed yourselves out trying to go it alone. It's completely reckless, what you've done."

"You haven't heard the worst part yet," said Kevin.

The man sat back. "I have a hard time believing that. Tell me. What's the worst part?"

"When we went downstairs in the safehouse to see if the FBI agents were okay, we found one of their duffle bags filled with cash. It had to be a payoff. How else would the killer have found us?"

Jonathan added a fact Candi hadn't heard before. "And I saw one of the guys who came after us today in the hospital when we were there after the prom. Someone's following us, and someone in the FBI is tipping them off about us."

"If someone's following you, they wouldn't need someone in the FBI tipping them off," said the officer.

"Yes, but how did they know about us being witnesses?" asked Candi.

"She's right," agreed Jonathan. "We hadn't yet met with the FBI about our role as witnesses. They called our house the afternoon of the prom and made arrangements to meet us the next day. But that night someone shot at Kevin ... or the person who they *thought* was Kevin. The only person who could have told them about us as witnesses was someone in the FBI."

"And we know that if we go to the cops, they'll just turn us over to the FBI, so we're screwed," said Kevin.

The officer was nodding, staring down at the table. Everyone remained quiet as he considered what they'd told him.

"So you were looking at law enforcement as people who would eventually get you killed," he finally said.

"Exactly!" said Kevin, sounding very relieved. "You totally get it. So now you know why we can't go with you or get arrested or do anything else that would lead these guys back to us."

"But your sister is in danger. She's going to be here for a week or so, completely unprotected."

"We'll protect her," said Candi, feeling very bold and sure of herself. When she was determined, she could do anything.

The officer shook his head. "I know this hospital very well. They don't allow overnight guests. She'll be alone every evening. If I were someone tasked with killing her by this Baskerov person, I could slip in and out without being seen without too much trouble."

Candi's blood chilled. "Why would you say such a thing?"

He threw up his hands. "To get you to see reason! You can't protect her or yourselves. Today should have proven that to you. You need help from law enforcement."

"We appreciate your enthusiasm, sir, but you can understand why we would choose to decline that offer," said Jonathan, sounding sad.

"I think there's something you're not understanding, though; and I'd be remiss in not giving you this information before you made your decision."

"What's that?" asked Candi, no longer trusting him so much.

"The FBI has regional offices - different ones in each city. Just because the staff in your area is questionable, it doesn't mean every office is under the influence of this Baskerov person. If we bring you to the FBI office here, and inform them of the facts that you've given me, you'll be protected by a different team altogether. And the ones on the original team will be placed into custody. The FBI doesn't mess around when it comes to that kind of thing. They don't tolerate turncoats or traitors."

Candi looked at her brother and Kevin. She wasn't sure about them, but she knew for a fact that she'd never considered that idea in just that way. She just saw the FBI as one big mass of people in black suits, all connected, all under the same orders and influences.

"I'd like to talk to my family," said Jonathan. "In private."

Officer Baker stood. "Be my guest. I'll be right outside."

"No," said Kevin, also standing. "You stay in here. *We'll* step outside."

Candi nodded, moving towards the door, happy that Kevin had made sure to keep them from being trapped inside. She was feeling nervous enough as it was. Maybe Kevin's plan was to just run; she wasn't going to argue if it was. She was totally ready to take off.

They stepped outside the door. Candi started to shut it, but Kevin stopped her.

"Leave it cracked. I want to hear if he's calling anyone on his cell."

Candi nodded, taking her hand off the door. "So what do you guys think?" she asked.

"I think he's being honest," said Jonathan.

"I do too," said Kevin. "But he may be underestimating the reach of Baskov. What if he's up here too?"

"Don't you think he would have heard the name?" asked Candi. "He didn't seem to know it."

"What if he's on Baskov's payroll?" asked Jonathan. "How

would we know? Maybe he flubbed up the name on purpose to throw us off."

"Paranoid much?" asked Kevin. "Come on, man ... this guy could have turned us in or arrested us ten times by now. We've been locked up in the room with him for a while now, and no one's come to arrest us. He hasn't made a single call."

"Maybe he's texting someone," said Candi, lamely. She knew Kevin was probably right, but she shared Jonathan's paranoia. She'd be much happier walking back to the cabin and setting up a fortress to wait for that killer who got away than sitting here waiting to be arrested. They could wait for Sarah to get out, steal another car, and go to California for real. Or Alaska, even ... start a whole new life.

"I know that look, Candi," said Kevin, pulling her in for side-hug. "You're thinking of going all reckless on us, like Baker said. I think we need to stop running. Sarah being hurt gives us no choice. That guy was right. She's just lying there, too easy to kill. It could even just be a fake nurse who comes in and injects her with something like in the movies. We'll never be able to protect her in here."

Jonathan nodded. "I hate to say it, but I'm afraid we don't have any choice. We have to put our trust in those who've sworn to uphold the law. There have to be some good ones out there who will believe us and protect us. We haven't done anything too wrong. I'm certain we'll find people who will want to help us do the right thing."

"But what happens if we do testify? What's to stop Baskov from coming after us to punish us? To prove to anyone else they should never go against him?" asked Candi.

"He'll be put in jail, and we'll be leaving for college next year," said Jonathan. "By the time he gets out, if he ever does, we'll be adults with families living somewhere else. We can change our names if we want. I'm not going to run for the rest of my life, Candi. I can't live like that, and neither can you. We just need to do the right thing and hope the universal laws protect us."

"I don't even know what those laws are, but I'm inspired," said Kevin, punching Jonathan lightly in the arm. "Come on, Gumdrop. Let's do this. I'll do everything I can to watch your back, I swear."

She smiled without much enthusiasm. "I know you will. And I'll do the same for you guys. Just promise me ... if the good guys go bad, you'll run and never look back."

"I promise," said Kevin, putting his hand out.

"I promise, too," said Jonathan, putting his hand on top of Kevin's.

Candi placed hers on the top of the stack. "I promise too. Let's go. One-two-three-break!"

They pumped their hands in time with her counting and then lifted them up on the last part. Smiling, they all entered the room. Officer Baker was standing in the middle of the space, sending someone a text message.

*****

Sarah moaned. The pain in her shoulder and abdomen was excruciating. She smacked her lips a few times, grossing out over the gooey, sticky sensation in her mouth. She tasted medicine and plain old stink breath.

"She just tried to say something!" said Candi's voice. It was coming from down on the ground.

Ground? Wait ... I'm not standing. I'm on my back. Candi's at my feet. Where am I? Sarah tried to open her eyes, but the effort required was too great for her right now.

"Try to say something else," said Jonathan. He was off to her right, possibly the one squeezing her hand.

She squeezed it back, trying to let him know she wanted to talk but couldn't.

"She moved! She gripped my hand! Sarah, I know you can hear me. You're in the hospital. You were shot, but you're okay now. You're okay! Did you hear me?"

She was too absorbed with the shock of what he'd said to let him know she'd heard. *Shot? Who shot me? What about the baby? Am I going to be blind from it? Did they sew my eyes shut?* The panic set in as she considered the fact that she might never see again. She moaned again, louder this time, determined to open her eyes if it was at all possible. She focused everything she had on forcing her lids open.

"She's trying to say something again," said Candi, her voice now on Sarah's left. "Sarah, say it again. We can't understand you."

"Eyes ... won't ... open ...," she said, barely able to get her mouth to form the words.

"Here. Let me help you," said Candi.

A blindingly bright light seared Sarah's eyeballs as her lids were forced open.

"Gaaaahhhh!" she screamed, praying for darkness again.

The fingers immediately left her face. "Ooops. Sorry. I was just trying to help."

"Water ...," Sarah whispered, just before the blackness closed in around her, sending her back into sweet oblivion.

*****

Kevin watched as his parents got out of the car and approached the front door, the Buckleys still struggling to get out of the back seat. Kevin and Candi were waiting for their parents in the living room of the safehouse they were staying in - one thankfully manned by the local police department and the local FBI office, working as a team. They hadn't been there a full twenty-four hours yet, but they'd made it this far without being shot or stabbed, so things were looking good. At least, as good as they could look, all things considered. Xena was still at the vet's office after her surgery, and James was being carefully watched by Candi. Sarah was upstairs.

Kevin sighed heavily as Candi's arm slid around his waist.

"Nervous?" she asked.

"Yeah. Preparing myself for my dad's usual bullshit. I'm afraid I'm going to end up punching him in the head at some point."

"He's not going to do anything to make you want to punch him," she said, a vague scolding tone to her words.

Kevin could tell - nothing was going to get her too upset today; she was too excited about seeing her parents. Kevin wished he felt the same about his own. "You don't know my father very well, do you?" he asked, wondering what the guy was going to do to embarrass him today. Sarah was probably still too sick in body and mind to even care what Frank did. That alone was enough to put Kevin on edge. One false move and his father was going to be one sorry mofo.

"I may not know him that well, but I know on the phone he sounded ... better," Candi offered.

"He was probably just behaving himself because he knew people were listening."

Frank was walking up the path to the door, allowing his wife to go in front of him while he carried a small overnight bag in his hand. The doorbell rang a few seconds later.

"At least he's not busting down the door." Kevin looked over as a uniformed police officer walked around the corner to invite their guests in. Kevin moved away from Candi's embrace to greet his father at the entrance to the room. *Might as well get it over with.*

The door opened and he listened as first his parents and then Candi's exchanged greetings with the officer. Moments later, his father appeared from the foyer, entering the living room.

Kevin expected there to be manly handshaking and possibly shoulder slapping as a greeting, so he was completely taken off guard when his father took too big steps and pulled him into a strong embrace.

"Son ..."

Kevin stood stock still, not sure what to do at first. As his father continued talking, he found his arms moving up of their own volition to hug him back.

"We were so worried. We thought you'd been kidnapped or ... worse." His voice caught, and he pulled back. His eyes were bloodshot and shining with unshed tears. "We're so happy you're okay."

"Yeah ... thanks. We're not exactly okay, though, are we?" Kevin felt the anger rising up in him. His father so carelessly disregarding his daughter's situation was enough to make him lose it. Kevin had never paid much attention to his sister and father's relationship before, but he sure was now.

"We heard about Sarah. They said she's here. Can we see her?"

"That depends," said Kevin, stepping away from his father. Before he could say anything else, his mother appeared at her husband's side.

"Darling!" she said, rushing over to hug him. Kevin accepted her affection and patted her back while she cried. "We were so worried! Worried sick!" She stepped back and looked up at him. "We assumed the worst. All those FBI agents killed! Murdered! The only bit of hope we had was there was no sign of ... you being hurt."

"Thanks to Sarah, none of us were." He glanced over at his father, giving him a hard look before going back to his mom. "If she hadn't taken our attacker down, we'd all be dead, just like those agents."

Kevin's mother threw her hand up to her mouth, a squeak of shock coming out.

Frank walked over to stand next to his wife, putting his arm around her waist. "Don't cry, now, Angie, we discussed this. We're going to keep our heads cool and help the kids figure out their next moves. Cool heads, remember?"

She nodded, wiping tears from her cheeks and clearing her throat. Kevin watched as she fought to gain control of her emotions, her expression so close to crumbling he knew just one wrong word and she'd fall apart.

"Where's Sarah?" asked Frank. "We'd like to see her if the doctor says it's alright."

"He's up there with her. You just have to knock on the door, and they'll either let you in or tell you to go away." Kevin sighed. "But Dad, listen ... maybe you shouldn't go up."

"Son, I'm going to go visit my daughter. She's been gravely injured, and she needs to see her parents. She needs our support."

"Yeah, that's true that she does need your support," said Kevin, his voice raising with anger. "She's needed it her whole life, not just now; but you haven't managed to give it to her before, so I'm not sure I trust the fact that you're going to give it to her when she's lying on her back in a hospital bed and not doing well at all."

Frank said nothing for a long while, just staring at Kevin and then at Candi.

Kevin watched his girlfriend lift her chin a little in response, and he was fiercely proud of her in that moment. She'd never let his dad intimidate her, which said a lot. Frank could be an overbearing prick sometimes, used to getting his way and not caring who he hurt in the process.

"Your father's not going to do anything wrong, Kevin, sweetie," admonished his mother. "You don't need to talk like that to him."

Kevin turned to his mother, his complete lack of respect for her evident in his expression. "Mom, I'm sorry to have to say this to you, but what the hell would you know about it? Dad's been treating Sarah like shit for years, and you've just stood by and let him do it. Or should I say, you *sleep* by and let him."

Angie's hand flew up to her throat. "What ...? What are you saying, Kevin? It's not like that ... I'm not like ... what kind of mother do you think I am?"

Kevin was happy to feel Candi's presence at his side. She'd moved closer, and her warmth was all the support he needed right now to lay out all of the truth to his parents. He noticed that the police officers who'd been on the perimeter of the room had quietly filed out.

"I think you're the kind of mother who cares more about appearances and material things than the happiness of her children."

"Kevin, don't talk to your mother that way," said Frank. He didn't sound mad, like Kevin had expected him to. He sounded tired.

"I'll talk to her any way I please. All I'm doing is telling her the truth, something she should have heard from me a long time ago. It never should have gotten this far. And while I'm on the subject, I have some stuff I'd like to say to you too, Dad." That word *dad* left a bitter aftertaste in his mouth.

Frank held up his hands. "You have every right to say what you want to say. But I have some things I'd like to say as well."

"Fine. Wait your turn. What I want to say is that the way you've been acting towards Sarah, towards the Buckleys - especially Jonathan - is inexcusable. I don't care what she's done, Sarah is your daughter, and she needs your love. Not your anger, not your criticisms, not your bullshit. I used to just ignore it and let her handle it, but not anymore. She's my sister, and I'm not going to let you bully her anymore." He stopped and then let out a huge breath. It felt like he'd vomited out about ten years of pent-up frustration at his parents, and while it was cleansing, it was also stressful. His pulse was pounding out of control, and all he wanted to do was finish off this little talk with a good tackle, pinning his father to the ground and pummeling him. But the feeling quickly dissipated in the wake of his father's response.

"You have every right to feel this way, Kevin. I'm man enough to admit that. You probably want to pop me right in the nose right now, and I don't blame you. I ... we ... didn't come here to fight or to lay blame or argue. We came to see if you and your sister were okay and see what we could do to help. Obviously, we have some issues to sort out. I take responsibility for that, and for our situation at home." He glanced at his wife who nodded while wiping tears off her face. "I've been under a lot of stress for the past couple years, and I've taken it out on you guys ... especially your mother and sister. I'm sorry for that, I really am."

"Everyone has stress in their lives. That's not an excuse," said Kevin, not at all ready to just forget everything his father had done.

"I know that. But some people handle stress better than others. It brings out the ugly part of my personality, unfortunately. But your mother has convinced me to get help." He held out his arm for her and she quickly stepped over to be with him. "I started to see someone ... a therapist. And I want you to know I'm going to keep going until I get everything worked out. I'm committed to it a hundred and ten percent."

"He's done really well so far, Kevin. You'd be very proud of him."

Kevin was more than stunned. His father had always talked really badly about therapists, calling them quacks and thieves.

Candi took a step towards Frank. "I think it's great that you're doing that, Mr. Peterson. Congratulations."

She squeaked in surprise when he released his wife and stepped up to give her a warm hug.

"Thank you, Candi. That means a lot." He let her go and walked back to be next to his wife. "We're really worried about Sarah. We'd like to see her. But if you think we should wait, we'll wait. Whatever you think is best - you know your sister better than we do. We don't want to cause her any more pain; I hope you can believe that."

Kevin didn't know what to say. If this wasn't a trick, it was maybe exactly what Sarah needed ... real parents. But if it was just his father being an ass, which he was really good at being, then it would be the last thing she needed. He shook his head. "Who are you, and what have you done with my father? You know ... Frank Peterson? Mister Hardass himself?"

Frank grimaced, raising his hand halfway. "Still me. Still a hardass. Only now I'm trying to channel it in other ways."

Kevin shook his head. "Let me go ask her. I'll be right back." He nodded at the Buckleys who were still standing in the front hall on his way up. The sounds of them greeting a jubilant Candi followed him up the stairs.

He took the stairs three at a time up to the temporary hospital room they'd made for Sarah in the safehouse. She was lying in an official hospital bed, wearing comfortable pajamas one of the agents had bought for her.

She turned her head as he entered. The doctor nodded and left them in the room together. "Hey, bro," she said in a soft voice.

"Hey, sis. Listen, I have some good news and some bad news."

Sarah looked at him blankly. "I'm not sure I can handle any more bad news in my life right now." Her hand went down to her stomach and rubbed it absently.

"Okay, I'll skip that part. Good news ... dad seems to have had some sort of epiphany and is no longer a flaming assbag."

Sarah remained quiet, her face impassive.

Kevin wasn't sure what to do with that response, so he talked some more. "He's seeing a therapist. Can you believe that? And he was really nice to mom, too."

"So?"

"So ... and here comes the bad news you didn't want to hear ... he wants to see you. They both do."

"No," she said turning away, but not before he saw the tears in her eyes.

"Come on, Sarah. Don't be like that."

She whipped her head back, glaring at him. "I can be any way I want! I don't have to see those jerks ever again if I don't want to!"

Kevin took her hand off the top of the covers, rubbing it awkwardly. "You're right. You don't have to. No one will let them up here if you say no. But I think you should let them up. Talk to them. For me?"

"Don't do that, Kevin. Don't ask me like that." She was crying now, letting the tears fall freely down her cheeks.

"If I thought for a second that he'd say anything rude to you, I'd beat his ass out on the front lawn myself. But I honestly think he wants to just apologize and try to be supportive."

She snorted angrily. "He doesn't even have a clue how to do that."

"He seems different." He squeezed his sister's hand to shut down the argument he saw coming. "I know it hasn't been very long, but maybe almost losing us made him see the light. I don't know. But seriously. Just give him one chance, and if he screws it up, I'll throw him out myself. I've got your back."

"I know you do," she said, sighing pitifully. "Fine. Show the assbag in. But don't you *dare* leave me alone with him."

Kevin looked around. "Where's Jonathan? I thought he was up here with you."

"No, he's in the other room using the FBI agent's laptop to surf the Internet. He's talking to Stephen, telling him we don't need him to be our messenger anymore."

"I hope someone contacts Jason, too," said Kevin, trying to be fair to the guy.

"He is. Candi made sure of that."

Kevin frowned but said nothing. His girlfriend had made it more than clear how she felt about his jealousy. He turned to go, using his best Terminator voice to say, "I'll be back," before going out of the room and back down the stairs.

His parents were standing in the living room, speaking with the Buckleys in hushed tones. Candi was next to her father, his arm draped across her shoulders. She was nodding her head at something Frank had said.

"Sarah said you can come up."

Frank separated himself from the group. "Mind if it's just me to start? Angie said she'd go second."

"Whatever. I'm coming with you." Kevin followed his father up the stairs, forcing himself not to crack his knuckles in preparation for a fight.

*****

Sarah was so nervous she felt like she was going to be sick. The sounds of footsteps coming up the stairs made her want to run. But she was wired to this stupid hospital bed and the machines around it, and too weak to pull all of it out and go. Sweat broke out on her upper lip, and she swiped it away angrily. She hated that her father could do this to her so easily.

The door opened slowly, and Kevin's head peeked in. "We're here ... me and dad. You decent?"

"Shut up," said Sarah, smiling even though she didn't feel like it.

He came in and her father followed.

Kevin was right. He looked different. *Weird. He looks like ... a wimp.* She was so used to her father being bigger than life, busting into rooms, talking in a voice that was always too loud and sales pitchy. Here was a man whose chest wasn't sticking out like a rooster anymore. He held a baseball hat in his hands, scrunching up the bill, folding it in half and running his fingers nervously along the edges.

"Hello," Frank said, his voice barely above a whisper. His gaze took in the machines beeping and the bed raised up high enough for doctors and nurses to manage her wound and other medical needs.

"Hi," she said warily. She was waiting for the scolding to begin.

He walked closer to the bed, stopping just at her side. "How are you feeling?"

"Like crap. Thanks for asking."

"Sarah ...," warned Kevin.

She scowled at him once before turning back to her father, waiting for his next move.

"We heard you were shot. We've been so worried. Worried sick, in fact."

"Yeah, well, we did what we had to do. Sorry I got mom all upset."

Frank reached out and took her hand. "It wasn't just your mother. I was upset too."

Sarah looked at the ceiling, ignoring his touch, not allowing herself to get set up for the fall that was surely coming. She'd spent enough years yearning for his affection to know that pain and disappointment were inevitable. "Well, as you can see, Kevin's fine, so you can go home now."

"But you're not. And that's why we're here. That's why *I'm* here."

Sarah said nothing.

Her father squeezed her hand, rubbing the back of it gently with his thumb. "I was a genuine asshole to you, Sarah. And to your mother and by extension to your brother, too. I'm sorry. I'm man enough to admit I've made some big mistakes. But I want you to know I'm trying to fix it. I'm willing to fix it. I want to do that. But it will make it a lot easier if you could find it in your heart to forgive me."

Sarah yanked her hand away, crying now and unable to stop it. "Did they tell you? Is that why you're here?"

"Tell me what?"

"About me? About the baby? I'll bet you're happy about it!"

The door opened suddenly and Jonathan came in. "What's going on here?" He strode over to Sarah's opposite side, positioning himself across from Frank. "Why are you crying?" He looked up at Frank. "Mr. Peterson, I think you should leave now."

Frank put his hands back onto his ballcap.

"He didn't say anything wrong," said Kevin. "He's just trying to apologize for being a dick."

Frank turned around to look at his son, but Kevin shrugged. "Sorry about the language, but it's pretty accurate."

Frank nodded, facing Sarah again. "He's right. It's accurate."

"Wow," said Jonathan. "Did you just admit you're a male's private part or did I misunderstand?"

"No, you've got it right," said Frank, sighing. "I need to apologize to you too, Jonathan." He held out his hand across the bed for a handshake. "I've been unfair. You've been very good to my daughter, and I owe you for that. You were there for her when I should have been."

Jonathan stared at his hand and then at Sarah.

She said nothing; she just watched him very, very carefully. Her emotions were on a roller coaster ride from hell. What he did right now would mean so much to her. She didn't even know what the right thing to do was, just that it would say something - mean something - to her.

Jonathan's hands remained at his sides. "Sir, I'd like to shake your hand right now, I really would. But until Sarah decides that you are forgiven in her heart, I cannot do it in good conscience."

Sarah started bawling, holding out her arms for Jonathan.

He leaned down without hesitation and enveloped her in his strong embrace, letting her cry all over his shoulder.

"What do you want me to do?" he whispered in her ear.

She got her sobs under control before answering. "Oh, just shake his stupid hand. Get it over with."

Jonathan gently released her and held out his hand. "I accept your apology."

Frank entered into the handshake. "Thank you." He turned to Sarah. "I'll give you all the time you need to figure this out. I don't expect the world. Just one chance, that's it."

"That's asking a lot," said Sarah in a voice barely above a whisper.

"I know. But I'm asking for it anyway."

"One chance," she said, her heart thumping painfully in her chest as she took in his earnest expression and tears.

He nodded once. "I'm going to get your mother. She's been worried sick." He turned to leave the room.

"Dad?" said Sarah as he reached the door.

He turned. "Yes?"

"I'm sorry too."

Frank came back to give her a hug. She cried with abandon,

for the baby she'd lost, for the years her father and she had wasted, for the huge ugly memory she'd always carry on her shoulder of the day she'd taken a person's life from him. She'd been reckless and paid for it, and she'd been thinking she'd never be able to recover. But feeling the safety and love from her father, the one who she'd thought had abandoned her forever, gave her hope.

Maybe ... just maybe ... there could be joy in her life again.

*****

Jonathan laid the flowers down on the tiny headstone, standing again to put his arm around Sarah's shoulders. They were alone in the cemetery, their armed guards standing near the parked cars, their family waiting patiently inside the black sedans with tinted windows.

"I didn't even get a chance to meet her," whispered Sarah.

"I know. But she'll always be with us. Our little Peanut." He was crying, but it was important that he get the words out, not just for Sarah but for himself. Strong emotion was never something he was comfortable with, but this expression of it was an imperative. This moment was a defining one in his life and Sarah's. They'd made a new, precious life together and it had been cruelly taken away from them. And now there was nothing tying this woman - the love of his life - to him but bonds that were forged during adversity and bad memories. He was afraid he was going to lose not only his baby but Sarah too, and he could barely stand the pain it caused.

"Do you think she knows about us? That we were her parents?" Sarah asked.

"I don't know," Jonathan said in a rough voice. "I want to think so."

"I do think so. I really do. I was her momma and you were her daddy. And we would have been good parents. Great ones."

"I know you would have been the best mother in the entire world. No one is more dedicated and loving and tough. You fought to save her life."

"And in the end, I lost it anyway. If I had just not ..." She couldn't finish. Her tears were too much.

Jonathan turned her to face him, staring her in the eyes. "Sarah, I don't ever want to hear you say that ... do you understand?"

She stared at him, tears and other stuff running down her face.

"You are *not* to blame for what happened. You did everything right. *Everything*. I've analyzed it eighteen times. I've factored in every variable I could come up with, and no matter what, it always comes out the same."

"You did?" she asked, a hint of hope in her voice. "You did that? Why?"

"Because. I knew it would be bothering you. I knew you'd blame yourself. You do that all the time. But you are not omniscient nor omnipotent. You don't have that kind of power. But you do have a strong moral compass and a personality that doesn't let you quit when things get tough. That's why ... that's why I love you. That's why I know you did the right thing. That's why I know that someday, not like we'd recently been planning, but someday, you will be the best mom in the world."

Sarah leaped into his arms. "You still love me," she said into his chest.

Jonathan frowned. "Of course I do, silly. Why wouldn't I?"

"Because ..."

"Because nothing," he said, cutting her off. "I love you, and that's all there is to it. I can't control it. It's perfectly logical, so there's no point in my fighting it. You're beautiful and wonderful and there's no one I'd rather be with. It's simple math, really."

Sarah stepped away, staring into his eyes. "I am so fucking lucky."

He smiled, feeling relieved over her use of foul language for some reason. "Are you back to swearing now?"

"Yes. Until I'm pregnant again. Which won't happen until *after* we finish college and *after* we're married."

Jonathan's throat was sore from holding back the tears, but he sensed Sarah needed strength right now, so that's what he gave her. "That appears to be a very sound plan. I'm fully on board if that's what makes you happy."

She reached up and patted his cheek. "Yes. It makes me very happy."

Jonathan took her by the hand, leading her away from the grave. "Are you ready to do this?"

She sighed heavily, looking back once before facing the cars again. "As ready as I'll ever be."

"I'll be right with you the entire way. Candi and Kevin will be too. Xena and James can't come inside, but they'll wait for us."

"I know. Our family and the dogs are the only things making any of this bearable."

They reached the cars, covering the rest of the ground in silence. Climbing into the limousine, they joined Kevin and Candi and the two dogs whose tails were going nonstop at their return. Both of the humans in the car had been crying.

"You okay?" asked Candi, searching both of their faces.

"As good as can be expected," said Jonathan, not trusting

himself to say anymore. He hadn't yet cried all the tears he needed to, in order to say goodbye to his unborn child.

*****

"You guys ready to testify?" asked Kevin. "That prep work we did with the lawyers didn't seem that bad."

The string of cars pulled away from the curb.

"I'm just glad they arranged the trial so that we could do this now and not wait anymore. I didn't realize they could have witnesses come in out of order," said Candi, stopping to blow her nose. She'd cried so many tears, she was surprised her body still had any fluid left to manufacture them. The sadness had hung over all of them like a heavy cloak for days. Even Sarah's parents doing a one-eighty and being loving for a change hadn't made it any easier. And she knew she was only feeling the sorrow of an aunt. It was nothing compared to the special misery reserved for parents of a lost baby.

"I wish they'd offered that to us from the beginning," said Sarah absently, staring out the window.

"There's no point in wondering why things happened the way they did. Let's just get through this and focus on unwinding this summer," said Jonathan, holding Sarah's hand in his lap.

"What are we going to do this summer, anyway?" asked Kevin. "I used to feel like doing a million things, but all I want to do now is disappear."

"Yeah. Back to our island," said Candi wistfully. Life was so much simpler there.

"Maybe we could take a vacation," said Jonathan. "With that reward money we're getting for furnishing information leading to the prosecution of Baskov, we can afford to go anywhere we want. We could even take a year off school if we needed to. Our parents already suggested it."

Candi shook her head. "I just need the summer. Then I'll decide about the rest of it after."

Sarah said nothing, her free hand gently stroking Xena's head. Xena rested her jaw on Sarah's lap, seeming to just know somehow that she needed warmth and love, not words. She ignored the bandages she still wore and the pain it obviously caused her to move around so much. Her only thought seemed to be for her humans.

They rode the rest of the way to the federal courthouse in silence, each of them lost in their own thoughts. Candi handed out tissues to anyone who teared up, eventually running out because everyone seemed to have some out-of-control emotions to deal with before the day was done.

They eventually pulled up in front of the courthouse, and the window dividing the front seat from the back rolled down. The agent who was riding in the front passenger seat turned around. "Stay here until we have your protection in place. We've already done a sweep of the courthouse and surrounding area. You'll be fine. We'll open the door when we're ready for you." He put the window back up, and the car rocked with him and his partner getting out and shutting the doors behind them.

*****

Sarah watched as the squadron of FBI agents gathered in a few small groups, several of them separating from the others to come towards the car. Her shoulder was burning like the blazes, and her arm stuck in the sling was sweating. It was a lot heavier than it should have been, but that was her secret to keep - one she'd continue to guard until she was safely inside that courtroom. She wasn't taking any chances. She'd already had too many things taken from her for one lifetime. She glanced up at the huge stone columns and hundred or so steps she'd have to climb before she would be comfortable about being out in public again. They were too vulnerable out here, outside the courthouse. The metal detectors that could sense hidden guns and knives lay just beyond the door that seemed so far away. Too far away. She wasn't going to lose anyone else she cared about if she had anything to say about it.

After a signal from an FBI agent, Jonathan got out of the limo first, holding his hand out for hers. With Kevin helping from behind, she was able to get out without jarring her injured shoulder too much. She grimaced with the small amount of pain she hadn't been able to avoid. "Stay, Xena. We'll be back soon." The dog climbed up on the seat where Sarah had been sitting, looking out the back window of the car.

Candi and Kevin followed her out, and they all stood in a tight group just outside the vehicle. They waited as the agents charged with their protection surrounded them in a circle. The one in charge, an agent Sarah recognized as being part of the other state's office, said into his sleeve, "Okay, we're ready to move in. Eyes on pedestrians, people, and windows."

Sarah's head whipped back and forth as she worked to follow his orders. She knew they weren't meant for her, but that wasn't going to stop her from doing everything she could to watch her own rear end.

Maybe if she hadn't been so paranoid and fired up about feeling like law enforcement had really dropped the ball on her, she wouldn't have noticed the bum sitting on the sidewalk to her left. But something about him was familiar, and it made her hesitate. She put her hand that wasn't in the sling inside with the injured one to calm herself.

The agent walking behind her stepped on her heel. "Excuse me," he said, righting himself.

Jonathan stopped and turned. "What are you doing? Come on, we need to stick together."

"That guy ...," Sarah said, not taking her eyes off him. *Where have I seen him before?*

"What about him?" asked the agent. "He's just a bum. Everyone present has been cleared by Agent Caffey as harmless. Ignore him and move forward, please."

"No," said Sarah, standing her ground, "I've seen him somewhere before."

"He looks like every other bum on the street, Sarah," said Kevin from up ahead. "Come on. It's dangerous to stand out here like this." He jogged to catch up to his girlfriend.

Candi had kept walking, oblivious to Sarah's concerns, so the single group turned into two. The agents split up, some of them remaining with Candi and Kevin, some dropping back to be with Jonathan and Sarah. Sarah glanced up at her brother and Candi as they rose up the stairs to the courthouse, noticing Candi looking back with a scared look on her face.

Sarah was just about to say something about how she and Jonathan were coming, when a loud boom sounded off to the right.

Candi screamed and ducked, throwing her arms over her head at the same time Sarah lowered her head down into her shoulders a little.

Kevin stood up higher for a second, trying to see over the agents' heads before ducking over Candi, shielding her with his body.

Another explosion came, this one again on the right, nearer the street.

All of the agents charged with taking care of them had closed in tightly, facing the right and talking into their sleeve-microphones and listening in earpieces for news of what was going on.

No one was looking at the bum anymore. No one but Sarah.

She had torn her gaze away from the smoke billowing up behind a decorative planter to their right in time to see the bum stand up, throw off his shabby, dirty blanket and pull out a semi-automatic rifle.

"The bum! The bum! He's got a ...!"

Before the rest of Sarah's words could make it out of her mouth, the weapon was spitting bullets at them.

The agents just on the outside of the circle near Candi and Kevin fell. The one on Sarah's left fell too, leaving her exposed to the killer's wrath.

She lifted up her elbow and pointed it at the bum. "Not today, asshole!" she yelled, just before she pulled the trigger of the handgun hidden in her sling.

*****

Jonathan heard the gunfire coming from behind him, fully expecting to see an FBI agent standing there defending them. But what he saw nearly blew his mind. Sarah was yelling like a crazy woman, shooting a homeless man holding a machine gun using her ... *sling?*

"Sarah!" he screamed.

Crimson spread across the man's chest. The large rifle fell from his hands to the pavement. He staggered forward three steps before falling to his knees.

Sarah kept yelling and shooting, causing the man's body to jerk like a rag doll, until all Jonathan could hear were empty clicks. But she kept walking towards the killer, looking like she intended to knock his head off maybe when she got there.

But five FBI agents had different ideas. Two of them sprinted over and grabbed Sarah between them, rushing her away and into the building. They pretty much carried her the entire way, with her yelling at them, using a stream of obscenities that was actually quite impressive in its creativity and breadth.

The three remaining agents converged on the bum, who apparently was not actually a bum, but someone they should have removed from the scene before escorting them out of the car.

"Where's Caffey?" yelled one of them. "Why didn't he clear this guy outta here?!"

Jonathan looked around as he was rushed by some new agents up the stairs. He didn't see the agent they'd met right after the prom anywhere. He could have sworn he'd seen him earlier.

Before he had time to think about it anymore, he was being pushed through the metal detector and into a small room with his sister, Kevin, and Sarah. They were all sitting around a table, looking shell-shocked - Sarah worse than all of them.

The door shut behind him, leaving two agents inside.

Sarah looked at the two of them. "You FBI agents listen up ... don't even think about trying to take us out. I've got weapons, and I'm more than happy to use them on anyone who tries to hurt us. So just go ahead ..."

One of the agents lifted an eyebrow. "And make your day?"

"Yeah. Exactly," she said.

Summertime

KEVIN LOOKED OUT OF HIS sister's bedroom window. She was still asleep, but she'd be getting up any minute. He'd set her alarm for an hour earlier than she'd planned, knowing Jonathan was coming over with a surprise.

The annoying sound of her clock went off, making Sarah reach over blindly to hit the snooze button.

"Wake up, sleepy head. Your boyfriend's going to be here in thirty minutes."

"What?" she asked, confused, squinting at her brother across the room.

"Yeah. Super secret romance plan. Better get your face on."

Sarah jumped out of bed and pushed him aside to get to her closet. "What should I wear?"

"Uhhh ... something that looks good."

"That's helpful, dipshit," she said from inside the closet.

He left the room saying, "My work here ... is done."

He pushed the door to his own room open, getting the card and envelope from his desk and quickly penning his name and a short message inside. Smiling at the picture on the front of it again, he slid it into the blank envelope, sealing it closed. Candi was going to be beyond surprised. He scribbled something on the outside of the envelope and went downstairs to wait for her and Jonathan to arrive.

*****

Candi got off the back of Jonathan's scooter, pulling the helmet from her head and doing her best to straighten her newly blond-highlighted hair. Sarah had sent her to her favorite hair dresser with strict instructions of what he was to do. Sarah had been a force to be reckoned with before, but now that she was some kind of hero, saving all of them and the majority of the FBI agents at the courthouse from being gunned down, she was unstoppable. Candi just stayed out of her way as much as possible.

Two weeks after returning, Sarah was in a better frame of mind. No longer seeing hired killers behind every tree and car, she was finally able to relax out in public. She still preferred to stay inside, though - mourning all that she had lost - so that's why they needed to go over to the Peterson's instead of meet at the mall like Candi had wanted.

"Come on, let's go inside," said Jonathan. "Kevin's expecting us."

"Oh. Did you guys plan this or what?"

"Yes, we did, as a matter of fact," he said, obviously proud of himself. "It's a surprise though, so don't ask me anything else."

"Does Sarah know about it?"

"No." Jonathan rang the doorbell.

The door opened to reveal Kevin standing there. He stepped out and picked Candi up in his big, strong arms, swinging her around in a big circle. "Hello, Gumdrop! Welcome to the Peterson house!"

She giggled, holding on for dear life. "You're happy today."

"It's a wonderful day for surprises, don't you think?"

"Uhhhh ... maybe." He put her down on her feet, and she held onto his arm until the dizziness faded. "I guess it depends on the surprise." She'd had enough of the bad ones to last a lifetime.

"Here," he said, pulling something out of his back pocket. "But don't open it yet."

"Awww," she said, her worry melting away at the sight of a small heart he'd drawn on the back. "K heart C. I love it." She reached up and kissed him on the lips, lingering a little longer than necessary. She heard Jonathan leaving to enter the house, but ignored him, enjoying the closeness with Kevin too much to stop.

A throat cleared behind them. Candi released Kevin, stepping out of his embrace and into the foyer. "Hello, Mr. Peterson."

"Hello, Candi. Nice to see you. Here for your surprise?"

She smiled. He wasn't nearly as scary as he used to be. "Yeah, I guess. What is it?"

"Dad ...," warned Kevin.

"I've been sworn to secrecy. Sorry, kid." Frank walked into the living room, leaving them in the front hall.

"Come into the kitchen." Kevin looked behind him to watch Sarah and Jonathan coming down the stairs. "Kitchen, you guys." He pointed into the hallway and started walking.

Candi followed, looking back at Sarah who seemed just as mystified as she was.

Once inside the kitchen, Kevin gestured for them to sit around the small round table that was at the far end of the room. He and Jonathan remained standing next to it.

"What's the deal, babe?" asked Sarah. "And FYI, this better be good. You woke me up from a sound sleep, and I was having some good dreams too."

Candi didn't comment, but she was glad to hear this. Sarah had been plagued with nightmares since the trial testimony started, and even with it long over, she still hadn't been able to sleep without being terrorized by her own mind.

"It's good. I promise," said Jonathan. "Kevin, would you like to start?"

"Sure, man." He cleared his throat and took a deep breath, letting it all out in one big huff. "Okay ... *phew*. So ... ladies. Jon and I were talking about how we've finished our junior year and how a lot of shit ... I mean *crap* has happened. And how we're all having trouble with sleeping and feeling safe and all that. So we decided that we need to just go away for a while. Right, Jon?"

"Yes. Exactly. We need to go somewhere where we can recharge our batteries. Sleep in and not worry about someone waking us up or wanting us to go somewhere or whatever."

"What do you mean? Like a vacation?" asked Candi.

"Yeah. A vacation or a getaway ... or whatever you want to call it," said Kevin.

"For how long?" asked Sarah, sounding suspicious.

"Well, here's the surprise ... we've put something together for a month. But we could extend it indefinitely, really," said Jonathan. "And we've already shared our proposal with all of our parents and they've all agreed that we should do this and without them along. Just the four of us."

"They'll agree to anything at this point," said Candi. "I think they just want us to be happy."

"Yes. And we've shown them we have thought of everything.

Even safety and things they'd worry about."

Jonathan took a card from his back pocket and laid it on the table in front of Sarah. "Open it," he said, smiling nervously.

Candi put her card on the table next to Sarah's. "Are they the same?"

"Kind of," said Kevin. "Just open them." He and Jonathan exchanged glances. They were like two kids in a candy shop getting ready to spend their allowance, they looked so excited.

Candi tore the flap off her envelope. Inside was a card that had a beach scene on the front of it. Four chairs were positioned in the sand, a palm tree partially shading them. She looked over and saw the same card in Sarah's hand.

Candi opened it slowly. Inside was a single paragraph, written in Kevin's boyish handwriting.

In three days we will leave on a plane from the airport. The plane will deliver us to the port where a boat with a captain will be waiting for us. He will take us to the island where we spent our best time together and leave us there with food, water, and everything else we need to stay there for a month. Then he'll return to take us back. We need this. Please say you'll do it with me. I love you. Kevin.

Candi looked up, her eyes bright with tears. Sarah put her card down on the table and dropped her face into her hands.

"Oh, no ... are you crying?" asked Jonathan. "I thought you'd be happy about this. We cleared it through everyone, including the FBI. They said we could do this."

Sarah lifted her face, nothing there but a smile. She was shaking her head slowly, her eyes glued on Jonathan. "I can't believe you did this."

"Is that a good thing or a bad thing?" Kevin asked, warily.

"It's a reckless thing. I mean, seriously *reckless*." She was still smiling. "We could starve ... get caught in a hurricane ... get bitten by a poisonous spider."

"So you don't want to do it, then?" asked Jonathan, visibly deflated.

"I didn't say that." She put her arm around Candy's shoulders. "What do you think, Sugar Lump?"

Candi shrugged, smiling now too. "It is reckless, I agree with you there."

"So what are we going to do?" asked Kevin, using his fired up voice. "Go safe or go reckless?"

They looked at each other around the table, the boys dropping into seats across from the girls. Each of them was weighing the idea, the consequences, and their need to do something, *anything* to get out of this funk that was dragging them down into pits of dark misery.

She couldn't wait anymore. She had to make a command decision and say what the hell. "I say we go reckless," said Candi, putting her hand in the middle of the table.

"Yes! Reckless. I'm in," said Kevin, putting his hand on hers.

"Reckless sounds like the best avenue at this juncture in our lives," said Jonathan, placing his hand over Kevin's.

"Well, I guess reckless it is, then," said Sarah, slapping her hand down firmly on top of the pile. She grinned at Candi, leaning into her. "Now get out of my way, Sugar Lump. I have to go pack."

Other Books by Elle Casey

War of the Fae: Book One, The Changelings
War of the Fae: Book Two, Call to Arms
War of the Fae: Book Three, Darkness & Light
War of the Fae: Book Four, New World Order

Clash of the Otherworlds: Book 1, After the Fall
Clash of the Otherworlds: Book 2, Between the Realms
Clash of the Otherworlds: Book 3, Portal Guardians

Apocalypse: Book 1, Kahayatle
Apocalypse: Book 2, Warpaint
Apocalypse: Book 3, Exodus
Apocalypse: Book 4, Haven

My Vampire Summer
My Vampire Fall

Wrecked
Reckless

Sign up for Elle's newsletter to be notified of new releases and promotions

www.ElleCasey.com/fan-club

About the Author

Elle Casey is an American writer who lives in Southern France with her husband, three kids, Hercules the wonder poodle, and Monie the bouvier. In her spare time she writes young adult novels.

A personal note from Elle ...

If you enjoyed this book, please consider leaving feedback on Amazon.com, Goodreads.com, or any book blogs you participate in. More positive feedback means I can spend more time writing! Oh, and I love interacting with my readers, so if you feel like shooting the breeze or talking about books, please visit me. You can find me at ...

www.ElleCasey.com
www.Facebook.com/ellecaseytheauthor
www.Twitter.com/ellecasey
www.Shelfari.com/ellecasey

Acknowledgments

Thank you to my readers first. Always, always, I thank you for supporting me and investing your time and money in my work. Your positive feedback keeps me going. Reader-love is my drug of choice. Thanks for taking a chance on an indie writer whose books aren't sitting on the bookshelf of your local bookstore - at least, not yet.

Thank you to my mom and husband, two people who are always there to lend a hand or an ear. Thanks to Theresa, my number one beta reader, always ready to jump on my manuscripts when they're finally ready. Thanks to www.editingbymargaret.com for the editorial help. Any mistakes in the books when I publish are mine, put in after Margaret's had her way with the red pen.

My children deserve a big hug for being so patient with their very busy mom. It's hard to see mommy in her room typing and fully appreciate that she's "at work," and I appreciate them trying and being such good sports about it.

Thanks to Manolo for working on my cover art font. Thank you to Claudia at www.phatpuppyart.com for her generosity and friendship. You rock the party, Claudia! Thanks to my author friends, Sweetapples, Jason Mullet Head Brant, Lady O, Amanda McKeon, and many others.

And thank you to the Beplates. No one parties like the Beplates party. Rock on, friends, and pass me the bubbly. :)

www.ingramcontent.com/pod-product-compliance
Lightning Source LLC
Chambersburg PA
CBHW031421240626
47154CB00001B/143